NIAGARA FALL

NIAGARA FALL

A Novel of Crime and Comedy

Stephen F. Wilcox

Mystery and Suspense Press
San Jose New York Lincoln Shanghai

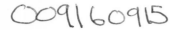
Niagara Fall
A Novel of Crime and Comedy

Mystery and Suspense Press
an imprint of iUniverse, Inc.

For information address:
iUniverse, Inc.
5220 S. 16th St., Suite 200
Lincoln, NE 68512
www.iuniverse.com

ISBN: 0-595-22146-7

Printed in the United States of America

As always, for Pauline and Bennett.

Prologue

❀

September 2000
Marla Ellen

Just past midnight in a handsome two-story tract house in the bedroom sub-urb of Eden, twelve miles northwest of Rochester, Marla Ellen Graycastle stood on the plush carpeting in her daughters' bedroom, the only respite from the darkness provided by the feeble glow of their Little Mermaid nightlight, and idly tapped an Easton youth model metal softball bat against her leg while she stared at her two sleeping girls.

Greta was six, Gretchen ten; both had light brown hair, almost blond, thin and wispy like their father's. Long, thin faces like Gary's, too, but Marla Ellen's brown eyes. They looked like angels sleeping there, tangled in their covers and whimpering softly, but their childhood innocence wasn't registering with Marla Ellen this night. What she saw in the bedroom's gloom was a little river of spittle trailing from Greta's half-opened mouth onto her crisply clean pil-lowcase, how in the throes of sleep Gretchen had kicked away her comforter and all her stuffed animals, which now lay scattered grotesquely across the floor.

Something else for Mother to pick up and put in its place, but did anyone care? Did anyone notice? Oh, all right, yes, Gary remembered to compliment her on the house, how tidy it always was, what a first-rate housekeeper she was.

A housekeeper! That was how he saw her, the only way he saw her, after eleven years of marriage.

The problem with Gary, good old smiley-face Gary, was that he was utterly satisfied. Satisfied with her, satisfied with the two children although hoping for more—which wasn't going to happen, thank you very much. Satisfied with the three-years-new house in Eden and her five-year-old Plymouth Voyager and the nine year old Toyota Camry he drove back and forth to work. Satisfied with the neighbors who shared the cul-de-sac, with their fellow-parishioners at Westside Wesleyan Methodist, with his golfing buddies from work and their PTA wives. Satisfied even with his job, an underpaid, overworked insurance agent masquerading as a financial planner.

Sometimes she felt like she'd died and gone to Utah, surrounded by Osmonds, all those dazzling teeth and not a clue in the bunch. She had to keep reminding herself that there was a world out there, of designer clothes and luxury cars and travel and money in the bank. People who didn't have to put all their change in a big coffee can for four shitty years to afford a trip somewhere, and then it turns out to be Orlando and all that Disney automated crapola. And Gary, naturally, surrounded by midgets in mouse suits and happy as a lima bean in butter sauce.

Marla Ellen Graycastle threw one last disapproving frown at her daughters and turned away abruptly, grinding her bare heel into the carpet as she spun a hundred-eighty degrees and strode from the girls' room, out into the hallway with its open view of the foyer below. Automatically turning to her left, she followed the Oriental carpet runner down past the main bath and the spotless guest room into the master bedroom.

She marched up to the right side of the queen-sized four-poster, Gary's side, and raised the bat high, holding it above her head with both hands, and glared down at her slumbering husband. Gary Graycastle's intermittent mewling snores echoed off the Navaho white walls and bounced down from the vaulted ceiling. Drool ran down his cheek and onto the pillow sham—goddamnit, he was sleeping on the sham again!

She raised the bat an inch higher and sucked in her breath and, as always, she froze there, overwhelmed with indecision and memories.

Not again. No. Be strong, Marla Ellen.

There were days, when the girls were in school, she'd call work to claim she had a migraine or that one of her kids was sick, then she'd drive out to Hamlin Beach State Park and stand there on one of the sandy bluffs overlooking Lake Ontario, all that gray-green roiling water, and just breathe; maybe pretend it was a cliff somewhere in England, the white cliffs of Dover, and soon her lover would return to her from across the sea. Days she just had to get out of that perfect twenty-four-hundred-square-foot builder's model, the house she herself had insisted they find a way to buy; when the walls were closing in too fast and she felt ready to shatter into shards right there on the kitchen's no-wax inlaid vinyl floor.

God, she'd like to plant that ball bat in the side of his head, put them both out of their misery. But she couldn't. He was her husband, and he couldn't help being—Gary.

With a shudder, she lowered the bat to her shoulder and rested it there, as if she were waiting her turn in the on-deck circle.

How appropriate. It seemed she'd spent her whole life waiting for her turn to shine, to feel fulfilled. And she was still waiting.

Anyway, even if she did have the guts to kill him, she'd never get away with it. She'd seen enough of the talk shows to know that. "Women who murder their mates; today on Sally Jesse Raphael." Nobody who knew Gary and knew Marla Ellen would ever believe he had abused her in any way. She couldn't get him to raise his voice, let alone his fists. Wouldn't keep a gun in the house, of course. He had his little insurance man statistics to back that one up. Too many accidental gun deaths had come across his desk, he'd say, for him to ever consider buying one.

Well, that was the idea, *Gary*; an accidental shooting whereby a small caliber projectile plows through your brain, sending you on your happy way to permanent, ultimate oblivion and leaving me with enough insurance money to make a new start, get a life for myself.

That's one thing he'd been very good about, overloading on life insurance. Sets the right example for the clientele, he liked to say.

But no, there'd be no guns in the house—one of the few things he'd ever put his foot down about—and so, no accidental shootings. That left the trusty ball bat they kept in the corner of the room, there to protect them in case a violent burglar broke in and threatened to heave baseballs at them, she supposed. Utterly worthless to her; try explaining that one to a judge, how you'd accidentally bludgeoned your husband to death one night, mistaking his thinning blond head for an incoming Roger Clemen's fastball.

She'd thought about it, too, don't think she hadn't. The possibility of maybe coming up with a whole new defense strategy, getting a syndrome named after her. The Marla Ellen Graycastle Defense. A woman who claims her husband's unrelenting good cheer had driven her to despondency and then to despair, nowhere to turn, no one to confide in, the horror of a scrapper like Marla Ellen being trapped in a relationship with an emotional pacifist like Gary. Bliss overload. Maybe stuff her face with Hostess Ho-Hos first, claim a glucose imbalance had screwed up her blood chemistry, leading to a hallucinatory episode ending in a tragic, entirely unplanned but fatal rampage—

Damn. Not even Jerry Springer's audience was dumb enough to fall for that.

"Hon?" Gary's big blue eyes pushed open, taking in her deflated stance there beside the bed, the bat lying across her shoulder. "Whassamatter, honeypie?" Mumbling, half asleep, that insipid smile beginning to seep across his face like spilled milk.

"Nothing, punkin. I—thought I heard a noise downstairs, but it was the wind."

"Huh. Like the other night? You should call me, sweetie-cakes. Man of the house and everything—"

"You need your rest. You've got work in the morning, Daddy. Early to bed, early to rise."

"Unghh, yeah, Momsy." He rolled over, purring as he sank back into sleep.

Marla Ellen lowered the bat to her side.

Nobody'd believe it for a minute. Besides, with a ball bat? The mess it would create on her Laura Ashley comforter sent a shiver of disgust down her bare arms.

It was a non-starter. She couldn't do it. No way.

So, she'd just have to find somebody who could.

CHAPTER 1

Big Man In Town

All the while he was talking, Jimmy Frat kept one eye on the guy in the tan jacket, sitting there kitty-corner on a bench the other side of the Indian statue, a nowhere look on his mug like some tourist waiting for the casino shuttle.

"So anyways," Jimmy was saying, "everybody thinks Frankie Valli was the key talent in the group, y'know? And I mean, yeah, sure, that signature voice and all, it was important, don't get me wrong. But *creatively* speaking, the guy you wanna talk about is Bob Gaudio. *Sherry, Big Girls Don't Cry, Walk Like A Man, Big Man In Town*—hell, you name just about any Four Seasons hit and Bob Gaudio either wrote it or co-wrote it with the group's producer, Bob Crewe. G'head, name a song."

Bona didn't wanna name a song, didn't know if he could even think of another freakin Four Seasons song, didn't even think they'd had any hits that weren't older than he was, but he figured he'd better give it a shot. All through lunch at the Hard Rock, listening to the oldies playing in the background while Bona had nibbled at his HRC house salad and soup of the day and Jimmy had scarfed a pig sandwich with fries and slaw and a monster chocolate shake, Jimmy Frat had kept up the Hit Parade chatter, naming this group and that group like he was in line for a prize from the deejay or something. The man had a serious jones for all that old Top Forty shit.

All the way out the door of the restaurant even and across Prospect Street into the park and onto the bench they now shared, all Jimmy Frat did was bark about golden oldies and acts he'd seen in Vegas or at Melody Fair or up at ArtPark or whatever. Bands that probably hadn't cut a record since before vinyl died, half of 'em most likely dead themselves. The freakin Everly Brothers? Some country cross-over tune they did in the fifties? How the fuck was Bona, age twenty-eight, supposed to relate to shit like that?

Still, the man was The Man. James 'Jimmy Frat' Fratelli was a capo with the Buffalo mob, no matter that it said general contractor on his tax returns; anybody could read the newspapers knew that. And this was more or less a job interview, so it's not like Bona had much choice but to try and play name that tune.

"Uhhhh." He leaned back against the slatted park bench and screwed his face into a fist and soaked in the early autumn sun while he tried to remember the name of one of the songs they'd just played over at the Hard Rock, something squeally with a huge backbeat. Clacks of tourists, mostly Asians, came and went from the park, passing by the bench. Behind Bona and Jimmy, a few hundred yards away, a mist billowed up from the American Falls. There was the sound of it, too, but it was so low and constant it was easily mistaken for the steady hum a breeze makes as it brushes the ears. Bona was aware of none of that, just the need to come up with a response for The Man. "Lessee," he said finally, "what was it—*Come a Little Closer?*"

"*Come a Little Bit Closer.*" Jimmy Frat gaped at him like he'd just failed to name the first president of the United States. "*Come a Little Bit Closer?* That's Jay and the Americans, for chrissake."

Bona almost blurted out a comeback, but he swallowed it. They'd played some U2 in the restaurant, *I Still Haven't Found What I'm Looking For*—talk about a soaring vocal—and Jimmy Frat didn't have a clue. When Bona tried to tell him what it was, who it was by, how the band was Irish with this lead singer named Bono and a guitarist called The Edge, Jimmy just gave him that wiseguy stare, like who gives a fuck, schmuck.

Bona gave a fuck, that's who. You could say the lead singer, Bono, was like his namesake—and it was pronounced BAH-no, not BOH-no like that dead congressman used to be married to Cher.

It was after he'd first started listening to U2 in a big way, right after The Joshua Tree came out, that he stopped going by Dennis Bonawitz and shortened the whole deal down to Bona. BAH-na, he told everybody, but everybody called him BOH-na anyway, including Jimmy Frat here, who seemed to think Bona was a guinea like him. A mistake that didn't need correcting, seeing as how The Man was about to put him on the payroll.

Jimmy Frat was distracted, eyeballing the guy in the tan jacket, who was pretending to look at the statue of the old Indian chief, but Jimmy wasn't buying it. Asshole had a fat camera strung around his neck, wearing a polo shirt under the jacket and dark cheaters and a pair of too-new jeans. Crisp white running shoes. Close-cropped hair gone mostly gray. He wasn't wearing anything in his ear that Jimmy could see; that'd be the clincher, the guy had an earpiece supposed to look like a hearing aid. Then he'd know he was a fucking Fed.

"Kid," Jimmy said. "Anybody ever tell you ya look like that singer, whatshisname?"

"Springsteen? Yeah, I get a lotta that."

"No, not him, the other one, wrote all those protest songs, can't sing for shit."

Bona was clueless, a not unfamiliar state. He shook his head. "I dunno. People say I look like the Boss—"

"Sinatra? That's a fucking laugh." Jimmy snapped his fingers. "Dylan, that's who you look like. God, I hate that guy."

Bona felt like saying thanks a lot, Dylan's an ugly fuck, not to mention he's like sixty something. Unless maybe Jimmy was talking about Jacob Dylan, the son, had that band The Wallflowers, but Bona didn't think so. He said, "Yeah, I hate 'im, too."

A girl in a pair of tight black jeans and a turtleneck sweater strolled past, grabbing Jimmy's attention. "Jesus," he said, not bothering to lower his voice, "you ever seen mambos like that on a Chinese broad?"

"Prob'ly implants."

"Yeah, so what? Too bad she didn't do something about her face while she was at it." Jimmy decided to give the kid the benefit of his expertise, vis a vis sixties pop music. He repositioned himself on the bench and leaned in a little bit closer, the hands going now. "Listen, comparing Jay and the Americans—which was a solid little group, don't get me wrong. Cut some nice sides. But comparing Jay and the fucking Americans to Frankie Valli and the Four Seasons is like comparing, hell, Jerry Vale to Sinatra. Like comparing the Cincinnati Reds to the New York Yankees. Fucking Subaru to General Motors. You see where I'm goin' with this?"

"I follow you, Mr. Fratelli."

"Good, cause I don't recruit no damn idiots into my organization. Not unless they're relatives anyway, *capisce?*"

Bona decided that was a joke and smiled. Jimmy Frat wished it was.

As much as anything it was his son-in-law—*future* son-in-law, Dale Maratucci, his Angelina's intended—that had him sitting on a hard bench in Niagara Falls State Park on a mild October weekday afternoon interviewing a prospective associate with a tin ear.

Dale. What the fuck kinda name was that for an Italian-American boy from Cheektowaga? He'd said to the wife, as soon as Angie got serious about the bum, You go look it up in the Bible and find me one fucking saint named Dale and I'll push a peanut down Delaware Avenue with my dick. To which the wife, that smart mouth of hers, said, You better make it a real tall peanut.

Dale Maratucci. Had a swagger like Deniro, a grin like Travolta, and a two-year degree in business from Erie County Community College, just enough higher education to land a job selling sneakers at the Walden Galleria and convince himself he was a genius—another Warren Buffet or Meyer Lansky—waiting to happen. One look at the punk and Jimmy figured he could wait until hell froze over and it still wouldn't happen, but Angie was ga-ga over him. They'd been going steady for like a year and the only good thing Jimmy could say about it was at least she hadn't let herself get pregnant. Now they were getting married, over the Thanksgiving weekend of all times, and Jimmy had the added *agita* of having to pay for everything. Which was one reason for the drive up to Niagara Falls, to check out the arrangements for the reception at a local party house owned by a third cousin's brother-in-law. Getting married at Niagara Falls, having their wedding pictures snapped overlooking the falls, or maybe over in the Wintergarden if the weather was too bad, this was his Angie's idea of an ideal wedding. Too bad he couldn't've talked her into spending the honeymoon here, too, maybe the bridal suite across the river at the Skyline, got the casino right next door. Save himself big bucks over two weeks at the MGM Grand in Vegas. But what the hell, like the wife was always reminding him, he only had one daughter.

Which dovetailed nicely with that other thing that had brought him up from Buffalo this morning. Niagara Falls on the Canadian side was doing okay, gangbusters in fact, what with the new Casino Niagara bringing in the tourists, hotels and motor lodges and chain eateries popping up like mushrooms in a damp cave. By comparison, the city of Niagara Falls, N.Y., over here on the U.S. side of the border, was for shit. It almost reminded him of some third-world country, Romania or some crap hole like that, all the vacant lots and vacant buildings and vacant looks on the faces of the locals. A town built on one natural resource, its famous falls, and two industries; tourism and the chemical-based companies that had moved in a century ago to take advantage of all the cheap electricity.

Problem was, neither industry was producing cash flow like in the good old days. Sure, the falls still pulled in ten, fifteen million visitors every year, but not many of them stuck around for more than a few hours anymore. It was a rush job, over to the falls to take a few snapshots, maybe a drive over to Goat Island, maybe a trip on the Maid of the Mist, then a quick hit at one of the souvenir shops to pick up some made-in-China memento of the Falls and everybody gets back into the car or the bus and takes off for the next stop on the itinerary; up to Toronto or down to the Finger Lakes, maybe on to New York City or Boston, some place with more to do than watch running water. Lately more and more of the suckers stayed and played over at the Casino for a few days, but the benefits were almost all across the river, in a whole other fucking country. The point being Niagara Falls, USA, wasn't a destination anymore, it was just a stop along the way to someplace else. Which meant the hotels and the motels were always half empty, and the same for the restaurants and the shops and the little museums and the tour busses.

Then you have to combine that with the loss of jobs at the chem plants and other heavy industries that lined the river bank out along Buffalo Avenue, your Carborundum and Olin Chemicals, Dupont and Elkem and Carbide. Your Oxy Chemical, which used to be called Hooker Chemical until the Love Canal scare came along in the seventies, forcing the company into a sell-off and a name change. But then, over the past forty years, there'd been lots of sell-offs and name changes and reorganizations in the industries along Buffalo Ave, and with every one it seemed a few hundred jobs went away permanently.

When Jimmy Frat was a kid in the fifties, his old man driving them the twenty miles up from the family homestead on Ramona Avenue on Buffalo's southside for a day's outing, Niagara Falls on the U.S. side was a city of a hundred thousand. A blue-collar city, sure, but working people with cash in their pockets, Italians and Poles mostly, folks who liked to wager some of that extra cash, whether it was at the church bingo games or a little special action at one of the "social clubs." But that was then. Now the city's population had shrunk by half, and the disposable income of those who were left had shrunk even more. Downtown was dotted here and there with razed blocks waiting for something better than an outlet mall to come along and fill them up. It had gotten so bad over the last twenty years even organized crime had largely lost interest. There just wasn't enough money coming in from various rackets to make a sustained presence worthwhile. So the Falls, what slim pickings there were, had largely been left to the scavengers, local guys like this kid Bona, to run their nickel-and-dime scams on the tourists, work a little insurance fraud here and there, sell a little dope, hustle a few girls.

But Jimmy Frat figured things might be ready to turn around. He saw himself as basically an optimist, a cup half-full kinda guy, and what else he saw was a booming cross-border economy between the U.S. and Canada all along the Niagara Frontier, fallout from this NAFTA deal that just about every union in Buffalo had come out against at the time. Truckloads of goods passing back and forth, busloads of American tourists heading north and Canadian shoppers heading south, Great Lakes freighters hauling holds filled with raw materials downriver from Buffalo's port on Lake Erie. What he saw was commerce, and commerce meant prosperity and, sooner or later, prosperity meant money in the pockets of even the little guys who loaded the ships and drove the trucks like his old man, or sold shoes like his intended son-in-law.

It was like Ronald Reagan had called it, that trickle down shit. Times were good just about everywhere else Jimmy looked, so how long could it be before the good times trickled down into the Falls?

And when the revival began, Jimmy Frat wanted to be on the ground floor, so to speak. He also needed something for his future son-in-law; a piece of something the kid could learn from and grow with. Learn from if he was smart, that is, or get lost in if he wasn't. Jimmy figured Niagara Falls might could be that place, if enough things fell into line.

The key was a casino, like what the Canadians built across the river. Casino Niagara was a cash cow for the Province of Ontario and the city of Niagara Falls, Ontario. Officials on the U.S. side of the border could only look across the Rainbow Bridge at NFO, see all those blazing neon signs, see the border traffic pouring into Canada every day, and salivate at the thought of what a similar gambling operation could mean to their city. Put a shiny new casino on one of those vacant downtown parcels and the rest would soon begin to fill up with resort hotels and chain restaurants. And that's where the biggest opportunity was for Jimmy Frat and his crew; major new construction projects. Hotels and restaurants, infrastructure improvements, that was his meat. Especially the state or federally funded projects, with their legally mandated union hiring. Anything that required crews of skilled tradesmen, yards of concrete and tons of steel. A fucking license to steal.

For ten minutes the asshole in the tan jacket had just sat there staring at the Indian statue, or pretending to. Now he started fussing with the camera, checking the settings without actually looking at them, the same for the lens. Jimmy Frat watched out of the corner of his eye while he changed conversational lanes with the new hire.

"So I mentioned Dale, right?"

Bona said, "The guy's marrying your daughter?"

"My future son-in-law, right. I'm thinking of doing some business up here and I'm looking to break the kid in while I'm at it, give him some experience. What I need is someone to show him the ropes, okay? Somebody knows his way around the Falls, can introduce him around, help him get the lay of the land so to speak."

"So you're planning to do some business up here, like on a regular basis? Because I can do you some good, Mr. Fratelli."

"Yeah, I know that, kid, otherwise we wouldn't be having this conversation, okay? Things fall the way I think they're gonna fall, this town's gonna open up again—"

"If they get casino gambling, you mean."

Jimmy Frat shifted his ass another half inch so he was almost facing Bona head on and, without raising his voice said, "Don't tell me what I mean, okay? Shut the fuck up and listen. I heard from our mutual friend you were a smart boy, did a good night's work and knew how to follow orders. Was it wrong, what I heard?"

"No, sir." Their mutual friend was Salvatore "Sally the Pig" Pignatti, another capo in the Buffalo mob. Bona hadn't actually met Sally the Pig, only seen him through the window of a truck stop coffee shop one time. But he'd done a couple jobs with members of Sally's crew, boosting trucks from the regional market. Bona's expertise was pinching bills of lading and shipping manifests from the offices, so the crew would know which trailers to target, which drivers to pay off, like that. Good work, when you can get it.

"I'm a real good listener, Mr. Fratelli."

"That's good. Things come up, we can always use a young guy knows how to take direction well and keep his mouth shut. But right now we're talkin' about an entry-level position, so to speak, taking Dale around and—" Jimmy Frat stopped abruptly and jerked his head around. "Fuck!"

The guy in the tan jacket had the camera up now, was snapping off pictures supposed to be of the Indian chief but Jimmy knew better. "Look at the son of a—hey! You think you're fooling somebody here?" he shouted, causing a group of Japanese tourists to take a wider berth as they passed the bench, their collective suspicions about the United States and every white devil in it graphically confirmed.

The object of his ire didn't seem to take notice. The joker in the tan jacket got up from his bench and walked calmly but purposefully toward the park exit, the camera bouncing against his chest.

Jimmy rapped Bona's arm with the back of his hand. "Y'see that asshole, taking my picture like that? *Minchia*, I can't even sit in a fucking park and have a conversation." He slapped at Bona again. "Go get me the film."

Bona was still trying to catch up with the program. "The film? You mean the guy over there—?"

"Yeah, him. Go take the fucking film out of his camera and bring it to me. I don't give a fuck he's a Fed or what he is, that don't give him a right to take my picture without my permission."

Bona licked his dry lips. "Well, maybe it does, Mr. Fratelli. I mean, if he really was taking your picture. Or could be he's just some lame-ass tourist—"

Jimmy Frat burned him again with that wiseguy who-gives-a-fuck-what-you-think stare. "Pricks getting away. Go get the fucking film off him and meet me back at the car, *capisce*?"

Bona rocketed off the bench, damn near saluted. "Absolutely, Mr. Fratelli."

CHAPTER 2

Walk Like A Man

"Get the fucking film, capeesh?" Bona mumbled, mimicking his new employer's gravelly whine as he hurried out of the park. "Fucking greaseball."

Jimmy could've sent his driver, Coco, if he wanted somebody braced in broad daylight. Fucking goon was the size of a refrigerator with a face looked like it'd been hammered out of bronze. One look at Coco and the guy'd hand over the film, his camera, his wallet, you name it. Instead the professional muscle sits there behind the wheel of Jimmy's Lincoln, double parked in front of the Hard Rock, while Bona, all one hundred forty-five pounds worth, has to chase down some asswipe who most likely wasn't taking Jimmy Frat's freakin picture in the first place.

That was the problem working for wops. You couldn't tell a one of 'em anything; they knew it all already. The money was decent, though. Those cargo heists he'd worked with some of the Pignatti crew were solid gigs, almost like having a regular nine-to-five job. You get your instructions, you go in and do your bit, and by the end of the week the crew boss, in this case Rick the Quick Lemongello, Sally the Pig's nephew, hands you an envelope with your action in it. The big problem was it wasn't a steady gig. The Pignatti crew worked a truck boost maybe once a month. A man couldn't make a decent living that way. To make ends meet, Bona had to keep putting small gigs together for himself, a burglary, a tourist mugging, a torch job; in the eleven years since he'd quit Niagara Falls High at seventeen, Bona had become a sort of jack of all trades crime-wise. And it was wearing his ass out.

Which is why he was bothering to chase some old dipshit half way across the city for a freakin roll of film. Jimmy Frat was holding out a chance for steady work, one of those little white envelopes with Bona's name on it every week. Something he could throw right back in Melody's face when she started in on him about paying the bills and his low-life friends and how if he had half a brain he'd go down and apply at fucking Carborundum or Oxy-Chem or someplace where he could get a real job, make an honest living.

"That'll be the fucking day," Bona muttered as he trotted across Prospect and headed up the pedestrian mall past all the souvenir shops. His quarry, the gray haired asshole in the tan jacket, was half a block ahead, about to cross over and—damn—cut through the Wintergarden, all those overgrown rain-forest plants and shit. Man, if he blew this Jimmy Frat would chew him up and spit out the pieces. So long steady gig, so long upward mobility.

Bona picked up the pace.

What Melody didn't understand about Bona, wouldn't ever understand, was he was incapable of taking a job at a place like Carborundum, even if they were dumb enough to offer him one again. His old man, Eugene Bonawitz, had spent thirty-eight years grubbing for a living over at the Buffalo Ave plant before retiring at a wore-out sixty-one and dying of brain cancer three years later. Grinders they called men like his old man, men who worked the blast furnaces and the crushers that produced silicon carbide and all the other abrasives that Carborundum marketed. Used to come home every freakin night with microscopic bits of silicon dust and other crap dropping out of his shoes and his pant cuffs and his hair, the old man did. Brag to Bona about this *special* job he was given, running the diamond crusher, how *rich* he was every day when he handled all those diamonds that went into his crusher. How the very dust he shook off on the kitchen's yellowed linoleum floor was diamond dust, the magic dust that dreams were made of. What grammar school boy wouldn't eat up stuff like that?

Then one day when he was around eleven, Bona went in to work with the old man as part of a school assignment and found out how truly full of shit he was. He remembered leaving the little house on 97th Street in the early morning darkness with diamonds gleaming in his eyes. His lunch bucket in his lap on the ride over; he could still smell the banana and the Twinkie. And then they pulled into the plant, and he felt the looming weight of the place bear down on him, all those old bricks and painted-over windows, the dense shadows the huge building threw on the men as they trudged in from the frozen parking lot. How hot it was around the blast furnaces and how cold it was everywhere else. Then he actually saw where his old man worked, the diamond crusher, this dirty, peeling piece of automated pig iron, and he saw the bin full of crappy looking little black stone chips. Industrial-grade diamonds, the old man explained with a grunt, as he loaded the hopper and pushed a fat red button, and then there was a noise louder than anything young Dennis Bonawitz had ever heard as the big piston driver came down, louder than Def Leppard with the volume on his stereo cranked up to ten. That's the day Bona promised himself he'd never work a day at fucking Carborundum or any place like it.

But seven years later, there he was, a year after dropping out of school, sitting in the personnel office at Carb, a job interview the old man had pulled strings to get for him. Sitting there in a straight-back chair while some four-eyed geek with a slide rule up his ass and a know-it-all smile quizzed him about his fucking career goals. Well, he just started laughing at the geek, laughing so hard he almost fell off the chair. The personnel guy accused him of being on something—which he was; dusted up to his ears—and tore up his application. So much for his old man's dream that they work side by side, two generations of grinders sweating their balls off for fucking Carborundum.

Three months after that Bona burgled the personnel guy's house down in North Tonawanda and took a shit on his kitchen table.

That was like ten years ago now. And here was Bona, still scuffling to get by. Chasing down some gray-haired fool for a fat little guinea with a Napoleon complex.

Bona cut straight through the Wintergarden, ignoring the side exits into the Rainbow Centre Outlet Mall, and came out onto Rainbow Boulevard North without picking up the guy. He crossed over to the pedestrian mall, still didn't see him, and, putting a little desperation into his gait, trotted east to Third Street and stopped. Took a deep breath and told himself to chill, take a good look around. He hopped up onto a bench, startling an old woman seated at the other end. Bona ignored her as she got up and shuffled away. He looked left first and then straight ahead, seeing nothing but cars and busses and the bobbing heads of tourists wandering around looking for something to do. Then he looked to his left and, after a moment, way the hell the other side of Niagara Street, he saw a tan jacket and gray hair walking north on Third.

Decker had popped into Norton's Newsstand and Stuff and was just then popping out again when he heard someone shouting. He looked back over his shoulder, saw a wiry, goateed young man in a black jacket simultaneously trying to negotiate Niagara Street against the light and waving in his direction, and realized it was the same kid who'd been seated with the man in the park. The fireplug of a man in the expensive brown suit who'd hollered something unintelligible at him.

Whatever it was, he wasn't interested. He kept on walking, past one of the many bars that lined that end of Third. When the shouts grew closer, accompanied by the sound of shoes slapping hard time against the pavement, he detoured up an alley.

Bona rounded the alley ten seconds later, saw Decker standing there next to a row of trashcans, and skidded to a halt like something out of a Roadrunner cartoon.

"Wow. Hey, man." Bona leaned over and sucked in some air and stuck on his best tourist grin. "Just the guy I needed to see."

Decker just stood there, calmly staring, his thumbs hooked on the pockets of his stonewashed jeans, a Nikon camera hanging around his neck. Bona stared back a couple seconds, then broke off. Guy wasn't quite what he was expecting. He'd seen him around before a few times, wandering around in the park near the falls, just sort of hanging around down there. There were quite a few local crazies like that, drawn to Niagara Falls almost like it was some mystical quest or something. Bona dismissed all of them as losers.

But this guy here, there was something different, something more. The short gray hair looked blonder close up, and the guy had a way of standing. Not as old as he'd thought, either. And those blue eyes, soft as the jeans he was wearing, but direct too. None of which would've mattered if Bona had had a good length of iron pipe handy, but he didn't.

"Look," he said, holding his palms up. "I need the film, okay?"

"The film?"

"In the camera. You took some shots a my boss back in the park and he don't like anybody doing that unless he okays it, okay? So I gotta get the film."

"I wasn't taking pictures of your boss."

"Yeah, well, I figured you were just shooting the old Indian chief, but Jimmy don't wanna hear that." Bona had his breath back and was sizing up his options. He moved a little closer, keeping up the spiel. "I don't wanna make a big deal out of it, man. Maybe I could give you somethin' for it, say ten bucks for a new roll of film."

Decker held fast, his gaze flitting from the kid's eyes to his shoulders and back. "There are no pictures," he said patiently. "There's no film in the camera."

"Aw right. Okay, fine." Bona turned half way to his left and bent slightly, his right foot kicking out, expecting to make contact with Decker's knee, but it wasn't there. He felt the heel of Decker's palm bang off his right shoulder and all at once he was the one who was down, face down on the alley's grimy macadam. He popped back up just as fast to have another go, tried to plant his back foot so he could get something behind the punch but the foot landed on something squishy and skidded and he went down again, harder.

"Shit!"

Decker, glancing down at the spot where Bona's foot had slipped, said, "No, actually it looks like a discarded coffee filter with the grounds still in it."

He made no move to press his advantage. He didn't appear to have moved at all, in fact; was still standing there, one thumb hooked in his jeans, the other hand holding onto the Nikon. Same contented look in his eyes.

Bona tried staring him down again, said "Fuck," and glanced away.

Decker said, "Whatever your problem is, kid, it isn't with me." He popped the back on the Nikon and held it out for Bona to see. There was no film in it. "Tell your boss I wasn't taking pictures of anything. It's too sunny out today. I was just—fooling around in the park."

"Yeah, right." Bona nodded miserably. "I can't hardly wait to tell him that."

🍁   🍁   🍁

Shuffling back down Third, curled over like a question mark, Bona thought about what he'd tell Jimmy Frat. Too sunny, what kinda crock of shit was that? The dude took the film outa the camera before Bona got to him, is probably what happened. Not that Jimmy was gonna be any happier with that particular deduction, either.

He was trying to think up an explanation Jimmy would be happy with, or one he'd at least like well enough to still put Bona on the payroll, when he came alongside Norton's Newsstand and Stuff, the hole-in-the-wall he'd seen the guy come out of. He stopped and stared at the familiar red-on-yellow Kodak logo in the corner of the front window, over a sign that read 24 Hour Processing. He straightened up, put on a befuddled expression, and went in.

The place had the dimensions of a shoe box, long and narrow, without being much larger. Newspapers from around the U.S. and Canada lined racks that ran down the center, with magazines and paperback books and maps and sundries displayed along the two side walls. The only person in the place was a short skinny guy, shorter than Bona by a good three inches. He had a pinched in face and close-set brown eyes and long brown hair pulled back into a pony-tail and looked a lot like that big talking rat in that Ninja turtle movie Bona'd bought for his kid. And there was something wrong with the guy's left leg; he moved with a serious starboard sway when he came down the counter.

Bona wagged a friendly finger at him. "You're—don't tell me. Norton, right?"

"Yeah," the little guy said neutrally. "Like it says on the sign."

"Right, but I seen you around the Falls, is how I knew. I got an eye for faces, but not always names." Norton didn't have anything to say to that, so Bona kept talking. "Like I thought I saw a guy I know come outa here a few minutes ago. A photographer type."

"You mean Monk?"

"Nah, not a monk. Guy with gray-blond hair, wearing a tan jacket. Takes pictures a lot down by the falls."

"Yeah, that's Monk Decker. Some of us call him Monk, 'cause he used to be one."

"No shit? What, with the long brown robe thingy and all that?"

"The whole nine yards."

"Jeez, I never would've guessed that." Bona rested his elbows on the glass counter. "Listen, you do picture processing here, right, Norton? How's that work?"

Norton Gage sighed. He got all kinds in his place, with a heavy emphasis on drunken wedding parties looking for smokes and rubbers and Japanese tourists snapping up maps and film and any little piece of cheap crap with "Niagara Falls, USA" printed on it. But when a guy who looks like Bruce Springsteen in his salad days comes in asking questions about people's names and photo processing and all, Norton's inner voice sends up a warning flare.

Still, it takes all kinds. And Norton had to make a living.

He pulled an empty processing envelope from under the counter and held it up. "You fill out one of these with your name and address, you pop in your roll of film, I give you a receipt and that's about it, friend."

"So what d'ya do with the roll after that?"

Norton sighed again, and half turned. "See that box there? Well, your film goes in there until I can send it out to the processing lab across town. And your name goes on file in this file box over here—hey!"

While Norton was talking, Bona had moved to the end of the counter and was coming around on his side. Norton tried to keep his eyes on him and search under the counter for his cut-down Adirondack bat at the same time, but it wasn't happening. Bona shoved him out of the way.

"Take it easy, gimp, I just wanna know what you did with this Decker guy's film."

"He didn't drop off any film—"

"I saw him come outa here, man."

"He ducked in to say hi, that's all. He's a friend of mine. You'd better get the hell out of here before you get yourself into real trouble."

"Yeah, yeah." Bona was rifling through the film box. "I just need the fucking film, okay? So quit dickin' me around here." Finding nothing with Decker's name on it, he started on the file box. "Ha! What's this here? You got a card for a Walter Decker on Walnut Avenue. Walter—no wonder he goes by Monk. Where's the film?"

"He didn't drop any film today, I'm telling you. He's a regular customer, I keep his name on file. But he didn't have anything for me today."

Norton didn't like the look the punk was giving him, so he kept on trying to convince him he didn't have any film and at the same time he tried to locate the truncated ball bat out of the corner of his eye. He was absolutely convinced he was about to get a beating, or worse. Then the bell on the door tinkled and a tall man with a black beard and a turban wandered in from the street. Norton was never in his life so glad to see a Third World impulse shopper.

Bona didn't care for the new odds. He slipped back around the counter, tossed a big smile at the snake charmer and a clipped salute at Norton and walked out.

❧　　　　　❧　　　　　❧

He was back across Niagara Street and heading toward Rainbow and the ramp garage when the champagne silver Town Car berthed at the curb. Coco was behind the wheel and Jimmy Frat was in back, gesturing for Bona to climb in front.

"J'get the film?"

"Not exactly, Mr. Fratelli." Bona had to fight to turn around in the soft leather seat, peering past the headrest as earnestly as he could while Jimmy Frat, the fat little sausage, sat there with a sour look on his pan. Had a whole fucking T.C. backseat to himself, but wouldn't share it with a peon like Bona. "He says he didn't have any film in—"

"'Not exactly'? Is that what you said? You keep me waitin' around for your sorry ass and you come back with 'Not exactly.'?" Jimmy's face was heading toward deep umber.

"Well, sir, what I'm trying to explain—"

"You're not *exactly* making a good first impression, Bona. Not fucking *exactly.*"

"I can get the film, Mr. Fratelli, if there's any film to get—"

Just as the color rising up from the little capo's collar seemed ready to blow off the top of his head, a new expression melted his features—maybe an aneurysm, Bona was thinking—and Jimmy said, "Shut up, shut up a minute and listen. Coco, turn it up."

The volume on the radio went up. Bona heard a semi-familiar oldie oozing from the Lincoln's nine-speaker sound system, some guy wailing about never getting married and maybe it's the best thing, and Jimmy Frat howling along like a wolf with its nuts frozen to the tundra.

"But it's the worst that could happen—to-oo-oo-oo me!"

It was enough to make a guy give fucking Carborundum a second look. But at least Jimmy Frat was smiling now.

"The Brooklyn Bridge with Johnny Maestro on lead vocals. Came out nine-teen-seventy-something. Coco?"

"I'm no good with dates, boss, you know that."

Bona, just to keep the ball rolling in the right direction, said, "Seventy four, I'm thinking."

"Yeah, around there. I think you're right." Jimmy scooted up to the edge of the seat. "Here's one I bet you don't know. Way back before he was in the Brooklyn Bridge, Johnny Maestro sang lead for another group had a big number one single. What was the group and what was the tune?"

"Uhhh—" Bona felt a drop of sweat pop out on his forehead. "Ummm—"

"Give up? It was 'Sixteen Candles' by the Crests. A classic, right?"

"Right," said Coco.

"Damn straight," said Bona.

Jimmy sat back again, exhaled heavily, and motioned for Coco to turn the radio down. "Okay, Bona, what's the deal on Alan Funt?"

Bona frowned, lost again. "Dude's name was Decker, Mr. Fratelli. Walter Decker, only people call him Monk on account of he used to be one."

"Asshole was a monk? Like, a real Catholic monk?"

"I guess. I've seen him around anyway. He's like one of the crazies who hang around the falls, y'know, communing with the thunder gods or whatever."

"He's just a local fruitcake?"

"Yeah, pretty much, I guess. I mean, why else would he be taking pictures with no film in his camera?"

"He didn't have no film in the camera?"

"Nu-uh. I looked."

"You check his pockets?"

"Yeah. I patted him down, like."

Jimmy Frat shrugged. "Okay." He'd almost forgotten the incident anyway; it was just waiting around for the kid to come back that had got him pissed. But he also didn't like being wrong about stuff, which is why he wasn't ready to let it go entirely. That, and it was a good opportunity to test the new kid a little more, see how resourceful he was. "Here's what I want you to do. Check out this monk of yours, make sure he is what he's supposed to be, flip his crib if you have to, bounce him around if you have to—but don't do no serious damage. Just make sure he's got no connections to the law, he's just some nut hangs around the park. And get back to me in a couple three days, *capisce*?"

Bona nodded. "No sweat, Mr. Fratelli."

"Coke, give him his envelope."

The giant behind the wheel reached inside his black leather car coat and pulled out a standard white number ten envelope and handed it to Bona.

"That's a taste," Jimmy Frat said. "For taking my future son-in-law around, showing him the town, like we talked about. Things work out, we find some work for you two to handle, you make yourself useful to me in other ways, show you're an earner, the envelope gets fatter. Understand?"

Bona said he understood just fine and thank you very much for the opportunity.

"Two things to remember, kid," Jimmy said, making heavy eye contact. "One, you don't get Dale involved in any of your penny-ante local action, not unless it's been cleared with me, *capisce*? I don't want him getting dirty for no dimes and nickels."

"Yessir."

"And two, don't do nothin' to draw attention to yourself, know what I mean? You get your mug in the papers for stickin' up a gas station, you're no good to me anymore. Do your business if you gotta, but keep it quiet, is what I'm sayin'. No cowboy bullshit. *And*, goes without saying, you tell noboby nothin' about what you do for me."

"You got it, Mr. F."

"Yeah, I do got it." Jimmy Frat smirked. "And I plan to keep it."

CHAPTER 3

Girl Come Running

The next morning at nine-fifteen, Decker sat in a back corner booth at the Metropolis Restaurant, finishing an indifferent breakfast of eggs and home-fries while Norton Gage told his end of the story.

"He comes on at first like he knew you or something, so, yeah, I gave up your name."

"Don't worry about it."

"Well, I am worried about it, man. Dipsoid bastard started pushing me around, then he digs into my files and gets your address, keeps saying he wants the film you dropped off and I'm all the time insisting you didn't drop any film." Norton threw up his hands, the ash from his thin cigar flying off and dropping into the empty booth behind him. "Christ, if a customer hadn't wandered in, I don't know what would've happened."

"Yeah, he came after me looking for the film, too." Decker sipped the oily black coffee. "Apparently his boss thought I was sneeking pictures of him and he didn't like it."

"What, some celebrity or something?"

"Not unless it was Joe Pesci. A real mob guy'd be more like it, I'd say. Maybe he thought I was a federal agent or something."

Norton squinched together his close-set brown eyes and peered down his long, narrow nose. "Yeah, man, I can see it. You could be a Fed."

Decker smiled. "If I was, first thing I'd do is bust you for contraband."

"What, for these?" Norton stared, incredulous, at the cigar between his fingers. It was a Cuban, part of a box he bought each month at a tobacco shop on Victoria Avenue, across the river in NFO, and brought over in a golf bag he kept in the trunk of his car. "That's the fundamental problem with law enforcement, going after the little guys on technicalities. It's stupid, anyway, embargoing Castro for forty goddamn years. Where's it got us, huh?"

"So you only buy those Havanas as a protest, right?" Decker glanced out the window. The Metropolis sat at the end of Main Street, near where it terminated at Rainbow Boulevard. Out across the restaurant parking lot and a vacant lot used to park tour busses, was a clear view of the Rainbow Bridge to Canada. A bit of the falls was on display, too, the upper portion of the American Falls, mostly veiled in mist. If he'd bothered to crane his neck around to the right, the panorama would've included a glimpse of the Horseshoe Falls and the Skylon Tower and Casino Niagara across the river, along with the hotels that clustered around it like piglets at a suckling sow.

That was half the reason he ate regularly at the Metropolis, its view and proximity to the falls. When the sun was right, you could see the top of the rainbow mingled in the mist from right there in that very booth. The other reason he came by regularly, for the last few weeks anyway, was just then tidying things up behind the counter. She was a tall honey blonde with hazel eyes, a mature body, and the muscled legs of a runner—or a seasoned waitress. Her first name was Suzzy; he hadn't gotten around to learning her last name yet. It had taken him two weeks just to work up to asking if "Suzzy" was supposed to be pronounced the same as "Suzy". She had given him a slow, butter melting kind of smile and said, No, it's pronounced like it's spelled, Suzzy, like Suzzy Roche, the folk singer. He'd never heard of Suzzy Roche the folksinger and he'd told her so, but that was as far as the conversation had gone, because a couple of loud truckers had come in just then and settled at one of her tables. He'd been thinking about picking up the discussion again when the time was right and, as he watched her now, fussing with the sugar dispensers along the counter, he hoped that time would come soon.

He turned back to his coffee and his friend. "This kid," he said. "You recognize him?"

"I seen him around before, but I don't know his name. Every lowlife in the Falls hangs out along Third Ave sooner or later, Monk, you know that. All the bars." Norton dragged the last puff from his cigar and ground out the stub in the plastic ash tray, then he picked up his coffee mug. "Look, man, I gotta get back to the newsstand before Lou screws something up. I just wanted you to know this punk's got your address. I tried calling yesterday, but you weren't around. You know, you should get a machine."

"What for? You're the only one ever calls and I see you just about every day anyway."

"Yeah. Which reminds me, you coming out to the garage this weekend? Cause I could use a hand."

"I'll be there."

"Good. We're running out of season, y'know."

Decker shrugged. "There's always next season."

"Yeah. Or not at all." Norton started to slide out of the booth, then paused. "You really didn't have any film in your camera this time? Or was that a line you gave the punk?"

"No film. Too sunny out. I was just playing around with the lens."

Norton shook his head, the wispy ponytail swinging in time. "So this entire hassle was for nothing." He struggled out the end of the booth, said, "Later, man," and trudged toward the front of the restaurant with that listing stiff-legged gait of his.

Decker wasn't the only one watching the little man go. Suzzy Koykendall had refilled to capacity every sugar dispenser at the short end of the ell-shaped counter and had moved on to the napkin holders. It was slow and quiet in the Metropolis that time of the morning. Steve Pellipollis wasn't around to pinch asses and brother Gus was back in the office grumbling over his account books. Besides Decker, the only other customers at her station were an old man eating a Danish at the counter and a tourist couple, Eastern Europeans by the sound of their accents, lingering over their coffees and cigarettes in one of the booths.

She snuck a look at Decker, seated alone now, and thought, Damn, what're you thinking of, girl?

She knew he liked her; the sidelong glances she'd catch him at, for one thing. And it sure wasn't the food at the Metropolis that kept him coming in every day, sometimes twice a day, always seating himself in her station even though it was the smoking section and she'd never seen him light up himself. So when the hell was he going to make a move?

Damn it, there you go again.

What if he did make a move? Or she did? What could come of it anyway? In her situation, the rules she was supposed to live by...

Oh, screw the rules. She had a right to *some* personal life, didn't she? A dinner date now and again? Even to get laid once in a blue moon, is that so terrible for a woman to want? Particularly a woman on the cusp of middle age.

At thirty-nine her biological clock was pounding like a jackhammer, loud enough to be heard all the way back to North Platte, Nebraska. She knew this for a fact because once a week her mother called to remind her of it. But this wasn't about that; whether or not she even wanted a husband and children and a permanent home. This was about another matrix of her biology all together. Urgings for human contact, conversation, and yes, sexual gratification.

And just look at him, sitting in his booth, so clean and calm and masculine. Short gray-blond hair, the soft blue eyes, that simple, direct gaze. She'd thought of Paul Newman the first time she'd waited on him. A forty-something Paul Newman with a somewhat larger, bent nose and a Kirk Douglas cleft in the chin.

Jesus Christ, Suzzy, why don't you buy yourself a copy of Tiger Beat while you're at it.

Sometimes you can think too much, she decided. She shoved the pack of napkins under the counter and grabbed the pot of coffee off the warming plate.

Decker was watching as she came around the far end of the counter and offered refills to the couple in the far booth. She topped them off and straightened, looking down his way. He smiled and picked up his cup, but she was already on her way.

"How was everything?" she asked, as she leaned over him to refill his cup. He could smell her scent, something lavender.

"Everything was perfect, Suzzy."

She felt little pin pricks at the backs of her knees when she heard him say her name, felt her face flush. This was goddamn ridiculous, behaving like a sixteen-year-old with a crush on the chemistry teacher.

"Well, can I get you anything else?" It came out harsher than she'd intended.

"Is something wrong? You sound a little upset."

"No, no. I'm sorry, I just—I guess I'm just tired. End of the week and all that."

"Understandable. You ever get a break?"

"Oh, yeah, sure. When it gets slow like this."

Decker hesitated, almost too long, then gestured to the seat opposite his. "Why don't you join me? I'll buy you a cup."

She felt a sense of relief wash over her, like when she got home at night and took off her sensible shoes. She gave him that slow grin. "Let me get my cigarettes."

❧   ❧   ❧

Suzzy made a ritual of sipping her cream-laden coffee, then carefully extracting a Virginia Slim, tapping the end on the table, slipping it between her lips and lighting it with a Bic disposable. She turned her head to the side to exhale the first puff. "Number two," she said.

"Two?"

"Sorry. Second smoke of the day. I only get five, so I need to make a mental note."

"How long you been keeping track?"

"Five a day? Oh, for years now. I read someplace that to be a moderate, low-risk smoker meant no more than five cigarettes a day, so that's what I do. I save 'em up mostly for after meals or with coffee breaks."

Decker shook his head. "I admire your self-control. I don't have that kind of discipline. I guess I'm basically a compulsive personality, either whole hog on something or cold turkey."

"Come on, you must be a pretty disciplined guy yourself. You were in a monastery for all those years—" She flushed. "At least, that's what I heard from somebody. Why folks call you Monk."

"Yeah, well, it's true. Sixteen years to be exact."

"Wow. That's a long time. Why'd you leave, if you don't mind my asking."

"Simply put, I left because I realized I had entered the order for the wrong reasons in the first place. I was living a lie, which wasn't fair to all the good brothers who were there for the right reasons. So I left, about three and a half years ago now."

"Any regrets?"

His smile was wistful. "Only that I didn't have the courage to leave sooner."

"Were there restrictions against leaving? I mean, did they try to stop you? I'm not Catholic, so I don't really know much—"

"No, there aren't any physical or legal restraints of any kind. A little peer pressure, is about all. I left when I did because I knew I had to. It became self-evident."

"How so? I mean, did something particular happen, or was it just an accumulation of things?"

"Both."

Suzzy sat back and puffed the Virginia Slim and waited. "So? Are you going to tell me the thing that happened?"

"Maybe. But not today. I don't know you well enough yet."

"You're making this seem awfully mysterious, you know."

"It isn't, believe me. It's just personal. And mildly embarrassing."

She shot forward. "Oh, now I really wanna know. Come on, Decker."

"When I know you better."

She locked onto his eyes. "When's that going to happen?"

"It's happening now," he said. "If you'd like to advance the process, maybe we could do it Saturday night? Over dinner? There's a little place over off Pine, if you like Italian. Rossi's—"

"I know the place. And I love Italian," she said, too quickly. "What time?"

"Uh, I can pick you up around seven—?"

"You know what, I'm gonna be out and about all day on errands Saturday. It might be better to meet at the restaurant, is that okay?"

"Fine."

They went back to their coffees and looked at each other across the table like business adversaries who didn't want the opposition to know how pleased they were with the deal they'd just cut. Suzzy eventually broke the silence with:

"Did I hear you tell Norton it was too sunny out to take pictures today? Or is my gift for eavesdropping fading on me."

"No, you heard right, but it was yesterday I was talking about." He gave her a summary version of the incident in Niagara Falls State Park and the subsequent confrontation in the alley off Third, finishing with Norton Gage's encounter with the same young guy in his newsstand. "Anyway," Decker concluded, "I don't know what his problem was, but I wasn't using film in the camera because it was too sunny out. I don't think that satisfied him, though."

"Some self-important jerk," Suzzy said, dismissing it with a wave. "I still don't follow about the film, though. It was too sunny out? Maybe it's me, but that sounds counter-intuitive."

"It does, doesn't it. But it's true if you're going for good fall foliage shots along the river. Y'see, the harsh sunlight reflects off the leaves and tends to wash out the colors. For best results you wanna go out in the morning, early, or late in the afternoon, when the sun's lower in the sky and being naturally filtered by more layers of atmosphere. It just makes for a more vivid photograph."

"That's interesting, but—didn't I hear you were a baker or something?"

"Yeah, I am. I supervise the bread-bake on the early morning shift at Pinto's, big commercial bakery up on Market. Photography is just a hobby really, something I started fooling with."

"And yesterday afternoon you were sitting over in the park by the statue of that Tuscarora chief, *pretending* to take pictures?"

He laughed. "It's not quite as nutty as it sounds. Or maybe it is. Look, it's kind of a long story."

Suzzy had one eye on the front door, watching as a pair of wide-shouldered men in dark business suits, one tall, one short, entered the restaurant. "I guess it's one more thing you'll have to save until you know me better, Decker. Saturday night, right?"

"Right. Seven o'clock at Rossi's."

"I'm looking forward to it." She hit him with the full-watt smile again as she slid from the booth. "Gotta get back to work."

But she didn't get straight back to work. Once back behind the counter, she watched the two suits nod at Camille, the hostess/cashier, and pass on back toward the office, where Gus Pellipollis was working.

She sidled up to the cashier's counter and said quietly, "Can you keep an eye on the counter for me a few minutes, Cammy? I've got to tinkle."

The other woman winked at her from under a pile of lemon-chiffon hair. "Sure, honey. Your handsome mystery man get you all runny, did he?"

Suzzy gave her a playful slap on the arm, then took her purse from its spot under the counter and followed the corridor back to the ladies room. She closed herself in the first stall, sat down, dug a small notepad and pen from the purse, and checked her watch. She wrote down the date and the time, then paused, thinking about what she needed to record next.

CHAPTER 4

Eddie and the Free Radicals

Eddie Touranjoe had been listening to Bona's rap on Corporate America it seemed like all night and he was getting very tired of it.

"Hey, Bona, what the fuck, eh? You think you're the only one ever been inside a factory?" Eddie flipped his cigarette butt out the passenger side window. "You never even worked a got-damn day at any production line, but I have, eh? So don't tell me what bullshit it is 'cause I already know more about it than you ever will."

It was only for nine months, and that was nearly nineteen years ago, but the thought of it still gave Eddie a chill. Up at Ford Canada outside Toronto, he'd worked as an apprentice spot welder at the front end of the assembly line. The big snake, they called it, this never-ending steel carcass, one van body frame after the other for eight fucking hours a day. All this time and he could still picture how that square welding gun used to hang suspended from the ceiling rack, the two-button set up, high voltage on top to join the metal, low voltage on the bottom to fuse it. How you'd stand on your little platform as the units moved up, and you'd make your welds, trying to ignore the incredible noise, keeping your mouth shut to keep from swallowing sparks. He figured it out once. Twelve-thousand, two-hundred twenty-eight times a day; that's how many times he had to pull that trigger every shift, hear that noise, smell the sparks burning the hair off his arms. Arms aching like hell after the first couple hours yanking on that welding gun. Going to the foreman to ask permission to take a leak, and him just as likely to smile at you and tell you to hold it until break. Nine months he'd lasted before walking out one day in the middle of the shift, couldn't take another got-damn minute of it. These days they use robots to do the exact same job, which tells you what kind of mindless, inhuman work it is.

Eddie had done jail time and he'd done time on the assembly line at Ford Canada, and the truth was he never, ever woke up in a sweat in the middle of the night dreaming about jail.

"Alls I'm saying," Bona said, "is that sittin' in a car all day staking out a guy isn't such a tough deal compared to working a crusher at fucking Carborundum for yay-many years, okay? Every line of work has its boring aspects, man, but we do what we gotta do. Things could be worse, a lot worse. Anyways, you invited yourself along."

Eddie grunted and slumped lower in the seat, his knees resting against the glove box. They were in Bona's beat Pontiac Grand Am, parked under a burned-out streetlamp on Walnut Avenue half a block up from the mark's apartment house. It was ten-fifty at night and they'd been sitting there for four and a half hours.

"That was before I knew the guy lived in a shithole like this, eh. What kinda cash a guy gonna have, he lives in a dump like this?"

"Hey, I never said it was a hot setup, did I? I told you I have to go in and toss the place for Jimmy, see what this guy's story is, *maybe* pick up a few goodies while we're inside. You're the one decided you had nothing better to do today. Shit, man, I been following Decker for two days, pissing in a Coke can. You oughta try that sometime."

"No way, eh. You had my equipment, you wouldn't be able to do it, neither." He took the packet of Player's from his shirt pocket, returning Bona's disapproving stare with one of his own as he lit up again. "Get over yourself, eh? You think you're gonna live forever or something, you don't smoke, you don't hardly eat red meat, you eat all those fruits and vegetables, you suck down all kinds of vitamins and shit. Everybody dies of something, eh."

Bona lowered his window a few more inches. "So why don't you just walk in front of a truck and get it over with."

"Yeah, that's what's gonna happen to you, eh? You'll spend all your time worrying about cancer and eating rabbit food and one day you'll get run over by a bus or some homeowner with a piece'll blow your fucking head off. Your ass'll be just as dead, eh, but it'll be even worse 'cause you missed out on all the good things in life."

Bona didn't bother to argue. Eddie Touranjoe was a friend, but he was a stupid son of a bitch and stupid people were all self-destructive. He'd already told Eddie, on more than one occasion, all about free radicals and the damage they can do to blood cells, how tobacco creates negative stresses and stuff like fresh fruits and leafy green veggies form the antioxidants that can fight back, keep the blood clean. Did Eddie care that statistics showed smoking and poor diet combined were a factor in like sixty-five percent of cancer deaths? Fuck no, dumb bastards like Eddie didn't care, never cared about stats and probabilities, because all that stuff was out into the future and ignorant people didn't think about the future.

Bona decided to change the subject back to Jimmy Frat.

"Listen, once I get rolling for the man, I'm gonna have opportunities coming out my ears, oughta be able to pass along some work."

"I hope it ain't shit like this." Eddie looked over at Bona and blew a smoke ring at him. He had a long, sharp face and a mouthful of crooked teeth that made all attempts to smile look like snarls. Not that it was a problem; Eddie was thirty-seven and had spent eight of the last seventeen years in various Canadian jails and prisons. Smiling was something he had gotten out of his system a while ago.

These days he was primarily a car thief and secondarily a meth mule for a Canadian motorcycle gang, Satan's Sons. He had an apartment above a body rub shop owned by a couple biker buddies on the Ontario side of the Niagara River. He had a Harley he hardly ever rode anymore except to motorcycle meets and a Jeep Grand Cherokee with phony VIN tags and a stereo system and a big-screen TV. Any time he wanted pussy or a blowjob, alls he had to do was walk down one flight of stairs and he had his pick of three or four sweet little bitches, farm girls from rural Ontario mostly, plump as summer sheep and just as easy.

He used to wear a beard and long hair, but he was a clean-shaven citizen these days, wore pressed denims and sweatshirts with Canadian sports teams logos on them, the easier to pass back and forth through customs at the Rainbow Bridge. It helped, too, that his Toronto boss, Miles Prevost, had some customs inspectors at both ends of the bridge in his pocket. But Eddie couldn't always count on getting a friendly face, so he dressed square and he kept the bike and the hot Grand Cherokee over in NFO and he usually walked across when he had business stateside. After all, what could a man in jeans and a pullover possibly have to hide?

It pissed him off no end that he had to keep coming over to the States to supplement his income, but that's how it was. An investigation into auto theft rings by the RCMP had caused Prevost to call for a stand-down for a few weeks till things cooled off. And the methamphetamine operation was a sideline, not something you could count on. Bona's action was mostly small-time, a burglary here, a torch job there, but it generated cash, and U.S. cash at that. Eddie figured every hundred bucks he stole in the States was the same as stealing a yard and a half in Canada, the loony being as weak as it was. Besides, there was something almost patriotic about it, ripping off Yanks and taking the money home to spend in Ontario.

"There's no guarantees what's in there," Bona said, "but like I told you, man, you keep the first hundred in cash we find. Anything over that we split fifty-fifty."

"Yeah, but you're takin' merchandise, too, eh. What if the guy's got no money in the house, but there's like a primo stereo system, eh? Then I get the shitty end."

"Hey, you want all the shit, go ahead and take it, Eddie. I'll even drive you over to my fence, you can unload it all, okay? Main reason I'm going in is to toss the place, see what I can find out about this Decker dude, maybe come up with a roll of freakin film for Jimmy. Like I said, for me this is just something I gotta do for Jimmy Frat, like an initiation."

Eddie, appeased for the moment, sank back into the Grand Am's seat and Bogarted his cigarette. "You really think this Buffalo wiseguy gonna put you onto some good money?"

"Hell, yes." Bona swiveled halfway around, his right knee banging the center console. "He's making me an associate, man. That's almost like being part of his regular crew."

"Don't you gotta kill somebody first? Make your bones, eh, then take some Sicilian blood oath or some shit like that?"

"I'm not talking about becoming a *made* guy, Eddie. Jesus, that's just for like the inner circle. But this is the next best thing, being a *connected* guy. Like those cargo jobs I worked with Sally the Pig's crew, only more regular stuff. I'm on the payroll now. I get an envelope from the man every week."

"Yeah? Bet your old lady's happy."

"Yeah, she likes seeing that cash come in. Far as the rest of it, what she don't know won't hurt her."

"Tell me about it. So how's little Brando doing? He's in school now, eh?"

"First grade already. He's great. A little hyper. Winnie's doin' nursery school this year, too, so Melody's home alone now part of the day. You'd think she'd like it, no rugrats under foot for a few hours, but she's talking about having more. Shit, I'm still payin' off hospital bills on Winnie. I told Melody we got one of each, healthy kids, why have more when they're almost both in school, she can think about workin' again part-time. Man, she didn't even wanna discuss that."

"Hey," Eddie said. "I only asked how the boy was doin', eh? I wanted to hear all this other shit I'd get married myself."

"Yeah, well, anyways, this is a good thing I got going with Mr. Fratelli."

"I thought you call him Jimmy."

"I do, but it's a respect thing around other people. Appearances are a big deal to these guys. I'll prob'ly have to buy some suits and stuff once we start doing regular business together up here in the Falls."

"I thought you were just gonna be driving his son-in-law around, eh?"

"For starters. His *future* son-in-law. He's bringing the kid into the Family business, know what I mean? And I'm helpin' break him in, showing him the possibilities."

"In this place?" Eddie grunted disdainfully. "What kinda money's the mob expect to squeeze out of the got-damn Falls? All the action's on the NFO side these days."

Bona wasn't about to let Eddie Touranjoe piss on his parade. He pushed himself up straight in the driver's seat. "Jimmy's got big plans for *both* sides a the river. He's gonna consolidate the rackets on both sides, control the trade unions, take a piece of all the new construction—that's for starters."

"There's some guys on the other side might have something to say about that."

"Oh, yeah." Bona laughed. "I'm sure the fucking Mafia is losing sleep over a bunch of Canuck mobsters. What're they gonna do, challenge 'em to a fucking snowball fight?"

Eddie, staring, blew another smoke ring in his direction.

⁂

They saw Decker come out of the house and climb into his car, an older blue Geo Prism, at eleven thirty-six. That fit with what Bona had put together.

"Okay, he's on his way to work at the bakery, won't be home before like eight-thirty in the morning." He made sure he had eye contact. "Now, we just walk up like we belong there and open the front door with the key the old lady keeps under the plant. She's got the whole first floor, but she's old and not too swift. We go straight up to the second floor. Decker's in the apartment to the right. Either there's nobody renting the other unit or they're dead, 'cause there ain't been any activity on that side, okay?"

"Yeah, sure." Like he'd never done this before, Eddie was thinking.

The key was under the empty terra cotta pot on the stoop, right where Bona had found it the previous night when he'd scouted out the place. They let themselves into the foyer and moved quietly up the carpeted stairs to the second floor landing. It was an old house, like most housing stock in the Falls, built sometime around the turn of the century as a single-family home. It had long since been cut up into an owner's apartment on the first floor and a couple of two-room units on the second floor. There was an old people smell to the place, like Lysol and boiled cabbage, that half gagged Bona. Eddie didn't seem to take notice of the odor or anything else but the scarred red-stained oak door to their right. At Bona's nod, he tried the knob—locked—then pulled a flat pry bar from under his sweatshirt and shoved the straight end in hard between the stop and the door at the level of the lockset. On the first push, there was a loud snap as the stop was crushed and part of the jamb broke away, but the door didn't swing in. He shoved the bar in farther and gave it another shot. There was a smaller noise as more of the jamb broke out and the door popped inward.

"Shit," Eddie said. "Look at it, eh. It's like…"

The word he was looking for was spartan. The apartment's main room had an efficiency kitchen on one wall, a small rectangular table with a Formica top, an old sofa, a hook rug on the floor, and a bookcase holding a table radio and dozens of mostly paperback books. The only decorations were a few color photographs of the falls and some familiar spots around the city, stuck into dime store frames and hung in a row along one of the beige walls.

"Not even a fucking TV."

"Check the bedroom," Bona said. He set to work on the kitchen cabinets, finding nothing but a few plates and cups, some flatware, sugar, coffee, the usual crap. There was a bundle of Kodak 35mm film in the refrigerator's tiny freezer, along with a tray of fuzzy ice cubes and half gallon of Perry's French vanilla ice cream, but the film was obviously unused. Bona took it anyway and shoved it into the Toy Story pillowcase he'd brought along.

"The bedroom's emptier than in here, eh." Eddie shook his head. "I used to keep more shit in my cell up at Kingston. I found a jar full of change and like seventeen dollars lying on the dresser."

"Once a monk always a monk." Bona was going through the shelves of books. Weird shit on God and philosophy and like that. He held each one upside down, riffled the pages, and dropped the book on the floor. "Anything else in there?"

"Just a metal box with some papers and a shoebox filled with pictures of the falls and the downtown area, touristy shit."

"You toss the mattress, too?"

"No, I forgot that, eh, 'cause I'm just a fuckin' dumbass Canuck. Course I tossed it."

"Well—why don't you check out the bathroom, just in case."

"Yeah, I need to take a leak anyway."

While Eddie Touranjoe was doing the head, Bona went into the bedroom and found the file box. Eddie had dumped it out on the overturned mattress.

The papers, in a loose pile, were the usual crap as well; old tax forms, pay stubs, an employee benefits package from Pinto's Bakery, a bunch of banking statements—

"Whoa, diggity." Bona took a second look at the figure at the bottom of the bank statement in his hand, then looked for the date of the statement before folding it neatly and sticking it inside his jacket. It was for a savings account at Marine Midland. As of a week ago Tuesday, Walter R. Decker's account was worth forty-two thousand, five hundred and fifty-three dollars and thirty-seven cents.

CHAPTER 5

Love Between The Thwarts

Doing it on the seat of Randy's F150 in the far end of the parking lot at the mall, Randy grunting and thrusting, Marla's bare legs sticking up, watching the stars twinkle through the windshield's tinted glass, made her think wistfully of her first time with Gary.

Not that it had started out promising. A dozen years ago now, that first date to go see Star Trek IV: The Voyage Home, followed by a late, spicy dinner at a Chinese restaurant, she knew then and there she could get him to marry her. She actually *wanted* him then. In her eagerness to land Gary she would've screwed him right there in the back of his Nova that first night, but it wasn't to be. He made only a tentative move in that direction anyway, which was just as well because Marla Ellen was you might say incapacitated, love-making-wise, at that time. A discharge down below, some viscous yellow-pink seepage from her honeypot, had started up the week before she met Gary, wouldn't you know. And so there she was, on the verge with a Chamber of Commerce type with a golden future, and her damn dripping fun factory wouldn't let her close the deal.

Luckily she'd had some extra penicillin tablets left over from when she'd had two wisdom teeth removed the previous winter, so the leaky honeypot problem cleared up in just a couple of weeks. Luckier still, sweet idiot Gary read her reluctance as a sign of her virtuous nature and, if anything, fell even more deeply in love with her.

They finally did it for the first time on their fifth date, in a rowboat at his cousin's cottage on Braddock Bay, a bright moonlit night like this one, the sounds of bullfrogs croaking in the mob of cattails they'd drifted into. Poor idiot Gary pretzeled ass-end-up between the thwarts while Marla Ellen lay under him, thrashing around on the bottom of that smelly boat like a fresh-caught large-mouth bass.

Why is it, Marla wondered absently as Randy began to pick up the pace, that the good times can't last forever?

"Oh, God, baby!"

"Uh-huh, uh-huh!"

"Oh-Marla-oh-yeah-yeah-yeah-Oh-baby-YEAH! Uhhhh-hhh."

Marla was not a cuddler. She let a respectful five seconds pass before nudging Randy off her, getting her panties and skirt back in place, and adjusting the rearview mirror so she could check her hair.

Randy leaned into her. "That was special, babe."

"Mmm." She gave him a peck on the lips, but turned away when he tried for more. "You'd better zip it, sweety. You have to get back to work soon and we need to talk first."

"Oh. You mean about…"

"Yes."

"Me killing your husband."

"Saving me from him, Randy. Saving one life—maybe three lives—by ending one person's existence."

Randy Post was a security guard at the mall where Marla worked part-time as a sales associate for a clothing store that specialized in petite women's sizes. He was presentable enough, fairly tall and slim and okay looking, but about what you'd expect in the emotional development department from a twenty-nine-year-old security guard who lived with his parents. For a month now Marla'd been bringing him along, doling out the ugly truths about her sad marriage to a cold, sadistic man, the sort of sicko who kept French lubricants and a cattle prod in the nightstand. At least, this was the truth she'd created for herself. When she put on her makeup and her high heels and her sexiest clothes and went to work at the Western Gate Mall, she liked to see herself as Marla Gray, glamorous fledgling romance novel writer, and poor Marla Ellen Graycastle, the mousy hausfrau from Eden with the husband from actuary hell, was merely her greatest literary invention.

Over the weeks of their affair she had told Randy how Gary had duped her into marriage, how he had fooled everyone into thinking he was this mild-mannered insurance agent when, in fact, every night behind the closed doors of their suburban contemporary colonial he transformed into a ranting beast. She was no psychologist, she told Randy, but her guess was that Gary's sterility and impotence had created such rage in him that he had turned to bondage and S&M and a hideous assortment of latex appliances to hide his shame. The girls, Greta and Gretchen, were, of course, adopted, taken in by Marla Ellen against Gary's wishes when her sister and brother-in-law both died of cancer some years before. She had planned at the time to suggest that, given these facts, she herself was practically still a virgin, but Randy was having trouble getting past the cancer thing.

"Jesus, they *both* died of cancer?" he had asked her, awed at the prospect.

Marla had nodded grimly. "Within three months of each other."

"Jesus. What kind of cancer?"

"Breast cancer," she'd answered immediately, before adding, "My sister had breast cancer. Her husband had testicular cancer."

"Testic—?"

"The balls, dearheart."

Hearing that last bit, Randy had cringed reflexively and dropped the subject for good.

Now, as he wriggled back into his navy double-knit trousers on the front seat of the Ford pickup, careful not to buck too hard and rupture himself on the steering wheel, Randy said the words that convinced Marla she'd been wasting her time with him for the past month.

"You know I love you, Marla baby."

Shit, she thought. Here it comes.

"But killing somebody—I mean, I still don't see why you can't just leave the son of a bitch. Take the girls with you and go. Hell, I'd even let you move in with me and my folks for a while, until we figured something out."

She stared at him. "We've already had this conversation, Randy. If I leave him, he'll kill me, he's said so dozens of times. He'd find me and kill me no matter where I went or what I did. He's obsessed with me. I've even looked into the Witness Protection Program, but they won't take me unless Gary does something federal, like embezzle money from a savings and loan or shoot up a post office. It isn't pretty, Randy, I'll admit. But after agonizing over this thing for months, I've come to the realization that the only way I can ever be truly free is if Gary is dead. That's all there is to it."

Well, not quite all; there was the financial component that had to be prominently factored in. But, naturally, she couldn't tell Randy Post about the company life insurance plan Gary had, with its two-and-a-half times annual compensation payout and double indemnity for wrongful death, which would make him worth like two hundred and fifty thousand bucks dead. Plus the mortgage insurance, which would pay off the house. *Plus* the retirement annuity Gary paid into every month, with its life insurance rider worth another hundred and fifty thousand. If Randy knew about all that, he was liable to get the wrong idea, consider killing Gary for a flat share rather than out of passion for her. Besides, he was a man, and Marla had been sure she could control him the way you control any man; from the crotch up. Particularly one whose middle name, she'd begun to suspect, was "Dumb As A".

And yet here the pig bastard was, turning her down even as he sat there sliding his wet willie back into his jockey shorts. She should've been livid, but she couldn't muster the energy. She'd had a long day, smiling as if she cared at short women with size P-four butts, and she only wanted to get to her minivan on the other side of the lot and go home. She'd just have to think of something else…

Randy was drumming his fingers on the steering wheel. "I was thinking."

"How'd that happen?" Marla flexed her ass muscles uncomfortably; she felt sodden with his bodily fluids.

"Don't bitch up on me, babe. You know I wanna help." He stopped tattooing the wheel and sighed, his vacant brown eyes glistening in the glow from one of the parking lot's numerous banks of overhead flood lamps. "There's this guy I know about in East Rochester. He might be able to point us to somebody could do—what needs to be done."

"Oh, my darling, I knew you wouldn't abandon me." Marla moved under the sweep of his arm, nestled her nose in against his throat, and purred.

CHAPTER 6

❀

Seen From An Italian Restaurant

"I don't mind the rain," she said. "It's the snow I dread. The harsh winters, all that cold Canadian air the weather guys are always talking about."

They had a window table with a view of the parking strip outside Rossi's and just a bit of Pine Avenue and a steady parade of cars. The rain streaking the glass made the cars seem blurry and far away and unreal.

Talk about unreal, Suzzy Koykendall thought. If Randall should ever find out she was dating a guy from the restaurant…

"Winter's long up here," Decker conceded. "But it's kind of nice, too, the way the falls changes its look. The way the lights play off the blocks of ice that form up at the bottom of the river gorge. Sometimes you can actually see the mist freeze in the air."

"God." She shivered. "Just picturing it gives me the chills."

"You ever see the falls from the Canadian side in winter?"

"No. In fact, in the three—" she almost said "months", but caught herself in time. "—years that I've lived here, I haven't even been over to the Ontario side."

"You're kidding. That's something we'll need to rectify one of these days. There's nothing to it you know, going through Customs. You can even walk across—"

"Oh, I know. I just never got around to going. I meant to. There just didn't seem much point, going sightseeing by myself."

She tasted her whiskey sour, Decker his scotch rocks, and they chatted aimlessly until the waiter came to take their orders; the house specialty, veal parmisan, for both, accompanied by minestrone soup, green salads and a bottle of pinot grigio.

She didn't want to talk about herself, nothing too far back or revealing, so she worked at getting him to tell about himself. He wasn't eager to go back too far, either, beginning his story from a point three and a half years ago.

"My second rebirth, you might say."

When Decker finally quit the monastery and made the move to Niagara Falls, he spent the first two years of his new life binging; overeating and getting laid. The two became almost interchangeable, whether he was scarfing down a whole pizza supremo or bedding a cocktail waitress; a 16-ounce King Cut prime rib and a baked potato soaked in sour cream *and* butter or a divorced school teacher from Wisconsin looking for a six-day, five-night all-inclusive summer passion fest. Along the way he ballooned up fifty pounds and contracted a minor case of gonorrhea. He looked at himself in the mirror one day, bloated, red-eyed and unshaven, and realized he was fast becoming a middle-aged version of what he was before he'd entered the monastery, and that was not someone he wanted to become again. So he cut back to the bone on everything, the overeating, the bar hopping, trolling for women. He started walking every day, down along the riverfront and the downtown district, and he lost half of the weight gain, which felt about right, and he compensated for the lonely times with a good book or fooling with his camera or a ball game on the radio.

And that was where he was, emotionally speaking, when he came across Suzzy working tables at the Metropolis; a man biding his time, almost holding his breath. Learning to discriminate.

He related some of this as the wine flowed and the courses came; the soup, the salad, the veal parmesan. He held back about the gonorrhea out of embarrassment and about the lonely times, also out of embarrassment. She listened with the reserved intensity of a psychoanalyst, or perhaps just a good waitress.

"Listening is part of the job description," she told him when he commented on it. "People talk to waitresses and bartenders. I guess we're cheap therapy, someone impartial who'll listen to a person gripe. Of course, we do it so we'll get a good tip. But it's actually one of the better aspects of the job, for me anyway. I like to listen."

Decker nodded, happy to turn the conversation away from himself. "And what are some of the worse aspects of the job?"

"Oh, God, don't get me started." She finished a small triangle of veal. "Well, let me see, my pet peeves of waitressing? I guess one is people who call me by everything except my first name. Miss, honey, sweetheart, ma'am—I *hate* ma'am. I mean, we wear those little name tags, you'd think people would get the hint. That's one of the things I liked about you right off. You called me Suzzy."

"After I found out how to pronounce it."

"At least you made the effort. Anyway, I also don't like that people make assumptions about waitresses. You know, that we do it because we can't do anything else. Like we're all totally desperate heads of single-family households with three fatherless kids at home and a collective IQ of seventy five. I'm not saying waiting tables is rocket science, mind you, but some of us have actually gone to college."

"Where'd you go?"

"Who said I did?" It came out defensive, and she silently berated herself.

"It's the impression I get. You don't hear words like 'counter-intuitive' used too often in a glorified Greek diner."

"Glorified?" She laughed. "What's glorified about the Metropolis?"

"The view. And certain members of the wait staff." He pinned her down with the soft blue eyes. "College?"

She sighed. "University of Iowa. I dropped out, though, in my junior year." A direct lie; she'd graduated Magna Cum Laude, but he didn't need to know that. *Better slow down, girl; the whiskey and the wine are getting you off your game.*

"How'd you get from Iowa to Niagara Falls?"

"That's a long story, Decker, which I think I'll save until I know you better." She smiled, tit for tat. "Tell me about being a monk."

There was a playfulness in her words that he chose not to pick up on. He sipped the wine, glanced out the streaked window again, before speaking. "Solitude, sign language, hard manual labor. Humility and simplicity, humbling oneself before God. Obedience to Christ. Respect for all living things. Abstention. These are the things that come to mind when I think about the abbey, the life of a Trappist."

"It sounds—difficult."

"Mm. You wanna know the most difficult part? For me anyway? It was getting use to the sameness of it. Every day just like the previous day, with no weekends off, no vacations to look forward to, no TV or movies. No women. Just that same routine of rising hours before dawn, eating the same simple foods, working in the bakery and in the fields, gathering to sing the psalms seven times a day, retiring to your cell at seven-thirty every evening—"

"A cell." Suzzy said. "How appropriate. I mean, it sounds like a self-imposed imprisonment."

"That's what it was for me. But then, I didn't join up for the right reasons. A true monk is someone looking to be seen by God, to prove that he's willing to sacrifice everything in his devotion to Christ. So he makes himself stand out from the crowd by taking himself away from the crowd and stripping away from his life everything that's extraneous or distracting. It's not so much a desire to get away from the secular world as it is a longing to get close to God. Does that make any sense, or am I just babbling, because that's what it feels like."

"No, no. I see what you mean. Monks hide themselves from society in order to be 'seen' by God," she said. "But that's how it's *supposed* to work. You still haven't told me what drew *you* to the monastic life."

"No, I haven't."

She waited for him to elaborate, but when he stayed silent, she tried filling in the blanks herself. "Were you in the military before? I mean—Vietnam maybe?"

His laughter was spontaneous and short-lived. "No, Suzzy, I wasn't a stressed out vet. I was never in the military. Quite the opposite. I was one of the bad guys, a punk." He gulped down his wine and re-poured and told her straight up. "I was part of a biker outfit. I made my living, such as it was, extorting money from people, kicking ass, selling coke and grass, putting young girls out on the street. That's what I did before I joined the Trappists."

Suzzy had fallen back against the booth's vinyl backrest. She should have known. Rule One of post-adolescent dating: If you meet a man who's too good to be true, count the silverware. Picture Randall getting hold of this; she's not only out with a guy who frequents the Metropolis, he's got a background that fits the profile. Or part of his background did. Still, just because Decker *maybe* fit the profile of the guys they were surveilling—hey, she was nuts to be out with him in the first place, so it was all just a matter of degree.

Besides which, he was becoming more interesting by the minute. After years dating only agency types—and where the hell had that gotten her? — maybe it was time to go off the reservation.

"So what happened?" she asked. "To make you change, I mean."

His shoulders heaved inside his navy blazer. Nice shoulders. The extra weight looked good on him, she decided. "Several things. My mother died, only I didn't hear about it for six months, didn't even know she'd been sick. My father died when I was a little kid, so losing my mother kind of—hit me, you know? I was suddenly a twenty-five-year-old orphan, caught up in a lot of bad shit that I was never going to be able to explain or make up for. Does that make any sense?"

"Yes."

"Anyway, it took another few months, after Mom died, for me to see the whole picture. I'd walled myself off for years emotionally, doing whatever I felt like whenever I felt like it without thinking about where it was all leading. But Mom's death—opened me up some. I guess I started taking stock, and what I toted up wasn't much. I had a '72 Harley Sportster, some worn leathers and jeans, and half a dozen handguns to my name. I was drunk or stoned or both most of the time. I didn't have a felony record, but it was only a matter of time, and time was running out. So I decided the first thing was to get clean and sober and give myself a good hard look. When I did, I didn't find much to like."

"So you decided to go a hundred and eighty degrees in the opposite direction, join a monastery."

"Not immediately. I walked away from the biker world first, did some wandering around, worked at odd jobs. One day I ended up walking down a country road in the Genesee Valley, forty miles or so south of Rochester, and there was the abbey. And all of a sudden I'm remembering simpler days, back when I was an altar boy and my mother was still proud of me." He shrugged again. "The Trappists took me in, gave me a place to sleep, shared their food with me, gave me some work to do. It grew from there. Eventually I became a novitiate, then a monk. I learned to make bread."

She waited through the last of the wine and the veal, the mutual decision to pass on desert and only have coffee, before picking up the thread again. She began by lighting a cigarette, number four for the day, and turning her head to expel the smoke.

"Are you going to tell me why you finally left, Decker, after sixteen years?"

"Didn't I already explain about that? That I never really fit in with the other brothers, who were there for the right reasons—"

"Yeah, yeah, but I mean the *specific* reason. The thing that put you over the top."

He grinned at her like a little boy with a toad behind his back. "You sure you wanna know, Suzzy?"

"I'm sure."

"Well—I guess you could blame it on the Internet."

"The Internet? Now I *really* wanna know the story."

The monks of the Abbey of the Genesee make bread—Monk's Bread—to support themselves, he explained, selling upwards of fifty thousand loaves a week through various supermarkets in central New York. One of his jobs, in addition to the grunt work of actually making the bread—loading the big stainless steel mixers with flour, greasing pans, washing raisins, racking the hot pans, running the slicer, hand-bagging and tagging; jobs shared by most of the abbey's three dozen monks—Decker was in charge of quality control testing.

"That became easier after Brother Erasmus brought in a computer. Brother Erasmus was the business manager for the bread operation. I learned how to use the computer to keep track of our control data—"

"Brother Erasmus, huh? What'd they call you anyway?"

"Brother Walter. That's my first name, Walter."

"Hmm." She looked at him through a squint. "Walter, Walt, Wally. I don't think so. Guess I'll stick with Decker. So, you were saying?"

"Well, we joined the computer age, and a few of us learned how to use the software pretty well. One thing led to another. Brother John, who was our resident computer whiz, came up with the idea that we go on the Net, have our own Web site, to use as a promotional device for our bread and other products as well as the retreats and seminars that are held at the abbey. So we had a lay person, a local programmer, come in and set one up for us."

"Mmm." Her thick red lips formed a pout. "And once you had access, the world outside the monastery was open to you, right? For better or worse."

"It was amazing, how much there was out there. And I mean 'out there'. Sites for alien conspiracy theorists, foot fetishists, curling, thimble collecting, tattoo art. I remember one of my first…encounters, you might say. I was at the computer, trying to follow some links from our new Web site to a site operated by some Buddhists in Montana and instead I ended up connected to this paramilitary group's home page, the Montana Minute Men Militia, or M-4. The lead item on the page was about Aryan domination of the Nobel Prizes. Then at the bottom was this article titled 'Eight Ways to Kill a Guy with a Spoon.'"

Suzzy laughed. "Jeez, I could use something like that. In the waitress game, you never know when some sicko trucker might come over the counter after you."

"Yeah, well, they padded the article a bit. I think number eight had to do with spooning arsenic into his Mr. Coffee. But anyway, my point about the Internet, I, uh, soon found my way to other interesting sites."

She arched a brow. "Eight Ways to Thrill a Gal with a Cucumber?"

"Yeah, more or less. I mean it didn't have to be kinky. After sixteen years of celibacy, just watching full-motion video clips of the old in-and-out was enough to put me in serious risk of spontaneous combustion."

"Uh-huh. Then one day one of the brothers caught you looking at porn—"

"No. I *almost* got caught once, by the abbot himself, but—"

"But that close call was enough in itself to convince you it was time to leave?"

"Well, no, not entirely."

"*Decker!*"

"You're sure you wanna hear this?"

"Goddamnit, Decker—"

"Okay, okay. Let's just say I became, uh, addicted to sneaking peeks at certain raunchy Web sites. Until it's all I could think about. Sex, I mean." She thought it was cute, the way his cheeks were pinking up. He let the last bit out all in a tumble. "One day I was at the midday meal, surrounded by my brethren, all of us silently eating our plain bread and vegetable soup and drinking our black coffees, and I looked over at Brother Monty and I said, 'Could you pussy the water jug, please?'"

Suzzy gulped in a lungful of smoke and began choking, then laughing, then laughing and choking, until finally she got both under control and took a sip of water, which started her laughing all over again, this time holding her hand over her mouth in consideration of the other diners.

"Major Freudian slip," Decker said, ruefully. "I meant to say 'Pass me the water jug.'"

"Yeah, I get it. Oh, God." She wiped away the tears with the back of her hand. Couldn't resist. "'Could you pussy the water jug, Brother Monty?'"

"Hey." He shrugged. "You asked."

Outside in the wet parking lot, just beyond the garish golden glow of a streetlight, they stood next to Suzzy's Nissan Pathfinder and tried unsuccessfully to avoid the exquisite awkwardness that comes at the end of every first date.

"Great meal."

"Yeah, it's a good spot. I've been wanting to share it with someone."

"Well, I'm glad you did. I had a very good time, Decker. I hope we can do it again."

"Me, too. Next Saturday?"

She was thinking, If not sooner. "That's probably good. Come by the restaurant during the week and we'll work it out."

She leaned in, but not too close, and kissed him lightly on the mouth. He put his hand on her elbow and smiled and for a moment she thought he was going to wrap her up in his arms and kiss her the way she wanted to be kissed, but he merely squeezed her elbow and released it.

He said, "I'd ask you up to my place, but—"

"No, that's okay. Another time, maybe." She hoped the disappointment didn't show, even though she really didn't want to go any farther with him. Well, she may've *wanted* to, but she couldn't allow it.

"Someone broke in last night while I was at work," he explained. "So the place is in even worse shape than normal."

"A burglary? God, that's galling. Did they take much?"

A shrug. "There's not much to take. They broke up the place some, probably pissed off because it was such a lousy haul. Sliced up the couch cushions and my mattress."

She didn't want to think about Decker's mattress. "Your camera equipment—?"

"Was in the trunk of my car, luckily. They did take a bundle of 400-speed film from the freezer."

"Film." The crease along Suzzy's brow deepened. "Makes you wonder, doesn't it? If there's some connection to the guy who gave you and Norton a hard time?"

"Yeah," Decker said. "It does make you wonder."

CHAPTER 7

Daddy Go Boom

"Dennis! Where the hell are you going now?"

Bona, his hand halfway to the door knob, heaved a sigh and turned around. "Out."

"Out, out. You're always going out when every other father on the block is coming in." Melody cocked her hip and crossed her arms. "It's Sunday night, for Christ's sake."

It made her look sexier, pushing up her boobs that way like one of those Wonderbras, if only he didn't have to listen to her running her mouth at the same time. It helped him remember how prime she was seven years ago when he married her, back when her jeans were a size six and she didn't need to buy them with that stretchy part in back. Granted, that was two kids ago, but still, she was only twenty-six freakin years old. What the hell did he have to look forward to in another seven years?

"Hey, I got a regular gig now. I gotta go meet a guy, is that okay with you, Mel?"

"Would it make any difference?"

"No."

"Well, fuck you, too, Dennis." She pushed back her bleached-blonde hair and tried to cut him with the green eyes, but the edge had worn off that look sometime back during the first pregnancy. Anyway, little Winnie ran up from the basement rec room to rat out her big brother. Bona caught her in mid-leap.

"Daddy, Daddy, Brando hit Connie." Her favorite doll. She pushed out some fat tears on cue; just like her old lady, Bona thought.

"Aw, he's playing around, kiddo, don't let it bug you. That's what he wants, y'know."

"He a freakin meany."

"Hey, now, where'd you get talk like that?"

"Jesus," Melody muttered. "Where the hell you think she gets it."

Winnie started in again, pouting and squirming in his arms, while the wife glared at him from across the room and from the basement stairwell came the unmistakeable din of six-year-old Brando trashing the rec room. Bona could feel the sides of the cramped ranch-style house begin to lean inward, bleeding shit through the walls like something out of the X-Files, conspiring with his family's needy demands and threatening to crush the youth out of him.

Breathless, he said, "I gotta go, kiddo," and put his daughter down on the carpet.

"Daddy go store?"

"No, not the store, Winnie." He grinned down at her. "Daddy go boom."

Out in the carport, while he fired up the Grand Am and let its sticky lifters warm up, he took a few deep breaths and tried to look on the bright side of a week that had started out so promising, but it wasn't easy.

Three hundred fucking dollars. That's all there was in the envelope Jimmy Frat had given him. Three hundred bucks in twenties so worn they felt like they'd been printed on old flannel. Okay, so he was the new guy, and playing tour guide for the boss's future son-in-law wasn't exactly heavy lifting, but shit. On top of that he cleared a lousy ten bucks on the bundle of film he took from the monk's crib. Eddie got the radio and the coffee maker and the loose change, which didn't amount to anything anyway, so fuck that.

But Bona did come out of that gig with one good thing—other than satisfying Jimmy Frat's paranoia about Monk Decker, that is. He had that bank statement from Marine Midland, the one showing Decker's savings account, with its measly two-and-three-quarter percent interest, was worth forty-two thousand bucks. He'd tucked that little piece of news into his pocket without

Eddie ever seeing it, which was another plus. Like having money in the bank his own self. All he had to do was think of a way to take it away from Decker.

❦   ❦   ❦

Dale Maratucci wrinkled his nose and said, "Hey, man, you ever clean out your wheels? Smell like you got some nasty booty stashed in here."

Bona glanced left and swung the Grand Am east onto Ferry. Which is the only way you can go since they made it one-way, further screwing up the city in Bona's opinion, but nobody asked him. "My kid pro'bly left a bologna sandwich under the seat or something."

"I told you we could've taken my ride."

"Yeah, and I told you it'd stand out too much, the job I gotta do."

"Leastwise it wouldn't smell like bad pussy, man." Dale played with the radio, stabbing all the pre-sets one after the other, then running the dial until he picked up some hip-hop crap on a black station out of Buffalo.

Bona had known Dale for about an hour and already he wanted to crack his skull with a tire iron. Fucking know-it-all disco-looking asshole with a forty dollar hairdo and an attitude, talks like he's some downtown shine 'stead of a punkass suburban wiseguy wannabe from fucking Cheektowaga. That, and the rest of the time he's making like he's fucking Donald Trump, spewing all this business shit he learned in JuCo. Christ, they shoulda taught him to use his brain once in a while. Asshole's driving a cherry red Trans Am with glass packs, you can hear it from four blocks away and see it from three, and he expects Bona to take it along on a residential job, a car anybody in the neighborhood would remember.

The shit he had to put up with to make a buck.

He looked over, gave the dipshit his best grin. "It's a nice set of wheels, all right. I betcha it moves along nice on the open road, huh?"

Dale snorted. If he had one bad feature it was that honker of his, had like a bony part halfway down that, looking at it in profile, reminded Bona of a speed bump. "You know how long it took me to buzz up here from the Galleria, man? Nine minutes, right up 290 to 190 to the Robert Moses."

"Wow, nine minutes, huh?" In a freakin Saturn rocket maybe. "That surely is a nice set a wheels, all right. Tell you what. Next time we go cruisin'? I'll leave the driving to you."

"I'm down with that, man. Nothin' personal, but you drive like my fuckin' grandma."

Bona let that slide and kept his mouth shut, letting the punkass flap his gums until they turned onto Twenty-seventh. That's when he switched off the radio and gave Dale the name of the cross street they wanted, a little busy work. Bona had already scoped the job out the night before and knew the exact house he was looking for. When they got to it, he pulled straight into the driveway, then backed out and parked across the street.

It was a house typical of the street, an aluminum sided Cape built on the cheap after the Second World War or Korea, affordable housing for all the returning GIs. The For Sale sign stuck in the front yard looked like it'd been there as long as the house. Properties like this were a dime a dozen in the Falls, almost literally. Sell for under thirty thousand, if you could sell it at all, which they obviously couldn't. Bona didn't know the particulars on this one, but he expected it was much the same story as others he'd done: The owners had probably moved out and rented the place for a while, until the tenants moved out, too, or trashed the place or otherwise became too big a nuisance to put up with anymore. That's when the owners go looking for a guy like Bona.

For five hundred down, against another grand when the insurance payment came through—minus the two bills he had to kick back to the dude who referred him—he could turn a troublesome piece of real estate into a hole in the ground.

"Okay," he told Dale. "Stay with the car. This shouldn't take long."

"Fuck that, man. Jimmy's paying you to show me how this burg works, this here is part of my education."

"Yeah, well, he also don't want you getting jammed up on any side jobs of mine and this is my side action here. So stay in the fucking car, okay?"

Bona grabbed the small canvas bag off the console and stuffed it inside his black leather jacket and got out. Dale slid out the passenger's side and followed him across the street, strutting like a rooster with a hardboiled egg caught up his ass.

"Okay, fine," Bona snapped at him. "Just stay behind me, keep quiet, and don't touch nothing, can you do that?"

"Twenty-four, seven, man."

"Yeah, right."

They walked up the broken driveway and went right for the side door as if they belonged. It was locked, but the key was stashed were it was supposed to be. The door opened into a small stairwell, three steps up to the kitchen, nine down to the low basement. Bona flipped a couple of switches—the basement light came on—went down, with Dale on his heels. It smelled of mildew and dry rot. Bona headed straight for the furnace, a rectangular gas unit that looked as if it had been replaced sometime in the past decade or so.

"Mm, good. No sweat," he mumbled as he inspected the furnace and the adjacent hot water heater, also a gas unit. "Wait here."

He started back up the stairs, but again Dale ignored him and followed.

"Look, make yourself useful," Bona said, struggling to keep it cool. "I need you to stay down here, tell me if the burner in the furnace fires up, okay?"

"Okay, man, sure." Dale shuffled back over to the furnace while Bona continued up the stairs. "Hey, I don't see a whatchamacallit in there, man. A flame? Maybe the gas is off."

"It's an electronic ignition," Bona called to him. "No pilot light. I just need to check out the thermostat."

"Copy that, man."

Bona rolled his eyes and kept walking.

This was an easy gig, if you discounted the aggravation from the dipshit in the basement. Some places, like with a real old furnace, or a house without gas service, he'd be stuck hauling half a dozen trash bags filled with gasoline into the living room and hooking up a timer with a heating iron plugged into it. But a house with a newish gas furnace like this one, it probably had an electronic set-back thermostat, too. If it didn't, he had one with him, could wire it up directly to the furnace and program it right there, have himself an instant time bomb. Nothing to it, really. First you set the thermostat way low, like forty degrees this time of year, so the furnace won't kick on. Then you set the correct time on the thermostat and program it to boost the temperature back up to like eighty degrees at, say, three in the morning. Then you create a gas leak in the basement, like break the connection into the hot water heater—first making sure that baby's off entirely—and you let the gas build up in the basement, up there in the space between the floor joists, for five, six hours. Then when the furnace fires up at three a.m.—ka-boom! No more house. Crackerbox like this would just about disintegrate, roof shingles and siding blown all over the freakin neighborhood. And the best part was, he'd be home in bed when it happened.

Bona found the set-back thermostat on the wall of the living room. It was turned down into vacation mode, as he'd figured. He pulled off the cover and read the directions printed on the back, then he poked in a few settings and called downstairs.

"Dale! Let me know if the burner lights."

"Okay. Alls it's doin' is like clicking, dude. Maybe there ain't no—whoa! Hey, there it goes, burnin' like a mothafuck!"

Bona smiled. Piece a cake.

❦   ❦   ❦

Forty minutes later they were back where they'd started, on a pair of stools at Packy's, a Third Avenue shot-and-a-beer bar. Dale, for once, was keeping his trap shut, trying to watch the Sunday Night Football match-up on ESPN, Seattle versus Kansas City, while Bona, still coming down off the high he always got after a job, was babbling on about cancer.

"You got your three legged stool of Big C prevention, man. There's diet, which is what I been telling you, lots of fruits and vegetables. Studies by the American Cancer Society show that a high-content fruit and veggie regime is effective on all different cancers, your lung and larynx cancer, oral, pharynx, esophageal. Just about everything except prostrate, for some reason, talk about a pain in the ass. Then you got your second leg of the stool, meaning dietary supplements. I do like a thousand milligrams of Vitamin C daily, six hundred IUs of E. And Beta Carotene, lots of that. And fiber supplements, which can lower the incidence of colon and rectum cancer, you do enough of it."

"Man," Dale said, not taking his eyes off the TV mounted over the bar. "All that fruit and fiber and shit, you must spend half your day on the can." Other than the fact that any football was better than no football, Dale's interest in a matchup between the lowly Seahawks and the K.C. Chiefs was directly proportional to the implications the game might have down the road vis-a-vis the

Buffalo Bills' chances to win a wild card slot. Kansas City was a definite contender for one of the playoff spots, which is why Dale was rooting for Seattle.

He sipped from his glass of Red Dog and, just to make conversation, said, "So what's the third leg, man?"

"The third leg. Of the stool?" Bona shrugged. "Oh, that's occupation and environment. What you do and where you live." He took a pull on his bottle of Bud Light. He didn't like talking about that third leg, even though he had the occupational part wired; no freakin factory exposures for him, that was for sure. But the environmental factor, that was always a sore point.

The house out on 97th Street, the one his old man had bought in the sixties, the house Bona had grown up in, was the very same house he lived in today. It was about the only thing his old man had left him when he'd died four years ago of brain cancer, which Melody, at the time, thought was a stroke of luck, since they were living in a one-bedroom apartment up by the airport back then and Brando was heavy into the terrible twos. So she wouldn't let him sell the place, and he probably couldn't've got anything for it anyway. Location, location, location, as the real estate assholes say: the little shoebox ranch was located smack-dab in the middle of the Love Canal neighborhood. Oh, it had a different name now—Black Creek Village—but that didn't fool many people, especially when they could drive down to the end of his street, right next to the boarded-over church, and look straight ahead at a ten-foot high chain-link fence plastered with warning signs and, inside the fence, a seventy-acre dead zone, all rolling green hillocks, looking like a golf course from Hell.

Bona was a little kid back in the seventies when the whole Love Canal stink broke in the papers, so young he still had stars in his eyes about his old man's "special" job, crushing diamonds at fucking Carborundum. He didn't understand the camera crews that began showing up outside his grammar school or the arguments between neighbors, those who believed the stories that Hooker Chemical had irreparably poisoned the land under their homes with years of dumping dioxin and a lot of other crap and those who thought the whole deal was just a bunch of whackoff scientists and liberal do-gooders crying wolf. His own parents had eventually split up over it, his mother insisting they take whatever loss necessary and get out, while the old man laughed at her and puffed on his Camels and refused to budge. Why, we're not even in one of the hot zones, he'd tell her, as if the five hundred feet between here and there was some kind of unbreachable gulf. Meanwhile, half the kids in Bona's class—the lucky ones—sold their "hot" houses to a government buy-out program and moved away and the school itself was bulldozed into rubble.

But maybe the old man was right, in a way. Bona's mom—no prize to begin with, as far as that went—had sunk deeper and deeper into a bottle of Polish vodka until one day she announced she'd had enough. She packed up her stuff and left Eugene and little Dennis in Love Canal and moved on down to Hollywood, Florida, where, a decade or so later, at age 53, she was killed when an eighty-seven-year-old retired CPA from Wilkes Barre, Pennsylvania, ran his Fleetwood up onto the sidewalk and through the glass doors of the medical office building where Rosalyn Bonawitz worked as a Receptionist/Medicare Forms Specialist. The old man, who escaped with a slight bump on his forehead from the airbag and three points on his driver's license, said he was looking for the Taco Bell drive-through.

So you just never could tell; maybe when it was your time to go, you went, and that was that. Maybe the Big Casino was already out there with Bona's name on it, hiding in a pile of dirt he played trucks in as a toddler or in the dark sludge he once saw oozing up from the sump pump hole in a friend's basement or the air he breathed running around the playground at the now-demolished 99th Street School. Maybe the cancer had gotten into his body then and nothing he could do now made a bit of difference. But Bona saw himself as a proactive type guy, a guy who studied the odds and did whatever he could to get them moving in his direction. So he watched his diet, and he took his handfuls of vitamins every day, and he tried not to think too much about the house he was stuck with on 97th Street, a stone's throw from twenty thousand tons of toxic gunk contained inside a state-of-the-art polyethylene wrapper; a giant garbage bag, basically, with a freakin twenty-year warranty.

For now, given his financial position and immediate prospects, he'd stay on in the little ranch on 97th. But someday, with or without Melody's cooperation, he planned to blow the fucker up. God, that was a comforting thought.

Ka-boom!

"What?" Dale turned from the TV set; it was half time.

"Nothing," Bona said, unaware he'd been mumbling to himself. "I's just thinking about shit. How you gotta be proactive in my business you wanna get anywheres."

"No shit." Dale raised his beer like in a toast. "Habit number one. Be Proactive."

"Huh?"

"Stephen Covey, man. The management guru, wrote 'The Seven Habits of Highly Effective People.' I did a term paper on it. Habit One is like the key to everything." He pitched his eyes toward the ceiling and recited. "'Our behavior is a function of our decisions, not our conditions.'" Then he looked expectantly at Bona.

"Freakin amazing," is all Bona could come up with.

Eddie Touranjoe eased onto the stool beside Bona while Dale was off to the head.

"That's your new babysitting job, eh? Looks like that Denny Terrio. Remember him, the Dance Fever guy? All those Solid Gold dancing girls, eh?"

"I ain't babysitting him, Eddie. It's a business thing, *eh*."

"You makin' sport of my Canadian ethnicity, eh?"

Bona took a slow drink. "Would I do that?"

"Not unless you want that bottle of piss shoved up your ass." Eddie was sensitive about his Canadian-ness. Also, he was more than a bit suspicious about what had gone down in Monk Decker's apartment. It's not that he had actually seen Bona take anything of value, but he could see, after they left, that Bona's mood had changed, that he'd had one of those I-know-something-you-don't-know smiles at the corners of his mouth. It had worked on Eddie for two days, this feeling that Bona was trying to get over on him, until he decided to cross the bridge tonight and put the question to him directly.

"You holding out on me, Bona? Because if you are, eh, that wouldn't be smart."

"Holding out on you?" Like he didn't have a clue. "Holding out what?"

"You know what I'm saying, eh. That apartment out there on Walnut, anything you took outa there you owe me half."

"Jesus Christ, man, you *saw* what was in the place, which is nothing. What d'ya think, I hid a big screen TV in my jeans and hauled it down outa there without you seeing? I mean, did you see something I didn't see in that fucking dump, because I didn't see squat."

By then Dale the disco punk was back from the shitter and Bona was doing an off-hand intro. Dale was more interested in watching the game, which was cool with Eddie. He never took his eyes off Bona. Deciding, reluctantly, that Bona was right. There'd been nothing in that place, so how could Bona have found anything of value?

The lying little fuck.

CHAPTER 8

Tell It To The Rain

"You don't have a VCR?"

"I don't have a television. Why would I need a VCR?"

"You don't even have a *television*? Decker, everybody has a TV."

"I had one when I first moved here, a little black-and-white number, but the reception was terrible with those rabbit ears, and then the picture went altogether and—" He shrugged. "I haven't gotten around to replacing it. I guess I fell out of the habit while I was in the monastery. Anyway, if I did have one, the clowns who broke into my place would've stolen it, so I still wouldn't have one."

"Well," Suzzy Koykendall said. "There's no law says you have to watch TV, I guess." It threw her, though. After Decker asked her out next Saturday for dinner and a movie she'd been building up this scenario; how about they rent a movie, an old classic, and watch it back at his place after dinner? Brazen, yes, but her hormones were absolutely shrieking at her every time she saw, or even thought about, Decker. Screw Randall and screw the job and screw her career, if she didn't get to screw Monk Decker pretty damn soon—

"How about you?" he asked her. "Do you have a VCR?"

"Me? Well, yeah, I've got one."

"So, maybe we could pick up a movie and go to your place?"

Good move, girl. Maneuvered yourself right into a corner. "Sure. That'd be great."

Decker returned her smile. It was a bit past one on a gray Wednesday afternoon and he was having coffee at the Metropolis's lunch counter. Suzzy was wearing her pink waitressing dress and a pair of white tennis shoes. Her honey-blonde hair was in a no-nonsense work do, coiled on the back of her head like a croissant. Her lipstick needed replenishing and the vanilla fragrance she'd misted on that morning had long since been submerged by the aroma of French fries. Decker wished he could reach over and pull her across the counter and gobble her up like a blue plate special. The heat of his gaze made Suzzy feel like a pat of butter sizzling in a skillet.

She slowed her breathing and said, "Can I warm that up for you?" It still came out too husky, but what the hell.

Decker looked down at his mug of black coffee and up at her. "Please," is all he said, but somehow, sparking along the rusted synapses that controlled the romance functions of his brain, it sounded to him like a tortured plea for intimacy. Suzzy didn't seem to notice, however, spinning neatly on her tennis shoes as she went off to fetch the coffee carafe. It provided him a few moments to pull himself up from the depths of her hazel eyes and focus on the booth at the far end of the restaurant in the no smoking area.

It was the kid, all right. Goateed little hustler in a black leather jacket, dark brown fly-away hair that looked like he combed it once a day with a wet hand, worn jeans and a pair of black shitkicker boots. Not unlike the uniform Decker used to wear in his pre-monastery days. Sitting in a booth opposite some woman, mid-thirties maybe, wearing a long lavender rain coat, stockings and heels, medium length brown hair with reddish highlights, a rather thick nose in profile but not an unattractive woman. Maybe she was his social worker or his parole officer.

Decker was thinking about going over—weighing the pros and cons of sauntering up and tapping the kid on the shoulder and saying something like "Find anything you liked in my apartment?"—when Suzzy was back with the refill. Bad idea anyway. He had no way of proving the kid had done the break-in and they both knew it.

"Hello, hello," Suzzy said as she poured. "Anybody home?"

"Sorry. I was—" He motioned her to lean in closer, then said quietly, "When you put the coffee pot back? Check out the corner booth over at the far end there, the kid in the leather jacket."

She snuck a glance, said, "Okey-dokey," and strolled back down the length of the counter with the carafe. She got a good look at the kid by the time she reached the coffee machine. Not the woman with him, all she could make of her was the profile, but the kid she could see plainly. And recognize. What the hell was his name? She knew she had him down in her notes someplace, a local punk, not a major player by any means but a player nevertheless. Bonawitz, that was it. Dennis Bonawitz, aka Bona. No criminal record as an adult, but she remembered he had a juvie sheet for the usual stuff—car theft, shoplifting—and he'd been interviewed on more than one occasion by the NFPD for various felony offenses, none of which had ever gone to court.

She retraced her steps back along the counter to Decker. "The one looks a little like a young Bruce, right?" At his blank expression, she added, "Springsteen? The Boss? Never mind, Decker. I've seen him in here a few times. Is he the one who gave you a hard time about the film and all that?"

"That's him."

"Well, I can't tell you anything about him, except I think I've heard people call him Bona."

❦   ❦   ❦

"Look, Mr. Bona—"

"Just Bona. BAH-na, sort of like Bono from U-2, see? Only with a soft 'a' stead of a hard 'o' at the end. You ever listen to any U-2 over there in Rochester?"

"Not me personally, no." Marla ran her tongue along her upper lip. It was the sort of thing that usually helped center a man's attention, at least it did with Gary and Randy and the other men she'd known. This one sitting across from her might be the exception. He couldn't be more than ten years younger than she, but he somehow seemed like he came from a completely different generation, possibly a completely different species. None of her feminine wiles seemed to faze him; he just sat there and took it all in like he already owned her, and the booth they were sitting in, and the entire world at large, as if he could do whatever he wanted with any part of it and no one could stop him. Come to think of it, the man who had sent her to Niagara Falls had some of that air about him, as well. A trait peculiar to the criminal element perhaps.

She found it very disturbing, encountering that sort of a man, having so little control, but also stimulating in some way. Marla licked her lip again, without premeditation this time.

"My husband hasn't been right since the war, Mr.—uh, Bona. He—"

"Which war would that be? The Gulf?"

"Vietnam."

"Whoa. How old's this guy?"

"Thirty-six. Gary is thirty-six and I'm thirty-four," she said, automatically knocking four years off herself.

"So he was in Vietnam when he was like ten years old?"

She blinked, twice, three times. "No, I didn't say during the war. He was there after the war ended, in the eighties, as part of an army intelligence unit gathering covert information on the communists. It was very stressful."

"Your husband, is he a slant?"

"Excuse me?"

"A gook. Does he look Vietnamese?"

"No." Insulted. "He's a regular white American."

"No wonder it was so stressful, sneaking around freakin Vietnam after the war, spying on all those commie slants. Poor guy must've stuck out like a sore thumb." He leaned in close, using his elbows to nudge away the plate with a remnant of banana muffin on it. "Look, lady, I don't give a rat's ass why you want your old man whacked. How 'bout answering the questions I'm asking for a change, 'stead of the ones you make up in your head? Think you can do that?"

He was right, she had gotten off the track a bit, feeling the need to explain herself. After all, it wasn't every day that a person walked up to another person and asked them to do a killing. Although, perhaps in this Bona's world, it did happen every day, who knows?

She fought to remember his original question, covering herself with a sip of her tea. "You wanted to know why Freddy the Fixer recommended you for the job."

"Close enough."

"He said you'd had—experience in this sort of thing, and he thought you might be available at a reasonable rate."

Bona stared at her, trying to get a read. Freddy McCoombs was a fixer and a fence that Bona had done some business with in the Rochester area a couple summers back. Mostly Freddy arranged cargo boosts, trucks filled with electronics or frozen foods. He liked hijacking loads of food best because food was harder to track; nobody put serial numbers on a frozen turkey or a TV dinner. Freddy would handle both ends of the job, figuring which trucks to hijack and making arrangements to deliver the load to repackagers, but he depended on crews—guys like Bona—to do the actual boost. Freddy the Fixer never came within shouting distance of a hot stereo or a frozen Cornish game hen.

Freddy sending this bitch to him was kind of funny, when Bona thought about it. It had to be because of the story he'd told one night when him and Freddy were hanging at a McDonald's south of Rochester, near the Thruway exit, waiting for a driver to show up with a manifest he was willing to sell. The guy was an hour late and Bona and Freddy filled the time bullshitting about jobs they'd done, or guys they knew, telling stories. Bona had come up with the time him and some guys from Sally the Pig's crew got questioned about a hijacking, a truckload of meat for Tops Markets, and how Rick the Quick Lemongello, Sally's nephew, got tipped by a guy in the Erie County DA's office that it was one of Rick's own men, a guy named Donny Pressi, who'd dropped the dime. The DA had Pressi on a drug beef or something, Bona couldn't remember, so Pressi decided to cut a deal by giving up the rest of the crew. Bona was there, in a warehouse in Buffalo near the waterfront, when Rick braced Pressi. Pressi denied everything, naturally, but Rick had his facts straight and that meant Donny Pressi was deader than that load of prime cuts he'd ratted them out on.

Bona could still see it, the swiftness of the move, as Rick's brother Tony pulled out a nine and kneecapped Pressi, both knees. Then, while the guy's curled up and crying and moaning there on that oily concrete floor, Tony hands the piece to Rick for a shot, then they pass it to each of the other three guys, including Bona. He was pretty sure the bastard was already dead by the time he put one into Pressi's chest; guy'd taken two in the head already and wasn't moving, wasn't even moaning anymore by the time Bona's turn came up.

That's what had gone down in that Buffalo warehouse three years earlier, but that's not exactly how he'd told it to Freddy the Fixer. He remembered leaving Freddy with the impression that it was him, Bona, who'd brought the nine along and who, at the signal from Rick Lemongello, had put the first pill into that rat bastard Pressi, ba-boom, right in the back of the head. In fact, he'd told it that way so well and so often he could see himself doing it, pulling the nine from his jacket, racking it and aiming it and firing, all in one fluid move, so fast Pressi didn't have a chance to turn around.

He may've also left Freddy with the impression it wasn't the first or the last time he'd done a hit, which accounts for why Freddy sent this Marla broad in his direction when she came looking for somebody to cancel her old man.

He stared at her for a long time, playing with his fork. She wasn't too bad looking, actually, for an older broad. Too much makeup, but Bona kind of liked that; it showed a woman was making an effort. Nice mouth.

He said, "How much can you pay?"

Marla sucked in her breath. This was it. She'd rehearsed it in her head over and over on the seventy-five mile drive over to Niagara Falls from Eden.

"I have to tell you, Mr., uh, Bona, I can't afford much. The thing is, I've had to put together the money a little at a time, in cash from my household accounts. Otherwise Gary would've noticed, him being a personal financial planning expert and—"

"How much?"

She hesitated an instant more. "I've managed to save up twelve hundred dollars." Three hundred of which she'd gotten from Randy Post. "It's all I can manage."

"Twelve bills? Jesus." Bona sat back. "Freddy told you I was reasonable, not a chump. You know, I usually get like five grand for something like this. And that's a local job. For this I gotta go all the way to Rochester."

"I'm sorry, but that's all I can pay." She was nearly whispering, but she still checked out the room; the nearest booths were all empty and their waitress was nowhere to be seen. "Look, if I tried to put together five thousand, I'd have to take it from one of our long-term accounts and that would leave a paper trail, you see? If the police investigate and find I've withdrawn a large amount of money—"

"Yeah, yeah, I get it." Bona went back to staring at her. Drumming the fingers of his right hand on the table. Sighing now and again like the put-upon man he was. Finally he said, "How 'bout some earnest money up front? Something to show me you're serious?"

Marla had about twenty dollars in her purse, enough to pay the check and to buy some gas on the ride home. "I don't want to do that," she said. "I think it's better we arrange something where you get the money all at once. I was thinking, Gary could have the money on him when you do him."

"We can work that out," he said. "But I still need *something* from you, you know? To prove your good faith. I'm not saying it has to be cash."

Marla arched one of her carefully plucked eyebrows. "What are you saying?"

"Well—how 'bout a blowjob?"

This time she didn't even blink once. "How soon can you do it?"

"The hit?" He shrugged. "Tomorrow night good for you?"

CHAPTER 9

❀

The Fool Killer

Suzzy had taken orders from a group of men in one of the booths, truckers and stevadores by the look and sound of them. She'd then grabbed her purse from under the counter and adjourned to the ladies room. Decker sat on his stool and idled over his coffee, checking his watch more than he needed to, killing time the best way he knew how until Norton Gage showed up.

He'd just glanced at the watch again when he saw the kid, Bona, and the woman slip out of their booth on the far side of the restaurant. He watched as the woman handed a few bills and some carefully calculated change to Camille, the cashier. As the pair made their way to the door he took a long drink of his tepid coffee, using the mug to obscure his face. It wasn't necessary; Bona never looked over his way.

While Decker sat there fidgeting, watching Bona and the woman walk down the sidewalk to the light at Main and Rainbow, debating whether to follow them or wait patiently for Norton, Suzzy returned from the ladies room and thereby made his mind up for him. "Listen," he told her as he dropped a couple of singles onto the counter, "when Norton comes in, tell him I went over to the observation platform, okay? He can meet me over there if he wants, or wait for me here, whatever."

"Okay. It looks like it might rain—" Suzzy said, but Decker was already halfway out the door.

🍁   🍁   🍁

The stairwell for the Rainbow Centre Parking Garage smelled like a four-story toilet. Decker took the steps two at a time and came out onto the second level breathing hard. Most traffic continued on to the third level, with its direct connection to the Rainbow Centre Outlet Mall, but he didn't peg the kid and his lady friend as bargain shoppers. If they were parked in here, it was likely to be in the first available unreserved slots, which were on Two.

He hadn't taken the time to explain his sudden departure to Suzzy because he couldn't adequately explain it to himself. Part of him, the part that used to rule him when he was a young turk running with the motorcycle gang, wanted to confront Bona and pay him back for the damage he'd done to Decker's apartment. Bounce the little peckerhead around the walls until he was ready to admit what he'd done, knock that cocky grin off his face in the process. That was the part of Decker that had hurried out of the restaurant in time to see Bona and the woman cross Niagara Street and enter the ramp garage via the stairwell.

But the other part of Decker, the part he'd worked to develop for years in the monastery, the part that had let the kid off with a shove the other week in the alley, was now telling him to cool it. Even if the kid *had* broken in, he wasn't going to admit anything, not with the woman there. He'd bluff and talk back and play tough to save face in front of her and Decker would be left with a choice; either push things farther than he'd intended, which would make *him* come out looking like the bad guy of the piece, or walk away with nothing accomplished but a lot of empty bluster.

"Damn it anyway."

He was walking past the backs of the cars parked along the right side, about to forget it and head over to the observation platform, when he caught some movement up ahead. A white minivan—a Plymouth or a Dodge, who could tell the difference? He saw it again; the back of a man's head and shoulders pressed up against the side window. He kept walking until he was directly behind the minivan. Looking through the back window, down the length of the vehicle, Decker could see in profile the face of Bona, sitting sideways in the passenger seat, looking down and nodding his head slowly. And the woman, leaning over the console in what had to be an uncomfortable position, her face, obscured by the shadows, buried in Bona's lap, her head moving up and down in short strokes like a well-oiled piston.

Decker felt a flush of embarrassment wash over him. He continued walking, briskly, all the way up the row and back down the other side until he reached the stairwell entrance, and on down to the street, across Rainbow Boulevard, past the vacant Oxy-Chem building and veering left as he crossed Prospect Street into the park.

He walked out onto the observation platform suspended over the Niagara River gorge and leaned his forearms on the railing and laughed, three short bursts. The people hugging the rail to either side glanced at him and moved away and he laughed again, shaking his head this time. Then he focused on the scene in front of him, the great sweep of the falls and the perpetual mists billowing upward and outward, and the tawdry image from the parking garage vanished.

It never failed to grab him, to raise a shudder that rippled down his body and came out the soles of his shoes and melted its energy into the steel and concrete deck of the platform. Listening to that continual thrum of the great Niagara, the "thunder water" as it was called in the forgotten language of a long-vanquished Indian tribe. Not just seeing, but feeling the force of it, the awesome relentlessness of the green and white water breaking over the dolomite lip and falling, falling, falling into a cold boil of spray and foam and rock at the base. The fearsome beauty often was softened by the appearance of a rainbow, but there was no rainbow this afternoon; too overcast.

Decker leaned on his elbows and studied the faces of the falls from left to right. First the American Falls, with its huge pile of jumbled boulders below, and beside it the delicate Bridal Veil. Then the intervening Goat Island and, beginning at its far side, the magnificent Horseshoe Falls of Canada, like a giant bite taken out of the Niagara River.

"Like going to church, ain't it?"

Decker glanced to his left. Norton Gage joined him at the railing.

"Better than church."

"Well, you'd know, I guess." Norton took out a cigarette, cupping his hand around it as he touched his lighter to the tip. "You been having second thoughts, Monk? Because I don't wanna—"

"No, no second thoughts." Decker pointed out at Goat Island. "I drove over first thing this morning, took a walk out to the Three Sisters."

"Yeah? What'd you think?"

"I think your theory is probably right. Course, some kind of test couldn't hurt, all those shallow rapids—"

Norton clapped him on the back. "Damn, Monk, it's nice to know you're still on the team. I was thinking maybe you were losing interest, what with a new lady in your life."

"Don't worry about Suzzy. One thing's got nothing to do with the other."

"I just thought, with a women to spend your money on now, you might be rethinking your financial commitment to our project."

"I'm in for half, Nortie. Partners, just like we agreed."

"Good. Great." A gust blew a combination of mist and rain into their faces. Norton turned his back to the railing and flipped up his collar. The pewter sky was changing to a charcoal gray out over southern Ontario. "I do believe a storm's about to blow up, man. How 'bout we hustle back up to the Metropolis and I buy you a wedge of pie?"

The thought of Norton Gage "hustling" anywhere on that game leg of his sent a spike of guilt through Decker. He hadn't been thinking of his friend's handicap when he'd told Suzzy to have Norton meet him at the observation platform.

Decker fell in to stride along Norton's right side and they headed out of the park, the little man swinging that stiff left leg of his in a circumscribed arc with every step. The rain came down harder, in large drops that splattered like robin's eggs on the blacktop pathway. All around them, gaggles of tourists popped open umbrellas or ran for their cars and busses, chattering away in a dozen different languages.

🍁   🍁   🍁

When Suzzy came by to offer a warmup, she said good naturedly, "What're you two up to anyway? Got your heads together, jabbering away like a couple mad scientists or something."

Norton grinned at her. "Entrepreneurs is more like it. We're trying to figure a way to corner the Falls market on rain gear."

His hair was soaked, right down to the ponytail, which was looking more like a rat tail at present. Decker's short gray-blond hair had been plastered to his skull when they rushed in from the storm, but now it was mostly dry. The difference between a wired-hair terrier and a collie, Suzzy thought, as she topped off their coffee mugs.

"Uh huh. It wouldn't have anything to do with this garage I keep hearing you mention, Norton?"

"What, you mean my workshop? That's just a place I keep my stuff, screw around with tools and so forth. Guy shit."

"Oh. Guy shit. That explains it." She looked at Decker, a wry smile lingering on her face. "I'll bet you're rebuilding some old hot rod, or a motorcycle. Is that it? You're rebuilding a Harley?"

Decker snorted. "Yeah, I'm fitting my old Sportster with a La-Z-Boy recliner. That's about the only way I'd ride a bike these days."

"Too old for that, huh?"

He looked at her over the rim of his cup. "Too sane. Which, I suppose, is a function of age in itself."

"What I'm actually building," Norton said, still playing with her, "is a full-size replica of the *Fool Killer*, gonna start up my own rapids ride. Give Marineland some competition in the thrills department."

"The what—*Fool Killer*?" Suzzy looked askance from Norton to Decker.

Decker said, "He's pulling your leg," and motioned her to slide in beside him, which she did.

"No, really," Norton said. "I'm gonna build it. You don't know about the *Fool Killer*? Boat originally built by a guy named Peter Nissen, had the idea he could start a passenger service to take folks through the Whirlpool Rapids. The first test run almost sank him, the second run tore off the boat's smoke-stack, rudder, and propeller and damn near drowned Nissen and his first mate. That was the end of that idea, for a good long time anyway."

"Somebody actually tried to take a passenger boat across the falls' rapids? When was this?"

"Hell, not the falls—nobody's that nuts. Through the *Whirlpool* Rapids, I said, a couple miles below the falls. Back in 1900."

"Oh. God, I thought you were talking about something recent."

"Most recent attempt to do regular passenger rides through the Whirlpool Rapids was in 1975, using a humungous rubber raft," Norton said. "Only the company that had that idea didn't stay in business too long."

"What happened?"

"Same thing that's happened to a lot of people that fooled with the Niagara River without knowing what they were doing. One day in August of '75 the raft went out with twenty-nine passengers and crew on board. Got flipped by a huge back-wave. Eighteen injured, three killed. Nobody's been allowed to try it again, and they couldn't get insured anyway."

"Norton's a walking encyclopedia on Niagara Falls," Decker explained. "Particularly when it comes to all the stunters."

"I've heard about people going over the falls in a barrel," she said, "but I didn't know they used to do stunts down at the whirlpool, too."

"Oh, hell, yeah. Stunters been challenging the Whirlpool Rapids almost as long as they've been doing the falls itself. Did you know the first guy to try and swim the rapids above the whirlpool was Matthew Webb, the guy who was famous for being the first one to swim the English Channel? It's true. Twenty-one miles across, that channel, and cold as a grave digger's ass in January. Yet he swam it and lived to tell the tale. Then, in 1883, he came to the Niagara and announced he was gonna swim the Whirlpool Rapids, which is only one of the roughest stretches of water in the whole damn world."

"I'm almost afraid to ask."

Norton snickered. "Yeah. He drowned, all right. Got pulled under by the first big piece of chop and disappeared. His body turned up four days later, way the hell down at Lewiston."

"That's awful," Suzzy said. "A fascinating story, though. I mean, the man who swam the English Channel, and then he comes here—"

"Hell, there's all kinds of interesting stories like that about Niagara Falls."

Decker shook his head. "Now you've got him started."

"Did you know," Norton said, "that the first person to actually go over the Falls in a barrel was a woman? Yeah. A sixty-one-year-old grandma, to boot. She sent her cat over in the barrel first, just to make sure it would work. The barrel made it over in fine shape. The cat died, unfortunately, but that didn't discourage old Annie Taylor. She hopped in that barrel of hers and, on

October 4, 1901, she went over the Horseshoe Falls and lived to tell about it. Numero Uno. First person, male or female, to go over the falls in a barrel."

"A grandmother?" Suzzy looked at Decker. "Is he kidding me?"

"Nope. It's true."

"These aren't even my favorite stunter stories," Norton said, his narrow face beaming with enthusiasm. "Back around the First World War this crazy Englishman, Charles Stephens was his name, gets the idea to suspend himself inside a huge oak barrel, so that his body wouldn't be touching the sides and he wouldn't get hurt, see? So he had his feet tied to a hundred pound anvil fixed to the bottom of the barrel, and his hands strapped to the inside of the lid of the barrel and over he went, against all the good advice anyone could give him. He was a stubborn bastard, this Limey."

"I'm *definitely* afraid to ask," Suzzy said.

"The only part of him they ever found was his left arm, still strapped to the barrel lid." Norton lubricated with a swallow of coffee. "Then, another favorite of mine, this happened just recently, back in 1990? This guy from Tennessee, supposedly an experienced white water kayaker, went over the Horseshoe in his kayak, if you can believe that. In the shank of the afternoon, with hundreds of tourists gawking at him. They never found any part of his body. Recovered the kayak, though."

Suzzy was shaking her head throughout the narrative. "Why do people do such crazy things?"

"Well," Norton said, "I've got a theory about that—"

"Which we'll save for another time," Decker cut him off. "Don't you have to be getting back to the newsstand?"

"Jesus, yeah," he said, glancing at his watch. "I leave Louie alone too long he'll dog-ear all the girlie magazines. Monk, I'll see you this weekend, then?"

"I'll be there."

After Norton was gone, Suzzy, sliding out of the booth, said, "So, you're not going to tell me what you two are up to in that garage of his?"

"It's no big deal. Just, you know—"

"Guy shit?"

"Exactly. Guy shit."

"And that's all you're going to tell me."

He shrugged. "We'll see. Besides, if I tell you all my secrets, you'll have to tell me all of yours."

"What makes you think I have any secrets to tell, Decker?"

He gave her that lazy Newman smile. "Everybody has secrets."

CHAPTER 10

❀

Divided Highways

All the way down 190, going in the opposite direction of the late-afternoon rush hour traffic, holding steady at sixty-five across Grand Island and down through Tonawanda, Suzzy Koykendall thought about secrets. Men, sex, career, and secrets. Right on into the city of Buffalo and to the employee parking lot at 111 West Huron Street, the walk into the lobby and the ride up in the elevator to the office where her regular Wednesday evening debriefings were held, her mind was cluttered with images of her ex-husband, of Decker and her deceptions, of her longing and her loneliness and the longing and loneliness she sensed in him, of fifteen years spent as a nomad in the federal law enforcement bureaucracy. Whether the trip down her particular career path had been worth all the twists and turns and dead-ends, the solo dinners, the parade of living spaces with off-white walls and too few accessories or memories to be called homes, her sex life reduced to one-nighters or the occasional three-week romance that died when the questions didn't get answered, or did.

And so it was that, when Randall sat her down and asked her how things were progressing at the Metropolis, she could only stare at him for several seconds as she struggled to get her mind back on business. A pause that not even J. Ellison Randall, Special Agent-in-Charge of the Buffalo Office of Investigations of the U.S. Customs Service, could miss.

His left eyebrow arched like the villain in a black-and-white B movie. "You okay?"

"Yes, I'm fine. Everything's fine." She wanted to add 'as far as the operation goes', but didn't. That would invite Randall to probe on a personal level, which might get her talking about her life outside the job, or lack thereof. Which would only give him an opening to suggest they renew their relationship. He'd be only too willing.

"I guess I'm just a little tired," she said, smiling wanly. "Don't ever let anyone tell you waitressing is a snap, Ellison. Some nights I go home aching from head to toe."

"A soak in a hot tub with some Epsom salts, is what you need. And some of that bubble bath of yours, too," he added. And he winked.

God.

Sitting there dispassionately across a desk from Randall, studying the ashes, it was difficult to remember what had started the fire in the first place. He was handsome enough, with a square, weathered face and cool gray eyes. His brown hair was thinning on top and she could detect, in the way the part along the left side of his head had crept south an inch or so, that he was already executing a minor comb-over to minimize the damage. But she didn't care about that, a little hair loss, a touch of vanity. There was the fact he was married. Suzzy had been able, in her need, to rationalize that little technicality when she'd started up with Randall. But when it ended, after little more than a month of sleazy trysts in even sleazier "honeymoon" motels out along Niagara Falls Boulevard, guilt over sleeping with another woman's husband had literally nauseated her, like a delayed reaction to a bad oyster.

But that wasn't the whole story, either. The real reason she had broken off with Randall was because she felt no passion for him, and she knew he felt little for her. It would've been worth risking the scorn of being labeled the other woman, the home wrecker, had there been a real connection there. But there wasn't. She didn't realize it at the time, but now she did. Now, thanks to Decker, she knew the difference.

"All right, Suzanne, let's get down to brass tacks then, shall we? Tell me what the brothers have been up to in the past week."

Suzzy crossed her legs and frowned, a reflex whenever she thought about The Brothers.

Gus Pellipollis and his younger brother Steve owned the Metropolis Restaurant outright, no mortgages, a pretty good trick considering that only twenty years earlier, Gus was driving a taxi in Athens and Steve was hustling British and German tourists down at the docks where all the cruise ships come in. Another immigrant family comes to America to seek its fortune and does just that, through diligence and hard work and an ability, unlike native-born Americans, to defer gratification, sometimes for years.

But the Customs Service suspected there was more to the Pellipollis family saga.

Like dealing in contraband, moving stolen or embargoed goods back and forth from Canada via the various entry points along the Niagara Frontier; the Peace Bridge in Buffalo, the Rainbow Bridge up at the Falls, and, a few more miles north, the bridge at Lewiston. Of the three, it was the Rainbow Bridge, located a veritable stone's throw from the Metropolis, that was the focus of the investigation. Such as it was.

"I still think a sting operation is in order—" Suzzy began, but Randall cut her off.

"We've been over this ground, Suzanne. A sting is out of the question. Besides, the brothers aren't the primary targets here. It's the compromised customs inspectors we're interested in nailing for the moment."

"But why not go after the money guys, the crooks responsible for bribing our inspectors in the first place?"

"Perhaps down the road, after we've identified and removed the bad apples at the border inspection site—"

"Oh, come on, Ellison." She uncrossed her legs, planting both feet firmly on the burgundy carpet. "Once you bust our people, a sting won't be possible, the traffickers will all be scurrying for cover. And if you get any customs inspectors to flip and name names, you and I both know the FBI will just swoop in and take the investigation away from us."

"Not necessarily."

"Yes, necessarily. We bust two or three customs inspectors on the take, then you send out a press release—'See, Mr. and Mrs. America, how effectively your tax dollars are being spent.'—and the Feebies catch a scent of the publicity and begin showing up on your doorstep in droves. That's how it'll go, Ellison, believe me. I've seen it happen before, when I was in Detroit. What we *ought* to be doing is setting up a sting centered at the restaurant. Let me get closer to some of the men the brothers are doing business with. Look, I could pretend I'm going with a guy who's got a truckload of unstamped cigarettes or liquor to unload—"

"Suzanne." Randall came out from behind the desk, propped himself on the edge of the credenza, sighed heavily. "Suzanne, please. Must we have this conversation every Wednesday? I'll say it one more time. This is not, repeat not, a sting operation. It's an in-house investigation of possible corruption—"

"Possible?"

"Of *possible* corruption among a handful of inspectors. Our job is to isolate which of our people, *if any*, are on the take. *Your* job, in particular, is—"

"I know my job, Ellison."

"Is to continue to keep track of the comings and goings from the Pellipollis's restaurant of those suspected traffickers whom we've identified. All you're to do is keep note of the names, the days and the times of their visits. Is that understood, Suzanne?"

"Yes, it's understood."

"Good." He went back to his desk chair. "It may seem dull, but what you're doing is key. You and the rest of the people we've got in the field, in the inspection station itself, doing surveillance on the streets. Once we get enough data, decipher all the comings and goings across that bridge, establish a pattern, we should be able to pinpoint which of our inspectors are dirty. It just takes time, right?"

"Right."

He broke out the room service smile. "Hey, I know it's not glamorous, waiting tables. But look on the bright side. At least you're not cooped up in an inspection booth, sucking in carbon monoxide all day long. *And* you get to keep all your tips."

Staring across the desk at him, she couldn't believe she'd ever actually put out for this guy.

At the same time Suzzy Koykendall was cruising down to Buffalo on the shores of Lake Erie for her meeting with Randall, Eddie Touranjoe, driving a Honda Accord he'd stolen off a lot four blocks from Casino Niagara, was breezing up the Queen Elizabeth Way at 125 kilometers per hour, through Hamilton and skirting the western edges of Lake Ontario to Toronto. With SkyDome and the CN Tower looming just ahead, he exited the Gardiner Expressway at Spadina Avenue and drove north several blocks, past Wayne Gretzky's restaurant, almost to the circle at the University of Toronto, before turning off at a narrow, crowded side street. The street was lined with older brick buildings, some of them still used as warehouse space, others used as offices, and a few converted to loft apartments. The building that housed the PreCan Shipping Company was a hybrid, half warehouse and half office space, with a large private suite on the uppermost floor for the company's founder and president, Miles Prevost.

The suite, despite its amenities—a large bedroom with bath, galley kitchen, living-dining room, the office study, and a billiard room with a view of the magnificent City Hall building—wasn't where Prevost lived. Not officially. That honor went to a newish brick and stucco mini-chateau shoehorned onto a forty-foot lot in Richmond Hill, one of the northern suburbs. But that was for the family, and the drive back and forth was worsening every year, so it was a convenience to establish this comfortable pied-a-terre in the city.

Eddie Touranjoe rode the freight elevator to the top and followed the distinctive sound of his boss's voice to the study.

"Ah, the prodigal son returns," Prevost said from behind his antique mahogany desk. The study, like the suite generally, was cluttered with shiny old furnishings that Eddie assumed were expensive antiques, but he didn't know for sure. The same with the fancy words Prevost liked to throw around. He could never tell if he was playing him or what, but he didn't ever push it because the man had always thrown good work his way.

"I left a message with Stef downstairs," Eddie said, feeling a bit defensive and hating it. "Called before I left NFO, eh, so you'd know I was on the way up."

"So you did." Prevost came out from behind the desk and motioned Eddie to a pair of leather wing chairs. After Eddie took one, he took the other, smoothing down the front of his pleated slacks.

Miles Prevost was particular about his clothes; he wore only silk or Australian wool suits, the fabric manufactured in Italy and custom tailored for him by a Honk Kong refugee with a shop in a fashionable arcade off Bloor Street. He was as proud of his speech and bearing as he was of his wardrobe, having patterned himself after actor Christopher Plummer, whom he superficially resembled. There was the aquiline nose, the long narrow face and slim body that suggested he was taller than his five feet ten inches. But most of all there was the accent, a kind of pure High Canadian, spoken without either the nasality of an American or the punctuating "ehs" in the cadence of lesser-educated men like Eddie Touranjoe. He had the usual pronunciations of standard Canadian—the hard 'O' in words like progress, the hard 'A' in again, to cite two examples—but had managed to avoid that peculiarity of speech that most marked the average Canadian; as a young man, bent on self-improvement, he had worked diligently to keep the keep the British and American 'ow' in words like 'out' and 'about', not, as most of his countrymen would pronounce it, 'oat' and 'aboat'.

Of course the key to his Plummerly tones was to be found in diction. He had trained himself to speak precisely, thanks to years of elocution lessons, pronouncing each and every letter of each and every word, no dropped 'gees' or smeared vowels for Miles Prevost.

"Let me guess, Edward," he said. "You're wondering when I'm going to allow you to resume stealing cars for me."

"Well, I'd like to know that, for sure, eh? But it's not the only reason I came up." Eddie tried on a half-smile without showing any teeth. He always felt like an aborted fetus around Miles Prevost. "Although I did bring up a sweet little Accord, eh? I figured one car here and there won't make a fuss."

"You *figured* I'd let you get by with it and pay you your finder's fee."

Finder's fee. That was another thing Eddie couldn't decide whether he liked or didn't like about the man. All these airy-fairy names for things, when it was best to call a spade a spade and a hot car a hot car. Fucking finder's fee. All he wanted was his fifteen hundred for bringing in the car, the going rate for Accords and Camrys.

"Well, I suppose you figured right in this instance," Prevost said. "As for the other thing, I expect we'll be back in the auto business for real in another two weeks or so. My informants tell me that's how long the Horsemen have left before the funding runs out on their surveillance operation in Hamilton."

"Ah, I need to get back to work. I say fuck them fuckers, eh?"

"Indeed. But in my experience, waiting them out is the better part of valor."

The Royal Canadian Mounted Police may appear to be a quaint and slightly antiquated organization to the tourists—just a bunch of square-jawed white men in red coats and Smokey the Bear hats—but to professional criminals like Prevost, the Horsemen, as they were called, were the fiercest group of gang-busters in Canada.

And if there was one thing Miles Prevost prided himself on, it was his professionalism. One didn't survive in the dynamic world of criminal enterprise without learning the rules of the game, developing an eye for detail. He'd started out thirty years earlier as a penniless confidence man, a typical rounder doing a bit of this and a bit of that, rigged card games above a gin joint on the Esplanade whenever the Royal York had a big convention crowd in, a bit of extortion among the immigrant shopkeepers near Kensington Market, simple smash-and-grabs in the trendy jewelry and art stores of Yorkville and Bloor.

It had taken years to build up the capital to open his own business, PreCan, an import-export operation that specialized in freight forwarding. An operation tailor-made for the lucrative business of auto theft, the cash cow of Prevost's empire and the linchpin in his plan to meld T.O.'s many crime factions into a cooperative, with Miles Prevost as its CEO.

It wasn't like the old days any more, back in the seventies, when three-quarters of the organized crime in Toronto and throughout Southern Ontario was controlled by the Calabrians. In those days, when Prevost was still a young rounder on the make, a pair of brothers, the Gallios, immigrants from Calabria in Italy, took a piece of everything and everybody, whether they had done anything to earn it or not. They had the muscle, so they took, just like their counter-parts in the States, the Sicilian mob. But times changed. New mobs moved into Canada from Russia and Southeast Asia, West Africa and

Jamaica and Latin America; mobs every bit as ruthless as the Calabrians, and with their own expertise and their own markets and constituencies to deal with. It had been Prevost's genius to recognize these new realities and to begin to forge connections whenever and wherever he could. Move some diamonds for the Russians, arrange to bring in a marijuana shipment at the behest of the Jakes, or a load of cocaine for the Columbians, or even human cargo for the Chinese tongs. All the while paying the Calabrians a percentage of his profits as protection, principally against them.

But as it turned out, it was the autos-for-export operation he started that proved to be his strongest link to the various factions. They provided the orders, he provided the cars. Stealing to order and then shipping overseas to Russia and the other new nations of the former Soviet Union, to the rich despots of a dozen different West African regimes, to Eastern Europe and Central America and Southeast Asia, expensive makes of cars and trucks swiped from the driveways and parking lots of Canada and the United States and whisked off to wealthy customers living in chaotic countries and willing to pay double, sometimes triple, the retail price for the car, no questions asked.

And the best part of all, it was so simple.

Prevost could write a book on the stupid things some people do to get their cars stolen. His men reported that nearly a third of the vehicles they boosted either had the keys in the ignition or had a second key 'hidden' somewhere, such as in a wheel well. Another sizeable percentage of the cars they stole came from keeping an eye on places like convenience stores and ATM machines and post offices. It's incredible how many people leave their cars running while they dash in to buy a paper and a large coffee.

Not that a fellow like Eddie Touranjoe needed any help. You give Eddie a long, flathead screwdriver and the cover of darkness and then point him in the right direction and he'll come back with a made-to-order stolen car every time. Simple. He jams the screwdriver down between the window and the doorframe, pushes a little lever that's down there, and the door is unlocked in five seconds. Uses the screwdriver again to pry off the plastic ring around the ignition lock—ten seconds, at the outside—and, lastly, shoves the screwdriver into the ignition and turns it. Engine fires up, thief drives away, elapsed time maybe twenty seconds.

The majority of the cars they brought in were carefully targeted: Accords and Camrys, Cutlasses, Mustangs, Jeeps and Ford F150s for the North American reconditioned parts market; Lexus, Mercedes, Acura Legends and Infinitis, big BMWs and high-end four-by-fours like the Grand Cherokee and the Toyota 4Runner and the Nissan Pathfinder for resale in the overseas luxury market.

Pearson International Airport was a popular spot for snagging the luxury models, what with all the up-scale Torontonians flying out every day to this or that business or vacation destination. Leaving their shiny almost-new Q45 or Eddie Bauer Explorer in long-term parking for a week or two. Piece of cake, as they say, for Eddie and his brethren to find just about anything they wanted out at Pearson. Then it was a short drive down the QEW to Hamilton and the freight docks, where there awaited row upon row of twenty and forty-foot containers for shipping overseas cargo. Many of those containers belonged to PreCan, and a select few were earmarked for special cargo. The thieves needn't even deliver the cars to the docks. Using his fleet of leased trucks, Prevost could arrange to drop a container anywhere it was needed, in a back alley or a dormant cornfield, in Canada or across the border in New York or Michigan or even Vermont. Eddie and his cohorts could fit up to four vehicles inside a forty-foot container simply by hoisting the front ends and stacking them like trained circus elephants. Fill the remaining space with rags or newspapers and padlock the doors. Then fill out the manifest—claim the contents to be family furnishings or household goods—and call the freight forwarder to pick up the container.

The ultimate beauty of the thing was how well-insulated Prevost was, since the freight forwarder—PreCan—has no responsibility for whatever is in the container, and thus no liability should the Horsemen or any other government snoops bust any of the shipments. No, no, we're merely a trans-shipper. If you want the guilty parties, gentlemen, you'll need to track down the fictitious names and addresses we were given on the manifests and deal with those people. If you can find them.

Miles Prevost chuckled, quite pleased with himself and life in general, despite the temporary disruption posed by the RCMP's latest attempt to tie him to the auto theft business.

"No, Edward," he said, flashing an avuncular smile at his ugly associate. "I believe we'll just wait out the Horsemen. As I say, it shouldn't be much longer. But it should be all right for you to drop off the Honda in Hamilton on your way back to NFO." When Eddie failed to take the hint, made no move to leave, Prevost added, "Was there something else?"

"Yeah, well, there is something else, eh? This friend of mine across the border, the one I do some work with, eh?"

"This would be the fellow you do burglaries with, I take it?"

"Bona's his name. Anyway, he's got a new arrangement you should know about."

"Oh? And why should your friend's new arrangement interest me?"

That's when Eddie told Prevost all about James 'Jimmy Frat' Fratelli, the Buffalo mob capo, and his expansion plans for Niagara Falls, including all of Bona's embellishments and throwing in a couple of his own. By the time he finished, Eddie made it sound as if Jimmy Frat had an army of swarthy troops massed along the Niagara Frontier, ready to invade not just NFO with its Casino Niagara crowd, but all of Southern Ontario, with a march on Toronto not entirely out of the question.

Prevost, for the first few seconds at least, was speechless. Years it had taken him to broker an arrangement with the Calabrians, to make a fragile kind of peace with the Chinks and the Jakes, to learn how to co-opt the Russians, and the Iranians, and the Vietnamese and all the other ethnic mafias, and now, when everything was falling into some sort of organizational equilibrium— loose, to be sure, but prospectively manageable—along comes a knuckle dragging, mouth breathing, garlic sucking Sicilian meatball of a Yank mafioso to upset the entire apple cart?

Not as long as Miles Prevost had a say in it.

He got up and took a stroll around the study, practicing the deep breathing exercises he'd learned as part of his elocution training, calming himself. What was needed, of course, was an object lesson for Mr. Fratelli of Buffalo, our Jimmy Frat. A rather sudden, loud, and obvious object lesson, subtlety being a waste of effort on Yanks in general and on people of Jimmy Frat's ilk in particular.

Yes. Something splashy.

Something pyrotechnic.

He was smiling again by the time he sat back down behind the desk.

"Edward, my man," he said archly. "How would you like to earn a few extra dollars, say five thousand, to see you through the next couple of week's inactivity?"

"Yeah?" Eddie Touranjoe started to smile, too, until he remembered his ragged teeth. "This five thousand, eh, would we be talking U.S. or Canadian?"

CHAPTER 11

Where The Streets Have No Name

"How fucking far is this anyway?"

"It's almost to Rochester, man, I told you. You wanted to drive, remember?"

"I'm just asking. You said Rochester and I'm down with that, but I didn't know it was like seventy miles or some fucking thing. We should've took the Thruway, man."

"Taking the freakin Thruway don't cut any miles off, not where we're going. These back roads here are the most direct way. It just sucks time-wise."

"Yeah, and mileage-wise, too. All these little fucking towns and speed zones and deer and shit like that."

They had almost hit a big buck a few miles east of Gasport, Dale standing on the brake and nearly sending the Tranny into a Godzilla-class storm ditch. They'd seen the doe first, just caught it in the headlights as it kind of tippy toed across the road. Then, while they were watching the doe dance by, the buck came following its mate, giant antlers sticking out all over its head like a crown of thorns, which made it all the more appropriate when they both yelled "Jesus Christ" as the Trans Am locked up and started into an ass-end slide toward that huge ditch.

Neither one of them had said a word for about a minute after that until Dale had the car back on the road and heading in the right direction. He said, "Mothafuckin' dark out here, man," and Bona had concurred. It was as dark as the end of the world out there.

They were driving along Rt. 31, dairy country mostly, dotted with small Erie Canal towns like Lockport and Brockport and, in between, a bunch of other little places with "port" in their names. Soon they'd be angling north to catch 104, the old Ridge Road, ride it right on into the town of Eden and Ben's ShopSmart shopping strip. That's where they'd wait for a certain Toyota Camry and, when it showed, Bona would tell Dale thanks for the lift and send him back to Buffalo. Give him the map and let him take the freakin Thruway, if he wanted to.

As if reading his mind, Dale looked over and said, "So you still ain't gonna tell me what this gig's all about, man?"

"Piece of business I gotta do. That's all you need to know."

"You know what Covey says in his book, about cooperative effort?"

"I don't give a flying fuck what he says."

Dale pouted. "I guess I won't tell you what Jimmy's got cooking for Sunday, you wanna be like that."

Bona kept his eyes front, staring out into the sweep of the headlights and the nothingness beyond, playing it cool. When the two of them had hooked up at Packy's earlier in the evening, Dale had handed over an envelope—another measly three hundred bucks—and an order from Jimmy Frat. Bona was supposed to meet a guy from Jimmy's crew, guy named Philly, down in North Tonawanda Sunday night at ten o'clock. That's all Dale told him, or knew to tell him, he said. Until now.

"I thought you didn't know what it was all about?"

"Ah, not officially. But I was over at the house last night watching some tube on the big screen with Angie? And when I went to use the bowl, I heard some stuff while Jimmy was on the kitchen phone with this Philly."

"What stuff?"

"Hey, f'getabotit. Why should I tell you, you won't tell me dick about this fucking safari into the wilderness you got me on."

Bona had thought it out before and decided Dale didn't need to know shit; he just needed to drive where Bona told him to drive and get lost when Bona told him to get lost. But all the while the whole deal was right there on the tip of his tongue, wanting to come out, just like the pistol was burning a hole in his pocket. It's like he had to tell somebody or he'd bust.

"This is part of my sideline business, like that torch job the other day, okay? Nobody needs to know about this except me and you."

"Hey, I'm down, man. Nobody gonna hear word one from me," Dale said, not even thinking about how he'd already told Jimmy and, later, Angie, all about the torch job.

"Okay. Here's the thing. I'm taking a guy out tonight." It gave him a charge just to say the words out loud, but Dale had to go and spoil it for him.

"Taking a guy out?" Grinning like an idiot. "What're you, a fucking homo, Bona? You're taking a guy out tonight?"

"I'm *hittin'* a guy, dipshit." He pulled the pistol out of his jacket pocket and held it up.

"Hittin' a guy? What, with that?" Dale laughed and slapped the steering wheel so hard they almost went into the ditch again.

Bona looked at the gun, nestled perfectly in the palm of his hand. "It'll do the job."

It was a Jennings .22 auto, a cheap little piece with a chrome finish and walnut stocks, a six-shot magazine and a two and a half inch barrel. He'd paid seventy-five bucks for it out of the trunk of a guy's car one night on Sixth Street, some home protection for Mel to have on hand when he was out, but she'd never given the gun a second glance and, to be truthful, he didn't worry all that much about her anymore.

"Where'd you get it from, a box a Cracker Jacks? That's a fucking girl's gun, man. Jesus, Bona, you sure you ain't a homo, drivin' out here to suck some guy's dick? Which, by the way, would prob'ly be bigger than that—"

Bona put the stubby barrel against the side of Dale's face, just behind the right eye socket. "I guess if I pull the trigger right now, this little bitty piece won't cut a tunnel right through your dumb fucking skull, huh?"

"Hey, Jesus, man."

"What're you sweatin' for, Dale? Little faggoty girl's gun like this?"

"You made your point, Bona. C'mon, man, I'm driving here."

Bona gave it another couple seconds and slipped the pistol back into his jacket. The silence that followed was a welcome break, but Dale never could keep his trap shut for long.

"So, uh—" He cleared his throat. "What's the deal on the hit?"

"The deal is you drop me off and get lost. That's the deal on the hit. What's the deal Jimmy's got me into for Sunday?"

"It's a break-in at a bar or a party house or some shit, I couldn't catch it. You're supposed to go in after-hours with Philly, look for some dirty pictures."

"Dirty pictures?"

"That's what I heard Jimmy say, man. Go figure."

❦   ❦   ❦

At nine o'clock that evening, as Gary Graycastle put his daughters Greta and Gretchen to bed and a sharp October wind whistled through the quiet cul-de-sac, Marla Ellen was in the kitchen, struggling to pack twelve hundred dollars in wrinkled tens, twenties, and fifties into a videocassette case.

"Shit, shit, shit!"

The problem was, she could fit the bills in nicely if she left out the video, a copy of "Shakespeare In Love". But that meant she'd have to destroy the video herself, there at home, and she didn't think even her top-of-the-line KitchenAide disposal could handle all that hard plastic. Additionally, the video case wouldn't feel right stuffed with money instead of a video cassette and, anyway, the case was semi-transparent; even the ever oblivious Gary would notice it was a bundle of cash he was carrying and not a rented movie.

Marla Ellen felt the tension streak down her arms and into her fingers, her choppy nails raking the solid surface veneer countertop. It had seemed like such a good plan when she'd laid it out for Bona yesterday afternoon in her minivan. She'd rent a video that day and "forget" to return it until late the next night—G-Day, Gary Gone Day, as she liked to think of it. She'd tell Gary to return it to the video rental shop at Ben's ShopSmart plaza. Inside the video-cassette, she'd told Bona, would be his fee for killing Gary. All Bona had to do was intercept Gary in the parking lot before he could get to the video shop's drop-off slot, and the rest was up to him—she didn't want to know about that part. It was too painful, she was still too conflicted about her feelings for her husband, to contemplate the precise manner of his undoing. Besides, the less she knew, the less she could get tripped up on later should the police get suspicious and make her take a lie detector test or something.

But now there was this annoying complication to deal with.

She took a moment and gathered herself, exhaling so hard it blew a couple of twenties off the stack and onto the floor. As she bent over to retrieve them, it came to her. She would rubber band the money to the *outside* of the video case, then tuck the whole bundle into a plastic Wegman's grocery bag and tie a good knot in the handles. Gary was pathetic with knots, as he was with anything involving the manual dexterity normally associated with males; he was just not handy. Rather than try and undo the knot, she knew Gary would simply shove the whole bag into the drop-off slot and let the video clerk sort it out.

Not that Gary would ever make it to the drop-off slot. Bona would see to that. And by, oh, an hour from now, poor Gary Graycastle would be yet another victim of a random crime and Marla Ellen, his loving and selfless wife of eleven years, would suddenly be a well-off widow with the world at her feet.

"Hey, punkin."

Gary came into the kitchen moments after Marla Ellen finished packing up the video and the cash. He was already in his pajamas.

She put on an aggrieved look, which came easy to her. "We forgot to return the movie, Gary. One of us is going to have to run it back."

"I can do it, honey bear. I'll just drop it off on the way in to work tomorrow."

"No, *Gary*, they'll charge us an extra three dollars."

"Isn't there a grace period or something like that? I mean, if it turns up in the return box before they open for business in the morning, you don't get charged for the extra day?"

"That's the *library*, pooky. Video stores don't give grace periods."

"Well, it's only three dollars."

"Fine." She slammed the Wegman's bag on the SSV countertop and walked toward the mudroom as if to get her coat. "I'll run it back myself."

"Oh, now, sweet knees—"

"Three dollars is three dollars, Gary. You remember two Sundays ago, when we were doing the collection envelope for church and we only had a five and a twenty, which you needed for gas money for the week? How you asked me if I had any singles lying around we could put in with the five, and then we ended up getting a couple of dollars from Gretchen's piggy bank?"

"All right, Marla Ellen, I'll take it back."

"All I'm saying is every little bit counts."

He went to the mudroom closet and took out his raincoat and slipped it on over his flannel paisley pajamas. As he picked the Wegman's bag off the kitchen's island, he put on a smile and said, "You're right, punkin, every little bit counts. Daddy'll be back in a jiffy."

Marla Ellen couldn't help herself. She threw her arms around him and buried her face against his neck and held him tight against her and tried not to sob.

"Hey," he said, chuckling amiably. "Easy there, you vixen. You'd think it was Saturday night or something."

That's when she let him go.

CHAPTER 12

Two in the Dome

"That it?"

"No, that's not it. That's a freakin blue Mazda. I told you a plum colored Camry."

"Hey, all these Jap traps look the same to me. The fuck color is plum anyway?"

"It's kinda between maroon and like a purple. I'll know it when I see it."

They were parked facing the video store, Dale killing time poking through the radio channels and running his mouth while Bona slumped quietly in the Trans Am's passenger seat and tried to keep his mind focused. Dale had picked up a hip-hop tune and then some swing from an alternative station, WBER, but the signal began to fade, so he'd switched to AM and a sports call-in program, amazed to hear how into the Bills and the Sabres the local fans were. But some idiot calling in about the Rochester Rhinos soccer team and a slew of commercials for mufflers and cut-rate auto insurance exhausted his patience and he switched off the radio. Now there was nothing to listen to but the ticking of the radiator as it cooled down and the sound of Dale's own interior monologues. Introspection was not a place he liked to visit often or for too long.

"So," he said, "you're really gonna grease a guy tonight."

Bona's grunt came from deep down in the Tranny's bucket seat.

"How you gonna do it? C'mon, man, gimme the four-one-one."

Bona didn't answer. He pushed up high enough to observe a dark green Lexus as it rolled by, then slumped back down.

Dale persisted. "Two in the back of the dome, that's how I'd do it. Quick-like and clean and I'm fucking gone. Only I'd use me a nine or a magnum, make sure that mothafuck was meat, man."

"Yeah, that'd be real clean, genius," Bona said. "He'd be freakin meat all right, meat all over the fucking windshield and the dashboard and every other fucking place, including your face, you try blowing a guy's head off from up close with a fucking magnum. Jesus."

"You know, you should watch the way you dis me, Bona. And that shit with the gun, shoving your piece at me. What up with that, man? You supposed to be taking me around, teaching me shit—"

"Lesson One: quit talking like a nigger. You don't come off authentic, you just look like some teen wigger struttin' through the mall with his pants fallin' off. So get a fresh act. Lesson Two: learn to shut the fuck up once in a while and let somebody else talk. There's a reason we've got one mouth and two ears."

Never having heard that one before, Dale assumed Bona had made it up on the spot and the profundity of it—one mouth and two ears, no shit—kept him quiet, thinking, for a good ten seconds. Then: "Alls I'm saying, man, is I ain't working for you, you're fucking working for me, is how I see it."

"Yeah? Well, the way I see it is I work for myself. And *sometimes* I do some stuff for Jimmy Frat and that's where you come in. But don't get confused, okay? In your normal babysitting deal, it's the babysitter who does the sitting and the baby who gets sat on."

"Fuck you, man."

"Good comeback, Dale."

The Camry showed up a few minutes later. Bona popped up like one of Brando's toaster strudels and was halfway out of the car by the time the Toyota was easing into the fire lane along the front of the video store.

"Take off," is all he said.

Dale leaned over as the door was swinging shut and yelled, "Hey, what'd you do with the fucking map?" But Bona was gone by then, tugging on a pair of leather driving gloves and slipping the gun into his palm as he fast-walked across the lot to the fire lane. The mark had parked and opened his door and was lowering one pajama leg to the pavement when Bona got there. He banged him on the forehead with the butt of the .22 and shoved him back behind the wheel, barking threats as he climbed into the back seat of the Camry.

"Drive."

Gary Graycastle was stunned, as much by the rudeness as by the blow to his cranial region. "What?"

"Drive, asshole," Bona hissed, and jabbed the gun into the back of his neck for emphasis.

"I-I'm s-sorry," Gary said, stumbling over the syllables. "You want a ride somewhere? Ow!"

"This is a fucking car jacking, okay? And this is a gun, so put this shitbox in gear and drive outa here before I have to shoot you dead and drive it myself. Capeesh?"

"Yes, yes." Gary put the car in drive and pulled away from the curb. "I w-was supposed to drop off a movie—"

"Lemme have it."

"What?"

"The fucking movie, man. Would you quit saying 'what, what, what'. You sound like a fucking duck."

While Gary handed back the Wegman's grocery bag with the video inside, Bona instructed him to drive west out of the shopping strip and to keep going on 104 until he was told different. Then Bona sat back and checked out the bag. He couldn't get the knot out of the handles wearing the gloves, so he took a hold on it and slipped a couple fingers in under it and he pulled until the bag tore apart like a pinata. Gary's eyes expanded in the rearview mirror when he saw the video case with the cash strapped around it.

"Is that—is that money?"

Bona was too busy counting it to answer. Old tens, twenties, a few fifties, making a neat little stack less than an inch high on his knee; a thousand and forty, sixty, eighty, eleven hundred, eleven fifty, eleven seventy, eleven ninety. That was it. She'd stiffed him ten bucks. Or maybe it had fallen on the floor.

He checked the matted carpet and felt around under the back of the driver's seat, coming up with an empty McDonald's drink cup and a Beanie Baby that looked like a frog, but no ten spot. The hell with it. He figured he'd keep the movie and call it even, until he checked the title, saw it was "Shakespeare In Love" and cursed.

Gary said, "That was money, wasn't it." Not really asking a question this time, but accusing.

"Don't worry about it. Just drive, and stay within shouting distance of the speed limit. I don't want any hick cops pulling us over."

"Where are we going?"

"Niagara Falls. Honeymoon capital of the world."

"I don't understand." Gary's blubbery blue cow eyes filled up the rearview mirror.

"Watch the freakin road, man."

"Why would Marla Ellen put all that money in a shopping bag?"

Bona didn't answer. He was sitting back, the stack of bills in his lap with the rubber band around it, looking around everywhere but the rearview mirror.

It took Gary another five minutes of silent driving to figure it out.

"You're going to kill me, is that it?"

Bona shot forward and rapped him with the Jennings. "Not if you shut the fuck up and drive, okay?"

It was a question he couldn't answer if he wanted to. All night he'd been studying the angles, looking to see which way was best to go on this deal. He could just walk. Have the asswipe drive him to Niagara Falls and drop him off near where he parked his ride, on Third. Then just walk away. He's got the money, and the bitch, Marla, there's no way she could turn him in to the cops. *'Scuse me, officer, but I think I've been defrauded by the hit man I hired to shoot my husband.* Don't think so.

Course, there was Gary here, the clueless hubby. Bona could just turn him around and send him home, probably the guy'd go back and divorce his old lady or crack her one upside the head and that'd be the end of it. Unless he was so pissed he couldn't leave it alone and he got wifey to give up Bona's name and he came looking for his twelve hundred bucks and a little payback…

Something else to factor in. What if the story got around, that Bona took money and didn't do the hit? What if Marla went back to Freddy the Fixer McCoombs and bitched to him about it? What would everybody think then?

Good for Bona, he ripped off some rube bitch for twelve hundred bucks? Or, Hey, did you hear about Bona punking out on a hit?

Something to think about, all right.

     ❦   ❦   ❦

Just north of Albion, along a particularly dark and empty stretch of 104, Bona whirred down the window and hook-shot the video and the case into a stubbled corn field. The sudden flow of cold air on the back of his neck seemed to shock Gary out of his stupor.

"I need gas," he said.

"What?" Bona leaned forward and checked out the gage. "Fuck."

"I've been on E for a while now. We'll never make it another forty miles—"

"All right, all right." They had passed a mini-mart a couple miles back. "Pull over. I gotta work this out."

What he came up with was to put Gary into the trunk, then drive back to the minimart and get some gas. Just before he closed the lid on him, he said, "Gimme some money."

Gary glared up at him from a fetal position. "I'm in my pajamas, for Pete's sake. I didn't bring any money. All I expected to do was drive to the ShopSmart and return a movie that I didn't even want to watch in the first—"

Bona slammed the lid shut.

At the mini-mart it got dicey for a moment when the kid behind the glass, goofy Alfred E. Newman-looking geek, got wise with him for only putting in three bucks worth of gas. Kid called him a big spender, grinning at him like that glass could protect him from anything, even a bullet, which maybe it could at that. Bona thought for a split second about flashing the gun, just to ice the punkass, but that would've been way too stupid. It was bad enough he'd called this much attention to himself, let somebody get a good look at him driving the mark's car, but that couldn't be helped. No fucking way was he going to put more than three dollars of his own money into somebody else's gas tank.

When he got a few miles down the road he pulled over again and got Gary out of the trunk and put him back behind the wheel. While he was making the transfer, Gary said only one thing to him—"Did she tell you why?"—but Bona didn't answer him.

They were all the way to Lewiston, angling south for the last few miles to the Falls, before anyone said anything. Bona was wishing they could go faster, wondering how it could take so long for ten minutes to crawl by in the dark. Gary, both hands draped over the steering wheel, was softly sobbing.

Finally Bona said, "Hey, man, c'mon. Show me some stones here."

Gary, blubbering: "How could she? How could she?"

Bona was only half listening. They were driving through a field of high-voltage trunk lines, part of a power grid that criss-crossed the area like a giant game of cat's cradle. What you had, taking in the hydroelectric plants on both sides of the Niagara River, was the largest generating complex in the world. There was poison in that shit, too, as far as Bona was concerned, no less dangerous than the dioxins the chemical companies had dumped at Love Canal. Electro-magnetic waves that fry brain cancer into your gourd without you ever feeling a thing, and he'd spent his entire life traveling under or living near those towering steel bastards. He could remember when Old Man Brinetti, down the street on 97th, would sit out on his patio with a piece of tin foil on top of his head like a soldier's cap and everybody would make fun of him. Everybody but Bona.

He rapped Gary again, but not so hard. "Y'know, your old lady'd never have the nads to do you like this if you didn't act like a fucking douche bag, crying and shit. I mean, it's like raising kids. You be nice-nice all the time and pretty soon they're walking all over you. You gotta let 'em know who's boss once in a while, man."

Gary sniffed, straightened a bit. "I put my foot down when I need to."

Bona laughed. "Look at you. You're in your fucking pajamas, taking back a fucking chick flick you didn't even wanna watch in the first place. You think you ain't a little bitty bit pussy whipped?"

Gary went to work on that for the next few minutes, hunched over the wheel and brooding as Bona gave directions. They came into the Falls from the north, all the way down Main Street, past the library and then city hall, making the lights at Pine and Walnut and Ferry, the traffic sparse at that hour on a weekday in the middle of October.

When they caught the light at Main and Rainbow Boulevard South, just down from the Metropolis Restaurant, Gary Graycastle said, "I could pay you myself. I have a 401-k at work that I could tap. I could give you twenty—forty thousand dollars. All I'd have to do is file a form, claiming a family medical emergency—"

"Yeah, right." He was supposed to hold a gun on the guy while he filled out the loan form, then keep holding it on him for another three to five working days while they waited for some bank doofus to cut a check. "I don't think we'll need to pursue that, man."

"But there's no reason to kill me—"

"Who said I was going to kill you? You're giving me a ride, is all. Maybe you and your old lady have some issues, but me, I've got what I signed on for."

"Really?"

"I got no reason to lie." The light changed. "Take Rainbow there and pull into the garage entrance, on the left."

"The parking garage?"

"Yeah. Drive up to the second level."

The parking was free, no ticket to take. The garage was nearly empty. Gary guided the Camry up the ramp and around, and up another ramp and around, until Bona tapped him on the shoulder.

"See that car parked over there? Go past it four or five slots and pull in."

"Is that your car?"

"No."

"It's nice. I've been thinking about getting a Taurus myself next time."

"Yeah, I hear it's a good family sedan."

Bona told Gary to turn off the Camry, told him to lay himself out across the front seats.

The fear welled up again in Gary's watery blue eyes. "Why do I have to lay down? The shifter's in the way."

"Well, curl around it or something. I want you down, so's you can't see which way I go. I'm gonna have you count to a hundred, okay?"

"You're not going to shoot me?"

"No."

"All right."

Gary stretched out as instructed, his rump pushed between the two seats, his face nearly touching the glove compartment, and began to count. Bona opened his door. He remembered the Beanie Baby on the seat and stuck it in his jacket for Minnie. Then he leaned over and thrust his right arm between the two front bucket seats and pushed the little pistol against the back of Gary's head and fired twice.

Pow, pow.

Two in the dome.

CHAPTER 13

Working For The Man

Eddie Touranjoe spent all day Thursday tracking down a home address for Jimmy Frat and all day Friday tracking down the dynamite he needed to earn the five K from Miles Prevost. He'd received half up front, in Canadian but that was okay. Eddie was as patriotic as the next guy. He'd then spent the daylight hours on Saturday driving himself down to Amherst in the northeast suburbs of Buffalo and casing out the neighborhood where Fratelli lived with his wife and daughter.

The house was a huge brick jobby with arched windows all over the place and a three-car attached garage. The rest of the winding street was filled with similar homes, mini-mansions on manicured lots heavy with ornamental trees and fussy topiary, not a one of them selling for under half a million, Eddie was willing to bet, and that was in U.S. funds. The whole place had the smell of money and privilege about it, and a smugness; the cop cars that routinely patrolled the quiet streets bore the slogan 'The safest town in America.'

When Eddie first saw that, a blue-on-white cruiser with 'The safest town in America' on the side in big block letters, all doubts about the assignment vanished; it was going to be a pleasure to blow up something—anything—in gotdamn Amherst, New York.

Problem was, on his first pass down the street around noon, there wasn't much of anything *to* blow up. If anyone was at home, their cars were hidden away in the garage; the parking area and the semi-circular driveway were both empty. This was something for Eddie to ponder. Prevost had said to do a car, the biggest and most expensive car on the property. Blow it up where it sat, as a warning to Jimmy Frat. Only the drive was empty. He could opt for a secondary target, maybe trim the bundled bomb down to two or three sticks and shove it through the mail slot in the front door. Only he couldn't get to the front door without crossing the open front lawn; it didn't have a nearby earth berm and hedge, like the driveway did. And besides, Prevost said to do a car and Eddie didn't like to improvise.

But then, on his second pass down the street at three, he saw there was a car in the parking area. A cherry red Trans Am. Probably not Jimmy Frat's. Probably belonged to his kid or the help or somebody. But at least it was a car and it was sitting out where Eddie could get at it. Things were looking up.

On his third pass-by at five, walking this time, hands shoved casually into the pockets of his jeans, cigarette dangling from his lips, like some local out for a stroll, Eddie was pleased to see another car in the driveway's parking area. A nice, new black BMW Z-3 sports car, like James Bond had driven in that movie, whatever the fuck it was called.

Despite the bad teeth, Eddie broke into a grin.

❧   ❧   ❧

There he was again.

Coco Pulli was pretty sure it was the same guy he'd seen earlier in the white Jeep Cherokee. The one with blue over white Ontario plates. Ugly, wedge-faced bastard in jeans and a blue windbreaker with a big red maple leaf on the back. Only he was walking this time, the guy.

Coco was seated in an Eames chair in Jimmy's den at the front of the house. He'd been seated there all day, except for a couple of breaks to go to the toilet and once, after lunch on a TV tray, to pace around the room for a few minutes to work the kinks out of his ass. It was the same place Coco always sat when the boss was home during the day. When he wasn't driving Jimmy, or handling some errand for Jimmy, or holding some guy's hands behind his back so's Jimmy could safely beat on the guy, Coco's job was to be around if needed but to stay out of the way. He liked to think he made himself handy in these slow times by keeping an eye peeled on the front door and the street. In ten years of watching, nothing had ever happened—except for one time when a carnival of local and federal cops had all tumbled out of a Chrysler Concorde and served some papers on Jimmy, and that was for some bogus grand jury investigation that never went nowhere—but you never could tell.

Now, on an otherwise sleepy Saturday afternoon at home, there was this possible problem with a rat-faced Canadian. Coco rocked back in the leather-clad Eames chair and, exhaling at the prospect, decided to give it some thought.

For a man his size, six-three and two-seventy, Coco had always been quick-reflexed. Bark an order, let the chrome of a gun barrel gleam in the wrong place at the wrong time, and he was in motion faster than you could say Dick Tracy. But throw *thinking* into the mix—give him time to confront a clear set of options and be forced to decide which alternative, if any, he was to exercise—and suddenly Coco Pulli was slower than tree sap in January.

Was this something important? Important enough to disturb Jimmy in the media room, listening to his CDs? God knows how Jimmy loves listening to his music. And maybe this guy, this rat face, was nobody. Just a wandering tourist, killing some time until his tour bus leaves for the Albright-Knox Gallery or something.

But then, on the other hand...

It was dark by the time Coco got done weighing the pros and cons and decided to go with full disclosure. He found Jimmy where he thought he would, in the media room off the back of the house, playing air guitar in a six hundred dollar burgundy silk bathrobe, looked like something Ric Flair would wear into the ring.

Roy Orbison was just then squeezing the last ounce of pathos from 'Crying' on Jimmy's twenty-thousand-dollar sound system. Seeing Coco come in, he killed the disc with the remote and took a Macanudo the size of a tomahawk missile from the humidor on the coffee table.

Jimmy, pointing at the Nakamichi CD player with the cigar, said, "Elvis himself called that man the greatest voice in rock and roll. Who's gonna argue with that, huh, Coke?"

"I guess nobody, boss."

"Bet your ass, nobody. Who's in the same class with Orbison, not including the King himself, I mean? Okay, maybe Gene Pitney came close on a good day." Jimmy broke into a spontaneous chorus of 'Town Without Pity'. Coco had never been partial to that song, particularly this rendition.

He said, "How about Jackie Wilson, boss?"

Jimmy scowled. "That's R&B. The woodpile's full of spooks can carry a tune just as good as fucking Jackie Wilson. You got Wilson Pickett, Sam Cooke, Percy Sledge. I could go on, but it's all R&B."

Coco, in all his years with Jimmy Frat, had never been able to grasp the fine distinction between rock and roll and rhythm and blues as defined by Jimmy, except that most R&B singers were black guys and most rock and roll singers were white guys trying to sound black. But he'd be the first to admit he didn't have a head for these things.

"Reason I come in, boss," he said. "I think we maybe got a lookee-loo outside."

Jimmy's large head snapped to attention. "Federal?"

"Dunno. I don't think so." Coco described the guy in the blue windbreaker with the red maple leaf on the back and the frequency of his tours through the neighborhood. "He looks more like a ex-con to me, boss. Could be he's casing the place for a rip-off."

Jimmy laughed. "He'd have to be an out-of-towner to be that dumb. All the local talent knows better than to come anywhere near my street." He touched off the cigar with a silver Dunhill lighter and blew an acrid cloud at Coco. "Prob'ly just a lookee-loo seeing how the other half lives. But I'll tell you what. You see him again, you go out and collar him, bring him in for a Q&A."

"It's pretty dark out, boss. Tough to see him if he ain't right under a street lamp. You want me to go out and lay for the guy?"

Jimmy turned it over. "Nah, fuck it. It's probably nothing. Jeez, the guy's *Canadian*, for chrissake."

Eddie waited until eleven o'clock to plant the bomb. The hardest part of waiting was staying away, laying low in a bowling alley bar, not risking another pass-by or two. It wouldn't do to be seen too often in the neighborhood. He just hoped, as he parked the Jeep around the corner and worked his way back toward the Fratelli house, that he'd still find the Beemer in the drive.

🍁   🍁   🍁

"Jeesh, remind me never to do that again." Jimmy Frat was in the master bedroom's changing closet, putting on his pajamas and working up a burp. The wife was in the adjacent bathroom, jellying her diaphram. An hour earlier, they had returned from a movie and a late dinner at a new place she had insisted on, the King of Siam.

"I thought it was very good," she said. "All those exotic spices. It's good to try something different for a change."

"Exotic? Everything was cooked in peanut butter. Hot, spicy peanut butter. Shit keeps repeating on me." He burped again. "Who the hell puts peanut butter on jumbo shrimp?"

"Well, the Thais do, I suppose."

"Yeah, that's another thing. The *Thais*. They're gonna spell it like that, it oughta be pronounced 'thighs.'"

"Speaking of thighs." The wife propped herself in the bathroom door jamb, wearing the black lace number Jimmy'd had Coco pick up at Victoria's Secret for last Mother's Day. Her left leg, encased in a sheer black stocking, was cocked provocatively, giving him just a glimpse of her bare bush.

"Whoa, mama." Jimmy whistled his appreciation. Not bad for a forty-six-year-old broad. He led her to the bed, fiddled a bit with the knobs on the console on the bedstand, dimming the lights to a pre-set level and turning on the tape loop to his favorite song for making love by, and climbed in with her.

Just as the scent of musk oil began to fill up his nose, the hidden speakers in the corners of the room trembled with the opening notes of 'Unchained Melody' by the Righteous Brothers. God, he loved that song, had even started thinking of the old lady's two milky orbs as Bill and Bobby, like in homage.

Talk about your white soul singers. Whoa, mama.

❧   ❧   ❧

It came as a huge relief to see the Z-3 was still sitting there on the parking pad, right next to the cherry Trans Am. Eddie, as he approached the end of the boxwood hedge that separated the house from its neighbor, didn't hesitate. He ducked onto the lawn, into the shadow of a Japanese maple, then onto his belly behind a berm of groundcover and low evergreens that acted as a buffer around the parking area.

The BMW was now just a few feet away. It would shield him from the house, while the Trans Am would block any view from the street. He crawled up and over the berm, almost snaring himself on a creeping rug juniper in the process but making it onto the blacktop between the cars without raising an alarm.

The bomb was stuffed into his jacket; six sticks of dynamite and a ten-foot fuse, held together with duct tape. Eddie rolled onto his back near the Beemer's rear tire, took out a pen light, and checked the undercarriage. The frame provided a ledge of sorts between the back axle and the gas tank. Perfect.

He took the bomb from his jacket and, after a couple of failed attempts, managed to wedge it in behind the axle. Then he carefully ran the loop out of the fuse and, holding the end, he rolled away from the car and onto one knee. He paused to listen for a moment; there was no activity coming from the house and no action on the street. So far, so good. He had to be back to his Jeep before midnight to beat the neighborhood's on-street parking restrictions. Last thing he needed was to draw the attention of a passing prowl car—but his time was good.

He waited five seconds more, taking a few deep breaths, letting the cool dampness of the ground work its way out of his back, swiping wet leaves off his ass. Then he took out his Bic lighter and, shielding the light with his hands, touched off the fuse.

Dale Maratucci was down in the Fratelli's basement rec room, under the pool table, putting the wood to his intended when the explosion rocked the house. His head came up fast and he cracked his skull against the underside of the table, a Brunswick Mediterranean model with oak framing holding up three layers of half-inch slate. The table didn't give an inch.

"Ming-yeow!" was all he managed to get out before the blow caused him to black out on top of Angelina Fratelli. His member was instantly as flaccid as the rest of him. Angie was disconcerted.

"*Day-yell*. I didn't even come yet. What the hell was that noise anyway?" She rolled her hips to the right, dumping him out onto the Berber carpet. He lay there like one of the yarn dolls she kept in her bedroom. "Dale? Dale, honey?"

***

Jimmy Frat was in the master bathroom shaking out a Tum when he heard it. And felt it. The wife never even budged. She was tucked in under the comforter, sleeping like she'd been shot in the forehead, as she always did after their Saturday night fluid exchange: wham, bam, thank you, ma'am.

First thing Jimmy did was he got out the piece he kept in the highboy under his socks, a SIG nine mm. auto, and checked the clip. Then he went out into the hallway, into one of the guest bedrooms at the front of the house and looked out the window. At first all he saw was a wispy white cloud kind of spiraling away down the driveway. Then he saw his daughter's BMW, the car he'd only just bought her last year. What was left of it anyway. Half of it had landed in the arborvitae. The other half was sitting on the hood of Dale's Trans Am.

His immediate thought was, Who did I piss off in the organization? But this was almost simultaneously dismissed by another thought: That fucking Canadian lookee-loo.

Jimmy was so angry he almost took a couple shots out the window at the smoldering hulk, but realized in time that that would only make things more difficult to straighten out with the cops, not to mention the goddamn neighborhood association, which was ten times worse. So instead, he bellowed an unbroken string of Sicilian and regular English curse words and called up Coco to get his ass over there ASAP.

***

It was after one in the morning by the time the cops left. Jimmy and the rest of the family were in the kitchen having coffee, which the wife had only grudgingly made. It had taken almost as long to revive her from her bed as it had to bring Dale around, sprawled out on the basement floor like a cheap throw rug.

"My car," he said now, elbows on the kitchen table, supporting a cup. "My bee-yoo-ti-ful car."

"*Your* car!" Angelina gave him a look he was starting to get used to. "What about my fucking car."

"Angie!" Jimmy gave her the exact same look, which really depressed Dale.

She had her old man's bright brown eyes and sharp nose and pouty lips, too, although Dale had to admit they looked better on her. The Fratelli big mouth was something else again. The big tits she'd definitely inherited from her mother. It was the combination, those big tits and the pouty lips, that had suckered him in that first time Angie walked into the store at the Galleria and had him fit her for a pair of New Balance cross-trainers. By nine o'clock that same evening they were jiggin' in the back seat of the Tranny and in five months were engaged. He'd had plenty of second thoughts since the announcement was printed in the Cheektowaga Weekly *Advertiser*, including at this very moment, seeing the both of them, father and daughter, glaring at him across the breakfast table. But who was he kidding? You don't break an engagement to a Mafia capo's daughter, not if one of your future goals in life is to keep breathing. Besides, career-wise it looked like a good move. He had enough business training at Erie County Community College to intuit that hijacking a whole truckload of shoes had to be more lucrative than selling them over-the-counter a pair at a time.

"Well, excuse me, Daddy, but I mean, my f-f-f-fouled up Z-3 is on its way to the scrap yard in a million f-f-freakin pieces and he's pissed off about a few dents in that stupid Pontiac of his!"

"Hey, babe. That car was absolutely mint."

"Oh, why don't you mint my ass. It didn't even have leather interior. Not only did my Z-3 have the Tanin leather seat package, they were *heated*!"

"Big fucking deal." Dale gingerly touched the back of his head and winced at the size of the knot. "Why don'tcha put a lid on it, huh, Angie? I think I got a concussion here."

"You don't tell me to shut up in my own house, Dale Maratucci—"

"All right, shut up the both of you." Jimmy ran a hand back through his dark, wavy hair. "I gotta think about this—situation."

Coco put his cup down on the island counter and said mournfully, "I'm sorry, boss. I shoulda braced that hatchet-faced bastard."

"Ahh." Jimmy waved it off. "Water under the bridge. Don't worry about it."

"I don't get it, boss. This Canadian. Did we do somethin' to piss off the Calabrians up in T.O.?"

"That's what don't make sense. Even if I stepped on some toes—which I don't see any way that I did—this ain't the Gallio brothers' style, not as a first resort. It's too risky, for one thing."

"Sometimes playing it safe is risky, according to Tom Peters."

Everybody glared at Dale. He couldn't help himself. He knew Jimmy hated it whenever Dale offered up any business advice, probably thinking it diminished him in the eyes of his daughter, but he couldn't help himself this time. His mouth was on auto-pilot thanks to the bump on the head.

"In *The Pursuit of WOW!*," Dale went on, oblivious. "My favorite chapter, 'Pens, Toilets, and Businessmen That Do It Differently'. Peters basically makes the point that if you play everything safe, you begin to lose your competitive edge. Next thing you know your competitors are eating your lunch."

"Dale," Jimmy said. "Shut the fuck up."

That's when the phone rang. Everybody, including the wife, stopped what they were doing and just stared at it for a couple more rings. Then, at a nod from the boss, Coco picked it up.

"Yeah? Who wants to know? Oh, yeah?" He held it out. "He says it's the boogy man."

"Oh, yeah? Son of a—" Jimmy got up and started to reach for the phone, then drew back. "Tell him to wait a minute. I'm gonna take it in the den."

In the den, he dropped heavily into his desk chair and pushed the star button and a pair of numbers on the telephone console. Then he grabbed up the handset. "This is Fratelli."

"Stay on your side of the Falls, Jimmy," said a cultured voice, vaguely familiar, like some TV announcer or somebody. "This is your first and only warning. Next time the car won't be empty."

Before Jimmy could respond, the caller hung up.

"Fucking amateur."

There was a little window on the phone console. Jimmy smiled grimly at the digital readout that filled the window. A phone number. Long distance. Canadian, in fact.

Jimmy Frat took a pencil from the desk drawer and a Post-it note from the pad and jotted down the number. Then he leaned back in the chair and called out, "Coco! Get your fat ass in here."

CHAPTER 14

Museum Of Heart

Saturday night Suzzy suggested they eat at the Hard Rock Cafe, mostly because it was loud and crowded and the service was quick, not a place that encouraged anyone to linger over coffee and conversation, which meant she and Decker could move on to what she hoped would be the more romantic part of the evening that much sooner.

They'd gotten an early start, too, eating around six, then heading back to Suzzy's at a little after seven to watch the movie she'd picked up earlier in the day, a tawdry little semi-classic she thought was just about perfect given their circumstances: 'Niagara', starring Marilyn Monroe and Joseph Cotten.

Decker, slumped on the leather couch beside Suzzy, began picking the movie apart from the beginning. The opening shot showed Joseph Cotten negotiating a path toward the rubble at the foot of the Rainbow Falls on the U.S. side of the river, but the next shot showed him walking up the drive of their motel, which, you could plainly see from the view of the falls in the background, was on the Canadian side.

"You know how long it'd take him to walk that far in real life?" Decker snorted. "All the way back up the gorge on the U.S. side and out of the park, walk across the bridge, then back up River Road to the Parkway. A guy in a suit and wingtips?"

"Hey, it's just a movie, Decker," Suzzy reminded him. "Least they didn't shoot it on a soundstage in Hollywood, some painting of the falls in the background."

Suzzy couldn't believe Decker had never seen it before; it was always turning up on American Move Classics or one of the other cable channels. See, Rose, played by Marilyn, is married to George (Joseph Cotten), who's a Korean War vet suffering from battle fatigue. He's also extremely jealous of his flirtatious wife. He knows she's a tramp but he's in love with her and wants to please her. So when Rose suggests they make a return trip to the site of their honeymoon, he agrees. What he doesn't know is that Rose and her lover are scheming to get rid of George by tossing him over the falls and making it appear to be suicide. So when they get to Niagara Falls Rose pushes all the right buttons to get George worked up, wearing tight dresses, going off alone on unexplained errands, making him crazy with jealousy so their neighbors at the motel can see how unstable he is. Then she arranges for George to meet her at a lookout point above the falls, only the boyfriend shows up in her place and supposedly tosses George over.

"It's the wrong guy, right?" Decker guessed when Rose was called in to the morgue to identify George's body.

"Shhh. Just watch."

When she sees it isn't George but her boyfriend lying on the slab, Rose faints dead away and wakes up in a hospital bed, at which point it was Suzzy who couldn't resist saying, "Hospitalized for fainting? I guess they didn't have HMOs back then."

So George had somehow turned the tables, killing the lover who had intended to kill him. Then he began to stalk Rose, finally cornering her in the bell tower of the carillon and strangling her under the bells. Then, with the Rainbow Bridge swarming with police, George, desperate to get back across to the U.S. side, steals a boat, only to run out of gas in the middle of the river and to become caught up in the treacherous current.

It was the most riveting part of the picture. Suzzy, as she sat there glued to the television screen, could sense that Decker too was absorbed by the images of the cabin cruiser bouncing helplessly in the rapids above the falls, Joseph Cotten desperately pounding holes in the hull to try and scuttle the boat, the spray washing over the sides and soaking him. She could hear Decker suck in a breath and feel him stiffen at the moment the boat reached the brink of the Horseshoe Falls and seemed to teeter for an instant, Joseph Cotten now resigned to his fate. And then it disappeared over the edge.

Suzzy said, "Pretty cool, huh?" But she looked at Decker and saw he had his eyes closed and saw that his lower lip was trembling slightly. "Hey," she added gently, reaching for his hand. "It's just a movie."

"Sorry. I guess—I just got caught up in it."

"Yeah, it is kinda sad. Poor George. He probably knew from the day he married her that Rose was out of his league. That she'd dump him sooner or later. And then, when it happens, she not only wants to dump him, she wants to drive him crazy and then kill him."

"That's the part I don't get. If she wanted to run off with the boyfriend, why didn't she just do it? Divorce George and take off?"

"For the money, Decker. Divorces cost money, whereas deaths *produce* money, from insurance settlements. Why go through all the time and riga-maroll of a contested divorce when one little murder can get you out from under right away, and with a stake to start a new life? That's where Rose was coming from."

"It still seems unbelievable to me, that a little money could make someone do something like that."

"Jeez, Decker, don't you read the papers? Don't you watch the news? Stuff like this happens all the time."

That same Saturday night, while Eddie Touranjoe was skulking around Jimmy Frat's driveway with a bundle of dynamite and Decker was at Suzzy's watching 'Niagara', Bona was out with his old lady at a Pizza Hut on the east side, supposedly having a good time, when he caught the face of Marla Ellen Graycastle on the television over the service counter.

The way it developed, Bona and Melody had just ordered a medium deep-dish pie, the meat lover's pizza except with mushrooms, and were helping themselves to the salad bar. Bona, after picking through the salad offerings with his nose in the air, goes over to the counter and asks to speak to the manager, who turned out to be the assistant manager, a pock-marked kid of maybe twenty or so. Bona started in on him, complaining about the salad bar's lack of cruciferous vegetables.

"Crucifer—what kind of vegetables?" The assistant manager wearing a half smile, not sure yet whether it was a put-on. This guy with the scruffy goat and the bomber jacket just trying to break his balls maybe, but no.

"Cru-ci-fer-ous." Bona broke it down into syllables small enough even for an assistant asshole at Pizza Hut to understand. "Your broccoli, your kale, your cauliflower, all sorts of different cabbages. Stuff like that's loaded with what they call phytochemicals that animal studies have shown can reduce cancer risks by up to 80 percent."

"Dennis." Melody was tugging at his arm. "Give it a rest."

"Hey, I'm just saying for $3.95 apiece for the all-you-can-eat salad bar, they got out chick peas and some creamy potato salad, freakin pickled beets even, they could at least have some fucking broccoli sprouts on hand." And then he looked past the assistant manager's ravaged countenance and up at the TV and there she was, looking a little washed out and definitely skankier than he remembered from when she was going down on him in her minivan, but it was her. Marla. Giving some kinda news interview. Talking about her husband Gary. Saying, with a Monroe County Sheriff's Investigator at her side, that anyone knowing the whereabouts of her missing husband should call a certain number at the bottom of the screen.

"Shit." Bona, without another word, took his salad and went back to their booth.

Melody finished loading up at the salad bar before sliding in across from him, starting in on him through clenched teeth.

"You know, Dennis, sometimes I swear you're fucking nuts."

"Yeah? Me, too." Mostly when I look at you.

"What was all that about anyway? One minute you're all worked up about cancer and everything, getting in the guy's face because his salad bar selections don't meet up with your high standards, and next you just walk away. What is it with you?"

"What it is with me is nothing. I just got things on my mind, is all."

"Yeah, well, if getting laid is one of 'em, you better stop acting like a mental case and start showing me a good time."

"Hey." He took a sip of his Pepsi. "We're out to dinner, aren't we?"

It had been two full days since he popped Gary Graycastle in the Rainbow Centre Parking Garage and, in truth, he hadn't really given it that much thought. Wondering once or twice when they'd find the body in there, expecting an item to show up in the *Gazette*. Other than that, though, he hadn't thought much about it, except maybe how easy it was, pow-pow, lights out. Like flipping a switch. He'd felt such a rush walking down out of the garage that night he almost forgot to lose the piece, but then he remembered, and he walked down to the bridge and halfway across to a spot where the tourists liked to snap pictures of the falls and he'd waited for a couple of dipshits with southern accents, a man and a woman, to get cold and move off. Then he pitched that little chrome Jennings over the side, two hundred feet down to the river at the bottom of the gorge and another hundred or more feet of river water below that. Then he'd walked back up to Third for his car and gone home.

He'd hardly given it a thought since, except for a certain smug satisfaction at the fact of his having done it. Took a guy out clean as a whistle, all on his own. The knowledge of it was like bubbles inside him, keeping him floating and at the same time wanting to come out. He wished he could tell somebody; could lean across the booth right now and tell the old lady something like, "Hey, Mel, you know I'm paying for that pie with cash I got for whacking a guy."

But Bona wasn't that stupid. He'd never tell anyone, especially not his old lady, what he'd done. Not in so many words anyway. There was ways to get the word out, when the time was right. Ways to promote yourself without actually copping to anything in a legal sense, and Bona planned to work that out sometime later. That was no problem.

But then there's this Marla bitch, going on TV to do some kind of appeal, and it being a slow enough news day for the Buffalo stations to pick it up from the Rochester stations—no, that still wasn't the problem. He knew there'd be media sooner or later.

The problem was Marla herself. Going on the TV like that to talk about her husband Gary with that big sheriff's stiff next to her. Talking about her poor missing hubby, who only went out to drop off a movie and then disappeared. Talking in that matter-of-fact monotone like she didn't really care and, worse, talking about Gary in the *past freakin tense.* Like that didn't sound to Bona and to the cop next to her and to the whole entire viewing public like Marla already knew he was dead.

Shit.

❧   ❧   ❧

Suzzy's biggest worry, bringing Decker over to her condo, had been how to explain the place to him. A two-bedroom townhouse condominium, hardwood floors all over, vaulted ceilings, ceramic tile in the kitchen and master bath, big-screen TV and a killer stereo system; all that on a waitress's take-home? But all he said, looking around when they first came in, was, "You must be raking in a hell of a lot of tips."

She'd given him the story then about the European history professor on sabbatical from nearby Niagara University and how she was house-sitting, which was actually the truth, except she wasn't staying there for free, as she implied. She was leasing for a year, paying the professor's monthly mortgage payment of almost fifteen hundred dollars, plus an association fee for maintenance and such.

Decker had seemed to accept that with no problem and they had settled in to watch the movie. Now, with 'Niagara' over and a stack of CDs on the changer, playing at random from amongst Shawn Colvin and Lucinda Williams and Dave Alvin and Dylan, she came out from the kitchen with a tray of munchies and two fresh beers to find Decker staring at the rack of audio-video equipment with a puzzled look on his face.

"Who's this again?" he asked her.

"The disc?" She listened for a moment; it was 'Stranger In Town' off the Museum of Heart album. "That's Dave Alvin. Used to play lead guitar for The Blasters back in the early eighties? Wrote most of their tunes before going solo."

Decker picked the jewel box from the pile and read it. "I haven't bought a record since, I don't know, probably the Allman Brothers. 'Eat a Peach.' I like this guy, Alvin."

"Yeah, great songwriter and a great guitar player." She put the tray down, feeling she was about to drop it if she didn't. Her arms felt weak, as if all the blood had been run out of them, and her legs, too. As if the heat of all that hot blood had rushed to her groin until she could do nothing but sit on the leather couch and cross her legs and force a casual expression onto her face. Anticipation breaking out all over her like a case of teenage zits. *Jesus, girl.*

Finally Decker put the jewel box down and came over to the couch and sat beside her.

"Drink?" she asked.

He smiled at her in that maddening way he had and picked up one of the bottles of Rolling Rock and took a long swallow. Then put the bottle down and leaned toward her and said, "I think I'm going to burst for wanting you, Suzzy." And kissed her, slow and soft.

❧   ❧   ❧

She called him some kind of heat-seaking missile and laughed. Shooting down her smokestack and exploding like ten tons of TNT in her boiler room.

He said he liked the phallic imagery—a guided missile.

"It ain't the size, Decker, it's the mega-tonnage."

"I would've thought the delayed detonation was key."

"Roger that."

Somehow they had managed to make it from the living room couch up the stairs to the master bedroom and the queen-size bed, Decker, between panting and thrusting, telling her, "If we tried this out in the yard somebody'd throw a bucket of water on us."

The whole deal hadn't taken more than ten minutes, from initial take-off to climax. Now, as they lay tangled in the bed covers and each other, exchanging kisses as freely as words, she felt a new warmth spread through her body, a sensation that threatened to extend deeper and stay longer, much longer.

She pulled him closer and met his tongue with hers, felt his cock against her thigh, already growing harder. There were moans of pleasure and expectation, his and hers, and then he was on her and in her again. This time there were no rockets; they were a train this time, moving slowly over a dark landscape, gathering momentum, building up steam.

🍁   🍁   🍁

"I have a ladybug on my ass."

"I noticed. At least, that's what I thought it was." A little, dime-sized tattoo high on her left buttock. Decker recalled kissing it in passing. "Not that it isn't cute, but why a ladybug?"

Suzzy stretched. "I dunno. I got it about five years ago, on a vacation. I kind of talked myself into going into the place, then I wanted to back out. So I picked the most unobtrusive design I could find." She paused before adding, "They're helpful insects, y'know. They eat aphids, keep roses healthy."

"Yeah?" Decker had two tattoos of his own. The name of his old motorcycle club, Nomads, was inked in blue on his right shoulder, a requirement of membership. On his other shoulder was a red rose, with the word 'Rose' intertwined. "That's nice to know."

"You gonna tell me who Rose is?"

"Yeah. Someday—"

"When you know me better." She playfully punched his arm. "Bastard."

"Ooh. Now you've gotta kiss it, make it all better."

"You wish."

He loved the fullness of her breasts and the smooth, long muscles in her thighs and calves. Runner's legs. She liked to run the Gorge Road in Whirlpool State Park on weekend mornings, she told him, from the Whirlpool Rapids down to the Devil's Hole and back. On workdays she had to settle for evening runs in the residential neighborhood around Niagara U's De Veaux Campus.

"What about you," she asked him, running her open hand across his abdomen. "What d'you do to keep in shape?"

Nothing really, he told her. "I walk quite a bit, is about all. Mostly from my apartment to the downtown area and back."

"To the falls?"

"Yeah. Sometimes I even cross over the bridge and take in the view from the Canadian side. It's the best angle, really."

She didn't understand the fascination with the falls, all that running water. To visit it, yes. Take a few snapshots, maybe do the tours, Maid of the Mist and all that. But to keep going back day after day to stare at the tumbling water, as if—as if what? It had some magic power to bestow on the faithful?

But she didn't want to tell him all that, to risk breaking the mood. So instead she probed gently: "I guess some people make a real visceral connection to things like that, natural wonders. Almost a religious experience."

Decker adjusted his pillows, put his hands behind his head. Smiled. "There's this thing the monks do called *lectio divina*. Means sacred reading. What it comes down to is a kind of careful, highly deliberate pondering of God's plan, traditionally achieved by reading over and over a passage in the Scripture. But it can be applied to anything. You can 'read' a piece of Gothic architecture, a stained glass window, for example, or an oak tree, or a field of corn. And it can take weeks or months. Even years. There's this one elderly monk at the abbey, Brother Jerome, a hermit, who's been studying the little copse of woods around his shack for over fifty years."

God. "How will he know when he's through?"

"In Jerome's case, he won't be through until he dies."

"What about you, Decker? You going to keep on baking bread at night and visiting the falls during the day until you die? Or do you see yourself doing something else next year? In the next five years?"

She knew even as the words tumbled out of her mouth that she was blowing it, becoming a woman on the make with a woman on the make's typically dumb questions and desperate concerns. She'd gone to bed with the man one time, the goddamn sheets were still damp, and just because she was in love with him didn't mean he had to suddenly *become* something. She had no right to expect any explanations from him, and he certainly didn't owe her one. But he gave her one anyway, of a sort.

"To be honest, I don't see myself staying here, no. I could. It's as good a place as any, I suppose. But down the road—I don't know. I see myself in a different place, maybe working on a ranch, or taking photos for a living, whatever. I just don't yet have any idea where that place might be."

He rolled onto his side, facing her, and talked about his job supervising the graveyard shift at Pinto's, how embarrassing it was to be paid so well to watch others work. How he put most of his pay into a bank account. "I've gotten used to living simply. Someday I guess I'll use the money as a grubstake, just quit Pinto's and move on until I find something else."

"Someday," Suzzy said. "In the meantime, you work, you walk around, and you study the sacred waters of Niagara Falls."

He laughed. "That's what I do. It's what got me into photography, for what that's worth. I used to just go down to the overlooks and stare at the water. Or sometimes I'd sit in the park and study the Tuscarora chief or the flowerbeds, the winter lights. Just doing my *lectio divina*, y'know? But I realized one day—actually, I think it was Nort who pointed it out—that people were seeing me as some kind of nut, a possible menace, sitting and staring like that all the time. So I bought myself a camera and a couple lenses, just as a cover, so I could study things and nobody'd be the wiser. Another shutterbug out looking for good saleable pictures." He rolled onto his back again. "Eventually I started putting film in the camera. So there you have it."

"Norton," Suzzy said, looking for a way out. "What's his story anyway? I mean, he's as wrapped up in the falls as anybody, isn't he?"

"Yeah. I guess it takes one to know one. Nort's lived in Niagara Falls his whole life. I think his interest in the history and everything came about when he messed up his leg. He was only about eleven or twelve when he took a bad fall in the gorge, down around the whirlpool someplace. He and some friends were playing on one of the trails and I guess some shale gave way and down he went. He told me his left leg was broken in so many places the doctors wanted to take it off, but Norton's father wouldn't let 'em have it. It never did set properly, as you can tell, but at least he's able to get around on it."

"No wonder he feels a kinship with all those old stunters."

"Yeah. He was laid up for a long time with that leg. He had plenty of time to read, and what he read about most was the Niagara River and the falls, its history, its geology. He can lecture for hours at a time if you let him."

"What about this mysterious project you two are working on in his garage?" Suzzy asked. "Does it have any connection to Norton's obsession with the falls?"

Decker took a moment before answering. An evasion would be the same as a lie, he decided, and he knew he didn't want to lie. Not to Suzzy. Not ever.

He looked into her hazel eyes and said, "Why don't you come out to the garage with me tomorrow, see for yourself?"

CHAPTER 15

Paradise and Brunch

They slept in late, Decker getting up first and throwing on some clothes and wandering out to the kitchen to figure out the German coffee machine. Suzzy woke in stages and luxuriated in the warmth of the bedding and the sunshine pouring in through the crack in the drapes and the general all-around wonderfulness of Planet Earth, until it occurred to her that Decker was poking around on his own out there and might inadvertently run across her laptop or her pistol or some of the work files she'd stashed in the dining room hutch.

She grabbed her robe and hurriedly brushed her teeth and hair, but she needn't have worried. She found him in the living room going through her rows of compact discs. She watched him in profile, enjoying the way his cotton shirt hung out, half buttoned, and how his brow flexed as he perused the backs of the CDs.

"This is some collection," he said. "How many of these d'you have anyway?"

"I don't know, a hundred fifty, two hundred."

"Some of these people I know from the old days. Dylan, Neil Young, Van Morrison, Joni Mitchell." He held up a jewel box. "I found your namesake, Suzzy Roche. And more Dave Alvin. Let's see, Elvis Costello, Tom Waits, Ry Cooder. I don't know where to start."

"Well, don't start with Tom Waits, not first thing on a Sunday morning. Put on some Cooder, why don'tcha," she told him. "'Paradise and Lunch', an oldie but a goody. That is, if you can figure out the player yourself. I need a coffee fix."

In the kitchen she poured a mug and took a first tentative sip and stared out the window over the sink, knowing it was time to think about things other than her satisfied libido and the morning after's illusion of domestic bliss. Now she was irredeemably in love with the guy, an impossibility founded on a major deception. Impossible except for one thing; it was a fact. It had happened, as she feared it would, as she planned for it to. So she just had to deal with it. The question was how? Her inclination was to march right in there and lay her cards on the table. I'm not a waitress, I'm a special agent with the United States Customs Service and I'm working an undercover operation at the Metropolis, but that's got nothing to do with you and me, although we do need to keep it just between you and me for the time being.

Just lay it out cold and see how Decker reacts.

Problem was, it was not only against department regs for her to reveal herself in the middle of an ongoing undercover investigation, it was actually against federal law. She could be fired *and* prosecuted for telling Decker about the operation. And yet, she couldn't tell him who she really was without explaining why she was slinging hash at the Metropolis. It was a conundrum, all right, made even more difficult by her fear that she might lose him if he knew. God knows, she'd seen it enough times in other men, men who showed plenty of initial interest only to cool their jets when they learned she was a federal law enforcement officer. Big Sister, one jerk had called her—"Like Big Brother, the government always watching, get it?"—and she'd never heard from the guy again. Which was great in that instance, because the guy was a total asshole anyway. But Decker wasn't. Decker was definitely a keeper.

On the other hand, if he reacted badly to her being a federal agent, was he really the man she thought he was?

Suzzy leaned against the counter and drank more of the hot black coffee, listening to Ry Cooder's mellow voice and punctilious fret work drift in from the other room as she let her thoughts drift back to her training days fifteen years earlier. The Federal Law Enforcement Training Center in Glynco, Georgia, down in the piney woods and the cypress swamps. Memories of sand fleas and huge cockroaches that the natives called palmetto bugs, of crewcut sunburned instructors, literally and figuratively rednecks, and the oppressive heat and humidity, mornings out on the gun ranges and the obstacle course and the drill field for hand-to-hand combat instruction, the driving course where she'd been trained in the protocols of a high-speed chase scenario. Afternoons spent mostly indoors in the classrooms, listening to lectures on interviewing techniques, federal statutes and criminal law, technical investigative equipment used in field operations, dynamics of terrorism, narcotics detection, and more. Sixteen weeks of intense work, at the end of which she'd left southern Georgia with a new job at a GS-7 pay grade level and a fiance.

She and her future husband, Bill Wyatt, had met down at Glynco, both of them on the training track for the U.S. Customs Service. In retrospect, after a rocky three-year marriage and a dozen more years to think about it, she realized it wasn't his lopsided grin or his unruly blond hair that had attracted her; it was how he had accepted her as an equal, in the classrooms, on the ranges, and later in the bedroom. While the other men in the program, instructors and trainees alike, had treated her and the three other women trainees with condescension and sometimes outright hostility, Bill Wyatt had rejoiced in finding a woman who could understand and share his enthusiasm to be a federal criminal investigator. And so they had fallen in love, and they had married in Washington, D.C., a month after graduation. And three years after that they were history, victims of the very drive that had brought them together in the first place. It had become impossible for both to pursue their careers in the Customs Service; career opportunities had them moving to different parts of the country. It came down to one of them having to sacrifice a good job in order to follow the other, and it always seemed to be Suzzy who was expected to make the sacrifice.

Well, she had done it once, going to San Diego with Bill, leaving a good job as a field investigator in D.C. to take a demotion to a glorified clerical position at the San Diego office of investigations, where Bill had been appointed an assistant to the special agent in charge. But later, when it was her turn, a chance to get back into field investigations in El Paso, Bill wouldn't even discuss the matter. She should be thinking about settling in and having kids, not chasing off to some dusty Texas border town to corral wetback smugglers, he had told her.

And she had told him good-bye.

A dozen years ago. A dozen long, lonely years. Enough time for any residue of glamour to have long since washed off assignments like El Paso and Detroit and now Niagara Falls. The so-called honeymoon capital of the world, and here she was in her Rayon/Dacron waitressing outfit taking orders on her pad and taking names on the sly and wondering, in those times of weakness she hated herself for, what it would be like to still be Mrs. Bill Wyatt of San Diego, with a ten-year-old in Little League and a six-year-old starting piano lessons.

A dozen years ago. And she hadn't really been in love since. Not until now.

But she was getting ahead of herself. She was a decent enough looking woman, yes, but one spin around the block didn't mean a man was ready to buy a car. Maybe all her agonizing over whether to tell him, when to tell him, was a waste of time. Maybe he'd make up some excuse after coffee and boogie on out the door and that's the last she'd see of him. It wouldn't be the first time.

It would be the first time it really mattered, though.

She sighed, put down her coffee mug, and found her pack of Virginia Slims on the counter. As she lit up—number one for the day—she decided to give him a little rope. After all, last night, in his post-coital high, he had invited her to come along to the garage with him today; Norton's precious garage and the 'projects' they whispered about like schoolboys. She'd wait and see if Decker followed through. If he did—well, there'd be plenty of time to explain to him about who she really was. Plenty of time.

❦   ❦   ❦

Decker stayed out in the living room, loading up the CD player and listening as he wandered around the room with his coffee, staying out of the kitchen. Letting Suzzy have her space. Anyway, he wasn't used to talking first thing in the morning. He lived alone, and for the sixteen years previous to moving to the Falls, he might as well have been alone. Signing to the other brothers over a pre-dawn breakfast of dry toast and black coffee and fruit juice wasn't much of a move up the scale of social interaction.

Besides that, he knew Suzzy had something going on. Something on her mind that she was struggling with. He had no idea what it was—maybe something to do with this place she lived in, an expensive townhouse packed with expensive consumer items. Maybe there was more to this college professor she was house-sitting for; a lover, perhaps? Or maybe Suzzy had some other sources of income, an inheritance maybe. He'd known of people who had problems with wealth, had to find ways to downplay it. Waitressing in a Niagara Falls diner seemed like an extreme remedy, but you never know. It was a crazy world and people did crazy things and the only thing Decker knew for sure was that he was crazy in love with Suzzy Koykendall.

And could only hope she felt at least halfway the same about him. Now, and later.

But he didn't want to think about later. Now was too good; the bluesy rock playing on the stereo, the coffee smells, the autumnal warmth of the sun slanting through the sliders. Suzzy coming out of the kitchen with her cigarette and coffee mug, her lips forming a smudge of a smile.

"You know how you look?" He asked her. "Besides gorgeous?"

"Frazzled? Bedraggled?" Bewitched, bothered, and bewildered?

"Hungry." He clapped his hands. "I can take you out for breakfast or I can fix it for us right here, provided you've got plenty of eggs, bread, some orange juice…"

"I've got a full fridge, but you don't have to—"

"Please. I brought in the paper, you've got your hot java, there's good music on the turntable—I mean the CD machine. So sit, my love, and soak up the morning while I whip us up a hearty breakfast."

She watched as his little khakied butt disappeared into the kitchen, humming as he went, and she thought, God, he *cooks*, too.

※   ※   ※

French toast. And it was delicious.

All she had on hand was regular white sandwich bread, Pinto's in fact, quite possibly a loaf he'd supervised into existence himself. But he said that was fine, you didn't really need French bread for French toast. The secret was a double dash of vanilla extract, along with just the right amount of milk to dilute the eggs. That and a liberal application of butter and maple syrup after. With melted butter and maple syrup on top, he told her, an old shoe wouldn't taste half bad. Especially the morning after a night like last night, she told him, and they smiled into each other's eyes.

"My brother's in Nebraska," Decker said when the conversation eventually moved around to other things. Suzzy had just mentioned childhood memories of big farm breakfasts out in North Platte, Nebraska, where she grew up. Farm-style breakfasts on the weekends, even though she and her family had lived in town, her dad the owner/operator of a hardware store. And Decker had brought up his brother.

"He lives in Omaha, a suburb anyway."

"Oh-my-god." Suzzy grinned. "That's what the old timers up our way used to call it. Oh-my-god, Nebraska. The big city. Course, coming from North Platte, where everything was either cattle or corn, it doesn't take a lot to impress folks."

"I visited David there a couple years ago. Met his wife and kids for the first time, my niece and nephew. It seemed like a nice enough place."

David was five years older, Decker's only close relative still living. Suzzy knew his mother died back when he was still a biker, in his twenties, and that his father had died when he was very young. A boating accident when I was seven, Decker said, shrugging it off, so she had left it there.

"He was in the air force, my dad," Decker said, sipping his lukewarm coffee. "After he died, my mom moved us in with relatives near Rochester for a few years. Then she remarried and we ended up living downstate for a while, my teen years. Until I busted loose and took off, fell into the biker life."

He wasn't sure why he was bringing up any of this, except that it seemed right. Life was a continuum; if there was going to be any future, there had to have been a past.

"I lost touch with my brother for a lot of years. I'm not sure how he ended up in Omaha, doing what he does. He says it was because we moved around so much when we were kids, following my dad from one air base to another, we never learned to speak with any kind of regional accent other than this sort of flat, straight-forward Middle American kind of sound. Anyway, I guess it was perfect for what he does."

"What does your brother do?"

"Oh. I didn't say? He's some kind of account executive with a big telemarketing firm. I guess he doesn't actually have to work the phones any more, but that's how he started out, calling up lists of names and reading a spiel to the people on the other end. 'Hello, Mrs. Jones, how are you tonight, and have you ever given any thought to the benefits of vinyl siding?' Or replacement windows, or Florida time shares. Whatever the hell they were being paid to sell to Mr. and Mrs. America."

Suzzy knew just what he meant. Omaha was to the telemarketing business what Orlando was to theme parks or New York City was to tall buildings. It was partly due to the local accent, or lack of accent, that neutral Middle American voice Decker had described. Television voices. Also, there was Omaha's central location in the country and the plentiful workforce of hard-working ex-farm kids looking to stay off the farm and in the city. But the real reason Omaha had evolved into the country's telemarketing center was because the nuclear weapons command center of the U.S. Strategic Command was buried out in the gentle hill country a few miles south of the city.

"I didn't know that," Decker said.

"Yeah. And because the command center requires a huge communications infrastructure to handle all the computers and the incoming intelligence data and all that, Omaha ended up with an overcapacity of the most up-to-date phone and data systems in the world." She turned up her hands. "Presto! American capitalism rushes in to take advantage."

"When I visited my brother," Decker said, "he was either at work or in his home office, doing something to spreadsheets on his computer. I got the feeling he'd do just about anything to see that he never had to go back to working one of his company's phone banks."

"Wouldn't be my cup of tea, either," Suzzy said, "cold-calling folks like that for minimum wage and commissions, selling some product off a sheet of paper."

She'd almost mentioned the Customs Service in an off-hand way, how telemarketing made airport baggage inspection sound exotic, but she caught herself. They decellerated into silence for a minute or so, finishing off the last of their breakfasts while listening to some Lucinda Williams from "Car Wheels On A Gravel Road."

"I really like all this music you have," Decker said, listening and nodding in time. Then: "Can I use your phone? I wanna track down Nort, find out when's a good time for us to swing out to the garage. I mean, assuming you're still interested..."

"Yes," Suzzy told him. "I'm definitely still interested."

CHAPTER 16

A Perky Gal In A White Convertible

Marla Ellen Graycastle couldn't help but wonder why everything was taking so long. Here it was Sunday afternoon, almost three full days since Gary had left, and they hadn't even found the body yet. It took every ounce of will not to scream at the officers that kept turning up at her door, How hard can it be to find a dead man in a nine-year-old Toyota Camry?

Anticipation was eating her up, that was the problem. She'd waited so long to be free, spent so many hours thinking about what it would be like to have some financial independence. Now, with her dreams so close to becoming reality, the discipline and self-control she'd shown for these many years was deserting her like battle-weary soldiers who could see the end of the war in sight.

Nevertheless, she had to maintain control over her emotions.

She stared at herself in the mirror, seeing that same pale, plain face stare back; the one that had appeared on the news the day before in an appeal for Gary. It had caught her by surprise, the policeman suggesting she make a statement to the news crew that had somehow heard of Gary's disappearance and had materialized on her doorstep almost as soon as the sheriff's deputies.

She'd been appalled at her appearance when she saw the piece, looking so haggard and washed-out. That was one mistake she wouldn't make again.

She took a white stretchy hair band from the drawer of the vanity and slipped it over her head, pulling her hair back away from her face. Then she took her jar of Ponds from the glass shelf below the mirror, dipped the tips of three fingers into the cold cream and began to rub it into her face in a gentle circular motion, first the forehead and working on down.

Emotions. That was another mistake she'd made in her interviews with the police and the media. She'd tried so hard to contain her excitement over her impending freedom, she had gone too far the other way, shown no emotion whatsoever for her missing husband.

They didn't believe her, she could see that in their eyes whenever she had to speak to them. Especially that sergeant, that sheriff's investigator. Chewing a stick of gum constantly and staring down into her face like it was Judgement Day or something every time he asked her a question.

Was there any personal strife in the marriage? Were you having any money woes of any significance? Is your husband the sort who might leave for a time without giving any notice, ma'am?

Always that little ma'am at the end, like something out of an old "Adam 12" episode. She hated that. Made her feel like she was a hundred and ten.

Did your husband normally run errands late at night? Was there an argument Thursday night prior to his leaving for the video store? What video was it, ma'am?

What video was it? Like, did she rent 'Dial M for Murder' or 'Double Indemnity', subconsciously attempting to give herself away. Is that what they were looking for? Is that how they were going to waste her time?

She snatched a tissue from the box on the counter and wiped away the cold cream. Taking out a clean washcloth, she wet it in hot water, squeezed out the excess, and thoroughly washed her face. Then she took an eyelash comb from her makeup box and ran it carefully through each lash. Next came her moisturizer, Oil of Olay, a dab on the finger applied to the face just as the Ponds had been, in gentle rounded motions.

You'd think they'd be grateful she was so composed. What did they expect her to do, break down and bawl and become hysterical like the girls had done?

Was that what the police wanted, a hysterical housewife who couldn't answer their questions? Thank God one of the neighbors had taken Gretchen and Greta off her hands today, after listening to them whine and wail all day Saturday for their missing daddy. Did they stop to think once about what their poor mother was going through, that she might need their support? All right, Marla Ellen wasn't really suffering over Gary's disappearance, but the girls didn't know that. It was thoughtless of them to carry on that way, as if their father was the only one who mattered.

She found her bottle of CoverGirl and shook it up, then used her middle finger to spread the buff beige makeup over her cheeks, chin, nose, and forehead, dabbing carefully under the eyes. Then she took her tube of Moisture Wear concealer and put a smear under each eye, working it in gently with a fingertip to hide the dark circles. And then she reached for the Pan-Stik, a bit more foundation for the cheeks, to give them a smooth consistency.

She knew the cops had already talked to the people at the video store, verifying that Marla Ellen had indeed rented "Shakespeare In Love" on Wednesday and that it had been due back Thursday but hadn't been returned. Learning nothing else; no one had seen her husband or remembered his car or seen anything that could be construed as an abduction. That was too bad. If they'd only caught a glimpse of Bona, not enough to recognize him but enough to give the theory of a random carjacking some weight, a rough looking young man in a leather jacket—but that hadn't happened.

They'd be out interviewing her friends by now, her co-workers at the petites shop. Checking her out, expending as much time and manpower on Marla Ellen as they would on looking for a violent hitchhiker or an escaped convict, someone who could've carjacked an unsuspecting man in his pajamas. Maybe more time. After all, it was easier to harass her than to go out and develop leads out of thin air.

She wondered for the first time if any of the other girls at the shop knew about her and Randy Post. That could get very bad very fast, if the cops found out about Randy, about their affair. If they actually pulled him in and interrogated him…

She took a brown eyebrow pencil and lightly drew in her brows, stroking straight across and then down for the last third. Followed by eyeliner, velvet charcoal shadow, a thin line just below the lower eyelashes and just above the upper lashes, with a slight extension of the line beyond the outer edge of the eye. She paused to inspect her work before continuing with her L'Oreal mascara, charcoal black, fussily brushed onto each lash, tops and bottoms, and then repeating the process for a second coat.

Real estate. She'd decided, that would be her field—as a sideline to the romance writing—when she was resettled somewhere, probably South Carolina. Definitely the Sun Belt. She'd never really considered real estate a glamorous career option until she and Gary had bought this house. Holly, their agent, was such a class act, a really perky gal in a white Sebring convertible, always wore red herself, usually a two-piece skirt and jacket. Always smiling and always doing business, on her cell phone constantly, chauffeuring buyers to this or that tract house, leading sellers by the hand through the closing process, and all the while collecting that six percent fee. As Marla Ellen understood it, Holly had to split that fee with her agency, but still. There were worse ways to make a living and Marla Ellen figured she'd already done three or four of them.

She picked up her compact, CoverGirl mocha mist, and pounced the brush in the blush, then applied it to each cheek with a motion that Gary, while watching her once, had said was like the Nike swoosh, whatever that was. After checking her cheeks in the mirror, she took out her lipstick, jungle red, and ran it expertly around her puckered lips, stepped back and tested out her Marla smile.

Yes. Now, there was a face that could close a deal.

She removed the hair band and shook out her auburn brown hair. It was time for a cut again, but that, too, would have to wait a little while longer. Only a little while…unless.

What if they did get to Randy? He'd talk. Of course he would, she had to be realistic. And once that happened, all the focus would be on Marla. The cops wouldn't look at any other explanation from that day forward. They'd try to get her to admit to a conspiracy to murder her husband for the insurance money. They could ruin everything, even if they couldn't prove anything. The accusations alone would be enough to delay indefinitely the insurance payoffs. The police would hound her, try to make her life a living hell, maybe even put her on trial, try to break her on the stand. She'd be all alone, cornered and alone, with nothing left except—Plan B.

Celebrity.

CHAPTER 17

The Frat House

Jimmy Frat wanted to kill the guy on the telephone, this Canadian fucker calling him up to threaten him, but that wasn't going to happen without he got a sanction from the don's council and that road was too touchy to even think about going down at the present time. You ask to whack a guy, an out-of-town guy, somebody looks to be connected to the Calabrians up in Toronto, all kinds of questions come up. Everybody's like, Why would this Canadian guy think a Buffalo capo was a threat to him and his people? You getting ambitious in your old age, Jimmy? Maybe thinking about stepping out on your own?

No way. Those kinds of Family troubles he didn't need right now; he had too many balls in the air as it was. So clipping the bastard—he took another squint at the name on the yellow Post-It—this Miles Prevost, was off the table, at least for now.

But the messenger was another story. This rat-faced Canuck Coco saw casing the house, this bomb-in-the-night sneaky son of a bitch was a nobody, on that Jimmy would bet good money. You always use lowlifes, disposable guys with a few handy skills, on a job like that. Which meant Jimmy could take him out without worrying it would make a fuss with the council. And take the ugly bastard out he would—that was a promise he'd made to himself.

He snatched up the phone, an old brown rotary model, and dialed the number again. Again he got a busy signal, and again he slammed the handset back onto the cradle.

"Who the fuck gabs on the fucking phone for an hour on a fucking Sunday afternoon?" Jimmy wanted to know. He was sitting at a round Formica table in the dining alcove, left foot tattooing the worn shag carpet.

Coco, hanging out by the picture window in the small living room, didn't answer him. The boss got this way whenever things didn't go exactly as he figured things should go, so you just had to roll with it. He'd been ranting on and off since late Saturday night after he got the number off the Caller ID feature on his phone. Calling people in the middle of the night until he tracked down a location for the number—a place up in Toronto, a business address for PreCan Shipping. An hour ago, working the phones, Jimmy'd come up with a name on the owner of PreCan. Now he was trying to get a handle on the hatchet-face who actually planted the bomb under Angie's car, but he was having a bitch of a time reaching some of his people, in particular the kid Bona up at the Falls, and his mood was getting uglier by the second. That's why Coco gave up answering every time the boss went off. Instead, he hung around the picture window and pretended to be absorbed in watching the street.

They were at a place on Buffalo's northeast side, the Frat House the crew called it, over near Riverside Park. Not an office and not exactly a safe house either, but a little house with a small neat yard and somebody else's name on the mailbox where Jimmy could meet with people when he didn't necessarily want other people copping to his whereabouts. The wife being one good example, whenever he got the itch for some strange, and the cops, too, who liked to spot check Jimmy's activities every now and again.

Nobody outside the crew knew about the place, just the key men, the ten soldiers who made up Jimmy's *decina*, each one of them a made guy. Not that this meant shit any more. Jimmy figured any of his guys would rat out this place and him and their own fucking mothers if enough heat was applied. You had to think that way to stay one step ahead in the rackets. Jimmy knew they'd rat him out if it ever came down to it because Jimmy'd do the same thing.

This is exactly why, over the last almost twenty years as a capo running his own crew, bringing in solid earnings for himself and for the Family, Jimmy never once put himself forward for a higher position. He knew for a fact he could've become consigliere to the new don after Don Stefano died, but he passed the word he wasn't interested. Same for any talk about him becoming underboss some time in the future. Alls he had to do was let people in the organization know he was content to be where he was. And loyal. Content and loyal and a good earner, that's how he wanted the don and the others in the Family to see Jimmy Frat.

And for good reason.

You engage in any business long enough, you go to school on certain people, people who know their way around, can teach you a thing or three about survival. Jimmy had gone to school on Salvatore Gravano. Sammy Bull was like a right hand to John Gotti in New York City, the Gambino Family, and Big John had rewarded Sammy big time; gave him his own crew, made him his underboss, cut him in on all his business. Sammy paid him back by selling Gotti downriver to Marion, Illinois, for life without parole in exchange for a chance at parole for himself and a spot in the Feds' witness protection program.

The Feds cut Sammy Bull this deal *knowing* he had a couple dozen hits to his credit—the son of a bitch copped to nineteen of them on the stand. But they cut him a deal anyway, this vicious little fuck in his high heel boots, because as much as they wanted Sammy the Bull Gravano, they wanted John Gotti—the fucking Teflon Don—even more. That had brought home to Jimmy one key truth: You don't ever want to rise so high in this business you got nothing to trade.

Besides which, Jimmy Frat had created a comfortable niche for himself in the local construction scene, taking a piece here, a piece there, doing a little business on the side when the right thing came along, putting some money out on the street, boosting the occasional big rig. He had the house in Amherst, the cottage down in the Finger Lakes, a legitimate investment portfolio and a not-so legitimate portfolio of real estate owned under different names and cash stashed in Caribbean accounts. Not bad for a *paisan* who started out muscling slow pays, getting general contractors to cough up the dough they owed to subcontractors and then collecting a percentage, usually twenty percent, from the sub. It was still a figure Jimmy liked to live by. Give him twenty percent of any deal he didn't actually have any exposure in and he was a happy camper.

Jimmy took out a Macanudo Robust, clipped it and fired it up. Leaned back as far as was wise in the dinette chair and blew a puff of smoke toward the popcorned ceiling.That reminded him of his early days, hanging drywall as part of Benny Shoes' off-the-books crew, doing those heavy texture jobs on the ceilings because it took too much skill and experience to do a smooth finish that looked like real plaster.

Jimmy, despite his mood, smiled at the memory.

The drywall work for his old capo, Benito 'Benny Shoes' Iuppa, was tied into a classic wiseguy scam called lumping. Say a big public building's going up some place, like a post office or a public housing project. Contracts specify that union labor will be used, because that's the law, whether it's a federal project or being funded by the state of New York. So you have to hire union tradesmen at union wages and the money's all figured in already as part of the bid. But what you do is, you get to a few key union officials and you pay them a gratuity to look the other way so you can bring in a non-union crew at half the price and pocket the difference. Lumping was still a very big source of income for Jimmy Frat, and he was looking forward to lots more of it when the Niagara Falls casino deal got off the ground.

Which got his mind off the ceiling and the old days and back to the problems at hand. He'd been working overtime to try and make things happen vis a vis the casino gambling proposal. Right now it was a cold war being fought on two fronts; by infiltrating the local Niagara Falls groups that had any kind of influence on the state legislature—your city and county governments, civic groups, chamber of commerce types, like that—and by lining up votes for the measure in Albany. So far Jimmy had a key upstate senator and three assemblymen in his pocket, each of them pushing the hell out of the idea to bring casino gambling to western New York State, specifically Niagara Falls.

It was going okay, too. Just a matter of time before all the underground maneuvering became a groundswell and the legislation could come up for a vote. Jimmy figured his biggest potential problem was the Indians. The Tuscaroras had a huge reservation just a few miles to the northeast of Niagara Falls. If those bastards got it in their heads to open a casino of their own, just like their blood brothers the Onandagas had done at Turning Stone, east of

Syracuse, Jimmy's whole scheme could go bust before it ever got off the ground. And those fucking Indians were tough to negotiate with. It'd take more money than the deal was worth to buy them off, he was sure of that.

Screw it. So far the Tuscaroras hadn't given more than lip service to the idea and half the tribe was opposed. Even if they did build one, that didn't mean there couldn't be more than one casino in the Falls. Hell, competition hadn't hurt Las Vegas any, right?

But, hey. One thing at a time. First thing was, Jimmy Frat needed to figure out who put a hair up this Canuck's ass, this Miles Prevost. Find out what the guy's beef was and deal with it before it became a distraction that could potentially complicate the casino legislation. But the *very* first thing was to find out who the bomber was, and where he was. Give him a send-off that would get his boss's undivided attention. Let him know just who the fuck he was playing with.

Jimmy parked the Mac in the ashtray and snatched up the phone again, dialing the number from memory. This time it rang at the other end. Three, four times before a tired-sounding female voice picked up.

"Gimme Bona," is all Jimmy said.

CHAPTER 18

Slowly She Turned

They came into the garage cooing like a couple of lovebirds, hardly able to keep their hands off each other. Norton Gage watched them stroll into the center bay through the opened overhead door, thinking, Man, has she got his dick tied in a knot or what?

He liked Suzzy, don't get him wrong. She was a classy, good looking lady, and if Decker was getting some steady action, more power to him. Just so long as it didn't interfere with his and Norton's pet project.

He himself was between girlfriends at the moment, in what you might call a romantic slump. A five-year slump, in point of fact, started when his ex-fiancee Mona hoovered their joint savings account one day while he was at the newsstand and hauled ass for the sunbelt in a rebuilt Camaro he'd been dumb enough to register in her name. It had put him off relationships entirely for a while and when he did step back into the ring it was limited to professional girls, escort service types you could negotiate a flat fee with and never mind dinner and a movie and all that other shit.

Not that he was bitter.

"You two oughta have tee shirts made up," he said, tossing the butt of his Cuban cigar into a five-gallon blacktop sealer can filled with sand. "'Guess what we did last night.'"

Decker rolled his eyes and looked at Suzzy. "This was your idea, remember."

"It's all right," she said. "I'll just pretend I'm at work and ignore him."

She was doing a pretty good job of it already, walking past Norton like he wasn't there. Right past and on up to the big rubber ball. It took up most of the back half of the center bay. The other two bays featured cars in various stages of reconstruction, a lime green '68 Dodge hemi on the left and a '65 Mustang convertible on the right. The garage, tucked away on a narrow northeast side-street crowded with small manufacturing firms, was operated by a couple of Italian brothers who specialized in custom work on classic cars. Norton owned the building, an investment he'd made largely so he'd have a place to quietly pursue his hobby, the big ball being a conspicuous example.

He tapped his foot to the music—a Styx classic—coming out of the grease-stained portable radio propped on a shelf beside a fat parts catalog and watched Suzzy's reaction with a big grin on his narrow face.

"So? What is it?" She stood there with her hands on her blue-jeaned hips, studying the huge black rubber-coated sphere.

"That there, m'dear, is a genuine, full-scale replica of French-Canucky Jean Lessier's famous six-foot Falls Ball. A near perfect copy, if I do say so, right down to the double-wall steel framing inside and the layers of inner tubes for the skin. Although, I'll admit I've used bicycle inner tubes instead of auto tire tubes, and I've had to double up on 'em. They don't make rubber as thick as they did back in 1928, y'know, so I figured I'd compensate, even if this one is just for display purposes."

Suzzy cocked an eyebrow, more than enough to keep Norton talking.

"I'm making it for one of the souvenir shops slash museums down off Rainbow Boulevard. They figure it'll make a nice tourist draw."

"You get paid for this sort of thing?"

"Hell, yeah. I've made up replicas of half a dozen different barrels and other contraptions folks cooked up to challenge the falls. I got a commission coming up to copy Dave Munday's red and white steel ball, the one he used for his historic second trip over the Horseshoe in '93. The real one's over in the Imax museum across the river, but my clients figure not too many folks'll know that, if you catch my drift." He threw in a wink.

"You mean they'll pretend they've got the real thing on display?"

"Well, let's say they won't necessarily label it as a replica. Just put it out in the window with some photos showing the real steel ball with Dave Munday in it being pulled out of the river. Let folks draw their own conclusions."

Suzzy could feel her law-enforcement gene kicking up a fuss in the pool. "Norton, you're perpetrating a fraud if you pass off these, these replicas of yours as the genuine article."

"Hey, girl, I'm not passing 'em off as nothing. I just make 'em up and sell 'em to whoever wants 'em. What happens after that is their business." He glanced over at Decker for support, but he was sitting this one out on a stack of tires. "I'll guarantee one thing, though. My replicas are so good, the stunters themselves couldn't tell the difference, not from the outside anyway."

"'What happens after that is their business.'" Try as she might, she couldn't shut herself up. "You sound like a guy who sells Uzis to skinheads out of the trunk of his car."

"Jesus Christ." Norton shook his head. "Lemme tell you a story about old Jean Lessier and that big old rubber ball of his. For a lotta years after going over the falls, he made a sideline business out of displaying his ball and selling off bits of the rubber for fifty cents each to the tourists. One day a fella came along and said to him, 'Y'know, Jean, for all the pieces of rubber you've sold off that ball of yours, I'm surprised there's anything left of it.' And old Jean smiled and admitted to the man that he'd been 'supplementing' his supply of rubber strips by going around to the local garages and collecting worn out inner tubes."

"Is there supposed to be a moral there?"

"Just that, even after word got around about what Jean was doing, people still kept coming around for a look at the famous rubber ball and to listen to his stories *and* to buy a strip of inner tube for half a buck." He limped over and gave his creation a fatherly pat. "People decide what they wanna believe in, Suzzy, whether you're talking DisneyLand or the Shroud of Turin or whatever. For half a buck, what the hell difference does it make?"

Suzzy let it go with a shrug. She was feeling way too good to let Norton's pettiest of larcenies change her mood. For Decker's sake, she gave the rubber ball another look, walking slowly around it to inspect every seam, and said, "So this is the project you two've been conspiring over? I mean, not that it isn't interesting. Sort of." Boys will be boys, she figured. They all needed hobbies, something to hold their interest when there wasn't a ballgame or a John Wayne shoot-em-up on the tube.

Norton, meanwhile, was trailing her with that bowlegged limp of his and simultaneously tossing furtive glances Decker's way, looking for a little direction, how he should play it. Decker picked up on it but didn't react right away. Then he came up off the stack of radials and said, "Actually, the sphere's not the thing we've been playing around with."

"Playing around?" Norton was indignant. "I wouldn't say it was exactly playing around, Monk, all the damn work I've put into the Torpedo, not to mention time and money."

Suzzy stopped circling. "The Torpedo?"

Decker cleared his throat. "A design idea Nort's been working on. For a self-propelled stunt vehicle."

"A self-propelled stunt vehicle."

"Yeah, and it's a thing of beauty," Norton said, clapping his hands with glee. "You wanna see it?"

Before she could answer he was leading her by the elbow, around the stack of tires and a large stainless pan for draining oil and a red metal roll-about tool chest almost as tall as he was, through a flush metal door in the back wall. It opened, not into an alley as Suzzy would've guessed, but into another workshop, this one half the size of the main garage but just as cluttered with tools and parts and trash, including its own out-of-date cheesecake calendar pinned to the wall. In the middle of the floor, resting atop a set of metal lifts, was a long cylindrical object—almost seven feet, it appeared—that indeed looked something like a torpedo. Provided a torpedo had a removable nose with a window in it and an outer skin that looked like some kind of processed cheese.

She couldn't help laughing. "You made a stunt vehicle out of Cheese Whiz?"

🍁　　　🍁　　　🍁

Bona wasn't in a laughing mood. The Robin Williams movie up on the big screen was supposed to be a comedy, but Bona didn't see that it was so funny, probably because the two turds sitting in front of him were making it impossible to watch the goddamn thing. Two fat-ass middle-aged women who came in late and plunked down right in front of him—the theater half empty on a freakin Sunday afternoon and they couldn't park their keesters anywhere except in his line of sight? And then with the talking, like this was brain surgery up there on the screen and the nasty old scag on the left couldn't figure out what was happening until the nasty old scag on the right explained it to her.

In the interest of keeping a low profile like he'd been told, Bona put up with the babbling bitches for a good ten minutes, but enough was enough. He leaned forward until his face was right between the two of them—he could smell the lilacs and popcorn butter—and laid on his best Jack Nicholson.

"How about I bring you two a couple TV trays and a remote control, make you feel like you're right back in your living room. Maybe a fucking afghan, huh?"

He'd bet the ranch neither of the old cows had moved that fast without a dinner bell being involved. They grabbed up their coats and their other crap and moved off into the darkness, huffing with fear and indignation, leaving Bona to watch the movie in peace.

And it still sucked.

Or maybe it was just the circumstances, Jimmy Frat calling him up and ordering him to get his ass down to the Maple Ridge 8 Cineplex in Amherst for the three-forty showing of whatever the fuck this turkey was called. Bad enough he had to give up his Sunday night to one of the man's schemes, now he was taking up the afternoon, too. Melody was perpetually pissed as it was, always threatening to take the kids and move back to her mother's, and him not spending any quality time with the family today wasn't helping. Just how much did that goddamn Jimmy Frat expect for a lousy three hundred a week anyway?

It almost made Bona laugh—almost—to think how paranoid Jimmy was, this tough Mafia capo. Won't talk business over the phone, won't agree to meetings that he didn't set up himself, always having meets in his car, which no doubt was swept for bugs twice a day. Shit, maybe it was better to be a small semi-independent operator like Bona. An *associate* of the wiseguys, sure, but still your own guy, you can go out and knock over a store once in a while, torch a house, whatever. There were always scores out there if a guy kept his ears and eyes open and his mouth shut. Like that forty-two grand sitting in that Monk dude's savings account at Marine Midland, don't think Bona had forgotten about that. Hell, no. He'd be getting around to that stash, soon as things slowed down a little and he had time to think up a plan.

Maybe the first thing he should do is tell Jimmy Frat to stuff his lousy three bills a week, go find himself some other sucker to chauffeur his future son-in-law's lame ass around town.

Yeah, right. Like that was an option.

Bona suddenly sensed something in the air, like a high pressure system moving in. Then a heavy hand encased his right shoulder. He half-turned and shuddered as he took in the face that went with the hand, like on one a those giant Easter Island statues.

"Hey, Coco. What's happening, man?"

The giant head jerked to the left. "Outside."

Bona squinted as they came out into the bright autumn sun. Across the way, parked illegally in a red zone next to a fire hydrant, was the champagne silver Town Car, Jimmy Frat slouched in the back seat listening to some dinosaur rock on the CD changer. Some hiccupping fruit singing about his Peggy Sue is all Bona picked up when he ducked into the front passenger seat.

Jimmy killed the tunes from in back with the remote.

"Hey, *paisan*," he said softly. "How they hangin' today?"

"They hangin' okay, Mr. Fratelli. Real good."

"Yeah? Well, mine ain't hangin' so good today, Bona." Same quiet tone. Then it started to climb. "In fact mine, you might say, are spinning in my scrotum like a couple *walnuts* in a *blender*. I got my *balls* in an uproar, account a some *Canadian fuck* blew up my daughter's car last night right in the middle a my *fucking driveway*, me and the wife inside in bed *trying to get a good FUCK-ING NIGHT'S SLEEP!*"

"Jesus, Mr. Fratelli." Bona fought not to shrink completely down into the buttery leather upholstery. "Who'd be crazy enough to do something like that to you?"

"That's a *good* fucking question. Let's explore it a bit, shall we? Coco, talk."

Like you'd order a dog to bark for a treat. Coco Pulli didn't seem to mind, though. He just started in talking, telling what he saw the day before, the rat-faced blond guy in the maple leaf jacket cruising the neighborhood, the white Jeep Cherokee with the Canadian plates, Bona listening attentively without actually looking over at the muscle or back at Jimmy Frat in the back seat. Definitely not making eye contact with Jimmy. And Bona getting that sinking feeling, thinking, What the fuck was that crazy Eddie Touranjoe doing, blowing up Jimmy Frat's daughter's car, for freakin sakes?

Jimmy leaned forward and started in again, this time punctuating every other word by flicking his index finger against the back of Bona's left ear. "I got some Toronto import-export asshole pissed off at me, thinking I'm about to move in on his action in NFO, so he sends somebody down with a message, *capisce*? What I wanna know is, how'd this Canuck Prevost get my name in the first fucking place? You been shooting your mouth off about my business, kid? Bragging around to your friends maybe, how you been doing a little work for the Organization? Huh?"

"No! Hell, no, Mr. Fratelli." Bona's face was turning puce, a mixture of rage and fear. Half his brain fervently wished he still had that little Jennings .22 auto, so he could turn around quick and unload it into Jimmy Frat's fat face, him and his flicking fucking finger. The other half of his brain, however, realized that the big ape behind the wheel would grab the gun and feed it to him before he could get halfway around. He calmed down by reminding himself that if Jimmy knew anything for sure about Bona's connection to Eddie, he'd probably be dead by now, and Jimmy wouldn't be along for the ride. He'd be safe and well-alibied back at the family mansion. So this was just a fishing expedition.

Something else Bona reminded himself: You decide to play with pigs, you gotta be prepared to eat shit once in a while.

"Honest, Mr. Fratelli, I don't know nothing about it. I swear it on my dead father's head." He remembered from somewhere, maybe he saw it in a movie, that guineas eat up bullshit like that, swearing on a dead parent's head. Bona'd swear on a head of iceberg lettuce if it got him outa that car in one piece. "I could check around for you, see if I can find out anything. I mean, I know a few people across the river in NFO. I maybe even seen this guy around, this rat-faced bastard Coco was talking about. I'm not saying I have for sure, but—"

Jimmy, who's finger had gotten tired, was laying back against the seat again, absently palming the CD changer's remote. He didn't entirely believe the kid, on the other hand he didn't entirely believe anything anyone ever told him. He was what you'd call a professional skeptic. Still, you had to gamble sometimes in this business, take people at their word and hope to God they didn't screw you too bad.

He exhaled, letting go all the bombast. "Here's the deal, kid. I figure this asshole most likely comes from just over the border someplace, somebody local enough to be comfortable slipping in and out easy. I got people checking out Fort Erie and on up to St. Catherine's. I want you to dig across the river in NFO. Use Dale to help you with the leg work. Come up with a name and address to fit Coco's description, there's an extra grand in it. You think you can handle that?"

"Yeah, Mr. Fratelli, I think I can handle that. It might take a couple days—"

"That's what you got, two days." Jimmy raised the remote and aimed it toward the dashboard. "Hey, you like Buddy Holly?"

❧   ❧   ❧

The Cheese Whiz crack didn't go down well.

Decker read Norton's scowl and decided to jump in. "It's foam insulation, the stuff they spray between the studs to insulate houses? Nort thought it'd made a good cushion, to protect the metal shell, right, Nort?"

"And add buoyancy. Two inches of this stuff bumps up the displacement on this baby by nearly fifty percent."

Suzzy nodded as if impressed.

"That shell underneath's made of an eighth-inch thick steel propane gas tank, and we've got another inch and a half of foam sprayed inside, specially molded to fit around and cushion the driver. And I use the word 'driver' literally." He had her elbow again and was leading her around to the rear of the thing, where a perforated metal ring encircled a small tri-blade propeller. "See that? Battery powered, operated with a foot pedal, just like the accelerator on a car, top speed about five knots. *And* I've got steering controls." He pointed out the metal fins attached to the sides of the contraption, about a third of the way from the front. "Those babies're operable with hand controls, using light-weight steel cabling. It won't be able to turn on a dime or anything like that, but they'll allow for course correction, to make sure the Torpedo stays on the correct line all the way to the edge of the Horseshoe."

"Why would they need to be operable in the first place?" she asked him. "I mean, if it's just another replica for show at some souvenir shop——"

"No, no, it's not a *replica*, Suzzy, this is something I've designed myself." Norton's eyes were shining like new pennies. Suzzy had seen the look before, most often on religious zealots and street people with a few screws loose. "It's a whole new concept in a falls vehicle. Unlike Dave Munday's steel ball, or Lessier's rubber ball or old Annie Taylor's wooden barrel, *this* is truly a vehicle. It isn't completely at the mercy of the currents, y'see, because it has *propulsion* and it can be *steered*. You know what that means?"

"Uh, no. What difference does it make, if all it has to do is drop over the falls?"

"Jesus Christ—excuse my French, but it makes all the fucking difference in the world." He appealed to Decker. "Explain it to her, man. She's your girl."

Decker held up his hands. "The Torpedo's your baby. You tell it."

Norton sighed and stared at Suzzy for a moment. "Okay. Look. I'll start with the basics. You know, of course, that when we talk about someone going over Niagara Falls in *anything*, we're talking about the Horseshoe, the Canadian Falls, right?"

"If you say so."

He gaped at her. "You didn't even know that? Hell, everybody can *see* that there's a forty-foot high pile of talus—jagged rocks—at the bottom of the American Falls and the Bridal Veil on the U.S. side, a pile of dolostone and limestone that'd crack any stunt vehicle open like an egg. Plus there's just not enough water flow over that side. Ninety percent of the water goes over the Horseshoe. You didn't know that?"

"I did not know that, Norton."

"Three thousand *tons* of water *per second* is what we're talking about, that's what goes over the Horseshoe."

"That's a hell of a lot of water."

"Yeah, but there used to be a lot more. In 1960 an agreement was reached that allowed the power authorities to divert more than twice as much of the flow as before. That means two things; that there's more exposed rock down at the bottom of the Horseshoe than there was in the heyday of barreling, and that there's less natural thrust provided by the river these days as the stunter goes over the lip."

"Natural thrust?"

"Right. When, say, Jean Lessier went over in his rubber sphere in the twenties, the heavier flow of water over the edge helped to thrust the ball farther out into the gorge before it descended, y'see? We're only talking a few extra feet, but that can make all the difference in the world. Like, a couple years after Lessier went over successfully in his rubber ball, a Greek chef from Buffalo, guy named George Stathkis, tried it in this huge one-ton barrel made of wood and steel. It made it over in one piece, but it was so heavy it couldn't take advantage of the natural thrust. When it cleared the lip, it went straight down, a hundred seventy feet or so to the surface water and then another hundred eighty feet to the bottom of the river."

Suzzy scoffed. "The idiot went over Niagara Falls in a barrel that wouldn't float?"

"No, the barrel would've floated fine if it had the chance. What happened was the Greek's heavy barrel went straight down and was trapped against the base of the falls by all that down-rushing water. It didn't work itself free and bob to the surface for twenty-two hours. And the Greek only had about three hours worth of oxygen inside the barrel, so he suffocated." Norton shrugged. "We learn from others' mistakes."

"Yeah, well, I'd think the main thing you'd learn is how stupid it is to challenge Niagara Falls."

"Maybe it was stupid to go to the moon, too, but it was a challenge and we did it, right, Monk? Anyway, the whole idea with my Torpedo is that it can overcome the problem of natural thrust by providing its own thrust. And with the steering controls, you can make sure you stay on the proper course right up to the edge, no getting hung up in the shallows or dropping too close to the talis pile below Terrapin Point."

Suzzy was tapping her foot impatiently. "You're actually planning on taking this contraption over the falls, aren't you?"

"Well, uh, I—"

"You're crazy, period." She turned to Decker. "And you. I thought Norton was your friend, but here you are giving him money to help him build this, this death trap? Encouraging this dumb stunt? You should be trying to talk him out of it, not *helping* him."

Decker sighed, stood as straight as he could, and crossed his arms over his chest. "In the first place, Suzzy, Nort doesn't need my money to do this. He owns this garage and half a dozen rental properties around the city, not to mention the income from his newsstand operation. As for me, I went in with him for my own reasons. Which brings me to the second thing." He paused, thought about taking her hand, but decided not to. "Nort isn't the one taking the Torpedo over the falls."

"Not that I wouldn't like to," Norton chimed in. He slapped at his rigid left leg. "Unfortunately, I couldn't even bend myself down into the thing, let alone work the foot controls."

Suzzy's wide-open hazel eyes swung from Norton back over to Decker. For a few seconds she just looked at him, reading his face until there could be no doubt.

Finally, she said, "Are you completely out of your fucking mind?"

CHAPTER 19

The Peeler and the Pervert

Twenty hours after the explosion and Dale Maratucci's head still ached, thanks to that crazy Angie and her thing for screwing every place but in a bed. There was a soft spot back there where his skull had come in contact with the Brunswick; his ears had a slight ring, too, and the corners of his eyeballs felt like somebody was pushing them in toward his nose. That's probably why it took Dale so long to realize that Coco's description of the bomber was somehow familiar, like he'd seen a guy like that someplace. Ferret-faced, short dirty blonde hair, a Canadian. Yeah. Seen a guy like that recently, like up in the Falls somewhere.

He pulled the big, sloppy Chevrolet into the Tops parking lot in North Tonawanda at exactly ten o'clock. Like driving a fucking bass boat, the way the Caprice rolled through the corners. He glanced over at his passenger, Philly, whose car this was, and said, "Hey, man, you oughta think about upgrading your ride. Somethin' with some nads, can haul ass in a hurry, considerin' the business you're in."

Philly looked over at him with dark, flat eyes. "You get yourself into a chase, you're already toast. Nobody outruns a police pursuit, kid. Only morons ever even try."

Dale wasn't sure at first if the little old bastard was calling him a moron. As he thought about it, he didn't think so. Guy didn't have the stones. When

Jimmy and him were going over the job earlier at a meet down in Amherst, Philly here had done just about everything but kiss Jimmy's ring, spewing out all the overly-polite chitchat like from a Godfather flick. And Philly knew he was engaged to Jimmy's only daughter, so dissin' Dale wouldn't be too swift. So he probably wasn't actually suggesting Dale was a moron.

"Your friend is late."

"He's not exactly my friend, okay?" Dale said. "He's hired help." He popped two more Ibuprofen tablets from the bottle on the dash and washed them down with a swig of Evian. "That's him pulling in now."

Bona rolled the rusting Grand Am up to the light pole with the large G on it and spotted Dale behind the wheel of the Caprice. Thinking, Great, that punkass Maratucci's the wheel man. That's just what I need to make my freakin Sunday complete.

"You're late." This from the little grayhaired asshole in the front passenger seat as Bona climbed into the back seat.

"Not according to my watch. I'm right on time."

"Your watch is two minutes slow."

"Says who? Maybe your watch is two minutes fast."

"Yeah?" The old guy jabbed a thumb at Dale. "And his watch is two minutes fast, too? And the clock in the dashboard? Maybe the whole world's two minutes fast and you're the only one with the correct time, huh, bub?"

Bona said, "Yeah, maybe. Maybe they fucked something up over there in Grenwich, England, and you guys just haven't got the word yet. Bub." He grinned; you never know what you'll pick up, watching the Discovery Channel with Brando.

The geezer gave him that yard stare they all do, then abruptly turned around and barked, "Drive," at Dale, who, after a five-second delay, did just that.

Seven minutes later they were in another parking lot, this one smaller and mostly hidden from view, tucked in behind a party house on the northeast edge of town. The party house consisted of two parts; the original building, a large two-story colonial home that had been converted sometime back in the fifties, and, tacked onto the back, a long, one-story addition with a flat roof.

Philly took a pair of palm-sized two-way radios from inside his jacket and gave one each to Dale and Bona. He twisted in the seat so he could stare straight at Bona. "The kid here's gonna keep six while you and me go in and peel the can."

"Hey," Dale said. "Keep six what?"

"Keep six. Means you're the lookout, okay? You stay in the car, keep your eyes open. You see anything ain't kosher go down, some prowler roll through or anything like that, you give your buddy here a squawk on the radio. Simple enough?"

Bona wanted to know why Dale got to sit around on his ass while he had to break and enter the premises. Just because Dale was the freakin' boss's daughter's fiancé—

Philly cut him off. "What're you, five-six, one-forty?"

"Five-seven, one-forty-five."

"Yeah. And the kid here is like five eleven, one seventy-five, around there." When Bona still didn't seem to get it, Philly added, "Burglary's a small man's job, okay?"

Bona ignored Dale's snicker. "So, what's my end in this thing anyway?"

"Jimmy didn't say?"

"Jimmy didn't tell me dick except to show up at the Tops lot and go rip off a place with you, supposedly steal some dirty pictures."

"*I* told you that part, man," Dale said. "Dude who owns the place is some big deal with the Niagara County Board, got a lot of juice."

Philly said. "I'm supposed to look for an album full of photos, is all I know."

Dale, despite the headache, liked being the only one in the car who had a clue why they were there. "Yeah, Jimmy says the dude wants a whole shitload of cash to vote the right way on getting a casino up at the Falls. Jimmy says the dude's into like kiddy porn – Jimmy owns a piece of the shop that sells some of that shit—so he figures he can save some money if he gets to the dude's stash, see? Give him some incentive to cooperate."

"That still don't tell me my end of the action."

Philly turned in the seat again. "I get half of any cash or valuables we take outa the place, over and above my standard fee that Jimmy's paying me. You two split thirty percent of the take between you."

"Thirty percent? What kinda shit is that? You get half, we should split the rest—"

"Jimmy gets twenty percent for settin' it up. That's standard. You wanna argue, argue with him." Philly faced front again. "Dale, pop the trunk."

Bona got out and followed the geezer around to the back of the Caprice. The guy was a shrimp himself, maybe five-three, one-twenty, skin dark and weathered like old redwood siding. He took a leather satchel from the trunk and jerked his head, Bona falling in step like a trained chimp, part of him wishing he was home playing Mario Karts on the Nintendo with Brando, part of him kinda curious about the gig. He'd never worked with an old-time safe-cracker before and it was kinda cool, even if the guy was a freakin midget.

When they reached the point where the single-story addition attached to the original house, Philly took from the satchel a coil of nylon rope with knots tied in it every three feet and a plastic-coated grappling hook on the end. A pull-down fire escape ladder was suspended about ten feet above them. The old man stepped out of the shadow of the building and began to swing the end of the rope with the grappling hook. He let it fly, catching the second-to-last rung of the ladder on the first try and slowly pulling it down.

On the roof, he used hand signals to direct Bona to a large metal exhaust vent, where they kneeled down, the leather bag between them. He spoke in a raspy whisper.

"See that window over there?" He indicated a regular double-sash window looking out over the flat roof from the original house's second floor. "That's the office, where we're headed. We're gonna get in through this vent here, God willing."

"What the fuck for? I mean, why don't we just jimmy the freakin window."

"It's wired. Whole place is hardwired, every window and door, with a silent alarm into the security company and an auto-dial distress call into 911 if we cut the wires. There's motion detectors, too, but they're aimed at the entrances. We can get past them no big deal."

"Yeah?" Bona felt a bead of sweat pop out on his brow, though it was a crispy cool autumn night. "How d'ya know? I mean, you cased the place your-self—?"

"Jimmy gimme the layout," he said, like that was enough.

"Well, how can you be sure he got it right? Where'd he get his information? I mean, if we go in and there's MDs you didn't know about, we're cooked." Bona'd done dozens of burglaries, but mostly of small residences, places too poor or cheap to have security systems and motion detectors and shit. He'd never knowingly gone into a place with a working alarm setup and he didn't much want any part of it now.

Philly stared contemptuously. "Listen, bub, if Jimmy gives you the layout, you can take it to the bank. That's all you gotta know." Philly himself couldn't say anymore because he didn't know the particulars. If he had to guess, he'd say Jimmy Frat owned a fire or health inspector or a meter reader, somebody could roam around the joint without drawing any suspicions. It's how the business went; you found a place worth knocking over, you hired somebody to case it, then you hired somebody like Philly to go in and make the extraction.

He rooted around in the bag again, coming up with a flat bar and cordless drill. He put a Phillips screwdriver head into the drill's chuck and used the softly whirring drill to back out half a dozen sheet metal screws from the vent cap. He and Bona gently placed the cap to one side. The vent shaft was about fifteen inches square, running straight down for about four feet to a set of fan blades. A screen was built into the vent shaft on the top, to keep rodents and leaves and such from getting in; Philly got that off in short order using the flat bar.

"Okay," he said, the rasp coming out a little faster now. "I gotta make a little noise. This here unit's right over the big cook stove in the kitchen. What I gotta do is have you hold my hands, lower me down so's I can kick out the fan, then pull me up." He indicated the coiled rope. "We'll lower ourselves in with that."

Bona didn't argue, thinking, Anything to get the fuck off this roof. He took the little man's rough hands and lowered him into the vent shaft, flinching at the noise when the fan fell free and bounced off the big Viking range below. He hauled Philly back up, they tied off the rope and dropped it down the shaft, then went down themselves, Bona following the old man and the leather satchel. It was greasy in the vent, but not as nasty as Bona was expecting, although he figured his jacket was going to smell like a freakin fish fry from then on.

"Okay," Philly said in almost a normal voice as he helped Bona climb down off the range. "You take the bag and follow me. *Don't* go off my path."

Bona gained a measure of respect for the geezer when he hefted the leather bag; it had to weigh thirty, forty pounds, yet Philly had hauled it up the fire escape ladder like it was his old lady's handbag. Staying close to walls, they moved out of the kitchen, around a corner near the restrooms, and up a set of stairs tucked away behind the bar. Philly had a penlight on him, but the ambient light from outside and from the beer signs and other small light sources in the place made it unnecessary. At the top of the stairs, Philly, without hesitation, opened the first door on the left and went through, with Bona and the bag right behind.

Light came into the office from a security lamp mounted on a pole out in the parking lot. Philly raised the blinds on the window higher to let in even more light, taking a glance down at the Caprice, parked at the back of the lot.

"Give the kid a squeal," he said. "Let him know we're on schedule here."

Bona put down the bag and took out the two-way and held it to his mouth, pushing in the button and talking softly. Dale's voice came back loud and sudden, like when you start your car and find out you forgot to turn off the radio from the night before.

"Jesus Christ," Bona said. "If you're gonna holler, why bother with the freakin radio?"

"Sorry, man. I didn't know these things had a volume control. How's that?"

"Yeah. Better. We're cool up here."

"Cool down here, too."

"Okay. Uh, out."

"That's a big ten-four, little buddy."

"Asshole," Bona muttered as he put the radio back in his pocket. Philly had spent the time profitably, moving around the small office to the corner behind the desk, removing some junk and a tablecloth off what looked at first like an end table but turned out to be a free-standing safe.

Philly held up the tablecloth. "This'd fool a lot of people, huh?" It was an older Sentry model, which seemed to delight the old bastard. "You ever crack a safe, bub?"

"Yeah, sure," Bona said. "Me and another guy took one like this out of a A&P once."

"Took it with you, huh. How'd you open her?"

"Hammered the door out with a sledge and a cold chisel." Actually, three cold chisels. It had taken them a week to do it and the fucking thing was empty except for two pennies and a cigar box full of coin wrappers.

Philly was shaking his head. "Waste of energy, moving a dead weight like this. Help me tip the son of a bitch on its front."

It took some time to get a proper hold on the thing, but within a minute it was lying face down on the carpet and Bona was sitting on the desk, catching his breath. The little man, meanwhile, was fishing in the satchel again, this time bringing out a short-handled axe and two pairs of Vise Grips.

"You never fool with the front of a can, bub. That's where they put all the muscle. You attack it from the back, see." He swung the axe hard, the blade landing at the midpoint of the back of the safe and putting a six-inch gash through the metal skin. "Most cans like this, all you got is a cheap layer of sheet metal over asbestos rock and wire mesh. We'll have this number peeled and plucked in twenty minutes."

❧   ❧   ❧

It took only eighteen, and six more minutes to get back to the Caprice.

"Drive," Philly said. "Slowly."

"You got the pictures?" Dale wanted to know. "Lemme see."

The photo album was on Philly's lap, along with a cash box. "Watch the road, kid. I'll do the honors."

Bona was eager, too, mostly to find out how much was in the cash box. He'd had a glimpse of the porn photos up in the office and wasn't interested beyond knowing they'd gotten what Jimmy Frat had sent them in after. He grabbed the back of the front seat and pulled himself forward, watching over the old peeler's shoulder as he popped the cash box's chintzy lock with a pocket knife. At first glance the take looked promising, two small stacks of bills rubber-banded together and some rolled coins. But by the time Philly counted it out and Bona did the math in his head, it was clear he wouldn't be retiring to Florida any time soon.

"Eighteen hun'erd and fifty, including the silver," Philly reported.

"Shit," Bona said.

"What's our end?" Dale asked, swerving over the center line as he looked over.

"Watch the goddamn road, kid."

"Five hundred and fifty five bucks," Bona said sourly.

"Apiece?"

"No. We gotta split it down the middle. That's two hundred seventy-seven-fifty each. Philly here gets nine-twenty-five *plus* his fee and Jimmy gets the rest, three hundred-seventy bucks." Bona shook his head. "I could make this much stealing shrubs over at the state park."

"Hey, bub, that's how the world works. Get yourself a professional skill like me if you wanna make the serious dough." He was thumbing through the photo album now. "Phew. Would you look at this crapola."

"Hey, lemme see."

"Keep your eyes on the road, kid."

Bona stared dispassionately over Philly's shoulder as he fanned the pages. The photos were all glossy enlargements, mostly in color, of pre-pubescent girls wearing little or no clothing, sometimes in pairs, sometimes using vegetables or household items as dildos.

Bona said, "At least the guy ain't a homo."

"Hey, bub, I got granddaughters this age. Goddamn weasel's a fucking pervert, oughta have his nuts cut off and shoved down his throat. We catch a guy like this in stir, that's exactly what we do to him."

"Yeah, well, look on the bright side, pops. Leastways Jimmy gets the leverage he's looking for. And as long as Jimmy Frat's happy—"

"Now you're learning, bub."

❧   ❧   ❧

Back in the Tops lot, Dale asked Philly to wait while he walked Bona over to his car.

"Listen up, man," he said, circling in close and invading Bona's personal space. "This bomber dude, the Canadian?"

"What about him?"

"I'm thinkin' it's one of your peeps, man. That ugly blond-haired geek you were hangin' with at Packy's last week, 'member? What the fuck was his name?"

Bona was thinking, *Shit, shit, shit*, but he tried a bluff anyway. "What blond geek? I don't hang with no geeks." Present company excepted.

"That Canadian dude, man. The one says 'eh' every other word. You guys took down some house or somethin'."

"Oh, yeah, right. I know who you mean, that guy I had a beer with at Packy's the other night? Eddie something. Yeah, he's like a cousin of a friend or whatever. We were on a job together with his cousin once, only that was like years ago." Bona paused to make it look good. "You know something, Dale. Come to think of it, you could be right. That guy does sort of fit the description Jimmy gave me. We'll have to check it out tomorrow night, see if we can locate the dude over in NFO." He nudged Dale's arm, like they were buddies. "Hey, maybe split another jackpot, huh? Jimmy's offering a grand for anybody can ID the mad bomber."

"Yeah, man—" Dale began to shake his head, then thought better of it, the pain shooting from the base of his skull straight into his eyeballs. "Truth is I'd go after this fucker for free. You oughta see what he did to my Trans Am."

"Yeah?" Bona grinning and thinking, *Too bad you weren't in it at the time.*

CHAPTER 20

Still Haven't Found What I'm Looking For

Bona had a system. Not a system, really, but a little game he played in his head whenever he was thumbing through a newspaper or a magazine or TV Guide or whatever. He'd come across a picture of a woman and he'd rate her, like would he do her or not. He'd refined it down to three basic categories: 1. Yes, he'd fuck her; 2. No, he wouldn't even do her with somebody else's dick; and 3. Blowjob only, which was self-explanatory.

This Marla bitch, when he'd first met her at the diner, he felt was like a toss-up between numbers one and three, and, given the time and location restraints, he'd settled for number three. Which, he had to admit, had gone just fine. Now, however, after seeing her on the tube again Sunday night, her giving that same zomby appeal for the return of her husband, Bona taking a really good look at her without any makeup, he decided she'd definitely been a blowjob only candidate at best and a strong possibility for not even with somebody else's dick.

He spent what was left of the evening listening to this running monologue in his head, and what he kept hearing wasn't good. By then it was a full three days since he'd popped the bitch's hubby and left him in his crappy Toyota in the Rainbow garage, and *still* the cops hadn't come up with the body. Which, he observed, said a lot about how bad tourism was going lately, a stiff laying around for three days in a public garage and nobody notices.

The main thing his inner voice told him was that he couldn't keep waiting around for Marla to get caught and roll over on him. He knew damn well she would, he could read it in her face every time he saw the news clip. The cops'd find some leverage to use on her and she'd fold; it was just a matter of time. And then Bona'd be in a jackpot of his own, not only with the cops but with Jimmy Frat, who didn't like associates making headlines.

Which is why, first thing Monday morning, Bona went out to Rent-a-Wreck and picked out a twelve-year-old Plymouth, and put his old man's deer rifle, a Marlin .30-30 with a scope and a five-shot magazine, into the trunk and then swung by the long-term lot at the Niagara Falls Airport and swiped a set of plates off a Chrysler. After changing the rental's license plates for the stolen ones, he popped his "Best of U2" tape into the cassette player and picked up Route 31, heading east.

An hour and a half later he was in Eden, northwest of Rochester, a quiet little suburban township that ten years before had been mostly cornfields and cowflops. Specifically, he was inching the Plymouth along down a meandering tract street called Pheasant Run, looking for an inconspicuous place to pull over, a spot that'd give him a clean sightline to 6 Grackle Court, realizing he wasn't going to find what he was looking for. Problem was there were no other cars parked on the streets. Plenty of vehicles sitting in driveways, yeah, mostly minivans and spanking clean SUVs, but nothing parked out on the street. He'd stand out like a nigger at a Klan rally.

Shit. It'd seemed so easy when he'd thought it up. What he didn't know at the time was that 6 Grackle Court was on a freakin cul-de-sac, one way in and one way out, with absolutely no trees or hedges higher than his knees to hide himself behind. And the rest of the development was more of the same. It wasn't like back in the Falls, all those old city neighborhoods with cars parked all over the streets and service alleys and high hedges and the occasional abandoned property; lots of places to lay up and wait for a clear shot.

Fucking suburbs.

He thought fleetingly of the Smith & Wesson in the glove compartment, little nickel-plated snubnosed .38 revolver they'd come across in the party house safe the night before, the only other thing in there besides the money box and the kiddy porn. Philly had let him take the piece, but with a small warning: "Coppers catch you comin' out of a place with that, bub, and you can add another dime onto your tab." Pictured himself parking in the drive at 6 Grackle Court, strolling up to the door and ringing. The Marla bitch opens it and *bam*, he drops her like a carnival duck and boogies on outa there.

Except it was a sucker's play. She sees him coming and calls the cops. Or he does her clean, but a neighbor sees the whole thing and has the neighborhood watch out circling the mini-vans before he can drive halfway out the tract, with all its crazy wandering streets.

The Best of U2 was on its third pass in the cassette player, the band cooking on "The Unforgettable Fire", lead singer Bono doing his thing, when Bona decided to haul his raggedy ass outa there before he drew too much attention to himself, one of these housewives possibly pulling herself away from Jerry Springer long enough to notice a shitty Plymouth sedan creeping down the street at ten miles per and take it upon herself to ring 911. He found his way back to the development's entrance and took a right onto the main road. A quarter mile down he passed a gravel track leading back into a wooded area and a sign next to it that read, "Coming Soon: Eden Woods Estates. Custom homesites starting at $169,900."

Bona pulled over, backed up, and read the sign again, while on the car's tinny sound system U2 swung into the single mix of "Sweetest Thing."

Something momentous was going to happen to Marla that day, she could feel it. Call it female intuition, or perhaps her new-found sense of identity had freed up some long-dormant psychic abilities. Whatever it was, she could feel it most profoundly. An expectant feeling, as if the phone were always about to ring, the doorbell about to buzz, and when she responded she would hear a voice or see a face and know exactly what the other person was going to say before they could even say it.

It was about Gary, she realized. Today would be the day they'd find his body. And then a couple of official-looking men from the police would come to her door and solemnly inform her that she was a widow, while the news crews would be right behind the police, clamoring for a statement. And she would be ready for them this time. Face made up, clothes carefully coordinated, sorrowful expression and anguished voice practiced in front of the bathroom mirror. She felt fully capable of looking directly into the camera lenses and presenting herself with just the right blend of pain and spunk.

"Yes, I am saddened beyond grief for my loss, sickened and confused that someone could just...snuff out a life like that, and for what? To steal a few dollars and an old car? I'd like to be able to crawl in bed and cry myself to sleep in the hope that this is all a bad dream and when I wake up, Gary will be sleeping beside me. But I know I can't do that, if only for the sake of my two daughters, Greta and Gretchen. I have to put up a strong front for them, to help them through this terrible tragedy.

God, just reviewing the words in her head started her tearing up.

※   ※   ※

Bona couldn't believe it. After fifteen minutes of circling around on that gravel track, in and out of the woods, past all these different stakes marking out this lot and that lot, finally pulling over at a likely spot and climbing up a little hill covered with bare trees and fallen leaves, he finds himself overlooking the ass end of 6 Grackle Court.

"Jesus," he muttered, taking in the scene, "fall in a barrel of shit and come up with a silver dollar, why don'tcha."

Actually, his vantage point was a little off to one side, but that worked out okay. He could plainly see the Graycastle's white mini-van parked on the drive in front of the garage, and the side of the garage leading back to what had to be the family room in back, with a pair of sliding doors opening onto a sizeable deck. He could also see a narrow window over the kitchen sink, and a much wider double window—the dining room, it looked like. Plus there were the upstairs windows, three of them across the back of the house.

Now if the bitch would just plant herself for a few seconds in front of one of those windows, or better yet, come out onto the deck—nah, too cool out for that. But with all those windows, or even if she came out to get the minivan...

Bona tramped back down to the Plymouth for the Marlin and then back up the hill, wishing he'd thought to bring along a blanket. He always carried one in the Grand Am for situations like this, case you gotta stake out a place all day or all night. This time of year in western New York, you could have yourself a nice Indian summer day like this one and then a cloud bank rolls in and the sun gets blocked and suddenly your ass is shaking like a bughouse rat, it gets so damn cold.

Back up on the hillock he made himself a little nest between two spruce trees, nestled down in the fallen needles, the bows of the trees floating over him so only his face and the barrel of the rifle were showing. He put the sight up to his eye and slowly panned across the back of the house, window to window, settling on the kitchen window over the sink as his best bet. With the scope he could even make out dirty dishes on the drain board. Looked like someone had had toast and runny eggs for breakfast.

❦   ❦   ❦

The waiting, particularly when you can't be absolutely sure what it is you're waiting for, is the hardest part. Marla tried pacing the living room for a while, one eye sneaking glances out the bay window toward the street, but that only made things worse. A watched pot never boils, as they say. So she sat and looked at a magazine, a month-old *People* with Leonardo di Caprio on the cover and a feature story on the world's most beautiful faces. Barbra Streisand? Get real. Sophia Loren, with those bulgy eyes and blubbery lips? Besides which the woman had to be eighty years old. Gwyneth Paltrow, maybe. Cameron Diaz, okay. Brad Pitt, definitely. Beautiful buns, too.

Marla sighed and put the magazine aside. Sometimes, when she was reading *People* or watching some celebrity thing on "E", she felt perfectly in tune, as though there, but for some accident of birth, go she. Not that she saw herself as beautiful; she knew she wasn't. But she was presentable, she had a certain presence; good clothes and the right attitude and money would make up the difference. Especially money.

There it was again, that feeling. As soon as she let her mind wander, it came back, the sensation that one of those benchmark moments in life was about to happen to her. It had to be about Gary, there was nothing else of that magnitude going on in her life, unless maybe Ed McMahon wanted to roll up to the door to award her the two million dollar first prize from the Publisher's Sweepstakes. Wouldn't that be sweet.

No, that's stupid. She hadn't even ordered any additional magazines, just renewals on *US* and *People*. They don't give those prizes away to people who don't order a slew of new subscriptions, she was reasonably certain of that. It had to be about Gary, this sense of anticipation she'd been wearing around all day like a housecoat. Maybe something to calm her nerves was in order. A Xanax. Couldn't hurt.

Marla pushed herself up from the couch and went to the kitchen for her pills and a glass of water.

❧   ❧   ❧

Nestled below the bows of spruce, Bona fiddled with the Marlin's leather sling, just for something to do. It was damp up there on that hill, and boring. Looking one-eyed through the scope was no freakin picnic, either. He'd given himself a minor headache already, panning across the back of the house from window to window, and for nothing. No sight of her. What the fuck was she doing, sleeping? It was ten-thirty in the morning, for chrissake.

He felt himself begin to nod off and snapped his head back. Needed a diversion, is what. His eye caught the roof of the Graycastle house, covered in your typical thirty-year asphalt shingles, decent stuff but nothing fancy. In one of the few legitimate jobs he'd ever had, Bona worked for a summer as a roofer's apprentice before coming to his senses. Jobs were costed out by the square, he recalled, a square being a ten-by-ten area of roof, or a hundred square feet.

He put the scope back up to his eye. If he counted the tabs on the shingles, he could figure about how many squares it would take to put a new roof on the place, not that it needed one, but it was something to—

Whoa. He picked up a flash of movement somewhere. He sighted along the second story windows, then moved down a fraction to the first floor. Nothing. Nothing. Noth—

There she was!

Standing at the kitchen sink, like he'd figured. Reaching up into a cabinet, probably for a glass. It was the Marla bitch, all right. No question. Bona took a deep breath and refitted his eye to the scope's socket, sighted the crosshairs on the window, on her dumb, unsuspecting face, and took another breath. Then held it.

Then let it out again in a whoosh.

"Jesus shit," he muttered. "Where the fuck did they come from."

𝖜 𝖜 𝖜

Marla's heart did a paradiddle when the doorbell rang. When she drew it open, the tableau in front of her was as if she'd painted it herself: that Monroe County sheriff's investigator, the big one with the aviator glasses and the wad of gum—Mulvaney was his name. Next to him a very dark black man with a long, rounded head and a thick body. Behind them, out on the sidewalk, was a young uniformed deputy, and behind him were two cars parked on the drive-way; a plain beige sedan and a red-and-white Monroe County sheriff's patrol car. All three men wore neutral expressions.

Mulvaney introduced the black man. "Sergeant Hazard of the Niagara Falls PD."

Niagara Falls. Of course, she should've guessed that's where—

"Ma'am, I'm sorry to inform you that your husband's body was found…"

The rest of it came and went in a drone. She listened, she nodded, she understood every word, but at the same time, she was someplace else. Outside of her body, looking down at the scene. Watching the policemen watching her.

Her tears came almost unbidden. "I've had a feeling. All day long—"

"Ma'am." Mulvaney again. If he'd been wearing a hat, he'd now be kneading the brim with both hands. "I know this isn't the best time. But, we'll have to ask you to answer a few questions for us."

"But—now?"

"Yes." The black man this time. Sergeant Hazard of the Niagara Falls PD. Staring at her with heavy, half-lidded eyes. She didn't care for those eyes.

"Well—" She sought out Mulvaney. "What kinds of questions?"

He cleared his throat. "To begin with, Mrs. Graycastle, I believe you know a man named Randy Post?"

𝖜 𝖜 𝖜

Shit, shit, shit, shit, *shit.*

Bona got himself down off the hill and the Marlin .30-30 back in the trunk and the rent-a-wreck Plymouth back on the road in a blur of anger and fright. He was still shaking fifteen miles up the road, heading due west on 104 toward the Falls.

That close. That close to getting rid of the dumb bitch before she could flip. Also, he realized, that close to nailing her just as a bunch of cops pulled into the driveway. He could picture himself trapped back there in the woods, cop cars blocking the gravel entrance to the new development, and him with no choice but to make a run on foot or give himself up. Fucked anyway you look at it. Thank God his peripheral vision was so sharp, picking up that red-and-white cruiser even before it turned in at 6 Grackle Court.

But he still had the Marla problem, that was the thing.

Going back some other day was probably a non-starter. Exposing himself once was one thing, but you start showing up in a place too often and people begin to notice. He'd had his chance and it didn't work out. All right, so you move on. Even if she named Bona as the shooter, it was still her word against his. What proof was there that Bona had done dick? Where was the murder weapon? And who says she could even ID him, he changes his appearance a little, gets a short haircut, a close shave, some preppy clothes. Go the whole nine yards, a dye job and a pierced ear, his own old lady wouldn't know him. Hey, man, who's this Bona guy you keep asking me about? My name's Dennis Bonawitz, and I live on 97th Street in Love Canal, and I'm a...a what?

Okay, so maybe he could use a steady job, something for a few weeks to make it look like he had what the cops call gainful employment. He could do that, hire on with his cousin's landscaping business maybe. Did they actually have any work in October, landscapers? Must be something. Burlapping shrubs for the winter, shit like that.

Yeah, it could still work out. Her word against his. And there was nobody who'd seen him with the dead husband that night.

Well, okay, so there was Dale Maratucci. But old Disco Dale, he wasn't a threat. He could be handled. One way or the other.

CHAPTER 21

Even The Tweety Bird Sings

Eddie Touranjoe was downstairs in the rub shop getting his knob polished by Tildy, a plump little blond farm girl from Goderich, Ontario, when Garth tracked him down.

"The man in T.O.'s been trying to reach you, eh?"

Eddie grinned without showing his teeth. "Maybe he wants to pay me the other twenty-five hundred he owes, eh? Like it's eating at his conscience?"

"Yah, right. Like he's got a conscience, eh? Anyway, he's on the phone in the office."

"Shit, man, I'm kinda busy right now, eh. Tell him I'll call him right back."

"He wants to talk now, man."

"Well, then, bring me the cordless phone, eh?"

"Fuck, man, I ain't no fucking slave. Get it your own self."

Eddie liked Garth. Not only were they brothers in the Satan's Sons motorcycle club, but Garth and his partner Evan had been renting Eddie the apartment over the rub shop at a discounted rate for three years. Not to mention all the action he wanted with the girls. All he had to do for it was act as sort of a night watchman and bouncer, help keep some of the unruly customers or the girls in line once in a while when Garth and Evan were off someplace on business or at home with their families out in NFO's suburbs. But Garth could be a prick when he wanted to be, which was often. You had to know how to play him.

"Hey, man," Eddie said. "I'm kinda in the middle of something here. Do a brother a favor, eh, just like I done you last month, taking that meth run when Posey got busted."

Garth crossed his thick, tattooed arms. "Ah, what the fuck, eh? I'll bring in the cordless, Eddie, cause you asked so nice, m'man."

"You're a prince, man."

Tildy, meanwhile, never missed a beat.

❧   ❧   ❧

Dale Maratucci, straddling a stool at Packy's on Third, said to Bona, "You didn't remember this dude? He was sitting right here, like a week ago. Eddie something, right?"

"I told you, I didn't make the connection at first. There's probably lots of guys fitting that description."

"Hey, who got rapped on the head here, you or me?" Dale was feeling much better since going to the doctor for a scan. A mild concussion was all it was, didn't hardly hurt anymore. "Hatchet-faced dude with short blond hair, around five-ten, skinny. Saying 'eh' all the time, like all those Canucks. What kinda car does Eddie drive?"

"I dunno, he usually walks across, I think," Bona said defensively. "Maybe a Jeep."

"See? A white Jeep is what Coco saw, man. And you didn't make the fucking connection?"

Bona wheeled around. "Hey, who the fuck are you, giving me the third degree? You think you're Jimmy Frat all of a sudden? Maybe I had my reasons for not copping to the guy right off, okay?"

"Yeah? Like what?"

Bona stared at Dale while he thought about it. Damn punkass Travolta clone, sitting there like he's got the world by the nuts, wide open as a whorehouse door. If he wasn't James freakin Fratelli's future son-in-law, Bona'd take a baseball bat to that pretty face then and there, teach the smart bastard a real lesson about life on the street.

"Like there was no percentage telling Jimmy right off that I had a line on this guy," Bona said. "If we make it sound too easy, just hand him a name and an address, he's not gonna pay us the extra grand, now, is he?"

"No. I guess not." Dale hadn't failed to pick up on that 'us' stuff. "He'd probably stiff us the bonus money, if he figured we didn't have to do any work to turn up this dude."

"That's right." Bona took a swallow from his glass of light beer. "Which is why we're gonna make a show of going over to NFO tonight, ask around a bit, make like we're working some leads, then check out this address I got for Eddie Touranjoe, make sure it's still good."

Dale smiled. "Very Covey, man. 'Begin with the end in mind.' Habit number two. It's like you got that vision thing happenin'."

"So, that means you're with me on this, right?"

"I'm down witcha, dude."

❧   ❧   ❧

"Edward?"

"Yeah, it's me."

"Sorry to tear you away from your recreation, Edward, but I have a request I'd like you to follow up on ASAP." Provost's mellow tones were even more pronounced coming over the telephone. Eddie wished the son of a bitch would back off with the fancy phraseology, though, not work so hard at proving what a got-damn Christopher Plummer he was. Like, okay, you got the job, so give it a rest, eh.

"What sorta request?"

"I want to talk to this American friend of yours, the one who told you about Jimmy Fratelli's plans for our side of Niagara Falls. I'd like to talk to him in person and I'd like you to make the arrangements for me. Can you handle that, Edward?"

Eddie sniffed. "You still owe me twenty-five hundred on the other thing, eh."

"Yes, and I'll get that to you after you handle this chore for me, along with a little extra sweetner. But right now I need you to concentrate on connecting me with your friend."

"Why d'ya wanna talk with Bona, eh?"

Prevost showed the first signs of pique. Eddie could hear him exhale in exasperation. "Because I do, Eddie. Is that all right with you?"

"You don't have to get pissy, eh. I was only askin'."

"It occurred to me your friend likes to talk, Edward. I just thought that, with the proper incentives, he might talk to me."

It took Eddie a few beats, but he got it. "You want him to like spy for you, eh? On this Mafia asshole?"

"Just set up a meeting, Edward. I'll do the strategic planning."

❧   ❧   ❧

They crossed over to Niagara Falls, Ontario, in Dale's mother's canary yellow Dodge Neon. Tweety Bird, Bona kept calling it.

"My Trans Am's gonna be in the shop for like two weeks," Dale explained for the fifth time, "so it's this piece of crap or I walk, and I don't walk, man."

"Yeah, well, with the grand we split for finding the bomber, maybe you can get your wheels outa hock that much sooner."

"It ain't the money. Jimmy's covering that. It's just they gotta put on a new hood and they had to order it."

"Bummer." Bona was doing his best to be nice to Dale, keep him thinking they were buds, partnering up on a little deal. Anything to keep the punkass from going to Jimmy about this Eddie screwup.

It took twenty minutes of creeping along in traffic three lanes wide on the Rainbow Bridge followed by another ten for a spot inspection before they cleared Canadian customs. Bona had Dale swing up past the casino and pick up Victoria Avenue, then cruise Clifton Hill real slow, Bona pretending to look for familiar faces, having Dale wait at the curb outside various tobacco shops and convenience stores while Bona ran in to ask about Eddie, Dale playing along for once without a lot of lip. It had started raining shortly after dark, a drizzily cold autumn rain that made Dale glad to sit behind the wheel while Bona did all the legwork. After an hour or so, Bona figured they'd made it look good enough. If on the off-chance Jimmy had a tail on them, all he'd hear back was that they'd canvassed NFO looking for leads on this rat-faced Canadian punk and had turned up the name Eddie Touranjoe.

He slid back into the Tweety Bird's passenger seat and shook off the rain-drops like a shaggy dog.

"I got an old address on Eddie. We better check it out, make sure he's still there."

Dale nodded cautiously, still leary of his recent concussion. "Which way?"

Bona directed him over to Stanley Avenue, north a few blocks to Kitchener, then south again, down a series of narrow streets packed with small houses, running him around so there'd be no chance he could find his way back again without Bona. They ended up almost back where they'd started, a couple blocks north of Victoria on a short street that was half old houses chopped up into small, mean apartments and half old houses converted into small, mean businesses. The address Bona had was a little of both, a two-story frame house with the bottom half given over to The Golden Palm Body Rub Shop and the upper half divided into two seedy apartments, one of which was Eddie's. Parked in the alley beside the place was a late-model white Jeep Grand Cherokee.

"Dis must be de place," Dale said, doing Amos and Andy without realizing it. "So, what now?"

"Now nothing. I thought I might have to go into the massage parlor, ask around a little to make sure Eddie still lives upstairs, but now I don't hafta. The Jeep is all the proof we need." Bona leaned back against the Neon's high seat. "We head on back to Packy's and give Jimmy the call he's been waiting on. Collect our grand bonus."

"I like the sound of that, bro." But he didn't move. Just sat there behind the wheel of the Neon, in the rain, parked at the curb across the way from The Golden Palm Body Rub Shop, waiting for God knows what.

Until Bona said, exasperated, "So?"

A know-it-all smile spread across Dale's face. "So, d'ya hear the news today, man? Falls cops found the little package you left for 'em in the parking garage."

Bona went all innocent, claimed he didn't know what package Dale was referring to.

"The dude you took out last week, man. C'mon, you know what I'm sayin'."

"You think the stiff in the garage was my guy?"

The smile became a full-bore smirk. "Hey, dude in an old Camry with a couple .22 slugs in the back of the melon, got abducted outside Rochester last Thursday night from in front of a video store. You think I don't know how to add two and two? I was a business major, 'member?"

Bona shifted around. "What I think is you better forget about doing any math, asswipe, unless you wanna count yourself in."

"Me? Fuck, man, alls I did was give you a ride."

"Yeah, and you knew why I needed the ride, which makes you an accessory, same deal as if you popped the guy yourself as far as the law's concerned. You wanna remember that, Dale. And forget about everything else."

"Shit, man, I wasn't gonna *tell* anybody."

"Then there's no reason to even be having this conversation, is there? So why don't you put this shitbox in gear and drive us back across the river."

        🍁   🍁   🍁

Not ten minutes after dropping the dime on Eddie Touranjoe, Bona's sitting at his usual stool at Packy's and who shows up?

"Hey, man," Eddie said, slipping onto the adjacent stool. "I been looking for you."

Bona glanced around nervously, but Dale had already taken off, back to Cheektowaga to get mommy her car back, and no one else in the bar showed any interest.

"Looking for me?"

"The one and only, eh." Eddie smiled through pursed lips. He tapped out a Player and fired it up. "Listen, you know the man I work for up in T.O.? The one I told you buys all the cars, eh? He's interested in setting up a meet with you."

"A meet. With me?"

"Right. I think he's got some work for you, eh."

"Yeah, right." Bona shook his head. "And I guess I'm just supposed to waltz on across the bridge, meet up at a bar someplace over there. Or maybe some alley. Then Prevost sends some goons—prob'ly you and your gearhead buddies—to kill my ass. That how it's supposed to work, Eddie?"

Eddie wasn't smiling any more. Things weren't going according to plan. For one thing, he'd been careful never to actually give Bona his employer's name, and yet here's Bona talking about Miles Prevost like he knows him or something. He took a pull on the cigarette, tried to think, came up blank.

"What the fuck're you talking about, eh?" was the best he could come up with.

Bona had been doing some calculating of his own. He knew the last thing he should do is let Eddie know they were onto him, that he'd just gotten off the horn with Jimmy Frat, giving him name and address on one Eddie Touranjoe of Niagara Falls, Ontario. What Bona needed to do was shut up and hear Eddie out, see what him and his T.O. boss were up to. But Bona didn't do that. He was too pissed and too anxious to do that.

"I'm talking about that dumb fuck of a boss you've got, man," he said. "You might wanna tell him we've got this new high tech thing going down here in the States, thing called Caller ID? Jimmy Frat had him made the minute he phoned his house, after *you* blew up his daughter's BMW, dickwad."

"Ooh."

"Yeah, fucking ooh. One a Jimmy's goons spotted you and your Jeep and that Ontario plate in like two seconds." Bona nipped at his glass of Miller Lite. "Some friend, man. I tell you a few things about my new gig and you go running off at the mouth to this Prevost prick, get him so worked up over nothing he sends you back down with a bundle of dynamite. Then you fucking waltz in here and try to set me up."

"I wasn't setting you up, man. Prevost wants to recruit you, is all. I think he wants you as his inside man, eh, keep him informed of Jimmy Frat's plans."

"Yeah, like I'm dumb enough to double-cross a Mafia capo."

Eddie's synapses may've been slow from too many years of alcohol and crank and inbreeding, but they eventually sparked. Suddenly the deeper meaning behind what Bona was telling him sank in.

"Shit, man. Jimmy Frat knows I'm the one did his car?"

"His daughter's car, which is like ten times worse. You threatened his only child, man."

Eddie started to check out the room from the corner of his eye. "It was just a message from Prevost, eh. Wasn't anybody hurt, wasn't anybody supposed to get hurt. You gotta tell him that for me, Bona."

"Oh, okay. I'll run down to Amherst and put in a good word for you, Eddie. Maybe then they'll just shoot you, 'stead of breaking all your bones first."

"This ain't funny, man."

"You see me laughing?"

"This whole thing's your fault, eh? If you hadna fucked me over on that break-in we did the other night—"

"Fucked you?" Bona was shocked. "That Monk guy's place? How'd I fuck you on that? There wasn't anything there."

"There was something there, eh. I just never figured out what it was."

"You better save your figuring for how you're gonna get your ass clear a this bomb mess you made, man."

Eddie dropped the cigarette on the floor and put his elbows on the bar and stared into the row of whiskey bottles lined up along the mirrored backsplash. Thought about his predicament and tried to think of a way out of it. Jesus Christ, a Mafia capo after his ass. Even Eddie didn't need long to figure this one out. He could try to cut a deal, or he could get the hell out of Dodge. One or the other.

Or maybe both.

Yeah. He could make a deal with Jimmy Frat. Maybe even turn the situation around a hundred-eighty degrees, come out of it smelling like a rose.

And if the Buffalo mobster didn't want to deal? Well, he could have his Jeep packed and on the road, headed north, in five minutes. Wonder what a winter in Sudbury would be like?

"Listen, Bona, you gotta talk to your guy for me. I got things he needs to know, eh."

"Like what?"

"Like lots of shit, about Miles Prevost's whole operation, up in T.O. and down here, too." Then he proceeded to give Bona the chapter headings; the car transport operation in Hamilton, the crystal meth factory down in Fort Erie, the illegal gambling rooms and the shakedowns in certain hotels around NFO, the mule train for cars, guns, drugs, tobacco, even girls, between New York State and the Province of Ontario.

"Prevost's got a regular little empire going, man, 'specially the luxury cars for export deal. I know how it works, eh. With Jimmy Frat's muscle, we could get rid of Prevost and take over everything he's got. You gotta go to bat for me, man."

Bona had no intention of talking to Jimmy Frat about any of this. That was the last thing he intended to do, give Jimmy any reason to believe that him and Eddie were anything more than casual acquaintances, guys who'd worked a job or two way back when. But that didn't mean he had no play.

"I think you're bluffing, man, talking out your ass. You don't really know shit about the guy's operations, 'cept how to steal cars from the airport for him."

"I know plenty, eh. I can give you the dock number up in Hamilton where we drop the cars, I can tell you how we work the manifests—"

He had more, but Bona cut him off. Give me something useful, he said; something he could check out himself, make sure it was solid, before he went to The Man for Eddie. That's when Eddie told him about the set-up at the customs stations at either end of the Rainbow Bridge. How he could get across without a search, no matter what he was driving or what he might have stuffed in suitcases in the trunk.

"We've got two guys in the bag," he said, warming to the subject with that half smile. "Maury on the U.S. side and Terrance on the Canadian, so we got you covered going in either direction."

Say you were bringing a trunk full of Cuban cigars over from NFO. All you needed to do was call Maury, the U.S. customs inspector, the night before and find out which booth he'd be working the next day. When you pull into his lane, you answer his question "Do you have anything to declare?" with "Not a blue nickel." That's all there was to it.

"Not bad," Bona said, nodding. "So what's the phone number I call?"

Eddie shook his head. "You wanna do a trial run, set it up and I'll make the call for you. But before I'll outright give you the number, you have to go to Jimmy Frat for me."

Bona made like he was thinking it over, then he started nodding his head real slow, like he was really taking to the idea. Then he stuck his hand out and grinned.

"Y'know something, I think Jimmy's gonna go for this, man. I really do."

CHAPTER 22

Working My Way Back To You

Tuesday, ten a.m. Decker was into Day Two of playing the love-dazed fool, holding down a stool at the short end of the counter in the smoking section of the Metropolis, waiting for Suzzy Koykendall to come by every so often to refill his cup of coffee without a word exchanged between them. Sitting there, as he had through three meals on Monday, with a hangdog expression, like Christ nailed to the cross, ready to do anything to return to her good graces. It wasn't working, but if he'd learned anything in sixteen years of monasticism, it was an almost saintly patience.

She had refused his calls Sunday night and had ignored his attempts at conversation at breakfast Monday morning, so a silent penance was about all he had left. Today he'd added a touch, a potted houseplant, an African violet that he placed on the counter as a love offering. It was still sitting there, as overlooked and pitiful as he was.

Suzzy, finding make-work as far from Decker's end of the counter as possible, was adrift somewhere between furious and heartbroken. Allowing herself to fall for an aging ex-biker goon, ex-Trappist monk bread maker who took pictures with no film and wanted to go over Niagara Falls in a self-propelled friggin propane tank—what in Christ could she have been thinking of?

And to think she'd almost told him the truth about herself, her real job, risking the undercover assignment at the Metropolis and her fifteen-year career in the Customs Service for the love of a goddamn wingnut.

The love of—

Love.

She felt her facial features beginning to slide again, but it was too soon for another quick retreat to the ladies room. Pull it together, you slobbering idiot. So you fell for a guy and it didn't work out. It's happened to you before and you survived; you've got the divorce decree to prove it. Better to find out now and cut your losses. Just move on.

If only he hadn't brought in that stupid little houseplant.

She snorted in a huge sniffle—loud enough to bring Decker's head up from his coffee mug like a birddog on the hunt—and grabbed her damp rag and attacked the counter. She would have gone on that way, rubbing the shine right off the Formica, but for the three men who came into the restaurant and took a booth in her area. One of them, she noticed immediately, was the young punk that had given Decker a hard time a week or two ago. Early Bruce Springsteen was the look, with the unruly dark hair and sideburns, the two-day growth, and the leather jacket; what was the name again?

Bonawitz, Dennis Bonawitz, that was it. AKA Bona. She remembered now, he was in a surveillance photo in her notebook, the principal target of the photo being one Eddie Touranjoe, a suspected car thief and mule for a Canadian biker gang. Touranjoe was considered a possible suspect in the Customs investigation; she'd recorded his name twice herself, stopping by the restaurant to see Gus Pellipollis. But Bonawitz wasn't on the primary list; he hadn't turned up enough times on the border crossing.

It was the other two men, particularly the smaller one, who really had her nose twitching. She got a good look when she served them coffees—an orange juice for Springsteen—and took their breakfast orders. The short dark stocky man in the expensive overcoat was familiar, but she couldn't place him. The other one, sitting next to Bonawitz and taking up four-fifths of the booth seat, was obviously paid muscle.

When she placed their order at the kitchen pass-through, she snuck a glance Decker's way; he was dividing his attention now between her and Bona.

She caught Camille's eye and pantomimed a cigarette, then took her purse with her as she went out back to the small loading dock where the restaurant's meats and produce were delivered. There was a kitty-corner view of the Rainbow Bridge from there, including the U.S. Customs booths and inspection station. Half the personnel from the station ate at least a few meals each week at the Metropolis, another reason it made for such a prime surveillance site.

Suzzy dug a Virginia Slim from her purse and lit up. The pack was almost gone. She'd given up counting her smokes in the last two days; she only had enough will power to kick one bad habit at a time and right now she was concentrating on rinsing Decker out of her hair.

Jesus. If only they made a patch for heartbreak, something she could stick on her arm and make her forget about the craving—

No! No, no, no, no. Do your damn job, that's all you need to think about.

She pulled her pad from the purse and scribbled in a notation. *10:15 a.m., Dennis Bonawitz and two possibles...*

✤　　　✤　　　✤

Bona didn't like any of this, didn't figure any of it was necessary. Didn't he call the night before and give Jimmy Frat the particulars on Eddie the Bomber? But Jimmy had insisted they meet up in the Falls that morning. And when Bona got to the arranged spot—the shrine at St. Mary's of the Cataract on 4th St. next to the convention center, Bona leaning against the high wrought iron fence near the fountain, having impure thoughts about the donations box—Coco pulls up in the Town Car and the back window whirs down and Jimmy says to get in, he's hungry and they can talk over breakfast. So they haul ass over to Niagara Street and hang a left and go on down to the Metropolis and there they were, Bona pinned into the booth by Coco's bulk, nothing to do but watch while Jimmy and his bodyguard each scarfed down the morning special; eggs, sausages, homefries and toast.

"Y'know, Mr. Fratelli," Bona tried again. "That address I gave you on Touranjoe is good, I checked it out myself. Me and Dale."

"So I heard." The booths each featured jukebox controls, put in a quarter and pick two songs from a flip chart of moldy oldies and recent hits, anything and everything from Patsy Cline to the Dave Matthews Band. Naturally, Jimmy Frat was thumbing through, looking for something to play, chortling—actually damn chortling—when he found a Four Seasons classic, 'Working My Way Back To You.' He inserted his quarter and punched in the letter and number, J-9. Then he put his full attention on Bona.

"So you're telling me this punk, this Eddie, isn't no friend of yours, is that right?"

"No, no friend at all. I hardly even know the guy. I mean, I know *of* him, sure, on account of he's around and I'm around and we both know some of the same people. But that's it. No shit, Mr. Fratelli, the guy's no friend of mine." Doing the big brown eyes bit the whole time, Mr. Sincerity, like he used to do when the school principal called him onto the carpet on suspicion of pulling the fire alarm.

"That's good," Jimmy said. "So you got no problem with whacking the puke."

"No, I got no problem with—wait a second, you mean *me* whacking him?"

Jimmy leaned closer. "Why not you? You never took anybody out before?"

"It's not that. It's just, you caught me off-guard." As he thought about it, he realized he should've seen it coming, Jimmy giving him some kind of loyalty test, see which way the wind was blowing. "I can handle it, Mr. F. If that's what you want. I mean, it might take a while to set the thing up—"

Jimmy's lip curled into what he liked to think of as his Elvis smile. "Relax, kid. You're just goin' along to finger the punk. I got somethin' in mind for Eddie boy takes a specialist." He blinked over to Coco. "You got our friend lined up for tonight, right?"

"Seven, boss, like you said. Meet the kid here at the shrine."

"You tell our friend I want the whole nine yards?"

"Everything. Including the spike. I told him."

Bona wanted to ask, The spike? But decided he didn't wanna know. He let his eyes and his mind drift away while Jimmy and Coco ravaged their cholesterol specials and talked some more about their "friend", the specialist. That's when he noticed the monk, whatshisname, down at the end of the counter, wearing the same tan jacket as on the day him and Jimmy first spotted the guy down in the park with his camera. Sitting there now like he'd just lost his dog, some kinda freakin flowerpot in front of him. Bona watched as the monk perked up when the waitress came out from the back. Same one that had taken Jimmy's and Coco's order, dirty blonde, tall, a little thick in the hips but not bad for her age. A definite 1, Bona decided.

Yeah, he'd bone her at both ends, all right.

The monk felt the same way by the look on his face. Guy was seriously smitten with the bitch, that much was obvious in the way he kept trying to catch her eye, get her to come down to his end of the counter. Fucking pathetic the way some guys let a woman jerk 'em around by their unit.

Bona felt a smile beginning to form on his face and, along with it, a grain of an idea.

🍁   🍁   🍁

Decker had noticed Bona right off, and he recognized one of the men with him, too, the swarthy, well-dressed character from Niagara Falls Park, the one who didn't like getting his picture taken. He mulled it over for about ten seconds, wondering what the pair were up to this time, but then he saw Suzzy take their order and he forgot all about them. When she disappeared into the back of the restaurant again, he thought about following her, maybe catching her taking a smoking break or coming out of the ladies room, but thought better of it. Let her anger play itself out. When she was ready to talk, to hear him out, he'd be there.

He had already decided on a course of action. This thing with the falls, he couldn't explain it to her with words alone and expect her to understand why a middle-aged man would feel compelled to risk his life on a foolhardy stunt. He couldn't put it into words, so he'd just have to show her. But to show her, he needed her to talk to him, to agree to come out with him one more time...

He had nearly six weeks of vacation built up. He planned on using some of it, beginning that night and for the rest of the week. He'd already gone out and done some shopping, picked up a few things for the apartment, and he needed to do some more. In between, he'd spend his time there on a stool at the Metropolis, waiting for Suzzy to soften up just a little bit.

🍁   🍁   🍁

"Hey! Bona! What's so fucking funny?"

He was still caught up watching the monk and the waitress, this little game they had going, like some master-slave thing with the waitress—Suzzy, he read from her nametag when she came around for coffee warmups; what the fuck kinda name was that?—her playing the role of the whip-happy dominatrix, while the monkster—Decker; that was it—was undoubtedly her willing whipping boy. Cute as custard pie.

Jimmy reached across and pinged Bona in the forehead with his index finger.

"I'm amusing you or boring you or what?"

"Hell, no, Mr. Fratelli." Bona had to blink a couple of times to refocus, remember where he was, wedged into the booth there beside giant Coco, Jimmy Frat glaring at him, that Four Seasons faggot whining out a high note on the chintzy jukebox speaker. A freakin dream come true. "I was just—I dunno, I guess I got distracted. That guy you had me brace for the film a couple weeks back? Monk Decker? I seen him sitting back there, is all."

Jimmy's brow folded. "What're you talkin', some fucking film guy?"

"The guy you thought was taking your picture over in the park, 'member?"

Jimmy hoisted his arm up onto the back of the booth and turned halfway around, scowering every face in the diner until settling on Decker. "What, that guy?" Still staring at Decker, who looked up and stared back blankly. "That's the guy from the park? I don't even remember him."

"That's him, Mr. F. Remember, he had on the same jacket."

Jimmy swung back around. "You checked the guy out, right? He's some kinda local nut, taking pitchers a the falls alla time, right?"

"Yeah, that's right."

"Then fuck him and pay attention to me, *capisce*? *Minchia*." He shook his head; try to find good help anymore. "So anyways, Coke here picks you up at seven, same place. That's tonight, got that?"

"Got it."

"Okay, then. You take Coco and our friend across the river to this Eddie puke's and finger him, they'll take it from there." He looked at Coco Pulli. "You know the routine, you got the address where to deliver the goods after."

Coco nodded.

Jimmy nodded, too. "This asshole Prevost thinks he's sending me a message, I'll send the prick a message he'll be dreamin' about for the rest of his short, shitty life." The dark eyes suddenly glowed with something approaching mirth. "Hey, I just thought a somethin' you can add to the list, Coco. Before you cross the bridge? Stop at one a those souvenir shops down along the park there…"

CHAPTER 23

※

The Friends of Eddie T.

Strategic thinking, thinking of any kind, had never been Eddie Touranjoe's strong suit. He'd always been a soldier, efficient at what he did but limited, not by a lack of willingness to do whatever it took to get over, but by a lack of imagination. It had never occurred to him before that he could put together his own action. Which was why turning on Miles Prevost was such a big deal.

Not that he owed the bastard anything. It'd be a pleasure, in fact, to see the snooty son of a bitch get taken down a few pegs, his little empire yanked out from under him. Eddie smiled: Yanked by the Yanks. Sounded like something Prevost himself would say, peering down his nose at you like it was a rifle sight and you were in the crosshairs. So, no, he didn't feel like he was doing anything except being smart, taking advantage of a situation.

Plus, there was the fact he didn't have a choice in the matter. It was Prevost's idea to go blow up a wiseguy's car in his own driveway. It was only fair that if someone had to get popped for doing it, it should be Miles. Talking Bona and Jimmy Frat into taking down his boss was, as far as Eddie saw it, a simple matter of doing what had to be done to survive. Any fringe benefits—like helping the Buffalo mob move in on Prevost's auto theft operation—was like a perk of doing business.

Eddie reminded himself of all this as he lit a Player's and placed a call to the man in Toronto. Yeah, the price of doing business. He was turning a corner here, career-wise, eh? Becoming a got-damn entrepreneur, is what.

"Yes?" was how Prevost answered his private line, that airy-fairy tone that said he was the fucking Duke of Windsor and the rest of us were around to sweep up the rose petals.

Eddie said, "I gave Bona your message."

"Yes. And?"

"And I'm still wondering about my other twenty-five bills, eh?"

An imperial sigh. "We'll call it three thousand, Edward—contingent on the arrangement you've made with your friend. You have set up a meeting?"

"I'm working on it, eh. These things take time."

"Well, how much time? If we string this matter out, I'll lose the edge I'm seeking."

"Hey, Bona's no got-damn idiot, eh. He don't wanna come over here and get whacked, y'know. You gotta show him some good faith, eh?"

"Good faith?"

"Offer to pay him for his time. Maybe show him a good time, like at the casino."

A pause. "How much are we talking about, Edward?"

Eddie tried to take the grin out of his voice. "Oh, like five hun'erd, eh, and you have him meet you at the blackjack tables, maybe spot him a few chips. Show him you got as much class as his wiseguy friends, eh?"

Prevost exhaled. This wasn't the sort of nuisance he needed—he had tickets for the Maple Leafs at the new Air Canada Centre Wednesday evening—but business was business, and this fellow Bona could be just the ace in the hole he needed. "All right, make the offer. I can be down to the Casino Niagara tomorrow night at nine. We can sort out the particulars later. But get on this ASAP, Edward."

"Absolutely."

Eddie hung up the phone and let the grin return. That should stall Prevost long enough for Bona to get back to him with an answer from Jimmy Frat, whether he was interested in Eddie's deal. And why the fuck wouldn't he be, eh, all the money to be made.

Meanwhile the only thing Eddie planned to get on ASAP was sweet little Tildy from downstairs.

❋   ❋   ❋

Coco Pulli, behind the wheel of an older Buick LeSabre, picked Bona up at seven p.m. at the shrine on Fourth and cut back around to Prospect Street, grabbing a spot at the curb and sending Bona into a souvenir shop for one of those little Canadian flags on a stick. Bona was back in two minutes flat with the flag and a question.

"What d'we need this thing for?"

"The boss said so." Coco was already on the move, taking the Buick up Prospect past the OxyChem building and hanging a left toward the customs station at the foot of the Rainbow Bridge.

While they waited to clear, Bona, his foot tapping a mile a minute, said, "We meet up with this 'friend' of yours on the Canadian side, huh?"

Coco grunted and rolled his window down, preparing to tell the Canuck in the booth they were both U.S. citizens from Buffalo, crossing over for a few hours recreation at the casino, yadda, yadda.

Once they were past Canadian Customs and cruising up Newman Hill, Bona said, "I gotta ask, man. The spike? What's up with that anyway?"

Coco didn't even grunt this time, his usually stoic slab of a face scrunched up in concentration, staring straight ahead as he struggled to read the unfamiliar signs in the feeble glow of the streetlights. After five minutes and a series of right turns he pulled the Buick into a nearly empty parking lot and paid the attendant with a couple of two-dollar Canadian coins. "Don't forget the flag," is all he said to Bona before getting out of the car and heading off down the sidewalk. A block farther on he stopped next to a gray van, rapped on the passenger window, and got in. The side door slid open and Bona, with a tentative glance around, climbed into the back. There were no seats back there, just a large red tool box tucked behind the driver's seat. Bona pulled it out a few inches and sat on it.

The driver was a skinny middle-aged guy with flat gray eyes and a grim little mouth. He reminded Bona of a costume he'd seen when he was in the souvenir shop, a garden variety Halloween ghoul. Coco said to him, "You remember the spike?"

The ghoul was offended by the question. "Course I remembered it." Voice as thin and greasy as the hair smeared across the top of his head. He reached down inside a gym bag wedged between the seats and brought out a hypodermic syringe, one of those big ones like they use to give hormone shots to cows. There was a cork on the end of the needle and a greenish yellow liquid inside the vial.

Bona said, "What the freakin fuck is that shit?"

The ghoul turned all the way around. "Bat'ry acid. You shoot it into this here artery in the neck, it eats up a man's brain from the inside. Nasty, nasty." Then he stuck out his tongue and scrunched up his face.

Bona remembered thinking, Jesus fucking Christ, what is it with these guineas? Can't they ever just shoot a guy?

❦   ❦   ❦

Eddie, in between boning Tildy, was bouncing some of his big plans off her while she watched MTV on the big screen Sony that took up one wall of the tiny apartment.

"I see myself opening a dealership, eh, late-model pre-owned luxury vehicles only, your Lexuses and Lincolns and the big SUVs, fully optioned. That way it's like a perfect front operation, eh. You bring in the stolen vehicles, you change the VIN numbers and give 'em new paper. All the while you're filling orders from Russia, Africa, countries like that. Anything you don't ship, you can sell right off the lot, eh, just like any legit operation. I don't know why Prevost doesn't do it that way now. Sounds like a good idea, don'tcha think?"

"Uh-huh." Tildy turned away from a Goo Goo Dolls video to say, "You wanna fuck me in the ass this time?"

Like she was asking him, "You want fries with that?" That's what he liked about her over the other girls who worked downstairs in the body rub shop. With Tildy, there was no games, no attitude. No rude remarks about his teeth.

"Yeah, sure," Eddie said, flashing back on his prison years. "Sounds good."

❦   ❦   ❦

Bona couldn't help but notice that the inside of the van was clean as a butcher's table, but it had this faint smell, like old blood and piss and disinfectant seeping from the framing. They were parked around the corner from Eddie's street, with a clear view of the body rub shop and the outside stairway to the second floor apartments. It was a slow night for massages and blowjobs by the look of it; the orange OPEN sign was switched on but not one person had gone into or come out of the dump in the twenty minutes they'd been watching.

Eddie Touranjoe's white Jeep Grand Cherokee was sitting in the alley, right beside the stairway.

The ghoul looked at Coco and said in that reedy voice, "Any quieter I'll nod off."

Coco said, "Yeah, we might's well take him in the apartment." He was wearing a burgundy leather car coat, from which he pulled a silenced Glock 9-mm automatic and checked the clip. He put it away and turned to Bona. "I need to see this asswipe's face first, to make sure it's the same guy I seen down in Amherst. The way we do it is, you go up and knock, get him to the door. I'm behind you and our friend here is behind me. I see it's the wrong guy, you make some excuse, we walk out. Otherwise, I tap you and you get the hell out of the way."

"Okay." Bona swallowed, just to prove he could. "What if Eddie—this asswipe comes to the door with a piece?"

"Why should he?"

"Well, hell, maybe he's nervous after doing the bomb, worrying about retaliation and shit."

Coco Pulli frowned minutely. "You just remember to get outa my way."

🍁   🍁   🍁

Tildy sprawled across the bed face down, blew out a breath, and rolled halfway over, one hand draped casually over her bare buttocks. "Y'know, you're a regular rooster, Eddie, just like my Uncle Parvo. He could get it up two, three times a session, too."

"Uh—thanks." Eddie decided just to accept the compliment and not dig any deeper into her family history. He was pulling up his briefs, looking around the cluttered floor for his jeans and his packet of Player's, when the knock came.

"Yeah, what?" Figuring it was Garth or Evan, wanting Tildy to get her ass back downstairs to work.

"It's, uh, Dennis Bonawitz. Is, uh, Eddie Touranjoe home?"

It took him a moment to connect the name Dennis Bonawitz to Bona, but when he did Eddie grabbed the knob and threw open the door with little more than a quizzical expression. "Hey, man, what's with the Dennis shit—"

The door flew inward, sending Eddie back against the dining table. Coco Pulli clipped him across the face with the barrel of the Glock, knocking him to the floor. The girl, Tildy, had rolled off the bed in the corner of the room and was standing between it and the wall, unconcerned with her nudity but shaken by the sight of the huge man with the gun. She sucked in a breath to scream but never got it out, as the suppressed barrel of the pistol swung in her direction and leveled off and, all in the sweep of a second or less, spat out two bullets. Tildy slammed backward against the wall as a pair of holes bloomed in the middle of her chest, just above a heart-and-arrow tattoo, and she was dead, eyes wide open, before her body came fully to rest in a heap on the floor.

⁂

By the time Bona ventured into the room, Coco and the ghoul were already making themselves at home. Music blared from a giant Sony projection television. All he could see of the dead girl was a smear of blood on the wallpaper and a bare foot poking out from behind the bed. The ghoul had his gym bag on the small round dinette table and was casually pulling on a pair of plastic gloves. Coco had put away the pistol and was dead lifting Eddie off the floor by the elastic in his underpants. He wasn't wearing anything else, except a red gash across the bridge of his nose and a doomed expression, thoughts of pain and his mother and how he wished he'd stuck it out at the Ford plant banging around in his head.

Bona felt his dinner do a summersault. Images of the Donny Pressi hit came back to him, how all the guys, Rick Lemongello's crew and him, took turns plugging Pressi's dead carcass, like freakin target practice on a piece of raw meat, the sounds the slugs made. Thinking how things were never really the way you remembered them. They were always worse.

"Bona? Man, you gotta do somethin' for me, eh." Eddie, being held up now by Coco, pleaded with him, the ugly face and teeth made even uglier by fear and desperation. "We were gonna deal—"

"Shut up! Shut the fuck up!" Bona landed a right hand even as the words were coming out of his mouth, and then another, and a knee to Eddie's gut as he went down, Coco letting him go and looking at him on the floor, and back up at Bona, saying, "Go ahead and stomp him, y'want. Save me some wear-and-tear on my shoes."

"Yeah, but don't kill him," said the ghoul, holding up the cow syringe. "Save some for me."

A rage came over Bona. The only reason he was in that shitty little room, the only reason anybody was there was all Eddie's fault, running to his boss with stories, coming around Jimmy Frat's house to blow up his daughter's car. Laying there now, trying to get his mouth working through the blood and the pain, still trying to drag Bona's ass down with him. Well, fuck him.

Bona drew his foot back and kicked him in the face, once, twice, three times.

Stupid. Motherfucking. Asshole.

Kicked him so hard he was out of breath when he stopped and Eddie Touranjoe's face wasn't Eddie anymore.

"Okay, we'll take it from here."

Bona's knees were wobbling like bowling pins. He fell back against the wall next to the big TV and worked on getting his wind back, staring at Coco Pulli so he wouldn't have to look anyplace else.

"You wanna hoof it back across the river, you can take off," Coco told him. "Me and my friend got a full evening still ahead of us."

Bona nodded, grateful for the dismissal. He started out, then turned back when Coco reminded him, "Hey. Leave the little flag."

🍁   🍁   🍁

At 8:14 on Wednesday morning, Miles Prevost was stuck in a traffic slow-up on the 404, the Don Valley Parkway, on his drive into Toronto from

Richmond Hill, when his dock foreman reached him on the car phone. He knew it was bad when the foreman refused to go into detail over the phone. And when he said they *think* it's Eddie Touranjoe.

It took another thirty minutes of herky-jerky on the parkway, his Lexus flanked on either side by Asians in sulphurous compacts, before the Don Valley began to flow again like a purged bowel. He thought about trying an alternate route through the city, but decided to stay the course, down to the Gardiner, then west to the Spadina exit.

They had moved the body from where it'd been found, lying at the foot of PreCan's loading dock inside two duct-taped black garbage bags. What was left of Eddie was now lying on a wooden pallet just inside the loading bay door, the garbage bags having been removed out of respect for the dead and in the interest of making a positive ID.

Miles Prevost stood over the body, his hands clenched, unconsciously grinding his back teeth as he looked over the remains; the nude white body a mass of jailhouse tattoos competing with bruises, the face a pulp of raw tissue, the spiky blond hair and snarling Doberman-like teeth blood-stained, eyes bulged out in an unimaginable agony. As if this wouldn't have been enough to enrage Prevost, there was more. One final slap in the face that made all the others, at least from Prevost's perspective, seem secondary.

Poking out from poor Edward's rectum was a small Canadian flag on a stick.

CHAPTER 24

❀

Sweet Dreams

"Women are trouble, Monk, specially if you go and fall in love with one. They think men are puppy dogs, you can pick one up at the A.S.P.C.A. for free, take him home and train him to sit up, roll over, fetch, beg, and not shit on the shag rug. Then they find out we've got independent will and there goes the honeymoon."

Decker wasn't so sure, particularly about that independent will stuff. He'd been running around for twenty-four hours doing things that he didn't necessarily want to do, beginning with all the new furnishings and other doodads he'd bought to spruce up his apartment just on the hope that it might help convince Suzzy Koykendall he wasn't a complete loser—if and when he was able to lure her over to his apartment, that is. Then there was that morning's excursion up to Lake Ontario with Norton Gage to test out the Torpedo. On the one hand, he didn't want to take the time away from his vigil at the Metropolis. On the other hand, there was no way he was going to ride the thing over a one hundred-seventy-foot plunge into tons of churning river without first testing its water-tightness and steering controls. And on the third hand, he was even less certain he wanted to do the stunt at all, not if it was going to cost him Suzzy.

He was a man cursed with two compulsions, each one pulling him in a different direction. Not a comfortable position, to say the least.

"She's got a right to be upset," he said. "It's not something a mature grownup does, going over Niagara Falls in a barrel."

"It's not a goddamn barrel, it's a highly engineered stunt capsule and it *works*. We just proved that." Norton took his eyes off the road long enough to glare over at Decker. "And I resent the notion you have to be some kinda immature goober to wanna do this. You, of all people, have legitimate reasons—"

"Yeah." Decker laughed, short and sour. "To vanquish old ghosts, huh? Make the recurring nightmare stop recurring. If it does. Or maybe I'll drown down there at the base of the falls. That'd certainly take care of the nightmare problem."

Norton turned his attention back to the road and shook his head. They were in a flat bed truck he owned, returning from an early morning trip to Wilson, a small tourist village on Lake Ontario up in the northeastern part of Niagara County. They'd used the truck's winch and PTO to launch the Torpedo at the public docks in Wilson, give it a shakedown cruise along the lake's calm, shallow shoreline with only a couple of gawkers on hand. Everything had checked out and now, late morning, they were headed back into the Falls from the north, under the miles of high-tension lines emanating from the Niagara-Mohawk power grid, the Torpedo secreted away under a tarpaulin. Norton should've been on an emotional high, breaking out one of the short dark Havanas in the truck's glove box, but his friend's funk had let most of the air out of his party balloon.

"I'd go myself if it wasn't for the leg," he said quietly. "And my claustrophobia."

"I know you would."

"Look, Monk, if you don't wanna go, we don't go. It's no big deal. You know me, I get all sorts of wild hairs up my ass, most of 'em going no farther than a few scattered parts on the floor of my shop. I don't give a shit about the time and the money we've put into this. Hell, we both know I'd be spending the money and the time doing some other dumbass project, so what's the difference. It's really no biggie, man."

Decker smiled. "Thanks, Nortie, but it's got nothing to do with your dreams. It's about my dreams, remember?"

"Yeah, I know. But—we've only got another week or so anyway, if you're gonna go. Last person to challenge Niagara Falls in the Twentieth Century.

Course we can forget it entirely for this season, reconsider it in the spring. First man over the falls in the Twenty-first Century—that's got a ring to it, too, huh?"

"Look, I know I need to make a decision soon, one way or the other. It's just, right now, this thing with Suzzy is filling me up. Somehow I've got to get her to come around."

"So why don't you just tell her? Explain it to her."

"I don't think I can convince her. Not just with words, anyway. That's why I wanna get her to go across the river with me, so I can *show* her rather than tell her."

"Well," Norton shrugged, "a picture's worth a thousand words, right?"

"Right. Specially when the picture's sixty feet high."

🍁   🍁   🍁

The very first thing Bona did Wednesday morning, after his shower and a breakfast of fresh fruit and Cheerios and a sniping contest with Melody over which of them was the bigger asshole, was he drove over to Military Road to a unisex place and got himself a complete makeover. Buzz cut and a blond tint job on what hair was left, a professional shave leaving only a short goatee and mustache circling his mouth, which he also had the girl dye blond. Then he went next door and had his left earlobe pierced and bought a little gold earring like on a pirate. Then he went down the street to the Prime Outlets Mall, to the Tommy Hilfiger Company Store, and got himself tricked out in a pair of khakis and a black tee shirt and an oversize shirt over that, a black and gray striped number that he wore hanging out and unbuttoned exactly like the mannequin in the window. And a pair of brown loafers from the Rockport Outlet to cap things off.

When he was done, he checked himself out in the mirror and thought, Damn, a card carrying member of Gen-X. The boy could do Pepsi commercials.

Yeah, a complete freakin makeover. Too bad he couldn't get a do-over while he was at it, like when he was a kid playing home run baseball over at Love Canal's now-demolished 99th Street School, the playground built on top all that Hooker Chemical dioxin. First thing he'd do over is tell Jimmy Frat to keep his shitty three hundred a week and his hot mob connections and get himself some other babysitter for his future son-in-law. Second thing he'd do over is he'd've taken that Marla bitch for the twelve hundred and the blow job and then let her pussywhipped husband go, let the two of them settle things themselves. Keep him the fuck out of it.

Bona never dreamed, but last night he'd dreamed. Dreamed like a bastard the whole night, tossing and turning, just about knocking Mel out of the bed one time. Nightmare was what it was, him looking down on the scene in this sleazy little apartment, a dead whore lying in the corner, Coco and the ghoul both holding onto this giant needle, some Canadian biker buddies of Eddie's bursting in laughing like it was a party, looking for their piece of the action. And on the floor, beaten bloody and begging for his life, wasn't no Eddie Touranjoe. It was Bona lying there, already in Hell and just waiting to die.

Worst dream he could ever remember, even worse than when he was a kid and used to picture himself working the graveyard shift on the crusher at fucking Carborundum, turning into his old man.

Only last night's dream didn't feel like a dream exactly. What it felt like was a premonition.

And that's why he'd made his mind up when he got out of bed that morning. He was done with Jimmy Frat and the Marla bitch and everything else. Life was too freakin short to spend it looking over your shoulder, some goddamn Mafia goon trying to cave in your skull or some invisible threat killing you slow, like the shit in the ground at Love Canal or the electro-magnetic waves pulsing over his head all over the city. Melody could have whatever she could get for the house on 97th. All she ever wanted to do anyway was take the kids and move back in with her old lady. So she'd get her wish and Bona'd get his; a fresh start. His skills, honed over a dozen years of house burglaries and snatch-and-grabs at convenience stores and special-order arsons, were completely portable; he could do insurance fraud or bust open an ATM in freakin Wichita Falls as easy as Niagara Falls. Alls he needed was a decent stake, something to get him across the country and set up in a new place, some new ID, enough money to live on while he got the lay of the land, made the necessary contacts.

Which is where Monk Decker's forty thousand dollars came in. He'd been half thinking about a way to get that money ever since he'd found out about it, and after seeing Decker in the Metropolis yesterday, drooling over that wait-ress, bringing her flowers even, Bona had an inspiration. It would take a little more planning, possibly a day or two to stakeout the target and get the setup the way he'd need it, but then he'd be ready. By the weekend, maybe sooner, he'd be free and clear...

Well, almost. There was one other potential problem. But he'd been half thinking on that, too, mulling all his options, and he knew now what he'd have to do about it.

"Sweet dreams are made of these," Bona sang along with the radio, an oldie by the Eurythmics, a tune he remembered from like junior high school. He was on Buffalo Avenue, driving downtown the long way around, not really knowing why he'd picked that route, past all the piles of red brick and vacant lots on both sides. Rubble and weeds that used to be manufacturing plants for Carborundum and Hooker and Olin and Dow and half a dozen other compa-nies that had downsized the city along with themselves.

Maybe he was just reminding himself that his life could be worse.

Or maybe he was just saying his good-byes.

❧   ❧   ❧

He brought her roses this time, a dozen blood-red tea roses in a small Irish cut-glass vase. The way the other diners stared at him, he began to waver as he made for his favorite stool, wondering if this wasn't actually a good way to prove he *was* a nut. But it was too late to turn back. She'd seen him come in, and even if she hadn't, there were two other waitresses eager to point him out to her.

Decker waited patiently for her to get around to serving him, surrepti-tiously watching as she handled the cash register and, it appeared, handled one of the diner's owners, who was standing closer to her than necessary. He let his mind go where it would, back over the same old ground, all the things he'd like to be able to tell her, some things he doubted he ever could. The bad old days with the Nomads when he was a user in every sense of the word, no direction and no thoughts of anything but himself, his own pleasure, the next woman, the next high, the next drunken bacchanal. The long years of exile at the Abbey of the Genesee, each morning rising in blackness at two o'clock to prepare for the day, a simple breakfast of coffee and thin juice and bread at three, followed by vigils, the first of seven daily gatherings in the chapel where the monks would pray and sing the Psalms. Three days a week he would begin his work-day well before dawn in the bakery, unloading hundred pound sacks of flour, cleaning and sorting raisins. By four-thirty, with the first bake ready, he'd move over to the ovens and unload the loaves from the hot pans, the worst job at the abbey, as far as Decker was concerned.

Until the summer of 1995, that is, and the gathering of the stones.

It had been decided that an extension would be built off the main building, a new conference hall, and fieldstone was needed for the foundation. Tons and tons of fieldstone, to be dug out of a hillside littered with ten-thousand-year-old rubble left behind by the recession of the glaciers at the end of the last Ice Age. At an abbey where the average age of the monks was well past fifty, it fell to Decker to handle the job of collecting the needed stones, with the help of two pious young novitiates, Simon and Jeffrey. Day after sweltering day, Decker and the two novices would scour the south-facing hillside for appro-priately sized rocks, then work them free from the sticky ground with long pry bars and roll them down the hill and into the bucket of the small Ford tractor, four or five at a time, and drive them down to the job site. Despite the advan-tage of the tractor, it was arduous, mind-numbing work, freeing up and load-ing the stones, and it continued on for weeks, all through the hot summer. For Decker it was as if each load of stones had become one large rock, and that one rock was always the same rock, and he had become Sisyphus in Hades, con-demned to an eternal, pointless toil.

His depression became so bad he finally went to the abbot for counsel.

Brother Walter, the abbot said to him, you have the wrong analogy entirely. Sisyphus was a bad king, a man without hope or redemption, condemned to his labors by the spiteful gods of the ancient Greeks. Pure mythology. You, my son, are a child of the one true God, a living testament to His glory. Each time you deliver your stones to the foundation site, you must look up to God and say a prayer and make your delivery an offering to Him. It's why we're all here, isn't it? To humble ourselves before God and our Savior?

So Decker went back to work, and he tried to put into practice the abbot's advice, but still he couldn't overcome the feeling of pointlessness. What did he—or God—care about a new conference hall? Why give us these free minds, these vivid imaginations, if we're expected to condemn ourselves to lives of drudgery? Shouldn't there be something more?

In the end it was not God but a woman who got him through that endless summer and set him on a path that eventually, a year and a half later, would see him leave the monastery and return to the secular world. He would never know her name, and she would never know he even existed, but she had been his salvation. He saw her only one time, coming out of the abbey's gift shop with her husband or boyfriend, a couple of tourists in a green sports car stopping by on a lark for some fresh bread and a jar of honey, perhaps a stroll through the wooded grotto for a few moments of contemplation at the carved Stations of the Cross.

He paused to watch her walk to the car, a woman of thirty or so, dark blond hair worn long and wavy, smooth tan legs tapering down from loose-fitting walking shorts, a sleeveless knit top. He remembered that it was red and that it clung closely to her bosom as she turned and lowered herself into the sports car's passenger seat. That and her easeful smile, as if the warmth of a sunny day and the prospect of a drive down a country lane with her lover was all anyone could ask for, or needed, in this life.

That nameless young woman snuggled into a corner of Decker's mind and took up residence, seeing him through the remaining weeks of toil on the hillside, as well as the long nights lying on the cot in his cell trying to fall asleep in the still-bright summer evenings. The conference hall foundation became the foundation of a cabin in the woods, where Decker and his fantasy woman would live together for all their days, and the gathering of the stones became a pleasure because he was doing it for her.

He wanted to tell Suzzy about the stones and the dream girl and how he'd been waiting for her to become a reality, not just a hazy recollection, a smile without a face. And how Suzzy had become that reality for him, from the first time she came down the long counter with a carafe of hot coffee in hand and that sly, knowing half-grin on her lips.

Don't call it love at first sight, he'd tell her, because I've seen you a thousand times in my dreams.

❦   ❦   ❦

Suzzy was standing near the cashier's counter, covering for Camille and fending off Steve Pellipollis, when she saw Decker come in with the roses. Steve, standing too close, was saying, "You could have this job permanent, y'know, babe, take the money from the customers and say 'How's ever'thing.' Pays good and alls you hafta do is smile and look pretty. You can do that."

"Wow, my dream job," Suzzy said. "And where's that leave Camille?"

"What the hell you worry 'bout Cammie? Girl's gotta worry about herself she wants to get somewheres."

"What I want, Steve, is for you to take your hand off my ass."

Both his hands came up, palms out. "Hey, I touch you and you'll know it, babe."

"And so will your wife, soon as I get to a phone."

"Ahhh." He called her a bitch and went back to the office, muttering in Greek as he went. Suzzy stole a glance down toward Decker at the far end of the counter, then turned her attention to a customer with the check and a ten dollar bill in his hand. She smiled automatically and took the money.

"Everything all right?" A question she could as easily ask herself, she thought, as she made change.

Suzzy's night had featured a dream, too. She was out on the deck at her townhouse on what seemed to be a summery afternoon. There was a man in the lawn chair beside her—she didn't see his face but they were chatting comfortably and she understood, in dream logic, that this man was her lover. Then the sky began to get darker; Suzzy looked up just as a large cloud passed over the sun. She could still see its brilliance, though, as if through a piece of gauze. As she gazed up at it, using her hand as a visor, the sun suddenly began to expand, becoming a splash of orange and red energy across the sky. And then the colorful flashes receded just as quickly and the sun was a glowing sphere again. But now it was diminished, less bright, and as she continued to watch in those few seconds, it flickered and flickered again and began to grow dimmer and dimmer, and already the air around her began to feel cold, until she realized that time had truly, finally run out on everything and everyone in this world.

Then she woke up, clammy with sweat and gulping for breath.

She'd been thinking about that dream all morning, and she'd thought of it the moment Decker came in with the roses. She'd made up her mind even before that, though; that she'd agree to go out with him again. She realized she couldn't just turn away, not without at least trying to talk him out of his plan to shoot over the falls in Norton's glorified tin can. If she loved him, she had to talk to him; if he loved her, he had to listen. While there was still time.

She grabbed a carafe of coffee and a clean mug and saucer and carried them down the length of the counter.

"It's becoming apparent to me, Decker," she said lightly, "that you've got a thing for roses."

He raised an eyebrow interrogatively. She placed the mug in front of him and poured it full.

"The rose tattoo on your shoulder," she said. "With Rose spelled out in flowery script. You promised to tell me about her, remember?"

"I remember. I said when I know you better." He added sugar, barely looking away from her eyes, recognizing his opportunity. "*Am* I going to get to know you better, Suzzy?"

She exhaled slowly to control her breathing. "We need to talk, Decker."

"That's what I'm suggesting. I want you to come out with me tonight, over to the Ontario side to see some of the sights—"

"Tonight?" She frowned, thinking about her regular Wednesday after-hours briefing with Randall down in Buffalo. She couldn't skip it, even if she wanted to. "I've, uh, got to do my laundry tonight or I won't have anything left to wear. Besides, it's supposed to be cold and wet later, maybe even a few snow showers."

"Okay, tomorrow then. I thought, if you could get somebody to cover the dinner shift for you, we could get something to eat first across the river, then do the town. There's—something in particular I want to show you."

"Just so long as it's understood—" She checked for eavesdroppers, finding none. "—we have to have a serious talk about this stunt idea of yours."

"Yes. Agreed." He smiled and nudged the vase of flowers toward her.

"A peace offering?"

"A love offering."

"You do make it hard on a girl."

"You make it hard on a boy, too, Suzzy."

"Ooh, smut talk. You been surfing the Web again, Decker?"

"I didn't mean it that way, but now that you mention it—"

"Down boy." She gently touched one of the rose petals, then moved the vase aside and rested her elbows on the counter, her face a foot away from his. Felt herself teetering like a diver on the brink. "Tell me about the tattoo."

He laughed ruefully. "Not much of a story there, I'm afraid. It was back in the biker days, a bunch of us got drunk and decided to get tattooed, I think it was down in Oceanside, New Jersey. I ended up getting this little rose thinga-majig on my shoulder."

"What about the name, Rose?"

"There is no Rose, never was. One of my compatriots, a fellow we called Hog, saw my new tattoo and claimed it looked like a pansy. I said it was a rose, he'd say it was a pansy. We went on like that for a while, as drunks will. Finally, I got sick of arguing so I had the tattoo guy put the name Rose across the stem, just so I could show it to Hog and say, See, it's a rose, dipshit. End of story. Dumb, huh?"

Her chin was propped on her hands. "You know, Decker, try as I might, I can't picture you as some bad-ass biker, hauling around on a chopper, all hairy and strung out."

"People change, Suzzy."

"Yeah," she said. "I'm counting on that."

✤   ✤   ✤

Distracted as they were by each other, neither Decker nor Suzzy noticed the other diners and the waitresses and Cammy the cashier watching them like it was a scene from a soap opera. And no one paid the least bit of attention to the slight, bleach-blond young man sipping the soup du jour at a booth in the no smoking section.

CHAPTER 25

❀

Stranger Than Fiction

Marla was back in her house at 6 Grackle Court working on a romance novel and trying to keep the world at bay. It was actually a kind of romance slash mystery novel, about a beautiful young housewife, Mary Beth Ponchatrain, whose husband, Gray Ponchatrain, was a pillar of the community by day and a sadistic sex deviant by night. In the first chapter, which is as far as Marla had gotten using Gary's old IBM Selectric typewriter, Mary Beth, desperate the morning after being thoroughly debauched and ravaged by Gray, seeks out help for the tenth time at the local police station only to be turned away yet again when in her modesty she refuses to allow a genital inspection. Now, at the beginning of chapter two, Marla has Mary Beth coming out of the police station and seeing at the bus stop a handsome young rogue in an orange jumpsuit who's just then been released from the county jail's Operation Clean Parks Program after serving six months of alternate weekends on a trumped up charge of assault and battery. Mary Beth offers him a ride in her Ford Windstar and he accepts with a coy grin.

"*Steed,*" *said the young man, offering her his hand.* "*Clint Steed.*"

"No, no, no, no." Marla backed up the carriage and Xed out *Clint Steed,* then sat back to ponder it. After half a minute, she said, "Ah!," and typed in *Cord Steel.*

The phone rang yet again, but Marla let the machine pick it up on the fourth ring. She'd already turned off the speaker, tired of listening to messages coming in from this or that TV station or her in-laws or snoopy neighbors pretending to convey their condolences over her loss. Phony bastards, every one of them. They all believed she was guilty, she could tell that by the way people looked at her. Stared at her whenever she went out in public, even as far as the end of the drive to get the mail; she could feel the eyes pop open all over the cul-de-sac, especially the vicious gossip next door, Jennifer, her former best friend who'd always been a two-faced bitch anyway. Give Jen an alleged murder for hire on her doorstep and it was like, like throwing raw tuna into a shark tank.

As a matter of fact, that wasn't a bad analogy for Marla's situation. Or for Mary Beth's, come to think of it.

Marla reached for her pen and her notepad and wrote down, on the page headed Story Notes, '*It was as if Mary Beth had become no more than a piece of chum tossed into a shark tank at Marineland, such was the frenzy of the media following her and Cord's arrest.*'

She read it—pleased with that word, *chum*—and put the notebook aside and went to the window. She was in the second floor guest bedroom, which doubled as a home office for Gary, a place he could work on his clients' policy updates and do a little cold calling. Marla pushed back the Laura Ashley curtains and carefully peeked through the crack in the sheers to the scene below.

Out in front of 6 Grackle Court, parked all along the curve of the cul-de-sac, were Chevy Luminas and Taurus station wagons and Dodge Caravans, not at all unusual in a development like hers, except these vehicles all had colorful logos painted on their sides and small satellite dishes mounted on their roofs. Marla recognized Polly D'Angelo, star reporter and weekend anchor from News10, and felt a frisson course through her body. There were some print and radio people, too, milling around together with their cheap Bic pens and slim notepads and portable tape recorders, but they didn't matter. It was television that could make or break a person; if it isn't on TV, it couldn't be important.

The exposure was a mixed blessing. On the one hand, the media crush and the notoriety was keeping her a prisoner in her own home, which was bad. On the other hand, it was giving her the forced discipline to get her novel written, which was a good thing. But it was making her look guilty, all those re-runs of her first appeal, with no makeup and no inflection in her voice, combined with standard footage of her being led into and out of the sheriff's office. Still, on the positive side, she hadn't been handcuffed, and besides, all this exposure should help her when and if she needed to recruit a high-profile attorney like Johnny Cochran or Alan Dershowitz to represent her.

Frankly, she believed Cochran to be a bit too ethnic and Dershowitz too annoying to have to spend any length of time with. She'd been thinking more and more of that youngish lawyer who was always defending Dr. Kevorkian, the Doctor of Death. Jeffrey Something.

But she was getting ahead of herself. The police hadn't even charged her with anything yet, no thanks to Randy Post and his big mouth and empty head.

She thought she was going to die the other morning when the sheriff's investigator, Mulvaney, came to the house with that black detective from Niagara Falls to tell her Gary was dead. Not at the news of his death; she'd been expecting that, naturally. But when Sgt. Mulvaney mentioned Randy.

Turns out it was a good thing they asked her to go downtown to the Public Safety Building in Rochester for questioning. The ride in gave Marla time to center herself, regain control. All they had was a case of his word against hers, and Randy was, after all, an idiot.

As she thought about it, the questioning had gone fairly well.

"Mrs. Graycastle, you do know a man named Randy Post? A security guard at the mall where you work part-time?"

"Randy the security guard? Oh, yes, I've seen him around. We shared a booth for coffee once at Friendly's, I remember."

"According to Randy you shared more than that, ma'am." Mulvaney, with his little 'ma'ams' every other sentence. She hated that, but she hated even more the other one, the black one from Niagara Falls, Sgt. Hazard, the way he stared at her like she was an open book. "According to Randy," Mulvaney continued, "you and him were lovers."

"Lovers?" Marla had been able to bring up a very genuine laugh. "Me and Randy the security guard? That awkward young guy in the blue double knits?

He hit on me once, that time we were having coffee, but that's it. I mean, even if I was interested, which I wasn't, I'm a married woman." She remembered to pause at that point and look down at her clenched fingers. "At least, I was. I suppose I'm a widow now. I'm—just getting used to the idea."

"Mrs. Graycastle, Randy Post also says you asked him to murder your husband for you. He says he gave you the name of a man in East Rochester, an ex-felon named Freddy McCoombs, also known as Freddy the Fixer. Guy's a fence. Allegedly."

"I don't understand. Why would I need a—a fence? If I wanted to kill anyone, which is ridiculous in the first place—"

"Freddy knows guys. He arranges things for people, that's why he's called a fixer. Randy figured Freddy could fix you up with a hit man to do your husband."

"Randy is insane."

"He says you later told him you'd seen Freddy and he'd given you a name to contact, but you needed more money. So Randy Post gave you all he had, three hundred dollars."

"And for three hundred dollars I hired myself a professional hit man? Drove all the way to Niagara Falls—"

"Nobody said you hired the hitter in Niagara Falls." It was her only major slipup and that black detective, Sgt. Hazard, jumped all over it. "So you drove all the way up to my town to meet with a guy Freddy McCoombs put you onto."

"I did no such thing."

"You just said you drove to Niagara Falls—"

"I was being, y'know, facetious. I was making the point that I don't think a person would have much luck trying to hire a hit man with three hundred dollars—"

"Forget the money for now. You could've had plenty more to add to the pot," said Sgt. Mulvaney, peering at her through those yellow-tinted aviator glasses like she was a clay pigeon or something. "You said 'drove all the way to Niagara Falls.' If you didn't hire the hitter, what makes you say you drove to Niagara Falls?"

"Well—it was a hypothetical. I mean, my husband's body was found in a parking garage in Niagara Falls, right? So I assumed the man who abducted and killed him probably came from there, that's all."

"But you said *you* drove to Niagara Falls."

That's how it had gone for the next hour and a half, the two burly detectives pounding away at her over the slip of the tongue on Niagara Falls and her denials and explanations. In the end, it was a stalemate. Marla was driven home, no charges against her, which told her that Freddy the Fixer, at least, was keeping his mouth shut; he obviously hadn't given them the name Bona or the phone number of the Niagara Falls bar where he could be reached.

But the grilling hadn't gone unnoticed by the media, which, feeding off a few well-placed leaks, had rushed to air in the past twenty-four hours with purely speculative stories, including hints at a secret lover and a paid assassin and some numbers on the possible life insurance payoffs that she only wished were true.

Thus the herd of reporters hanging out on her cul-de-sac like—like—Well, she couldn't think of a decent simile, but then she'd been writing her heart out all morning and was just too wrung-out to care.

"The hell with all of you," she whispered through the veil of the sheers.

Marla dropped the curtain and returned to the little desk and the typewriter and sighed wearily. She couldn't kid herself; she knew, before this was all over, she'd have to go through more interrogations just as nerve wracking and humiliating as Monday's.

But then, look on the bright side. If nothing else, she'd gotten a character out of it for her novel. A brutish police detective—patterned after both the tall, hulking Sgt. Mulvaney and the chunky, brooding Sgt. Hazard—who hounds Mary Beth and Cord after her husband, Gray, turns up dead in a Dempsy Dumpster at a resort hotel in the Adirondacks, his body half-eaten by scavenging bears. Only instead of Mulvaney or Hazard, her brutish police detective would be called Melvin 'Third Degree' Burns.

Marla positioned her fingers on the Selectric's keyboard, closed her eyes a moment, then opened them and began to type.

CHAPTER 26

O, Canada

Toronto was enveloped in a cold gray mist all day Wednesday, something to do with what the weathercasters called an inversion layer. Miles Prevost called it fog, as did most of his fellow citizens, all of whom were used to occasional banks of the stuff blanketing the city, usually when the water temperature out on Lake Ontario was warmer than the surrounding air and the wind directions were right. Prevost could recall a family trip years before out to the old unlamented ballpark at the Exhibition Grounds, a cool September Saturday afternoon, the Blue Jays versus the Seattle Mariners in a battle of expansion franchises, when a great cloud came in over the left field grandstand and settled on the place like a lid on a sugar bowl. They'd had to delay the game for an hour and a half until the wind changed direction and blew the fog back out onto the lake. He couldn't remember anything else about that game, not even which team won; only the fog.

It was in a personal fog that Prevost walked east along College Street toward the subway entrance at Queen's Park, his Burberry raincoat cinched, the collar turned up against the autumn chill. On a warmer day, and when he had more time, he might've elected to walk the twelve additional blocks down to Front Street for his luncheon meeting, but not today.

The luncheon invitation—a command in the form of a suggestion—had surprised him, frankly. It had been his call that initiated it. A courtesy call, to let the Calabrians know of his intention to retaliate against Mr. 'Jimmy Frat' Fratelli. He'd been severely agitated at the time, naturally. After all, he'd just supervised the loading of Eddie Touranjoe's tenderized carcass into the trunk of a 1973 Mercury Cougar, which was at that very moment on its way down to Burlington, where it would be stamped into a meter-square block of scrap metal and shipped to a steel re-processor in Guatemala. You don't witness something like that and then just trot gaily off to tea time.

"A lesson has to be made," he had said to Gianni Gallio over the phone. "This insult cannot be allowed, not unless we're ready to simply surrender all of southern Ontario, maybe the whole of Canada, to these Buffalo gorillas."

What are we talking about here, Gianni Gallio had said, and, when Prevost told him what had instigated the trouble in the first place, and what he now had in mind for Jimmy Frat, the Calabrian crime boss had cut him off in mid-syllable.

"Lunch," he said brusquely, his words carrying the operatic rhythms of the old country. "Onna me. Twelve-thirty." He named a place, a little trattoria on Scott Street near the theatre district, and abruptly hung up on Prevost.

And Prevost had come. Despite his anger, despite the disruptions he'd already suffered that morning, he had pulled on his raincoat at the appropriate hour and headed out to the restaurant. They may have gotten older and they may have seen their grip on the city loosened, a finger at a time, by all the foreign gangs that had moved in, but the Calabrians were still the Calabrians.

What was especially galling, Prevost thought, as he found a seat on the subway car and settled in for the short ride south, was that this day should have been a triumph for him, worthy of a gourmet meal somewhere special, say Truffles or Scaramouche. He'd just worked out a cloning deal with an extended family of blackmarket entrepreneurs down in Mexico; they were to receive a shipment of two-hundred-fifty legally obtained used cars, each with an accompanying certificate of origin, which would supposedly be filed away by Mexican customs officials once the cars were off-loaded. But this enterprising family has brothers and cousins working for Mexican Customs, making it a simple matter to keep the certificates of origin and mail them back up to Toronto, where Prevost can use them to "authenticate" a shipment of two-hundred-and-fifty stolen automobiles. A triumph of organizational networking. But now there'd be no time to savor the simple elegance of the thing.

Prevost frowned and watched the advertisements and the station names glide into and out of view—St. Patrick Station, Osgoode, St. Andrew—letting his thoughts wander for a moment. To be a Canadian and a Torontonian were one in the same thing in his mind. He loved the city, its civility and cosmopolitanism, the blend of old and new architecture, the museums and sports franchises, the world-class restaurants and thriving theatre life. Even the steely winters with their Great White North windchills were manageable; one could spend the entire day working and shopping and dining in Toronto without ever stepping foot outside, thanks to its ten-kilometer network of underground shops and tunnels in the central downtown area. Hadn't Canada, for something like the sixth year running, been named the best country to live in by the United Nations' index on social and economic progress? And wasn't Toronto, with its growing millions, the undisputed premier city of Canada?

And yet some pasta puking meatball snappers from of all places Buffalo, the sphincter at the butt end of the state of New York, with its greasy chicken wings and loser football team and shrinking population—these Sicilian organ grinders have the temerity to believe they can polka into Canada and knock it over like it's some Mom-and-Pop store in the next neighborhood.

Just who in the fuck do these people think they are?

"Really, Gianni, I'm asking. Who do these Buffalo wiseguys think they're fucking with here? They must think we're all Red Green and the McKenzie Brothers, fools and pushovers. Well, enough is enough. We need to draw the line down in Niagara Falls, right there in front of the casino, show these smirking bastards that Canada is already taken, thank you very much. And I say we start by turning this Jimmy Frat into a bowl of minestrone soup."

"You through?"

Prevost wasn't sure if he meant with the tirade or with the pasta primavera. He retreated to his glass of wine and took a tactical sip. Their booth was tucked into a special alcove in the tiny restaurant, away from the bustle and noise of the main dining room. Like the table location, the service was special for Mr. Gallio; the waiter, a Calabrian himself, hung just out of earshot at all times, ready to answer every whim.

"Look." Gianni Gallio's saturnine face attempted an avuncular smile. "It ain't like inna old days, Miles, you working your sucker games on them Kiwanis types at motels out along the airport strip, me and my brother busting a few heads over the Market. You ain't a two-bit rounder no more and me and Matteo ain't paid muscle. We come a long way, all of us, done okay for ourselves, uh? And gonna do better still. But there's a one thing we all need to remember." Gallio paused long enough to draw Prevost all the way into his dull brown gaze. It was the only part of him that didn't go with the expensive blue pinstripe suit, those eyes, and marked him as something other than the simple businessman he pretended to be. "You're an important and valued business associate, Miles. But you ain't essential."

Prevost sat back in the cushiony booth as if he'd been kicked in the chest. "I'm—shocked, Gianni. We're partners, you and Matteo and I. And yet you threaten me?"

"It ain't a threat, Miles, come on. We're just a talking here, and I'm trying to tell you what's what, okay?" All the while Gallio's small hands fluttered the air like hummingbirds. Now he pushed aside his plate of raviolis and laid the palms flat on the table. "First off, you and me, Miles, we ain't partners. Show me the papers, okay? You don't got any. Me and Matteo, we're partners, because we're brothers and that's blood and that's different. Otherwise, I don't got *partners* like you mean it, what I got is business arrangements. You do very good by this arrangement, Miles, all them hot cars you move back and a forth from the States, in and outa Canada, all over the world. You move some product for us sometimes, too, and we both do okay. But you, you do better'n okay with the car thing, alla them big shipping containers down there in Hamilton, you think we don't know how that works?"

The implication was clear; they could take over his auto operation and run it themselves if they wanted to. Not that it came as a surprise. The overseas markets for stolen autos had gotten so large, the profits so high and the relative risks so low, that Prevost knew of some major drug traffickers who had switched over and were now dealing only in hot cars. It was only a matter of time before the greedy Gallio brothers decided to increase their piece of his action. Prevost understood that, was even expecting it. But to try and nudge him aside, with his contacts, his expertise, it simply wasn't a good business move, not in a market where everybody, through cooperation, stood to make big profits.

Prevost started to speak, but was cut off with a slash of one of Gallio's dainty hands.

"*Second*, Miles, you ain't the only business arrangement we gotta think about. These Buffalo *La Cosa Nostra*, the ones your Jimmy Frat belong to, them Magganos, they're connected to the Gambinos and the Commission down in New York City, okay? And me and Matteo, we got arrangements down in Connecticut with some cousins got their own interests with them Gambinos. Y'see where I'm goin', Miles?"

Prevost prided himself on his self-control, but he was barely able to keep the rage from his voice. "You're telling me we have to rollover, we lowly Canadians, to a bunch of cheap Buffalo mafioso because they're connected to an even bigger bunch of spaghetti-sucking pricks down in New York. So as not to step on any Sicilian toes, we're expected to bend over and let Jimmy Frat, some low-level capo, fuck us over, steal away a cash cow like Niagara Falls—" He stopped himself, realizing he'd begun to lose the polished Plummerly diction and was slipping backward toward his old street-wise patois.

"Miles, Miles, Miles." Gianni shook his head. "After you call me this morning, I make a few calls myself, okay? Word I got is nobody's tryin' to cut us out of NFO. At worst, we got a mid-level guy, a capo like you say, maybe lookin' to muscle us a little."

"A little?" Prevost leaned as far across the table as he could. "Gianni, they took one of my best boosters, broke him up like a bag of potato chips and shot him up with acid. They stuck the Maple Leaf up his ass, for pity's sake, used our national flag like it was toilet tissue. They're pissing in our faces, Gianni, yours and mine."

"I don't feel a thing. You?" Gallio spread the palms up. "They wanna rub it in, make a point, so what? You the one started it, sending that Eddie, that *stronzo* motorcycle fuck, down there to do a bomb at the guy's a house. Alls this Fratelli did was let you know shit like that ain't gonna fly, the way I see it."

"Gianni—"

"Ah-ah." Now the hand went up like a traffic cop's. "Okay, they went too far. Some payback is in order maybe. But you don't whack a made guy over a dead motorcycle bum. It ain't whatchacall proportional."

"What then?"

Gallio shrugged elaborately. "Pick somebody else to make your point on. Di'nt you say this Eddie a yours was s'posed to be recruiting one a Jimmy Frat's people for you? And you figure it was this other *stronzo*, this—"

"Bona something."

"This a Bona, 'stead a comin' over to you, he ratted out your boy Eddie. So, I was you, Miles, I'd find this a Bona and do unto him, so to speak."

"Yes." Prevost was nodding, starting to accept it, to see the possibilities. "Yes. I suppose that would be, as you say, proportional."

CHAPTER 27

Last of the Independents

Melody freaked when she saw the new look, just like Bona figured she would.

"What is this, something fresh for all your girlfriends? Or, no, maybe it's the cops're after you. Or your new Mafia friends, is that it, Dennis? You don't wanna be recognized by somebody you screwed over so you go and do this MTV shit?"

Hey, he had told her, it was just time for a freakin change, is all. Don't make a federal case out of it.

"Oh, right. You needed a change, so you just go out and get your hair done, some gold jewelry, a stop at the Outlet. But if I wanna get *my* hair done, buy *me* some new clothes, it's 'Whaddya think, Mel, I'm made outa money?' All I ever get to do is your goddamn laundry and pick up after you and feed you, and I don't get a fucking dime for myself."

He almost told her she always wanted him to go legit so bad, why didn't she get a job herself, quit complaining about how much she already does. Here they're living in a twelve-hundred-square-foot crackerbox ranch looks like the Unibomber just came through and she makes out like she's been cooking and cleaning for the freakin Brady Bunch all day.

Instead he said to her, "You wouldn't need any new clothes you lost a few pounds off your ass."

The ass reference was a proven method for getting her off his ass and over to her mother's with the kids for at least two days, which was just how Bona wanted it. A man couldn't think with kids screaming and a wife yammering in his hear. And Bona had things to think about. Like getting Decker's forty thousand out of his Marine Midland account and then boogying out of town.

But there was one other thing that needed attention first. A loose end, you could say.

Bona'd seen an old movie on the cable the other night. That old actor, Walter somebody, usually made sappy comedies, but *Charlie Varrick* had to be about the coolest flick he ever made, in Bona's opinion. He plays this ex-con crop duster out in New Mexico who sticks up a small-town bank with his partners, only to find out later the bank was a mob laundry. Varrick, who calls himself the Last of the Independents on his business card, he sees what the mob's hit man does to his partner and he figures its time to get the hell outa town, but he's got an angle, a way to get away with the money and get the wiseguys off his case at the same time. Very, very slick indeed.

Bona liked to see himself that way, too: The Last of the Independents. Fuck Jimmy Frat and his three hundred bucks per. What Bona needed was a fresh start in a new place, with money in his pocket and nobody dogging his ass.

It wasn't the cops he was worried about, either. If there's one thing he'd learned from doing Gary Graycastle and seeing Eddie Touranjoe go down, it was that killing somebody was easy. Even a messy deal like that, that little apartment splattered with blood, Eddie and the whore whacked, Bona hadn't seen shit about it in the papers, and he'd checked the NFO rag, too. Not word one. Like a couple lowlifes like them don't count, just get cleaned up and tossed out somewheres and forgotten about. And the garage hit was still in a holding pattern, too, that dumb fuck Gary. Something showed up in the *Gazette* every morning, first a big story on Page One and then a much shorter piece on the inside of the local section, a bunch of crap about police officials concentrating their investigative efforts in the Rochester area for now, which Bona figured was like a code for saying they were looking hard at the dead guy's wife but so far she wouldn't crack.

So far.

Still, the cops weren't close to him yet. Bona had a sixth sense about shit like that, could always feel when a deal didn't look right or he was under the microscope. It's what'd kept him out of jail all these years. More than once he'd begged off a job only to find out later it was a sting operation, or something else would go wrong and everybody involved got busted later. He didn't have that feeling about the Marla thing, not yet anyway. He had a little time to play with there.

What was worrying Bona right this minute was Jimmy Frat. Unlike the cops, you can't outrun these Mafia motherfuckers no matter how hard you try, not if they think you screwed 'em over. After seeing what happened to Eddie Touranjoe, Bona's main concern was getting out of town without Jimmy finding out how tight him and Eddie really were, how it could maybe be interpreted that Bona's loose lips had kicked off the whole bombing thing with this Canadian mobster, Prevost. The only way to make sure that didn't happen, far as Bona could see, was to shut up the one guy who knew him and Eddie were buddies.

Beauty of the thing was, the same guy who knew about him and Eddie was also the only guy who could put Bona in Rochester the night of the Graycastle hit. Nobody else—short of the Marla bitch herself and she was a known fucking liar anyway—could connect Bona to the killing. And the *other* beauty of the thing was, this little war between Jimmy and the Canadians made a great smokescreen.

🍁   🍁   🍁

Early Wednesday evening Decker was in his apartment, cleaning the lens on his Nikon with a special cloth and half watching the local news, some female anchor pretty as a bowl of waxed fruit, on his brand new twenty-seven inch Zenith stereo television. The salesman had tried to get him to go "big screen", this thirty-two inch behemoth, but Decker had thought a twenty-seven-incher was plenty big enough for his little living room and seeing it sitting on an oak "entertainment center" ten feet away convinced him he was right.

The television and cable hook-up were only the tip of the iceberg. In the past three days he'd bought himself a new Bose home stereo system and a VCR, both of which shared the entertainment center with the TV; a matching chair and sofa in a kind of soft denim fabric, with an end table and coffee table of painted pine; a queen-sized bed that took over two-thirds of the bedroom; a wool Persian-design area rug for the living room, machine-made but still thick and rich looking; and he'd had several of his better shots of the falls and the city enlarged and matted and framed, and he'd hung them on the walls. He also had new towels in the bathroom and a handful of CDs to play on the new stereo system, all titles he'd already listened to at Suzzy's except for a reissue of an Allman Brother's greatest hits album.

And, his final purchase, the installation of a dead-bolt lock on his apartment door, now that he actually had some stuff worth stealing.

In all, he'd spent a little under forty-five hundred dollars and he didn't feel as guilty about it as he thought he would. He wasn't a monk anymore, after all; he needed a home guests could feel comfortable in. Especially Suzzy.

He checked his watch again, as if that was going to make the next twenty-four hours fly by. He had the whole night ahead of him and all day on Thursday to fill, the first vacation time he'd taken in years. You'd think a guy would know what to do with himself, especially with all the new toys to play with. But Decker felt—adrift. All the new gear, the new furnishings, were of little interest unless he got to share them with her. And whether he ever got to do that was riding on tomorrow night, Thursday, their date over across the river in Niagara Falls, Ontario.

The anticipation and anxiety were pushing at him like schoolyard bullies, refusing to let him go.

He'd already made some plans for tomorrow, weather permitting; he'd have breakfast at the diner and then spend most of the day shooting along and in the river gorge, only he'd go north a few miles this time, up around the whirlpool and the rapids and Devil's Hole. Entering the fourth week in October, the maples and ash and oak and the other deciduous trees were just past their peak colors, but that was worth capturing, too, the beginning of the end of the season, when the branches begin to thin out of their leaves and the light, if he can capture it just right, has that brittle quality to it that signals the imminence of winter.

Speaking of which, it was already feeling a bit sharp out there. Suzzy had been right about Wednesday's weather, unseasonably cold and blustery, with rain or even snow showers called for by mid-evening. Decker had turned off the stereo and one of his new Dave Alvin CDs to watch for a weather report on the television, hoping tomorrow's forecast wouldn't be a repeat. He put the Nikon on the coffee table and gave his full attention to the smooth-talking woman on the screen.

"*On that apparent robbery-murder of a Rochester man whose body was found in a Niagara Falls parking garage on Monday, Todd, it's being reported by our sister station in Rochester, WOKL, that police there now suspect the deceased's wife, Marla Ellen Graycastle, may have hired someone to murder him.*"

As the news anchor read her teleprompter, a photo of Marla Ellen Graycastle appeared over her left shoulder. Decker looked at the photo with little interest beyond curiosity. Then found himself leaning forward, looking harder. Something familiar about that...

"*WOKL reports that an unnamed source close to the investigation has revealed that Mrs. Graycastle is suspected of coming to Niagara Falls sometime in recent weeks to hire a hit man to kill her husband, Gary, allegedly so that she could collect on his life insurance. Official police spokespersons both in Rochester and in Niagara Falls are refusing to comment at this time...*"

Now the pretty news anchor disappeared from the screen entirely, replaced by footage of a woman, identified as Marla Ellen Graycastle, being helped into the back seat of a sheriff's cruiser. The cameraman shooting the video must've been half sprawled across the trunk of the cruiser to get this angle, looking through the back window at the woman as she turned half way to the side and then ducked her head down, trying to hide her face. It was at precisely that moment that Decker, who didn't realize he had crept to the edge of his new sofa and was in danger of sliding off, made the connection.

The woman he'd seen with the punk Bona at the Metropolis, and out in the minivan at the Rainbow Garage. Looked like her, anyway. It *was* her. He was almost positive.

Almost.

He found the phone and dialed a number from memory. Suzzy had seen her, too; maybe she'd remember. The phone rang and rang and rang...

Hours after her phone stopped ringing, Suzzy Koykendall was finally on her way home. The late hour was her own fault. After a rather stormy meeting with Randall at the Custom Service's Buffalo offices on West Huron, she'd felt the need for a long, hard workout in the third-floor employees gym. By the time she'd finished her cathartic workout—including a full routine of punches and kicks on the heavy bag—and taken a shower, she was ravenous and decided to grab a drink and a bite at a cozy tavern around the corner from the federal building.

Now, past nine o'clock, as she drove up 190 over the North Grand Island Bridge and neared the exit onto the Robert Moses Parkway, she could think back over her meeting with Randall with some perspective.

"You smell like a plate of fries," is what he'd said to her by way of a greeting, and it had gone downhill from there.

In her mind, she divided the meeting into thirds; a third of the time she spent fending off Randall's veiled sexual references, a third of the time she spent thumbing through the mug books while Randall yapped away about the need for diligence in the surveillance operation up at the Rainbow Bridge, and a third of the time she spent arguing for an expanded undercover operation against the Pellipollis brothers and their associates.

"Suzanne, please." Randall at one point fixed her with his cool gray eyes. "Can we have just one debriefing where you don't importune me to expand the operation?"

Importune. The pedantic son of a bitch. Suzzy, still busy thumbing through the mug books, didn't answer. Randall interpreted this as strong-headedness tinged with insubordination, which he wasn't about to stand for. Particularly since they weren't sleeping together anymore.

"Look, Suzanne, you can purse your pretty lips and pout all you want, but this operation is not—I repeat not—aimed at the Pellipollis brothers or their associates. Not directly anyway. Our primary objective is to identify compromised customs inspectors at the Rainbow Bridge station. That's the angle we're working from. If we make a bust and we can use the dirty inspectors to make a link back to the Greeks or anyone else we've surveilled at the restaurant, then we will pursue it. But—"

"Hey!" Suzzy lifted her head from the mug book. "I found the guy I was telling you about, the one came into the Metropolis yesterday. Look here."

It was a two-shot of James Fratelli, taken by Buffalo police some years earlier on an arrest for extortion that was later kicked out of court. Jimmy looked a bit younger and a bit thinner in the jowls, but the cocky smirk was exactly the same.

"I *knew* I'd seen him somewhere. Jimmy Frat, a capo in the Maggano Family, suspected of labor racketeering, extortion and graft related to the building trades, cargo theft, loan sharking, and no doubt a few murders."

She looked expectantly at Randall, who shook his head, then self-consciously patted his comb-over to see it was still glued in place.

"Congratulations," he said dryly. "But what do you really have? Even mafioso are allowed to go out for breakfast once in a while."

"What, are you saying this was just a coincidence? Him coming into the Metropolis with a bodyguard and a known Niagara Falls career criminal, that Bonawitz I told you about?"

J. Ellison Randall, Special Agent-in-Charge of the Buffalo Office of Investigations of the U.S. Customs Service, refused to be impressed. "Did Fratelli go in back to the office with either of the Pellipollis brothers?"

"Well, no."

"Did he at any time make an effort to contact one of the brothers, or perhaps pass along any information?"

"Not that I saw, but there could be some kind of signal—"

"In other words, Agent Koykendall, you saw him do nothing except eat breakfast, is that not correct?"

God. There were days, lots of them, when she'd like to give him a good swift kick in his management level balls. She exhaled slowly, like a steam engine. "Yes, that is correct, SAC Randall."

"Besides, you said it yourself. Jimmy Frat makes his money off extortion and racketeering in the building trades and the occasional truck heist."

"He has to move the stolen cargo, doesn't he?" Suzzy tried. "So why not into Canada for re-packaging—"

Randall cut her off. "Even if that's true, he wouldn't be using the Rainbow Bridge. *Think*, girl. The Niagara Falls bridges are closed to heavy truck traffic.

The big rigs have to go north to Lewiston-Queenston or use the Peace Bridge here in Buffalo. You really think Fratelli's going to try to move a trailer load of stolen frozen foods in the trunks of passenger cars? It's ludicrous."

Of course it was. Suzzy should've remembered about the weight limit on the Rainbow Bridge. But she was too angry to give Randall the satisfaction, so she turned away from him like a petulant child and stared at the maps of the Buffalo shoreline on the far wall.

Randall went around the conference table and stood in front of her, looking directly down at her. "Let me make myself perfectly clear on this, so we can avoid future miscommunications. You know what your role is in this operation. Observe and take names when possible, keep track of the Customs personnel who frequent the restaurant as well as any known felons who interact either with our personnel or the Pellipollis brothers. Do not—I repeat, do not—take one step beyond that assignment. Do not attempt to develop any independent sources. Do not make any overtures to anyone you've observed and do not do anything that might expose who you are and risk the integrity of this operation. In short, do not go cowgirl on me and charge in with guns blazing. Are we absolutely clear on this, Agent Koykendall?"

Suzzy slammed shut the mug book. "That's a big ten-four. *Sir.*"

CHAPTER 28

Luna Island

Dale Maratucci had on a red and blue Buffalo Bills parka and a Sabres knit cap and still he was bitching about the cold.

"Man, I'm tellin' you, even my dick is freezing."

"Yeah, well, you shoulda worn gloves, you're gonna be playing with yourself."

"I'm not playing with myself, asshole, I'm adjusting. Some of us got enough down there it gets out of alignment sometimes, we gotta push it back up into a proper upright position."

"What is it you got down there, a dick or one a them airplane trays?"

"Never mind what I got, fuckin' homo. You and that sweet faggot dye job."

Bona just kept on walking, head down against the biting wind, thinking, You're making this easy, punkass.

They were on Third, leaving Packy's and heading down the block and around the corner to where Dale parked his old lady's yellow Neon. The night was as pissy as the predictors said it would be, a Canadian cold air mass sweeping through, bringing a severe temperature dip and the kind of snow flurries that come at you hard and horizontal, stinging the face like a carpet burn. If anything Bona was dressed worse than Dale, an old navy pea jacket and his thin leather driving gloves and no hat, but he was handling the weather better.

The secret was to put yourself in a better place, don't think about the cold and the wet, think about something warm and pleasant. Bona was thinking about a desert someplace in the southwest and a condo development with a big Olympic pool. He could see himself living there, making a new start. A stripper for a live-in girlfriend, maybe two even, a blonde and a redhead, could do each other when he was too busy to do the both of them. Or a blonde and a Chinese broad would be good, one with long silky black hair and a skinny little-girl body, but not too skinny. Get one with implants so long as they were decent, didn't bulge out like frog's eyes and feel like a couple shrink-wrapped whiffle balls.

They were coming to the alley. Bona looked up into the driving flurries just in time to see two big hairy bastards coming toward them down the street. There was nobody else out on such a shitty night, a fact Bona was counting on. The pair came down the sidewalk and Bona could see they were wearing biker jackets, smelly black leathers, and he could see they were as interested in checking him and Dale out as he was in looking at them. The biggest one, with a red beard sprouting like a furry rash over the lower half of his face, was vaguely familiar, but Bona couldn't come up with a name.

It was too late to do anything but keep walking, the two bikers eyeballing him and Dale as they drew even, then went past. Thank Jesus, they didn't recognize him with the new blond do. Bona congratulated himself, his instincts paying dividends again.

He stole a look at the backs of their leather jackets—Yep, Satan's Sons—as he hooked Dale's arm and pulled him into the alley.

"What the fuck? You really are some kinda homo—"

"Hey, didn't you see those two guys?"

"What two guys?"

"The bikers. They just walked by, giving us the evil freakin eye."

Dale hadn't seen shit, his head pulled down into his parka's collar like a turtle in its shell, staring down at the pavement while he put one foot in front of the other.

"A couple bikers, man, big fuckin' whoop."

"Canadian bikers. From Eddie Touranjoe's outfit." He grabbed Dale's arm again and hurried him down the alley and out into the parking lot to the Neon. Inside, he got the engine going and revved it a few times to warm it up. From his coat he pulled a fifth of blackberry brandy and held it out.

"What's this shit?" Dale grumbled, hunkered in the passenger's seat, but he took the bottle.

"A little warm-up, man. Thought we might need it for this gig." Bona watched Dale take a long pull on the bottle, only halfway thinking about the trip over to Goat Island and the story he'd fed the punkass. The rest of him was still back there with the two bikers. What the fuck were those two up to on a night like this, on the U.S. side of the falls, unless it was looking for his ass, looking for payback on Eddie.

But the assholes didn't recognize him, and now he knew enough to stay out of their way, avoid his usual hangouts. That was worth something, just knowing. Plus there was a way he could use this, now that he thought about it.

He said to Dale, "You got your cell phone with you?"

"Yeah, I always got my cell."

"I want you to call Jimmy—"

"Call Jimmy? What the fuck for? He ain't even home tonight, I don't think." Dale took another swallow. "Him and the wife had some function, is what Angie told me."

"Well, call his machine and leave him a message." Bona squared around behind the steering wheel, making sure he had Dale's attention. "Those bikers, man, they're sent over here by that Prevost guy up in Toronto. They're looking for *us*, man, to get back for the hit Jimmy ordered on Eddie."

"Us? I didn't have nothing to do with that."

"You rode with me over in NFO when we checked out the address. You took credit along with me for fingering Eddie. Anyway, these guys don't care who they grab, they just wanna grab somebody off Jimmy's crew and take him out."

"Shit. You think?"

"Lookit, call the house down in Amherst, let Jimmy know what we saw, these two bikers working for Prevost, looking for trouble. Give him a heads-up on these guys so he can warn the rest of his people to keep their eyes open."

"Yeah," Dale said, tucking the bottle between his legs and fishing out his phone. "He'll wanna warn his peeps."

Bona sat back in the warming car seat and listened as the punkass called and left the message on Jimmy's machine, making it sound as if it was him, Dale, who'd spotted the two bikers and thought to report in. Perfect.

"So, dude," Dale said as he tucked the phone back inside his Bills parka, "maybe we should cancel this deal tonight, huh? I mean, considering."

"We can't just cancel. The guy's probably already over on the island waiting for us. We don't show, there goes five grand, good-bye."

"I was just sayin', what with these Canucks on the prowl and the shitty weather—"

"Hey, aren't you the guy was telling me about all them highly effective habits of successful people, that part about discipline?"

"Yeah, Habit 3: Put first things first." Dale squinched his eyes as he pulled together a paraphrase. "Covey says management is discipline, meaning you gotta decide what comes first and learn to establish goals and set priorities."

"Exactly. And we got a goal here gets priority. Five thousand bucks, easy as stealing candy off a baby. You don't really wanna walk away from that?"

"I was just sayin' it's pretty damn cold—"

"Cause you can wait in the car, man, while I go out and tap the dude. Course, I won't split the money with you, maybe just you give a little something for your time—"

"No way, man, I'm in. Just fucking drive."

❦   ❦   ❦

Garth and Evan blew into Packy's like a pair of vikings sweeping into an English seaside village. A deserted village. There were three people in the place counting the bartender and he was the only one sober enough to listen, let alone answer any questions.

Garth knocked a chair over for the hell of it on his way to the bar. He planted both elbows and leaned forward and smiled with a complete lack of sincerity.

"Lookin' for a guy called Bona," he said, loud enough for the two drunks at the end of the bar to hear as well. "Skinny little shit with dark curly hair, wimpy beard. A smart-ass, eh."

It was how he remembered Bona from the one time he'd seen him, hanging with Eddie Touranjoe over in NFO. He'd already tried it out in two other bars with no luck so far and the lack of success was only making Garth angrier. Even the five grand Miles Prevost was paying them didn't help. It wasn't Eddie so much—the guy was a brother and all that, but he was also a dumb fuck who was bound to get himself killed or locked away again. What really hurt Garth and Evan was Tildy getting herself killed. She was a good girl, that Tildy, who did what the customers wanted and didn't argue about her cut and didn't open her mouth much at all, except when the job required it. And at nineteen, she still would've had two or three good years left sucking off tourists at the body rub shop.

The apartment—there was another source of irritation. For a little chick, Tildy had bled like a punch in the nose; whatever kind of wadcutters they'd shot her with had gone right through and out her back, leaving Garth and Evan a major spackle job on that one wall. The fucking carpet was a total loss, between Tildy and Eddie both bleeding all over it, and on top of it all they'd had to get rid of her body, which meant using up a favor with a pig farmer out near Hagersville.

If there was any silver lining in this, far as Garth was concerned, it was the bonus he was promised for snatching this Bona and bringing him across the river. Prevost had given Garth a name and a number to call, somebody from Canadian Customs he'd bought off, so getting Bona over to NFO in the trunk of Evan's Caddy shouldn't be a problem. And once he had him across, Bona's ass was all his; Prevost promised him and Evan they could kill the punk any way they wanted so long as it was nasty and they captured it on video. How 'bout being torn to pieces by a two-hundred pound fighting dog, Garth had told him. That nasty enough?

Evan couldn't give a shit about the dogs other than making a few bucks on side bets here and there, but Garth was a fanatic. He loved the action, loved the rush of seeing one of his animals take and destroy somebody else's pride and joy, clamp down on some scabby-ass pit bull's neck and shake the mother-fucker till he was limper than a rag doll.

The undisputed king of Garth's stable was Terminator, a crossbreed bred from a bull mastiff, for superior size, and a pit bull, for its tenacity and its leg and jaw strength. And it wasn't purely breeding; he trained the hell outa that animal, running it on a treadmill to build muscle and endurance, a live cat dangling from the arm supports to keep the dog interested. Afterward, Terminator does a good workout, he gets the cat for fun. Garth had paid three thousand for the dog and he was worth every penny, already earning back twice that much in fights in The Pit, an empty gas station on NFO's north side, the former grease pit used as a ring. But it was getting harder and harder to line up any fights for Terminator, such was his reputation. The dog was in danger of losing his edge, he didn't get some action soon.

That's where Bona came in. Garth couldn't hardly wait to find out what would happen when he tossed Bona's sorry, stomped ass down in the pit with a hungry, mad-as-hell Terminator. And to capture it on video yet; what's that gotta be worth, you run off a few thousand cheap dupes and sell 'em through the Internet to all the true dog-fighting fans out there?

But first they had to find the little prick and this bartender with the slow mouth and the sleepy eyes wasn't helping.

"Bona, you said?" He blinked slow, too, like a lizard. "I'm not sure I can remember anybody by that name."

Whether he was looking to protect the guy or just wanted a few bucks for the information, Garth didn't know and didn't care. He snatched the bartender's shirt and pulled him halfway across the bar and shoved his face into a bowl of stale popcorn.

"You think I'm fucking around, eh? That I won't bust every fucking bottle in this place, eh, and your head as well?" Garth continued to grind the bartender's face into the bowl while Evan stared at the two drunks, who didn't deign to stare back.

The bartender tried to shout something, but it got lost amongst the butter-soggy kernels. Garth jerked the guy's head back up.

"He was here, you just missed him." Spitting bits of popcorn with every syllable. "You prob'ly walked right past him outside."

Garth frowned and ran a hand over his wild red beard. "Nah, the asshole in the fucking Sabres cap? He was too tall, eh."

"The other one—"

"He was a yellow-haired faggot," Garth roared, and hit him squarely in the mouth, sending him back against the beer cooler and down.

Through his bleeding lips, sitting on his ass and leaning against the stainless steel cooler, the bartender said, "He changed it, got a buzz and a dye job, is what I'm telling you."

"Oh. Yeah? So that was him, eh?" Garth took a ten dollar bill out and laid it on the bar and said, "Buy the house a drink, eh, on me."

The bartender waited until they'd left before getting to his feet. He glanced at the ten on the bar and shook his head in disgust. It was Canadian.

🍁   🍁   🍁

Dale made Bona explain it again on the ride over to Goat Island, Bona driving slow in the swirling snow flurries and talking slow. Taking his time to reassure Dale and, at the same time, let him get a few more good swallows of the brandy.

"Like I said, the guy wants his wife killed, okay? Ten grand for the hit, including five in advance tonight, which is why the guy's meeting us out at Terrapin Point, to like nail down the particulars and exchange the cash."

"Uh-huh." Dale took another pull. "Only we ain't really gonna do the hit."

"No way. What we're gonna do is, we're gonna take the five grand off the guy and knock him around a little—just to scare him, y'know. And then we book." He guided the canary yellow compact over the bridge and followed the familiar signs to the right and under the bridge to the loop road that ran around the perimeter of the island. "It's a piece a cake, man. The guy can't even report us to the cops. How's he gonna explain walking around a state park on a night like this with five thousand cash in his pocket?"

"Long as the dude can't come back on us."

"That's what I'm saying. Guy's got no recourse."

"I just don't know why we gotta meet way the fuck out here, hangin' over the fucking falls in all this freezing shit."

"A public place that's also got some privacy, is what the man said."

Goat Island was part of the state park that surrounded the falls on the U.S. side. At the west end the island formed the dividing line between the American Falls, including the Bridal Veil, and the Horseshoe Falls on the Canadian side of the Niagara River. Bona's destination, Terrapin Point, at the southwest tip of Goat Island, was an overlook right on the brink of the Horseshoe Falls' northern terminus.

The visitor's parking lot was nearly empty, not a surprise on a cold, stormy late-October night. Bona parked the Tweety Bird and led the grumbling Dale

Maratucci across the park road and down the wooded path past the now-closed Top of the Falls restaurant and gift shop. They passed one couple coming up the path, an older man and woman with chattering teeth who nonetheless smiled cheerily and said it was worth the effort. Bona nodded and Dale ignored them and they continued on, the roar of the falls a constant now, the white spray forming a wall ahead of them, obscuring all but the brightest lights on the Canadian side. Bona could make out across the river the Skylon Tower, the Casino Niagara, big signs for Planet Hollywood and a couple of major hotels along River Road.

They took the broad macadam path downhill toward the roar. The air was like breathing in the frost on a beer mug. At the base of the hill, Terrapin point leaned out over the plunging, mad water like an epaulet hanging from a general's shoulder. Dale, despite the cold and his nature, was drawn right to the edge, beside one of the twenty-five-cent viewers, leaning fast against the three-foot high extruded metal railing, awed at the power and majesty of all that water rushing straight down one hundred-seventy feet, right there at his feet.

Bona, watching Dale lean out, in perfect position, could only curse his luck.

A family of tourists, Pakies by the look of them, were manning the rails to either side of the punkass, oohing and ahhing in English and jabbering in whatever language it is Pakies talk to each other in and snapping pictures like Kodak was giving out free film. Freezing their brown little asses off obviously, but just as obviously showing no signs of heading back up to the minibus.

Bona, like a true Niagara Falls native, thought, Jesus Christmas, people, it's just a bunch of freakin water.

Dale came off the rail after a minute and sidled in next to Bona, asking, So where the fuck was the guy with the money. Figuring if any of these Pakies had that kind of cash they'd use it for a downpayment on a seedy motel.

"Oh, man," Bona said, resisting the impulse to slap his frozen forehead for effect. "You know what it is? This is Terrapin Point, right?"

Dale said, "The fuck you think it was?"

"I remember now, the guy mentioned Terrapin Point, right? But then he changed his mind and said Luna Island. On account it would be quieter and all."

Bona raised up his brows and stared earnestly at Dale, his eyeballs getting pelted by little bits of frozen mist and flurries. The punkass cursed a couple times and glared back at Bona. Then he took out the bottle of brandy from his Bills parka and took another long swallow and said, "Now how the fuck do we get to Luna Island?"

Bona clapped him on the back and urged him back up the macadam path toward the restaurant and gift shop complex. It wasn't far, Luna Island, maybe a quarter mile along the pathway, through the woods, down past the elevators for the Cave of the Winds tour and the snack shop, all closed at that hour. Bona led the way, keeping up the chatter, herding Dale along like a 4-H kid urging his favorite cow onto the trailer.

Luna Island was maybe fifty yards wide and a hundred and fifty long. Connected to Goat Island by a foot bridge that spanned the churning river rapids, Luna divided the American Falls and the slim, graceful Bridal Veil, and provided an intimate and dizzying vantage point from which to observe both.

On that night, however, no one had chosen to take advantage of Luna Island's charms; no one except Bona and Dale.

"Fuck, man, he's not down here," Dale bitched, after they came down the stone steps and crossed the foot bridge. "What a fucking waste of time, Bona. I oughta kick your ass, gettin' me out in this shit."

"Hey, we've still got time. Guy said between nine and nine-thirty, okay? We can give him a few minutes, check out the view."

Despite his mood, Dale was drawn to the railing again, first on the Bridal Veil end, then around to the edge of the American Falls. The big iron observation platform was visible through the clouds a few hundred yards straight ahead of them. Immediately below them, mostly obscured by the mist and the foam of rushing water, was the talus pile, boulders that had piled up at the foot of the falls as the dolostone caprock had been undercut over the years.

Dale was leaning over, staring down, the nearly empty brandy bottle in his hand, shouting something that couldn't be heard above the thunder of the Niagara.

Bona looked through the snow and mist back toward the bridge and the stairs, seeing no one, hearing no one. He was three steps behind Dale but he closed the distance quickly, pulling from the pocket of the pea jacket the S&W

.38, snuggling it in his gloved hand and bringing it up above his head. He swung his arm in a downward arc just as Dale began to turn toward him, the butt of the gun not connecting as solidly with the back of his skull as Bona had planned but sort of bouncing off Dale's Sabres cap like a stone skipped over water.

Bona, panicked, stepped back and fumbled with the gun, trying to bring it up and work his gloved finger inside the trigger guard and get off a shot, but he stopped with the S&W pointed at Dale's chest, didn't fire.

He watched, fascinated, as Dale's shiny brown eyes rolled back in their sockets and he took two faltering steps in a semi-circle, like an old man with a walker, and then collapsed, one arm hooking the railing and preventing him from slumping all the way down to the wet macadam.

And there he hung, staring but not seeing, Bona looking from the punkass to the butt of the .38 and thinking, Jesus, just like in the freakin movies. One little tap is all it takes. Not realizing, as he put away the gun and grabbed Dale by the shoulders and manhandled his body up and over the railing, sent it tumbling into the spray and the darkness, that he'd hit him in precisely the spot where only four days earlier he'd suffered a concussion when he struck his head on the Brunswick in Angie's basement, causing a subdural hematoma.

Bona took one quick look down at the talus pile, but couldn't make out any sign of the body in all that froth and foam. He noticed the brandy bottle on the ground and kicked it over the edge. Then he stepped back and pulled his collar higher and headed back up the path, where he would continue over to the main island and then down to the pedestrian bridge and across to the city again. A long cold walk ahead of him but, hey. You do what you gotta do.

CHAPTER 29

❀

Love on the Rocks

On Thursday morning a middle-aged couple from Bremen, Germany, Helmut and Marie-Gert Freitag, were the first to spot the body wedged between two huge dolostone boulders. While on the Cave of the Winds tour with a busload of other tourists, they had donned yellow rain slickers and descended down an elevator and then along a sloping tunnel to a network of platforms and board-walks near the base of the Bridal Veil.

It was Marie-Gert who, having wandered away from the group to the far-thest platform, was able to make out a slash of red and blue up there in the rocks below the American Falls, but she assumed at first it was simply a marker of some kind or perhaps someone had lost a coat in the swirling winds up above. Nonetheless, she shouted and waved until she caught Helmut's atten-tion through the constant thunder and spray and he joined her, changing the wide lens on his Sigma for a 90-mm telephoto to get a better look. Only then did it become clear to the Freitags, and soon to the entire tour group, that it was a human body they were seeing trapped amidst all that furious foam.

The word went up the line to the tour operator, then the park police, then the river rescue people. By ten-thirty a boat had been dispatched and by a quarter after eleven, using long grappling lines and precise maneuvering in the treacherous currents that swirl continuously at the base of the falls, a rescue team was able to dislodge the body and return with it to the docks along the

U.S. side of the gorge, where a wallet jammed into the back pocket of a pair of thoroughly waterlogged Slates slacks identified the deceased as Dale Maratucci, 24, of Cheektowaga.

Dale's mother got official word of his death at 12:34 that afternoon and almost immediately called Angelina Fratelli to share her grief. Jimmy Frat, pacing in his study at the time and half listening to some Neil Diamond being piped in from the media room, heard the wail go up somewhere at the back of the house and he knew what it was about without anyone having to tell him.

Dale never showed up at home last night. This Jimmy already knew because Dale's mother had called the house first thing in the morning, wondering if her boy had spent the night. She was concerned about her son, sure, but Jimmy had the feeling it was her car that was uppermost. By then, Jimmy had played back the message on his machine, at first angry that his thoughtless son-in-law-to-be could be stupid enough to leave such a detailed message on a recording, where any technically proficient Fed with a wire-tap authorization could maybe retrieve it. Now, with Dale dead, his irritation with him was gone, replaced by a fury of such depth and dimension that, like a volcano, it had to be let off in short bursts lest it blow up all at once and destroy everything in its vicinity, including the mountain itself.

The initial burst he let off in the privacy of the study, picking up a snow scene paperweight from the desk and hurling it, smashing it against the hunt green flocked wallpaper and, in the bargain, dislodging a print of red-jacketed limeys on horseback chasing a fox over a fence. He hated the fucking picture anyway; it was just part of the crap the decorator had hauled in there, along with the leather-bound Great Books series and the reproduction antique globe. Jimmy looked at the print lying in broken glass on the forest mist cut-pile carpet and remembered the arguments he'd had with the wife and that fag decorator she'd hired—trying to keep his faithful old Eames chair out of the study so it didn't "mar the 18th Century gentleman's salon look"; Jimmy saying over his dead body—and he wheezed out a chuckle.

In truth, he wasn't that crazy about his future son-in-law either. The kid was strictly flash, all sizzle and no steak. The original idea, sending him up to Niagara Falls to keep him out of the way, maybe teach him some basics about the family business, seemed ridiculous now that Jimmy thought about it.

What he should've done, if Angie insisted on marrying the dummy, was put him in a union job, give him a little desk and a clipboard, send him out to audit compliance at job sites around town. See if the kid had any stick-to-itiveness, any long-term potential, which Jimmy seriously doubted, but still. That would've been the thing to do, for Angelina's sake.

Thinking about his daughter and her broken heart and the wedding that wouldn't happen now led him to remember the deposit he'd already laid out for the reception up at the Falls, three grand that was supposed to be non-refundable. Happily Jimmy Frat didn't believe in non-refundable deposits where his cash was concerned, and the manager of the party house wouldn't believe in them either once Jimmy sent Coco Pulli up there to get it back.

The thought of Coco getting his dough back made Jimmy feel better, too, and he chuckled again. After all, he wasn't so much losing a son-in-law as losing another freeloading mouth to feed.

But his mood swung just as quickly in the other direction, thinking about Miles Prevost, that Canuck prick who so far was just a faceless name up there in Toronto. That bastard had blown up his daughter's car and now he'd sent a couple more of his goons to toss her fiance' over Niagara Falls like a bag of garbage and, even if Dale was a pain in the ass and a potential burden to Jimmy, that prick Prevost didn't know that. Alls he'd been after was a way to intimidate Jimmy, scare him off, win by default some war Jimmy didn't even know what it was they were fighting about.

But that didn't matter anymore, either. Whatever this thing was about, Jimmy Frat intended to come out on top.

He checked with the wife first, made sure she had Angelina and the arrangements and everything in hand, then he got on the horn. Coco was no problem, picked up the phone on the first ring like he always did and said he'd be over to the house in ten minutes. That was good. Jimmy had places to go and he didn't like driving himself. What he especially didn't like doing himself was going out to the garage and starting the Town Car for the first time, not on a normal day and certainly not with all this Canuck shit flying. That's what he had Coco for.

The second call didn't go so well. Jimmy'd been trying to reach that Bona at home since first thing that morning, after he listened to Dale's message from the night before. This was well before he found out Dale was out of the picture. Now, listening to the phone ring and ring in an empty house, a little bit of anxiety seeped in to season his anger.

Jesus Christ, maybe the Canucks had got themselves a two-for-one, grabbing Bona and Dale both off the streets up there, the Bona kid's body still pinned down in the rocks below the falls or maybe drifting downriver, on its way out into Lake Ontario, food for the salmon and the walleye.

Or maybe the little shit just took off. Found out the Canucks were on the prowl and decided to see the U.S.A. in his Chevrolet.

Jimmy slammed the phone down and began to pace the room, then dropped into the Eames chair and slumped and pushed out his lower lip. It wasn't fair, this Prevost fuck coming out of the blue and messing up his life, screwing with his livelihood. Alls Jimmy was trying to do was do some business, get a casino bill passed, see the local economy get revved up a little, start a building boom could put a lotta people to work, most especially some of his non-union tradesmen. Just do his job; be a good capo, keep his people busy, be a good earner for himself and the organization. How the fuck did life suddenly get so fucking complicated?

He leaned back against the headrest and closed his eyes and, for a moment, let himself get lost in the music pouring from the Mission in-wall speakers. Neil Diamond was never a favorite of Jimmy's until sometime in the early eighties. After Elvis died in '77 Jimmy stayed away from Vegas for a few years, like outa respect, but then the wife started complaining how sick she was of Atlantic City, it was too cold, it was too run down, the acts weren't as good, so he agrees to take her back to Vegas one January and there's absolutely nothing happening show-wise. You had your Sigfried and Roy, your Steve and Edie, and that was about it, Tom Jones being on the road and Wayne laid up with the flu or some fucking thing. Except for Neil Diamond, who was doing major business at the Grand. So Jimmy takes the wife and, whadd'ya know, turns out it was a fabulous show and Jimmy'd been a Neil fan ever since.

"She got the way to move me, Cherry—"

He was rolling his head side to side against the leather head-rest, softly singing along, when his phone warbled. "Shit."

Shit, for sure.

The unmistakeable voice at the other end of the line belonged to the don. Not the asthmatic wheeze of Marlon Brando doing Don Corleone, a mouth full of cotton balls, but the local don's staccato bleat, incomplete sentences delivered in bursts like slugs from a Mac10.

Tragedy about the boy, Jimmy. Condolences to Angelina, the missus. Our friends downstate concerned, your welfare. All a misunderstanding, see? Gotta talk, Jimmy, you and Mick, plus two, the fly spot. Ciao.

The fly spot meant a certain dark, cool lounge out near Buffalo International, owned by a friend of the Family, so to speak. Plus two was a standard code used by the don and all his key people when talking over the phone. All you had to know was the starting point, which was one o'clock p.m. Somebody says to meet at plus two, he's saying three o'clock in the afternoon. He says meet at, say, minus four, he means nine a.m.

Simple. Some would even say a little paranoid. But not Jimmy.

Jimmy'd seen and heard about too many wiseguys taken down by the Feds, using that RICO law and all sorts of James Bond spy crap, to feel completely safe anywhere. These FBI guys and DEA types and Treasury had surveillance toys NASA'd be envious of. The fucking Feebies even had their own crew, the Special Projects Unit, worked out of a place called the Q building down there in Quantico, Virginia, where they built special equipment just to catch guys like him, transmitters hidden inside fake olives, pencil-sized video cameras you could hide in a hatband or up some call girl's whazoo, you wanted to. Jimmy himself had a second cousin in Jersey got nailed taking down a warehouse full of electronics at three in the morning, no moon. A surveillance unit in the back of a van parked three blocks away. *Three fucking blocks.* They got him and the whole crew on video using a special nitrogen-filled lens and a 25-mm intensifier tube can see in the dark up to half a mile.

So nobody had to tell Jimmy Frat about taking precautions.

He walked into the lounge behind Coco, as was his custom, and moved to the side of the door and waited there near the coat rack while his eyes adjusted, also his custom. The place was nearly deserted at that hour; only the bartender, who nodded but otherwise kept his mouth shut, and two guys in a side booth. He recognized both immediately. The thin studious one in the mousy brown suit was Mick Amalfi, the don's consigliere, the bruiser in the plaid jacket was Mick's brother and guardian angel, Bobby.

After the usual formalities, Jimmy told Coco to go watch the door and Mick sent Bobby to the bar for a round of drinks.

The first thing Jimmy said as he sat down was, "This place been swept lately?"

"Twice a day, every day. And I got a man patrolling the block with a scanner as we speak." Mick was good, that much Jimmy had to give him, even if he did look like he belonged at a small college some place, teaching math or whatever.

He said, "It's your dime."

Mick nodded, the bones in his thin face seeming to become more pronounced. "When your daughter's car was bombed, you made out it was no big thing, some personal vendetta you could take care of yourself, no big deal."

"That's all I thought it was at the time. I didn't know, maybe I aced out some Canadian in the building trades, cost him some money. Whatever. Alls I did, Mick, was move on the asshole who came onto my property and did Angie's car. That should've been the end of it, far as I was concerned. Until this, today."

"From what we're hearing second-hand from our friends in Toronto, you did more than move on the asshole. You made it very, very personal with this Prevost. You challenged the guy, Jimmy."

"What'dya expect me to do, send him a fucking forget-me-not bouquet?"

The bartender brought the drinks on a little round tray, a Johnny Walker sour for Jimmy and straight Stoli's for Mick. Bobby stayed at the bar, sipping a glass of syrupy Sprite.

Mick and Jimmy continued the silence for a long time, using the drinks as a buffer. Finally Mick said, "It has to stop here, Jimmy."

"Says who?"

"Don't be fucking obtuse, Fratelli, you know fucking well who. And it goes much farther than that even, all the way downstate, okay?" The flash of anger passed and Mick became the don's consigliere again; cool, measured. "Any whiff of this gets out to the media, Jimmy, how d'ya think that'll effect casino legislation in Albany, a gang war along the Niagara Frontier? Have you thought about that, the big picture?"

Jimmy worked over the cocktail napkin, twisting it, shredding it, letting his anger leak out through his fingertips. "What is it you want me to do?"

"Set up a meet with this Prevost."

"Awww, shit, Mick—"

"This is what we and our friends want, Jimmy. Also the Calabrians. Meet with the man, settle your differences. A negotiation. Let tempers cool, everybody get back to doing business. We know, through our friends, that Prevost will be amenable to this, a face-to-face."

"Sure, he's amenable. He got last ups, put my future son-in-law into the fucking Niagara River."

"The word we have is that they're denying it, claiming they didn't hit anyone on our side."

"Course they're denying it."

"Jimmy."

Jimmy looked at Mick, really looked, and the message was clear. No more words. You get your marching orders from the don, you start putting one foot in front of the other. Or you become a liability.

Jimmy Frat let his breath out slowly. "All right. I'll arrange a meet."

Mick leaned across and tapped him on the wrist lightly. "Just between you and me, Jimmy? This Prevost moves a lot of cars and other merchandise for our Toronto friends. He makes a lot of money for them, and even more for himself. But that arrangement is currently under reevaluation and, in the next few months, is apt to undergo fundamental restructuring."

For the first time that day, Jimmy grinned. "Are you saying the Calabrians are planning a hostile take-over?"

"I am indeed."

"Well, zippity fucking doo-dah."

CHAPTER 30

The Big Picture

They started the evening early with a stroll through the bustling Casino Niagara, pausing long enough on the smoke-free second level to lose a few quarters in one of the casino's twenty-seven hundred slot machines, then down to the third level for drinks at the in-house Hard Rock Cafe. From there they wandered over to Clifton Hill, NFO's main tourist drag, passing on Ripley's Believe It Or Not Museum and Castle Dracula and Guiness World of Records but stopping in for a quick tour of the celebrity effigies at Tussaud's Waxworks.

By then it was almost seven-thirty. Decker retrieved his Prism from the lot and they drove a few blocks west to Murray and took a glass elevator up to the revolving restaurant at the top of the Skylon Tower. The previous day's cold front had moved off, taking with it the gray cloud cover and sleet, leaving in its wake a soft fall evening, clear as lead crystal, their table near one of the windows affording them a three-hundred-sixty degree view of both cities of Niagara Falls as well as the falls themselves and the Niagara River Gorge, the basin below the falls bathed in the white glow of dozens of strategically-placed spotlights.

Suzzy sipped her wine and smiled tentatively and looked gorgeous in a moss green silk pantsuit that perfectly complimented her hazel eyes and honey hair, a braid of gold around her long neck the only embellishment. Decker, his blond-gray hair freshly trimmed, wore tan slacks and a light blue Oxford shirt under a navy blazer. He was as nervous as a schoolboy on a prom date. They chatted politely through an appetizer of snails baked in Thousand Island garlic butter, the French Onion Soup au Gratin and simple garden salads, and the house specialty, Le Carre' d'Agneau Dijonnais; New Zealand rack of lamb baked with Dijon mustard and herb breading. By the time coffee and desert was served—Chocolate Wafer Torte Terrine for her and French Brulee for him—the careful small-talk, along with most of the two hundred dollars Decker had changed over to Canadian currency, was used up.

Decker put down his fork. "Suzzy, I—you must be wondering what the point of all this is, my insisting we come over here tonight."

"Well, I assumed the idea was to wine and dine me and get enough alcohol into my system to get me into bed later." She was smiling wryly as she said it, but Decker's kind blue eyes seemed to be focused on something else. She added lightly, "It's working, if that helps."

He tried a smile of his own. "I can't think of anything I want more than to make love to you. But not just for one night. What I'm trying to say, the reason for all this—" He paused to drink from his water goblet. He could feel the sweat rising under his arms and on his forehead, recognized the shallow breaths of an incipient anxiety attack. Recognized all the old psychological warning signs that had bedeviled him for so many years whenever he tried to put into words his secret dread; his Niagara Falls nightmare. "Wow." He laughed pathetically. "If I haven't already convinced you what a basket case I am, this performance—"

Suzzy reached across the fine white linen table cloth and covered his trembling hand with hers. "You don't have to 'perform' for me, Decker. That's what I've been trying to tell you. Whatever this is about, you don't have to prove anything to me."

The warmth and strength in her grip brought him to ground. "No, not to you, Suzzy. But to myself."

He turned to the window, urging her to do the same. Below, just coming up on their right in the restaurant's slow revolution, was the brightly lit dome of the IMAX Theatre a block away. The marquee read, 'Niagara: Miracles, Myths & Magic.'

"We have to see the show," he said. "That's the only way I can do this."

Suzzy, not understanding any of it, nodded her head and said, "Of course."

❧   ❧   ❧

Bona had tailed the two love birds as far as the Rainbow Bridge before deciding to turn back. Now he guided the Grand Am along the back streets of the city, up Niagara Street to Tenth, on past the Memorial Med Center and right on Pine, left again a few blocks down onto Seventeenth Street, cruising by the shuttered City Market. A couple more turns onto side streets and he was there, his temporary home away from home.

He parked in the alley next to an empty storefront that had once been a butcher shop. Walked behind the building through permanent shadows, his loafers crunching on gravel and chips of broken green glass, to a break in the old board fence that buffered the commercial building from the residences on the next street. He slipped between the missing boards into a small gap in the cedar shrubs that had been planted by the homeowner as an additional barrier. The back yard of the property was an overgrown jungle of neglected evergreens, fifteen-foot-tall rhododenrons competing for space with bushy yews and waist-high boxwood, all of it once shaped into fancy topiary by the original owners, who had long since sold the place and moved to a mobile home park in Seminole, Florida. The current owner was one of those get-rich-quick-with-no-money-down assholes who buy a set of tapes off the TV and think they're gonna make millions renting out chintzy cracker boxes to working stiffs with shit for brains.

The asshole had overextended himself, naturally, and had been trying for a year and a half to sell this and four other rental houses scattered around the Falls, with no takers. It was a familiar story to Bona, one that almost inevitably led to his getting a phone message at Packy's, the desperate landlord wanting to discuss Bona's "special services", see if an accident could be arranged that would get him out from under and immediately improve his cash flow. Bona telling him, You know what they say; accidents happen.

You could say this particular house was an accident waiting to happen. Waiting because Bona had another use for it, temporarily. Until he could get his finances in order and relocate to another part of the continent. Which, he figured, better happen pretty freakin soon.

He let himself in the side door with a key, playing it cool, acting as if he belonged, even though the house next door, another dump with a For Sale sign in the yard, was as empty as this one. He moved through the now-familiar small rooms, not bothering to turn a light on until he was in the first-floor rear bedroom. He hit the switch and a round ceiling fixture came on, illuminating the room's faded blue wall paint and stained oatmeal carpet and the thin curtains—sea horses on a rust-red background—hat draped the only window. On the floor were Bona's things; a sleeping roll and a radio, a cooler containing a few pieces of fruit and bread and peanut butter and juice and vitamin bottles, a cardboard box with some of the items he needed to carry out his plan. He took from his coat pocket a six-foot extension cord and clipped off the female end with a pair of wire cutters and tossed the cord and the cutters into the box next to the roll of duct tape and the can of black spray paint, some clothesline, his old man's old Polaroid camera and a set of channel-lock pliers. His hand automatically went under his jacket to check for the Smith & Wesson; it was tucked reassuringly in his belt.

Bona sat down Indian-style on the bedroll and again inventoried the box, nodding his head approvingly.

Outside of a little luck, good timing, he couldn't think of anything else he'd need.

꩜   ꩜   ꩜

They spent a few minutes in the IMAX Daredevil's Museum first, killing time before the show started.

Killing time. A poor choice of words, Suzzy thought, as she let Decker lead her around all the old photos and the genuine stunt vehicles on display; none of Norton's replicas here, he assured her. No, just a collection of giant metal spheres and rubber balls and wooden barrels that, for all their diversity of shape and color and materials, looked the same to Suzzy; like coffins for lunatics.

They filed into the theatre amidst a few handfuls of tourists and took seats halfway up the steeply sloped auditorium. The layout reminded Suzzy of the lecture halls at the University of Iowa, except for the huge, concave screen that made up the facing wall. Six stories high, according to the disembodied female voice that seeped from the theatre's myriad hidden speakers. The voice droned on, explaining what the audience was about to see, in six languages. Decker held Suzzy's hand throughout, his grip tightening as the house lights finally lowered and the film began.

Suzzy sat in the dark, her eyes trying to take in the entirety of the huge screen while her ears were assaulted with the sound of the falls, comparing it in her memory to the great rolling thunder that preceded the late-summer storms of her childhood out on the Great Plains. Only there was no break in this sound, she realized; it was a constant, day and night, year after year, one millennium to the next, since the last great Ice Age, and probably until the next. She watched as the story of the river and the falls unfolded, from geological times to the early Native Americans, who named the place "Great Thunderer of Waters" and coined the legend of a young Indian woman who sacrificed herself to the river and became The Maid of the Mist; to the French explorers accompanying LaSalle, who were credited as the first Europeans to see the falls; to the taming of the Niagara Frontier after the War of 1812 and the coming of the Erie Canal and settlements and, inevitably, beginning in 1826 with a brash young man named Sam Patch and his trained bear, the daredevils and stunters eager to challenge the mighty Niagara.

There on the screen was Blondin, the dashing young French aerialist who in 1859 was the first to cross over the gorge on a high wire. Annie Taylor, the barreling grandmother who made history in 1901. Jean Lussier, the Quebecois in his rubber ball. Englishman Charles Stephens and Greek George Stathakis, local stunters like Red Hill, Jr. and Dave Munday, and a dozen others, some of whom survived their folly and some of whom did not. And none of whom found more than passing glory for their risk, a few lines in a Chamber of Commerce brochure, a dusty display in a tourist museum.

Fascinated as she was by the images of the river up on the giant screen, Suzzy was ever more aware of the sense of foreboding weighting down her heart; that whatever Decker expected her to take from the film, it hadn't worked. It all belonged to another time, it seemed to her, men in funny bathing suits in old black-and-white photos, these Niagara stunters and their

contraptions. Desperate people living in the Great Depression years and earlier, before pensions and unions and Social Security.

But, even if there was anything tangible to be gained by such a stunt,
Decker wasn't particularly interested in money or fame. She felt she knew him
well enough to know that. So what could he possibly be thinking?

He let go of her hand suddenly and took a death grip on the sides of his
seat. She glanced at his profile, noticed the sheen on his forehead. He looked at
her for just a second and smiled, but it was the smile of a man about to go
under the knife.

"Watch," he said.

She followed his gaze back to the screen just as the narrator began the final
chapter of the saga, the true story of the only person ever to survive a trip over
Niagara Falls without protection.

*It is the summer of 1960 when a father sets out on the river with his two sons
in a borrowed boat, a fourteen footer with a small Evinrude outboard engine. At
the deceptively calm Grass Island Pool, the river begins to run faster as it
approaches the rapids above the falls; buoys warn of dangerous waters ahead, but
for whatever reason, the father, Stanley Beidecker, chooses to go on. In the bow of
the boat is his oldest son, David, 12, and in the stern is his seven-year-old son,
Walter, both of the boys wearing life vests...*

Walter Beidecker, age seven? Suzzy's synapses began to spark, but the connection wasn't quite there yet. Brother David, age twelve?

*As they near the rapids, Stanley Beidecker begins to turn the boat back, but he
turns too sharply and a wave of water washes over the engine, stalling it. He desperately struggles to restart the engine as the little boat drifts faster and faster into
the rapids, but it won't start and, in moments, it makes no difference. They are
already passing the Three Sisters Islands and moving into the heart of the rapids,
the tow of the river too strong and violent for any boat engine to resist, let alone a
small outboard; this is the part of the river experienced Niagara River men call
the point of no return.*

*Furiously attempting to steer the wildly careening boat with oars, Stanley
manages to get close enough to the extreme end of Goat Island for his oldest son,
David, to leap into the water and pull himself painfully from rock to rock while
scores of sightseers at Terrapin Point urge the boy on. At the last moment, only*

yards before he would've gone over the brink, young David is able to grab a camera strap dangled by one of the onlookers and is pulled up to safety.

Suzzy, without taking her eyes from the screen, put her hand over Decker's, thinking, Walter Decker, whose father died in a boating accident when he was only seven...

Under her grip, she could feel Decker's shakes grow with the relentless roar coming out of the sound system while, up on the screen...

As Stanley Beidecker moves toward his youngest son, undoubtedly hoping to try and throw him as close to the Goat Island shoreline as possible, the boat hits a rock and pitches upward and then over, spilling both father and son into the remorseless current. His hand upraised and beseeching, Stanley disappears over the edge just before, moments later, little Walter Beidecker is shot over the lip like a champagne cork and drops from sight, some 170 feet into the mist below.

The screen showed a reenactment; a close-up of a young boy in turbulent water, screaming, then a long shot of an aluminum skiff floating upside down over the falls. Decker turned his hand over and curled his fingers around Suzzy's, his palm slick with sweat.

Now the film changed point of view, the scene was at the base of the falls, the picture grainier and the color washed out and the camera was bouncing; original footage, Suzzy realized. Someone on the tour boat with an old movie camera.

A few precious minutes later, a hundred feet out from the base of the Horseshoe Falls, passengers aboard the Canadian tour vessel Maid-of-the-Mist spot the boy, terrified and battered but otherwise unharmed, floating out of the foam in his orange life vest. Walter Beidecker remains, to this day, the only person to go over the falls accidentally—and live to tell the tale!

The shot zoomed in on the bobbing figure in the water, and Suzzy could see the boy's shocked face looking up and, even with the span of forty years separating them, she recognized the boy's face as Decker's face.

As the music soared and the credits rolled and the house lights came up, they both let out a long exhalation and continued to hold hands and continued to stare at the screen until Decker broke the silence.

"'Battered but otherwise unharmed,'" he quoted, shaking his head wryly. "They should see the psychiatric bills."

❀

CHAPTER 31

Fate, Revelations and John Calvin

"They say it was my light weight that saved me. I was barely fifty pounds. The life jacket kept me high in the water and when I got to the edge the powerful flow just spit me out, far enough so that when I dropped I was clear of the undertow and the tons of falling water, some of that natural thrust Norton was telling you about. Of course that was 1960, which happens to be the last year before the agreement was reached to divert so much more of the flow to the power authorities, so today there's a lot less water going over the Horseshoe and there wouldn't be so much thrust and—who knows if that'd been the case back then? I might not've lived to tell the tale, as they say."

Decker had started talking in the parking lot at the IMAX and barely let up on the drive home. Suzzy encouraged him with a nod or a brief comment here and there, suspecting it'd had been a long time, if ever, since he'd opened up about his brush with death at Niagara Falls.

"My father was—I loved my father, but he was a reckless sort of guy. At the time I just thought of him as cool and funny and sort of swashbuckling, if you know what I mean. I remember him as always driving too fast, or standing too close to the rim, like when we visited the Grand Canyon when I was five. Showing off. He was a sergeant in the Air Force, was in charge of ground crews, but he had the same cockiness you associate with the pilots." He shrugged. "Maybe that's where he got it. Trying to prove he was just as good as the officers he worked for, just as gutsy. Anyway, it finally cost him his life, his showing off in a borrowed boat, and it cost me and my mother and my brother plenty, too."

They were crossing the Rainbow Bridge and pulling up to the inspection booths on the U.S. side, half a dozen cars ahead of them in the line.

Suzzy said, "You resent him. For taking the boat too close to the rapids that day."

"It was a stupid thing to do, two kids in the boat. I guess what I've always resented the most is how dumb, how thoughtless it was."

"It was a momentary lapse in judgement. He wasn't familiar with the river—"

He turned to her. "He put his children at risk, Suzzy. That should've been the first thought in his head, the first thought in any father's head; keep the kids safe. But, no, his immaturity overruled everything."

They cleared customs and Decker picked up the Robert Moses northbound. He'd hoped to take Suzzy over to his apartment, show off some of the improvements he'd made, but she'd wanted to go to her place and he wasn't going to argue. She'd see his apartment another time, he hoped.

"Anyway, the nightmares started almost immediately. I'll see myself in the rapids, my mouth wide open but no sound coming out—nothing but the roar of the falls. I see my dad kinda floating at the edge of the falls, like a ghost, smiling and telling me I'm on my own, I need to be a man. And then I feel the world start to slide out from under me and I'm dropping, dropping—sometimes I wake up on the floor, I fall right out of the bed."

"And you still get these nightmares?"

He nodded emphatically. "Almost forty years now. Not every night, but— often enough. I had psychological counseling when I was a kid, but it didn't help. Then, just as I was turning into a teenager, my mom remarried and I rebelled against my new step-dad, so things at home were pretty ugly for about five years until I finished high school and took off with the Nomads. My bad-ass stage. I was about eight years with them, mostly getting high or drunk, but still I'd get the nightmare. Even at the monastery later, all those years, I'd wake up on the floor of my cell once or twice a week." He looked over and grinned ruefully. "So, you can see, Suzzy, I've tried Freud and I've tried God *and* the devil. No relief."

"So now you wanna try confronting the demon head on."

He didn't answer right away. "D'you believe in fate, Suzzy?"

She didn't answer right away either, knowing a trick question when she heard one. She watched the black trees fly by along the side of the highway. Finally: "I believe that some things happen beyond our control, and we have to accept that. If you wanna call that fate—"

"Let me tell you what I call fate." He began slowing down for the De Veaux Campus exit. "When I decided to leave the monastery, I needed a job. The only offer I got was from one of the abbey's biggest lay supporters, Gabriel Pinto, to come work at his bakery here in Niagara Falls. After I took the job and moved here, it took me a month to work up the courage to go and see the falls. While I'm standing there at the overlook in the park, trying to keep myself from barfing, I meet Norton Gage, looking to talk someone's ear off about the mighty Niagara. So I lent him my ear. When he hears my name—Walter Decker—he immediately makes the connection. 'Hey,' he says, 'there was a little kid named Walter *Bei*decker went over the falls back in '60, he'd be about your age now.' So, naturally, I had to confess I was that kid. We become friends. He eventually tells me about his secret ambition, to design and build a stunt vehicle like no other stunt vehicle and have someone pilot it over the falls." He turned up his hands.

Again Suzzy didn't speak right away. A man who'd been having nightmares for forty years wasn't going to be easily swayed. Maybe he shouldn't be. But she felt it was worth one more try. "I was raised a Presbyterian, Decker, had old John Calvin's tenets hammered into me, most prominently the one that says we live and die only by the grace of God, the path He sets for us. So I'm not gonna get into a debate about fate. But I will say this: You can choose to ride that contraption of Norton's over the Horseshoe, and you may live or you may die. But if you live, it's no guarantee your nightmares will end, Decker, because I don't think your nightmare's about Niagara Falls. It's about your father, how he failed you, and the only way you can get past that is by seeing it and facing it and dealing with it in the here and now."

They were on her street. Decker pulled the Prism into the driveway of her townhouse and switched off the engine. "I know, at its root, that it's about my father; my feelings of abandonment, resentment, all that. The shrinks pointed that out to me a long time ago. But in order to get past it, as you say, I have to explore my deeper feelings about him. And I can't do that now, Suzzy, because my memories of my father always trigger images of that last day, those final seconds on the river as we're both swept over the falls. And when I think of that, I have nightmares and anxiety attacks and I no longer want to dig into my psyche to deal with my father, because it's too traumatic."

He reached out in the dark, cramped interior of the car and took her hand. It was soft and warm, and her fingers curled reassuringly around his.

"What I'm hoping," he said quietly, holding her eyes, "is that by confronting my physical fear of the falls, by taking on the Horseshoe on my own terms, I'll be able to clear it away. And what I'll be left with is just my dad and myself. Then I can begin to work that relationship out."

"If you're still alive."

He shrugged. "I think I will be or I wouldn't consider going. Nort's really put a lotta thought into the design, and nobody knows the subject better than he does. Look, I'm not suicidal, Suzzy. Especially not now, now that I've got you in my life."

This last was said with a bit of hopeful expectancy. Suzzy stared into his stonewashed eyes and squeezed his hand harder.

"When will you do it?" she asked.

"Well, soon, within the next six days. The power authorities get to reduce the flow by half after October 31, for the winter season. We'll wanna do it while we've got the best thrust at the top. Otherwise we'll have to wait until spring, April 1st or later, when the flow is increased again for the main tourist season."

"You've really thought this thing out."

"Yeah, we have. I told you, Suzzy, I don't have a death wish."

The moment she saw his little-boy face up on the giant screen, struggling and terrified, she'd known that, whatever happened, she loved him and she would have to stick by him, even if it meant risking his loss. Knew, too, that it was her turn to reveal herself and, ironically, that she might lose him anyway.

She said, "You'd better come in." And, although it sounded like an odd way to phrase an invitation, Decker didn't question it. They got out of the little blue Prism and he followed her to the door, neither of them noticing the dinged, rusting nine-year-old Grand Am parked down the block in the deep shadows of an ancient silver maple.

✤   ✤   ✤

Decker asked to use the bathroom and when he came out, he saw the telephone sitting on the kitchen peninsula. It reminded him of the previous night, how he'd tried to call her several times without an answer, and why he'd tried to call her. He'd put it out of his mind before, not wanting her to think he was checking up on her, wondering where she was and what she was doing. But now, he brought up the call.

"I was out," Suzzy said. She was taking a couple bottles of Labatt's Blue Lights from the fridge, moving deliberately. "Down in Buffalo. It's a regular meeting I have every Wednesday night. That's what I want to—"

"Reason I was calling," he cut in. "You been following this thing on the news? The body they found shot in a car in the Rainbow Garage? Turns out it was some guy from Rochester, and now it looks like they suspect his wife hired a local gunman to kill him."

Suzzy, distracted by her own thoughts, said, "No. The man they found dead in the garage? I heard about that, that he was from Rochester. They think his wife had him killed?"

"That's what they reported on the news last night. Only speculation, I guess, but I saw a picture of the woman. That's why I called here, I wanted to see if you saw it and thought the same thing I did."

Suzzy frowned. "Thought what?" She used a dishtowel to grip the bottles and twist off the caps, sliding one across the counter to Decker.

"The woman, this Marla Ellen something." He picked up his beer and swallowed deeply. "I'm almost certain it's the woman I saw with that punk Bona in the Metropolis that day, remember?"

"You're kidding."

"No. And I wondered if you'd seen her on TV and made the same connection. Obviously not."

"I haven't seen the news, but it wouldn't matter. I have no recollection of the woman he was with. I'm surprised you do, Decker. They were sitting a long way away."

"Yeah, but I saw 'em when they paid the check," he said. "And again, later. I, uh, followed them over to the Rainbow Garage."

She gave him a look. "Thinking about some payback for his robbing your apartment?"

He tossed his head. "Something like that, I guess. At least let him know I suspected him. Anyway, I saw them in a minivan in the garage. They were— she was, uh, going down on him."

"Well," She put the bottle to her lips to mask an incipient grin. "I'm guessing that's not the first time that drippy old garage has seen some action."

"Suzzy, I'm serious. I think it was the same woman. And the news report said the police think she hired a local guy, from here in the Falls, to kill her husband."

Without thinking she went into law enforcement mode, her brow furrowed, and shook her head. "Bona a professional hit man? According to his sheet he's nothing more than a small-time career thief, a few arrests but no convictions since he was a juvie." She turned it over again in her mind, oblivious to the questioning look she was getting from Decker. "On the other hand, I *did* see him in the restaurant just a couple days ago with a known Mafia figure."

"Wait a minute," Decker said, putting down his beer. "Whaddya mean, 'his sheet'? How do you know so much about him all of a sudden?"

"I—it's what I was going to tell you, babe." She walked around the kitchen peninsula into the dining room, moving as if in a dream. As if she could change the moment if only she took enough time. But when she got to the hutch she realized she was out of time, and she went to one knee and moved aside her laptop and her holstered weapon and brought out her three-ring notebook and a leather case containing her official ID and shield. She brought them back to the kitchen side of the peninsula and set down the notebook and fanned it open, Decker following every move wordlessly.

When she found the surveillance shot with Bona and Eddie Touranjoe, she spun the notebook around. "There's your guy, right?" Without waiting for his answer, she turned the notebook back around and paraphrased the information printed below the photo. "Dennis Bonawitz, aka Bona, lives on 97th Street in the former Love Canal neighborhood, age twenty-eight, height blah-blah-blah—"

"Suzzy, what the hell—"

She sighed and flipped open the case, laying her ID and shield in front of him. "I'm a special agent with the U.S. Customs Service, Decker, working undercover at the Metropolis to try and identify a smuggling ring that we believe is being operated out of the restaurant. Primarily we've been trying to identify which of our own inspectors may've been compromised, but we try to follow up on any known or suspected lowlifes, which is how Bona got snapped. It's actually the other guy in the picture we were interested in."

Decker leaned back as far as the stool would allow. His nervous fingers had stripped most of the label from his Blue Light and now he pushed the bottle away. The stonewashed eyes drifted from her face to the ID and back to her face. She waited for him to speak, but he didn't, and she knew if somebody didn't say something she was going to start bawling.

"I'm sorry, babe, I wanted to say something sooner but I couldn't. I mean—" She felt moisture welling in her eyes and blinked and went on, her voice businesslike again. "It's the job. We're under orders not to reveal ourselves to civilians during a covert operation."

Special agent. Covert operations. Mafia figure. Surveillance photos. Decker felt a gang of jumbled emotions mugging him as this woman in front of him, the woman he was in love with, became someone else with each foreign phrase that came out of her mouth. Went from being Suzzy the waitress, a vulnerable but loving woman with a carafe of coffee in hand and a lopsided smile on her face, to Suzanne Koykendall, a special agent of the federal government. As if the woman of his dreams, the woman he'd gathered stones for, had transmogrified from Donna Reed to Wonder Woman. Everything he'd revealed of himself…

Almost involuntarily he slipped off the stool and mumbled, "I think I need to call it a night." And crossed to the foyer and let himself out.

Suzzy held herself rigid on the stool and told herself she was all right and didn't allow a single tear to fall until she heard the door click shut.

CHAPTER 32

Snatch

Suzzy had run extra hard that morning and was walking it off the last quarter mile, moving a little rubber-legged in the pre-dawn gloom of the streetlights, her thoughts on Decker a million miles away across the city, when Bona stepped out of a hedge and braced her with the .38.

She wouldn't have recognized him, and there wasn't time anyway. In that fraction of a second after he appeared before her, her brain registered bytes of relevant information—*blond, gun, slim, cocky*—and formed an immediate impression—*rapist.* Her muscle memory and Glynco training took over from there.

"No noise," is all he managed to say before she pivoted forty-five degrees on the ball of her right foot as her left foot shot out, catching him not in the gut as she'd intended but a bit higher, just below the heart. He fired once as he went down and Suzzy felt a flash of heat sear her upper arm followed by raw pain, like sucking in cold air over a tooth's exposed nerve. She fell onto her other shoulder, the right, and grimaced as she tested the left arm's mobility and began to roll away, but by then it was too late. He was on top of her, pinning her good arm with a knee and slapping away the injured arm with the gun, then jamming the gun hard under her chin, leaning over her close enough she could smell the stale spearmint on his breath. A drop of sweat fell from his nose onto her cheek.

"Just fucking move again, cunt," he hissed at her. "Gimme a fucking reason to blow your fucking head off your fucking shoulders."

She stared up at him, at first seeing only the rage in his dark eyes, the rage and the desperation about to explode. Then her view widened and she took in the short blond hair and the blond goatee and saw the black stubble of beard that had filled in the rest of his cheeks, giving his face a cartoonish aspect, as if a child had mixed up her crayons and colored him in badly. Only on the third take did Suzzy register the shape of the face and put it together with the unbleached stubble and his compact size.

"You!" she blurted.

"Yeah," Bona snarled down at her. "Fucking me."

       ❦   ❦   ❦

He'd come within a few inches of blowing her away and that wouldn't have been cool at all, not at all. He needed the bitch alive, at least for a little while longer. She'd been tame enough getting into the trunk, but getting her out was tricky. She tried kicking him again and he'd had to punch her in her wounded arm, not wanting to risk a fist to her face because he didn't want her looking too bad for the picture. That's all it took, though. She was bleeding like a stuck pig until he had her rip up the tee shirt she had on under her sweats—flashed him those nice titties—and wrap it tight around the crease on her upper arm.

"A freakin flesh wound, they call that in the movies. Bruce Willis wouldn't even bother wrapping it. You're lucky I didn't kill you, kickin' me with that kung fu shit. I'm gonna have a motherfucker bruise."

"Alla unnna mmaa—"

"Shut the fuck up." He gave the arm a twist and her knees buckled in agony. He had her on the landing now, duct tape run tight around her wrists and around her mouth, pushing her dark blonde hair up in the back. "And watch your step. We're goin' down."

He led her down the steps into the low basement, the only light provided by two high, narrow windows. Her nose twitching at the fug of mildew and decay and old plumbing, he deposited her onto a torn sofa cushion along the far wall. Running up the wall next to her was the house's heavy black iron waste pipe, running vertically from the concrete floor and disappearing into the framing overhead. He had his box of materials down there already, on the makeshift workbench built of two-by-fours. He took out the length of clothesline and the roll of gray duct tape. He taped her ankles together, then looped the nylon rope around her already-taped wrists and ran it four times around the waste pipe before tying it off. Lastly, he ran more tape around the wrists and around the pipe, covering both knots.

Bona was whistling softly as he worked, something only he would ever recognize as a U2 tune. He rummaged through the box again.

"Here, hold this up." He tossed that morning's edition of the *Niagara Falls Gazette* onto her lap. "Oh, you can't, can you, all trussed up like that. Well, lemme see." He pulled her around so that her back was against the wall next to the pipe, her legs pulled in. Ignoring her grunts of pain, he shifted her around until he could prop the newspaper in her lap just so.

He got the Polaroid and knelt in front of her and framed the shot so he had her face and shoulders and a good close-up on the paper's masthead, showing the date.

Suzzy's eyebrows knitted themselves into a chevron, more a look of confusion than fear, Bona decided. "It's for your boyfriend, bitch. He's gonna see this and he's gonna go to the bank and get out forty k to buy you back."

The expression in her eyes turned to incredulity and she shook her head and grunted. "Unngh-uhnng."

"Hey, don't tell me you don't know about your boyfriend's money, honey. Y'mean you're sucking his dick just for the fun of it? I'd let you do mine if I wasn't runnin' on a timetable here." He checked his watch. "Yeah, bitch, your holy man's gonna finance my move to greener pastures. Alls you gotta do is lay here on that sweet ass and wait for him to come rescue you. After I get my money, that is. Now, I got one last thing I need from you and I'm gonna hafta take the tape off your mouth, so don't give me no trouble, okay? You scream nobody's gonna hear you and it's only gonna piss me off and I'll have to hurt you, so do yourself a favor."

He went back to the box first and got out the portable cassette recorder, a last-minute addition. Kneeling again, he placed the recorder on the gritty floor and took out a pocket knife and cut away the duct tape, nicking the skin next to her mouth.

"Nother flesh wound," he said, grinning at her. He held up the cassette recorder. "Okay, lady, when I give you the word I want you to say something like, 'Monk, honey, give him the money so they'll let me go.' Can you do that?"

"Listen," Suzzy began, sucking in air, "you have no goddamn idea what you're getting yourself—"

He backhanded her across the face. "Shut the fuck up, bitch, and do what I'm telling you or I'll do you right now! Now talk into the fucking machine. 'Monk, honey, please give 'em the money so they'll let me go.' Do it!"

Suzzy's tongue flicked out and whisked away a drip of blood. "Monk, honey, give 'em the money so they'll let me go.'" Voice flat as her native Nebraska.

He clicked off the recorder. "Good. That's real good, lady, now turn toward the wall."

"What're you gonna do?"

"I'm gonna tape your pretty mouth shut again, okay? And I don't want you spittin' at me, so turn around and look at the fucking wall."

She turned, grimacing as her damaged arm rubbed against the waste pipe.

Bona wrapped the duct tape around her face twice and cut it with the knife. Then he reached into his jacket pocket and took out the Smith & Wesson and swiftly brought the butt down hard on the back of her skull.

She slumped into a heap immediately, no three-second delay like when he'd hammered Dale, and once again Bona thought, Jesus Christ, it really *is* like in the freakin movies. One little tap.

❀   ❀   ❀

Suzzy stayed as still as she could, crumpled up there on the couch cushion with her head and right shoulder hard against the damp concrete block wall, and stifled a groan. The back of her skull throbbed, as did her arm.

She chanced opening the left eye just enough to let light in; she could see Bona's back, his arms raised, hands fiddling with the bare bulb light fixture attached to one of the joists. Removing the unlit bulb. Plugging in a short white extension cord into an outlet on the side of the fixture—an extension cord with bare wires at one end?

She closed the eye as Bona turned and went back to his box on the workbench. He was out of her line of sight back there unless she moved her head, which she wasn't going to do. If he wanted her to be unconscious, she would be unconscious. It was far preferable to being dead.

He was softly whistling again. She heard him scuffle back to her side of the basement. When she eased open the eye she could him see through the filter of her lashes, twisting together the wires of the maimed extension cord and looping the cord up between the ceiling joist, around and around the cross-bracing, right above the furnace. From his jacket he removed something else—steel wool?—and stuffed that up into the cross-bracing as well.

He started to turn and she closed the eye again. Listened as he moved around behind her and back again. She heard the scrape and whine of metal on metal and risked another peek, seeing Bona use a large pair of pliers on a piece of pipe, a joint, running up from the top of the furnace. His hand suddenly plunged forward and there was a low hissing sound and she thought with a shudder, *Gas*.

He went back to his box. She allowed the eye to close and this time she heard a rustling followed by the unmistakable rattle of a can of spray paint being shaken. Listened to him move around the room and spray something with the paint, then cracked her left eye just enough—the light was dimmer now—she could see him as he went to the high window at the back of the basement and repeated what he'd just done to the only other window; blacked it over with the paint.

A moment later, he took his box of materials and, with one last glance her way, he clopped up the stairs. She heard him pause for several beats of her heart on the landing beside the side door, then he was out the door and the place was quiet. Quiet but for the low, sibilant menace of escaping gas.

❦   ❦   ❦

Decker was chagrined that morning. He'd spent a rough night rolling in his new bed, getting up, pacing the living room, falling back in bed again only to dream fitfully, not of Niagara for once but of love lost in a moment's confused indecision. He'd tried calling Suzzy first thing in the morning—explain how sorry he was for his mute reaction to her revelation; how it didn't matter to him if she was J. Edgar Hoover—but he had gotten no answer at her condo and now, at the Metropolis, nearly nine-thirty and she hadn't turned up for work, hadn't called in sick.

Leaving Decker feeling sick. And chagrined. She was at home, possibly, not answering her phone, too busy dealing with her own heartbreak; that, Decker figured, was the best-case scenario. Otherwise she was probably packing her things, figuring she'd blown her cover or whatever they call it in the Customs Service and all she could do was write off the operation and get out of town. Write him off, too, while she was at it.

God *damn* it anyway.

Well, he'd just have to go find her, he decided, sliding off the stool and leaving a couple of dollars for his coffee. It'd make him feel like a fool, but he'd do it once again, open up his jumbled mental attic to her and try to explain his life-long aversion to authority figures, particularly people with uniforms and badges, something one of his shrinks had claimed went all the way back to associations he forged during his trauma at the falls; to his own father and his Air Force uniform and to all the cops who'd taken him in hand after his miraculous recovery from the gorge...

Shit.

Even saying it in his head sounded lame. Suzzy was gonna think he was a total basket case, one neurosis after another, when the truth was the only thing driving him crazy any more was the thought of losing her.

He came out onto the sidewalk, zipped his jacket, and turned left up South Main, wishing for once that he'd driven the eight blocks from his apartment instead of walking. Not that it wasn't a good day for it, crisp and sunny and dry. The weather somehow gave him optimism. He threw his shoulders back a fraction and softly hummed a song from one of his new CDs.

He'd gotten only about a hundred feet when a young man, leaning against a Pontiac parked at the curb, casually came off the car and blocked his way.

Decker stopped short and looked at him without alarm or anger; young guy with a bad blond dye job, lots of black stubble in between, probably looking for a handout. Then he heard the voice.

"Hey, man, we meet again."

Decker's eyes widened a bit. "Dennis Bona-something, isn't it?"

"Bona's close enough." He didn't like that the guy'd been checking up on him, knew his real name. "We've got some business, you and me. You wanna step into my office?" He gestured to the beatup Grand Am.

"I don't think so." Decker started to move around him, but Bona stepped back.

"Think again, asswipe." With his left hand he held up the Polaroid photo of Suzzy in her duct tape, with the right he pushed back his jacket and pulled the .38 Smith & Wesson from his belt. "Get in the fucking car, man. Behind the wheel."

Decker did as instructed. His hands gripping the steering wheel at ten and two, he looked at Bona in the passenger seat. "You're out of your mind. If you've done anything to her—"

"Yeah, yeah, yeah, I know. You love her, want no harm to come to her—why d'ya think I snatched her in the first place?" As he spoke, Bona leaned across with his left hand and switched the ignition key to accessory. A cassette tape was sticking half out of the built-in dash deck. He turned a knob and pushed the tape all the way in. Immediately loud, distorted rock music blared from the speakers. Bona said, "Wait." A few seconds later, the music cut out as abruptly as it had begun and Suzzy's voice came on, flat and angry and alone.

"Monk, honey, give 'em the money so they'll let me go.'"

Bona turned off the tape. "Okay, here's the deal. You got forty grand sittin' in a savings account over at Marine Midland. I get the money, you get the girl."

Decker stared at him as he processed the information. "So it *was* you who broke into my apartment."

"I confess. I'm a bad element, you could say." He waggled the gun. "Hey, man, you don't know what to do with all that freakin money anyway, you got it sittin' in a bank for like two, three percent interest. You might's well give it to me."

"Yeah." Decker, still staring, almost added, So you can beat it the hell out of town before the cops nail you for a contract killing. But he decided it wouldn't be productive to let Bona know that he knew how desperate he must be. "There's not quite forty grand anymore," he said. "I bought some things—"

"Fuck!" Bona's face puckered into a pout. He felt proprietary about that money, like it was rightfully his, the whole forty grand; where'd this asswipe get off spending *his* cash like that. "How much you got left?"

"Mm, I guess about thirty-eight thousand and change."

"Yeah?" Thirty-eight thousand. Didn't have the same ring to it as forty grand, but fuck it, close enough. "Close enough. Take out the thirty-eight and leave the change, don't close out the account."

"What happens then?"

"Then I tell you where your lady is and you get to play Sir Lancelot, as in she digs your lance a lot." Bona's grin faded. "That was a joke, assface."

"Funny."

The gun came up, leveling off at Decker's ribs. "Start the car, dickwad."

CHAPTER 33

Jimmy and Miles and Kilometers

The face-to-face was set for an abandoned chemical plant out on Buffalo Avenue, three free-standing walls of softening brick with no windows and no roof and no local ownership anymore; nobody to give a shit if a couple gangsters needed to use the place to settle their differences.

It hadn't been easy getting even that far, agreeing to the location. First Jimmy Frat said it had to be on the U.S. side and Prevost said no, he was thinking Fort Erie. Then Jimmy comes back with Buffalo, along the waterfront, and Prevost says he'll give him the U.S., but if he must cross over, it has to be up in Niagara Falls. So finally, a little more give and take, some boilerplate threats, and they settle on the derelict chemical plant on Buffalo Ave, only two, three miles from the Rainbow Bridge.

Jimmy looked him up and down disdainfully and showed his teeth. "So you're the big Toronto hotshot, huh? Prevost—what is that anyway? Jew?"

"It's Canadian. Can we dispense with the petty posturing and get down to business?"

Miles Prevost was dressed typically and in silk: custom-tailored suit in indigo, custom-made shirt and a designer tie from a small, exclusive Yorkville haberdasher. Standing in front of his Lexus, one hand in his pocket, one leg slightly bent, he resembled an *Esquire* ad aimed at successful fiftyish professionals. Only Garth, standing a few paces to his left, his red beard matted, his gut protruding from his unzipped leather jacket, marred the picture. Or per-haps merely lent it an Annie Leibowitz quality, Prevost decided.

Jimmy Frat was in his usual duds, too; a three-piece Hickey-Freeman suit of navy merino wool with a chalkstripe, crisp white shirt, rep tie and black Bruno Magli shoes that shined like obsidian. Feet splayed a shoulder's width apart, thick legs set into the ground as implacably as tree trunks. Immediately behind Jimmy, with the Town Car's hood between them, was Coco Pulli, look-ing broad as a billboard and almost twice as animated in gray slacks and his favorite maroon leather car coat, the better to conceal his Glock 9-mm.

A gap of twenty feet separated the cars.

"Business," Jimmy said, tasting the word like it was hard candy. "Yeah, let's us talk about *business*. Starting with why you sent that lowlife prick, that fuck-ing wedge-faced ugly fuck, after me and my family. Tell me about that little piece of *business*, why don'tcha."

Prevost sighed and tilted his head a fraction to the right. "Is that what this is going to be? Recriminations followed by more recriminations? I'd say you exacted more than your share of revenge on Eddie Touranjoe, Fratelli, so why not move on and—"

"Oh, we handled that fuck, yeah." Jimmy took a step forward, prompting Garth to stiffen and slip a hand around to the back of his jacket, which caused Coco Pulli to make a countermove, sliding his hand inside the car coat. Both sides had agreed to come unarmed and accompanied by only one bodyguard, but neither man had ever intended to honor the agreement and would've been amazed if the other had. In addition to the firepower Coco was packing, Jimmy had his own nine auto in a shoulder rig. Prevost had a lightweight .32 in his jacket pocket and Garth had his Colt holstered at the small of his back along with a baby .25 in his right boot and a hog sticker in his left. Both men also had people posted outside the crumbling factory walls, just in case.

"What I haven't done," Jimmy went on, "is I haven't exacted any fucking revenge on your ass personally, Prevost. Fucking recriminations? You're lucky I didn't walk in here and shove a piece up your ass and blow your shit into next week. Fact I still might, you two-bit carny hustler, whaddya think about that?"

"Well," Prevost said equitably, "some might say that *would* make us even. True, I'd be dead—but you'd still be in Buffalo."

"Oh. Right." Jimmy nodded, his normal ruddy tan darkening toward violet. "Now it's with the Buffalo jokes. Hey, leastwise it's part of the United States of America, pal, not some fucking country kisses the Queen of England's wrinkled ass and calls its money the fucking loony, for fuck's sake. Thinks a fucking slice of ham is bacon. I mean, Canada, who gives a flying fuck? You could blow up the whole fucking place and all it means is we'd hafta start gettin' lumber from our own trees again."

Prevost refused to rise to the provocation. "Some of us like it."

"Yeah, well, some guys like to suck dick and go to the ballet, too." Jimmy was on a roll now, beginning to enjoy himself, glancing back at Coco for an audience and also just to make sure he was backing him up. "You can keep your fucking so-called music while you're at it. The fucking Guess Who and them country songbirds, fucking Anne Murray and that new one, Shinola Twain or Shania Twang, whatever the fuck her name is."

Prevost rolled his eyes heavenward. "Could we simply accept that you don't like me and I don't like you and get on with this? We're not free agents, either of us, Fratelli, or we wouldn't even be standing here talking. You'd be trying to kill me and I'd be trying to kill you—and, believe me, killing you would be the highlight of my year. But unfortunately, I have business partners who don't wish to see a border war break out, and you seem to have associates with similar concerns." Never raising his voice above a weary baritone, a paragon of self-control. "So, please, dispense with the hackneyed dago posturing and let's get on with things, shall we?"

Seeing the guy and listening to him talk in that television smoothee voice, Jimmy realized, made him wanna kill the fucker even more. Just pull out his piece and kneecap him, pow-pow, and then have Coke break his teeth off one by one with a pair of ViseGrips while he bleeds out. That's what he'd *like* to do with Prevost. But he had his marching orders and to go against the will of the don and that smartass Mick Amalfi, the don's consigliere, was suicide, both professionally and health-wise. There was a time when a two-bit hustler like this wouldn't raise his eyes, let alone his voice, in front of a made guy like Jimmy. But those days were pretty much gone, along with American-made TV sets and full-service gas stations; it was the fucking globalization of crime, is what it was. Everybody's a fucking entrepreneur.

If there was any satisfaction for Jimmy Frat, it was the knowledge that Prevost was on his way out anyway, soon as the Calabrians got around to foreclosing on his dumb ass and taking over his operations.

"All right. Let's talk business," Jimmy said, then he made them wait. Moving very deliberately, he took from inside his jacket a Macanudo Prince Phillip Robust, seven and a half inches of rich hand-rolled Dominican tobacco at a dollar per inch, and stripped off the cellophane. A guillotine-like cutter appeared in his right hand and he neatly clipped the end of the cigar, rolled it between his lips, and exchanged the cutter for a silver Dunhill cigar lighter.

"First thing," he said as he took a puff, "is you owe me compensation for my future son-in-law."

Prevost shook his head. "I truly wish it were otherwise, but we had nothing to do with his death."

Jimmy jumped up and down. "Fuck you. Fuck—you! I guess he just picked last night to go and.dive over Niagara Falls, huh? And I'm supposed to believe that shit even though he fucking *called* me and told me you had some of these biker fairies of yours—" He stabbed the Macanudo in Garth's direction, prompting a low growl. "—out looking to grab one of my guys. For all I know you owe me for two, 'cause I got a second guy missing."

"Would that be a punk named Bona, by any chance?"

Jimmy's face didn't change expression. "Yeah, that would be him."

"He was the one my people were looking for, to make an example of. He was an old friend of Eddie Touranjoe's, they worked some jobs together on both sides of the falls. He's also the one who fingered Eddie, am I right?"

"Old friends?"

"Garth here can tell you. Your Bona used to hang around Eddie's apartment once in a while, above Garth's body rub shop. That's why I sent him and an associate of his over here Wednesday night to try and track down Bona."

"It don't scan," Jimmy said, even though he knew that it did. "What's the kid got to do with any of this? He's nothin'. A local I hired to do errands, show my future son-in-law the ropes. My *dead* future son-in-law, who you fucks tossed over goddamn Niagara Falls."

"You don't give me much credit for imagination, Fratelli. Really, after what your people did to Eddie, do you think I'd only have your son-in-law tossed over the falls? We had something much more spectacular planned for the man we were after—Bona, the Judas."

"So, who the fuck did Dale then if it wasn't you guys?"

Prevost's slim shoulders rose and fell elegantly inside the indigo silk suit. "If I had to guess, I'd say your boy Bona did the deed. He was the one who told Eddie about your plans to make a move in NFO—"

"I told the Calabrians, I'm not interested in the Canadian side, I'm only trying to get a casino for us."

"That's not what Bona told Eddie. He made it sound like you were mounting a D-Day invasion. Maybe the other one—Dale?—knew that Bona and Eddie were friends and that Bona'd been telling tales, so to speak. If he threatened to tell *you* about it, well, I doubt Bona would've wanted that to happen, particularly if he was aware of what you'd already done to Eddie."

Jimmy still didn't wanna believe it, not coming from this faggoty fuck Prevost. It took Coco Pulli, hemming and hawing from behind the Lincoln, to seal the deal.

"Bona did know this Eddie better'n he lets on, boss. Leastwise, this Eddie knew Bona, that's how it looked. When we went to the door of his apartment? Bona used his real name, said like, 'It's me, Dennis Bonawitz.'"

"Dennis fucking Bonawitz? I thought his name was Bona." Jimmy was bewildered, unaware of the ash from the Macanudo dropping onto the trousers of his fine Hickey-Freeman suit. "He's a polak?"

Coco nodded, abashed. "That's what he called himself, boss. Dennis Bonawitz. And this Eddie came right to the door. And then—" He snuck a peek at Prevost. "—while we were hammerin' him, he starts beggin', sayin' like 'I thought we had a deal, you gotta do somethin' for me.' To Bona, he's sayin' this shit. So, y'know, I think they prob'ly knew each other pretty good, boss."

Jimmy glared as only he can, his eyeballs as fat as hardboiled eggs. "Why in the name of all the fucking saints in heaven didn't you tell me this before, you dumb fucking moron?"

"I dunno." Coco dropped his eyes. "It just din't come up, I guess."

Prevost tossed in the capper. "And now the boy seems to have disappeared on you."

"Bona." Jimmy began pacing between the cars. "Bona. That fucking little prick weasel." The more he turned it over, the more it made sense. The bastard got too big for his britches, bragged about his connection to Jimmy Frat, built it up into something it wasn't, bah-dah-bing, the Canucks get worried and send a message, Jimmy retaliates, Bona sees he's playing monkey in the middle and decides he better get lost. But first he's gotta get rid of Dale, who's been riding around with him for a month, seeing too much and hearing too much, so he tosses him over the falls and figures the blame'll go to the Canucks. And while the gang war breaks out full scale, he slips outa town. "Goddamnit, I'll have the little fucker's head on a fucking platter."

Prevost said, "Now that we've agreed on the target, we'd better move fast. If Bona hasn't already taken off, he soon will."

"Hold it," Jimmy said. "What's with 'we'? I don't need no help with this."

"Don't think of it as help, think of it as giving me my pound of flesh." Prevost stared down his long, patrician nose at the mafioso, his eyes hard as blue steel. "I won't be swayed from this, Fratelli. You will not fuck me out of what is rightfully mine. I want a piece of Mr. Bonawitz as payback for my man—a big piece, you understand? I want to hear him beg for my mercy and I want to be looking into his eyes when he realizes he's utterly beyond hope. And when he's finally dead, I will piss on his corpse."

"Jesus Christ," Jimmy said, impressed. "For a Canadian, that's pretty fucking cold."

"It's a pretty fucking cold country," Prevost said. "At any rate, you'll need us along. Bona's undergone a makeover and Garth here is the only one of us who knows what he currently looks like. So that settles that, correct?"

Jimmy, caught a little back on his heels, merely nodded. For a moment he was reminded of a favorite old movie, *The Bridge on the River Kwai*, with Miles Prevost cast in the Alec Guiness role of the batty English colonel. Only he looked more like that other actor, the one from *The Sound of Music*, what the fuck was his name?

"Good. The only other matter before we go is to decide how to dispatch Bona once we grab him," Prevost said briskly. "Now, there are a couple of options *we've* considered. Garth has a collection of fighting dogs over in NFO, one in particular, he tells me, a crossbreed—"

"Wait a minute, you're gonna take him across the river into Ontario? While he's still alive?"

"Of course." Prevost squeezed out a thin smile. "It wouldn't be nearly as interesting for the video cameras if he were not alive and—kicking, in a manner of speaking."

"And what about if the customs guy decides to spot check your car?"

"That's not a problem, I assure you."

"*Marrone.* It's one helluva fucking problem, pally, if you get caught."

"I have people at the Rainbow crossing," Prevost cut in impatiently. "There's no risk to me, either from Canadian or U.S. Customs."

"Ahh." Jimmy's furry black brows shot up. That could come in handy, having a couple border inspectors in your pocket. He wondered if the Calabrians knew who Prevost had on the take, hoped they'd be smart enough to beat it out of him during their hostile takeover. He considered his cigar for a moment.

"I still don't like it," he said. "Even if he's knocked out, he could come to in the trunk and raise a racket. Believe me, I seen it happen. Anybody besides your people hear it you got a major problem. Anyway, it ain't necessary. I got a gravel pit picked out with Bona's name on it – whatever his fucking name is."

"I have a compromise that may be better." Prevost carefully removed a folded map from his jacket and gestured for permission to spread it out on the Town Car's hood, which Jimmy granted with an imperious nod.

"There's an island, Navy Island, out on the river almost directly across from this location," Prevost said, pointing it out on the map. "It's in Canadian waters and it's a nature preserve, no development on it at all. I can have one of my people come up river with a skiff and meet us, we have the body dumped over there and in a few days or weeks, depending on the efficiency of the turkey vultures and the crows and the other scavengers, there won't be anything left of your cheap little flunky."

Jimmy looked out through the missing wall of the factory past the Conrail tracks to the Robert Moses Parkway and the river beyond that. "What, so we schlepp this dead fuck across four lanes of highway to get to your fucking 'skiff'? You think they post fucking signs out there, Slow Down: Stiff Crossing?"

Prevost just stared at the squat Buffalo capo for a moment, thinking not for the first time, Americans, how can they possibly be leading the world in *any-thing*? Then he went back to the map. "It's a small boat. He can bring it right up Gill Creek here, *under* the parkway, and pick up the carcass. After that it's a quick run back down the creek and across the river to Navy Island, no more than a kilometer and a half or so—"

"A kilometer and a half," Jimmy mimicked. "Which is like a mile, right? So why the fuck don'tcha just say so? Fucking kilometers."

But he did like the idea, dumping the body over on the Canadian side of the river where nobody'd bother looking for the little puke. All those fucking birds and animals and shit picking him apart, that had a certain appeal, too.

"Tell you what. You guys can have the body," Jimmy said. "But I still want the fucker's head."

CHAPTER 34

The Hissing of the Gas

At the moment Jimmy and Prevost were deciding his future, Bona was sitting in his car backed into a space at a Wilson Farms convenience store kitty-corner to the main Marine Midland office on Niagara Street. It was a wide street, four lanes divided by a median, and Bona had to strain his eyes to clearly see the people coming into and out of the bank entrance, but he wasn't worried about missing Decker. The guy was too hopped up about his girlfriend to do anything stupid, Bona was pretty sure of that.

After waylaying Decker outside the restaurant, Bona had him drive back to his apartment on Walnut to get his account book and all the ID he could muster. Then, figuring branch banks might not be as quick to handle a transaction that large, Bona decided to have him drive back downtown to the big Marine Midland building. Now he sat up straighter as he saw Decker, in that tan jacket and jeans, come out of the bank and make for the crosswalk, holding in his left hand one of those zippered nylon pouches with the bank's name and logo on it. His whole freakin future riding in that little zippered pouch.

Come to papa.

Bona ran his tongue over dry, chapped lips. He was so close now. The home stretch. Get the money from the monk and give him the address on the north side where he can find his bitch and, while Decker goes off to play hero, Bona hauls ass down to Buffalo International, but not to catch a plane. He'd never flown in his life and he didn't intend to start now. No, he'd go to long-term parking and exchange the Grand Am for something finer, something new into the lot, dust-free, something the owner wasn't likely to miss for days, and he'd head south and then west, taking his time, seeing the country.

He figured he'd have maybe a two-day head start before Jimmy worked anything out on Dale and at least a week before the cops could sort out the other thing; Decker and the waitress, what's left of them, in the wreckage of that house.

Bona allowed himself a grin for his cleverness as he watched Decker cross the street. The arson investigators call it a low-order explosion and nine times out of ten write it off as accidental; a natural gas leak in an old, poorly maintained house causes a build-up, something creates a spark and ka-BOOM. You get what's called a diffused blast, the force pushing outward, collapsing the roof and the upper floors down into the basement where they tend to burn hot and quick, like kindling at a weenie roast. Big motherfucking weenie roast.

He'd been making insurance companies pay off on deals just like this for going on ten years, although in this case the owner of the house, the no-money-down asshole, was no doubt gonna get stiffed, what with the bodies inside. No way the arson guys'd write this off as accidental. Too freakin bad for Mr. Easy Money.

Bona glanced at the clock in the dash. Three hours and forty minutes since he'd cracked the line in the basement, started the gas leaking out of the pipe, floating up, lighter than air, to fill the spaces between the floor joist. A good four hours of buildup before Decker could get over there—that should be enough. Bona could see the whole scenario playing out in his head. Decker rushes to the house and goes in the side door off the driveway, onto the landing, three steps up to the kitchen or nine steps down to the basement, but naturally he wants to go down into the basement because Bona told him that's where the girlfriend is. But it's dark down there, too fucking dark. So he sees the light switch on the wall and he flips it on and he'd get some freakin light, all right. Like a starburst. The light at the end of the tunnel. Just like that, he's history, and his lady, too, if breathing the gas hasn't already killed her. Either way, they'll never know what hit 'em.

They could say whatever they wanted about him, but nobody could tell Bona he didn't know his freakin business.

❦   ❦   ❦

In the stale decadent gloom of the basement, Suzzy Koykendall struggled. Struggled with her mind, to keep it focused and away from the pain at the back of her head and in her joints and wounded arm. Struggled with her breathing, shallow and low to the floor on her smelly sofa cushion, the better to avoid the sickly sweet gas that continued to hiss somewhere above and to her left. Struggled with her bonds, rubbing the nylon clothesline up and down in short strokes along the back of the black waste pipe, down at the cleanout fitting near the floor where she'd found a small jagged burr in the metal.

Up and down, up and down she sawed, but not too rapidly or she'd raise her heart rate and her breathing, be forced to take in more air. More gas.

Had to keep moving the rope over the metal burr, slowly. Had to remember to breath slowly, evenly, through her nose. Had to remember to think, make her mind work along with her arms.

The light bulb socket mounted on one of the joist overhead, the extension cord she'd seen him plug into it, the bare wires at the stripped end poked up into the joist with the bunch of steel wool, the gas building up…all it would take was a spark. The steel wool would heat up and flame, the flame would ignite the gas…The spark…the spark…

Her eyelids began to droop again, her hand motion slowed, slowed. Stopped.

Her head dipped in increments until it clunked gently against the cinderblock of the wall and she snapped back to alertness.

But not all the way back.

With each lapse her recovery was limited, like the recoil of a bungee cord snapping back half again and half again, losing a bit of her resiliency, her mental strength, with each nod.

Losing.

To the hissing of the gas.

❦   ❦   ❦

Bona grabbed the bag as soon as Decker slid into the passenger seat.

"You got it all?" he demanded, fumbling with the zipper. "How much?"

"Thirty-eight thousand, like you said."

Decker watched Bona work open the zipper and run a thumb over the edges of the bills, hundreds and fifties mostly, with some twenties mixed in, a wad as thick as a man's wrist. Bona giggling at the sight of all that cash, completely oblivious when Decker pulled his right fist back to his shoulder and threw a short, straight punch at the side of his face. Bona's head bounced off the driver's side window and came back on the rebound and Decker hit it again, like a return of volley, the flat of his knuckles making a pleasing splat against the meat of Bona's cheek.

Bona sputtered. His forehead fell and came to rest on the steering wheel, his eyes glazed under half-closed lids, a string of spittle hanging from the corner of his mouth. Already the red splotch on the side of his face was beginning to discolor.

By the time he got his senses back, sat up and shook his head and clawed at his lap and turned his head painfully to the right, there was Decker with the money pouch in one hand and the Smith & Wesson in the other.

"Oh, man. *Fuck.*"

"Take me to her," Decker said. "Now."

Bona bought time by looking wool-eyed into the barrel of the gun and up into Decker's wooden face and down the barrel of the gun again, and he made a decision. The very worst the ex-monk would do is shoot him dead and that would be the end of it. If Bona didn't get that money and get as far away from Niagara Falls as fast as possible, if he fell into Jimmy Frat's or the fucking Canadian's hands, a sudden bullet would seem like a luxury.

He blinked once, languidly, and said, "Fuck you."

Decker backhanded him with the money pouch, catching the tender cheek. "You're not in charge anymore, shithead."

Bona blanched and tenderly felt his cheek. "I think I am, if you want the lady back, Decker. You wanna shoot me, go ahead. If I don't get that money I'm fucked anyway. You wanna take me to the cops? Same deal. Only you should know something." He reached out and tapped the dash clock. It read ten-thirteen. "We're on a timetable here, man. I don't get this money free and clear and get a call back to my partner by ten-thirty, your girlfriend's as fucked as me. He'll kill her, man, and book."

"You're a liar."

"Yeah, I am, when I hafta be. But not this time. You want me to play the tape again? She said 'they', 'member? 'Give *them* the money'. Who you think that means, man?"

Decker raised the .38 and held it an inch from Bona's face and thumbed back the hammer. Bona's eyes swam in their sockets like a pair of turds floating in a toilet bowl but he didn't flinch, didn't give in to the cold bead of sweat that ran down his spine to the crack of his ass. Told himself if he'd made the wrong call, not given this douche bag enough credit for balls, he'd never know it anyway. Wouldn't even hear the shot.

But he didn't make the wrong call.

Decker lowered the gun.

"That's cool." Bona put out his hand. Decker handed over the money pouch, but not the S&W.

"You don't get the gun back," he said. "No way."

"Now, that's not cool. I need the piece, man, for protection."

Decker gestured toward the money. "Buy yourself a new one."

"I can't do that, man. I need to like keep a low profile right now."

"I don't doubt it, but you're not getting the gun back. So, how do we complete this? Where's Suzzy?"

"Fuck kinda name is that anyway, 'Suzzy'?" Bona could see he wasn't gonna get an answer, wasn't gonna get shit from Decker but a hard stare, so he said, "Okay, how it works is, you get outa the car and start walking home. You get to your place you'll find an envelope stuck under the windshield on that little blue crapster a yours, envelope has an address on it. That's where your girlfriend's being held, in the basement of this house. Meantime, I give my partner a call from that phone over there—"

"I don't like it."

"I know you don't like it, man, but you don't hafta fucking like it, it's how it is."

"How do I know the envelope will be there? Or that it's the right address?"

"Because it is, okay? Look, man, alls I want is the money and to get outa the Falls." He threw up his hands. "If I wanted to kill her, I'd kill you, too, right? But I didn't do that, did I?"

"You didn't get the opportunity. I took the gun away from you."

"Yeah, well, true." Bona sat back and sighed. "We're back to square one here. You're just gonna hafta believe me. The envelope's there, man. Lookit, all I want's the money. I got some problems, okay? And I need to get the fuck outa Dodge pronto."

Decker stared at him, thinking, The Rochester thing. He's worried the cops are getting close on the contract murder and he's blowing town. He said, "Drive me back to my place."

"Aw, man—"

"Drive me back." Decker raised the gun again. "If the envelope's on the windshield like you claim, you can take off."

Bona pretended to think it over, then started up the Pontiac. "Just remember," he said, nodding toward the clock on the dash. "You're on a timetable here, man. Tick-tock."

Floating.

She could feel herself floating, rising to the top, lighter than air, and for a moment she saw herself in the Niagara River Gorge at the base of the falls with Decker, the two of them laying out on the Torpedo like sunbathers, bobbing in the green water...

Clunk.

Her head banged the wall again, harder this time. She snapped to, blinking her eyes rapidly in the near total darkness. Only a thin blade of light managed to make it into the basement from the stairway landing, just enough for her accustomed eyes to make out gray shapes: the workbench on the back wall, the cylindrical water heater, the big boxy furnace.

Her lids began to droop again and she shook herself like a dog drying itself after a dip in a pond. Had to concentrate.

The gas continued its low sibilance.

Helpless.

Hopeless.

Easier just to dream. To lay back and let the weariness take her...

No! Goddamn it to hell—no! Don't die, girl! Don't give that slimy little scum-sucking parasite the satisfaction.

She banged the back of her head against the wall, once, twice, the pain from the knot on her skull shooting through her, making her eyes water. Forced herself to feel the burn of her chafed wrists, forced herself back down onto her scraped elbows and once again found the burr in the metal of the waste pipe and began to saw.

So close now, more than halfway through the nylon rope...

❧   ❧   ❧

Bona watched Decker jump from the Pontiac before it came to a full stop and dart across the street, his mind on nothing but the yellow legal envelope stuck under the wiper of his Prism. He waited until Decker had his hands on the envelope, then he gunned the engine and took off up the block, hanging a right at the first cross street and another right onto Pine Avenue.

Heading east, toward the 190 and freedom. He had it all now. Had it all.

He looked at the money pouch on the console. Picked it up, laughing, and tried to zipper it open, just wanted another look, but couldn't get the zipper to budge with one hand on the steering wheel, had to swerve to miss a car turning left, and decided to pull over. Just for a minute.

He turned into the lot of a strip mall and found a space away from the other cars. Took the pouch in both hands and worked back the zipper. Spread it open.

"Ahhhhh."

He could smell it, a feint but rich aroma of ink and chemical dyes.

Had to count it, feel it on his fingers. Had to.

Reverently he pulled the wad of bills from the pouch and began counting it off into stacks on the console; hundreds here, fifties here, twenties over there. He'd never seen this much cash up close before, thirty-eight grand even. His best payday ever, by far. Buy him a year, a year and a half if he's careful, out west somewheres, getting set up, making contacts.

He saw himself sitting around that desert swimming pool again, the two big-titted strippers lounging next to him sipping fruit drinks. The air clean, the soil made up of nothing but empty sand, no freakin dioxins, no fucking huge powerlines overhead. The picture of health, he'd be, three thousand miles away from Jimmy Frat and Niagara Falls and brain cancer and all that shit...

A shadow passed across the piles of cash. Bona's head swiveled quickly, sending a blade of pain up the right side of his face where Decker's fist had punished him. Outside the car, leaning in and learing at him, was a bum, a stubble-faced drunk, must've staggered out from behind the dumpster at the end of the lot.

The rummy rapped the window glass, said, "C'mon, buddy, lemme have some a that. I ain't et in a week."

Bona reached for the gun in his belt, realized it wasn't there; Decker had kept it. *Fuck.* He felt bare without it, especially now that he had something to protect. Had to do something about that; couldn't drive cross-country with no protection at all.

He remembered his old man's Marlin .30-.30, back at the house. Risky, going back there. Riskier still trying to connect with any gun sellers in town right now, guys operating from the trunks of their cars, make you wait out on a street corner while they check you out.

Had to have *something* along.

"Get the fuck away from the car," Bona hollered at the drunk. He stuffed the money back into the pouch and started the Pontiac and roared out of the lot, still heading east on Pine, but now planning a little detour back out to Love Canal.

🍁   🍁   🍁

Decker had the envelope in his hand and was reading it, re-reading the scrawled address on it, when he realized Bona had taken off. The Pontiac was already a half a block away and turning the corner, its brake lights shining, by the time Decker looked up.

He told himself it didn't matter; he had the address now, could go find Suzzy. There was no room anymore for doubts—but still, they were there. Had he played it right? Would she be waiting for him, safe and sound? Or was it all a game, a trap set by Bona? Maybe he should've beaten the location out of him, forced him to take him there—

No. He would've had to torture him. He could see it in the other man's eyes, the resolve forged from desperation. Bona wouldn't have given in unless Decker had shot or beaten him to within an inch of his life. He couldn't do that, not as long as there was an alternative, and both men knew it.

He checked the address again, but didn't recognize it. Moving quickly, he ducked inside the Prism and dug the city map from the glove box and unfolded it over the steering wheel. His finger glided down the street index, finding the name and the coordinates. Somewhere on the near north side. *There.* Near the City Market. Five, six minutes away with any luck.

He threw the map aside and fumbled his keys from his pocket, glancing at his watch. Ten-twenty. No problem. He'd make it.

He had to make it.

※   ※   ※

Sawing and sawing. Up and down, up and down. Leaning back to pull the clothesline rope tight against the backside of the waste pipe. Sawing and sawing, even as her head began to loll to one side. Up and down, moving to a rhythm she no longer consciously controlled, like a perpetual motion machine. No longer aware of her actions, her surroundings.

Not even hearing the hissing of the gas.

Suddenly the last strand of the rope gave way and she fell backward off the cushion and onto the dirty floor, banging her head yet again, little pink and yellow balls zipping across her field of vision. She struggled to rise, but couldn't summon the strength. Her wrists and ankles were still bound with duct tape and more of the stuff was wrapped tightly across her mouth. With the shred of energy and awareness she had left, she drew up her legs and pushed off against the floor, sliding forward on her back a few inches, while, with her broken fingernails raised up to her mouth, she picked at the edges of the duct tape as if it were a scab.

※   ※   ※

He missed the street on the first pass and had to circle the block. It wasn't much of a street at all, a handful of small shabby post-war Capes, several of them empty or for sale, sandwiched between commercial buildings and a sad little playground.

The house he was looking for had an overgrown, weedy lawn with a real estate sign listing to port and a cracked and rutted driveway on one side. Decker skidded the little car to a stop on the crumbling driveway and jumped out and charged up to the side door. If anyone was to ask him later what color the house was, or if there was a house next door, or if the sun was shining, he couldn't have told them; he was focused only on that door, getting inside, finding Suzzy.

He practically tore the pitted aluminum screen door off its hinges and shoved open the inner door, banging it against the wall. He was on a small L-shaped landing, three steps up to another door, maybe ten steps down into a gloomy basement. Bona had said the basement...

His hand automatically reached toward the switch plate, even as his nose was twitching, registering the smell of gas. His finger found one of the two switch toggles and, with a flick, flipped it upward. Nothing. He reached for the other switch.

⚘   ⚘   ⚘

From a long way off, Suzzy heard the door bang the wall. So far away, it almost slipped by, part of her dreams, lost in her delirium. But then her brain managed to encircle the sound and squeeze it and hold on.

The door! Somebody came in the door!

Her cramped, aching fingers clawed at the duct tape at her mouth, yanking it down, down onto her chin and, with every ounce of lung power she could muster, she screamed, "*Don't hit the light switch—there's gas, a booby trap—don't turn on the light!*"

A beat of near total silence—only the hissing of the gas—and then she heard her name called. "Suzzy!"

"*Don't touch the light switch—gas—gas—*"

The clop-clop of shoes on the tired wooden stairs, a silhouette of a man, the voice calling out to her again as if in her dreams: Decker!

And then he was lifting her over his shoulder in a fireman's carry, up the groaning stairs to the light of the landing and out the door, where she could open her lungs and breathe again.

CHAPTER 35

❀

Love Canal and Other Euphemisms

Decker barely had time to strip the duct tape off her and hold her close for a moment before Suzzy pushed off to arm's length.

"We don't have time for this, I love you, but we don't have time. You've gotta go find a phone, tell Niagara Mohawk to get over here and turn off the gas, then call the city police, tell 'em about Bonawitz and have 'em meet me out on 97th Street—"

"Suzzy, Suzzy, whoa!" He gently gripped her under the elbows and guided her back against the Prism for support. "First off, what makes you think he'd go back to his house?"

"It's a starting point, is all. Maybe he left behind information, an airline stub—"

"Sweetheart, you can barely stand up. You can't go running after bad guys like this."

She stared at him, taking the time to get her breathing under control, suck in the cool head-clearing air. It wasn't so bad: no worse than the buzz from half a bottle of red wine. "Decker, listen to me. I'm a federal law enforcement agent. This is what I do. It's who I am."

"I understand that. It's great, what you do. But you've just had a traumatic experience here. Christ, you're wounded—"

"Decker." She reached out and touched his cheek. "Baby, I'm fine. And I have to do this. You understand?"

He held her eyes for a beat longer, then shrugged, a small acquiescent lifting of one shoulder. "I guess you'll need my car?"

"Yes. I'll drop you at a phone along the way."

"And you'll need this, too." He took the S&W revolver from his waistband and gave it to her. "I took it off our sick little friend."

She smiled, patted his cheek again. Then: "C'mon, let's go. I'll drive."

❧   ❧   ❧

She dropped Decker at a convenience store two blocks away and drove out Pine until it became Niagara Falls Boulevard, weaving the blue Prism through the crawling traffic just like she'd been taught down at Glynco, Georgia, on the slalom course. She didn't know exactly where 97th was, had never driven this far east in the city, and for a few seconds she thought she was in trouble when out beyond Military Road the numbered streets disappeared. But she took a right and circled back into a residential neighborhood and there they were again, the numbered streets; 94th, 95th, 96th, 97th.

It was a short street strung with small inexpensive houses, mostly ranches, most with carports instead of garages. She slowed as she came down the block, trying to remember the house number for the Bonawitz place, trying to ignore the throbbing of her head.

Just ahead, about halfway up the block, a car began moving, backing out of a driveway. A pitted old Grand Am—she recognized it—and without hesitating she floored the accelerator, drove up over the low curb and down the sidewalk, and slammed on the brakes, sending the Prism into a power slide that stopped abruptly five feet behind the Pontiac.

Suzzy was quick coming out from behind the wheel, but Bona was quicker. By the time she had the gun lined up on the Prism's roof, he was already two lawns away, heading south at a gallop.

Suzzy pulled down the revolver and took off after him.

❧   ❧   ❧

He ran up the block to the cross street, checked traffic, and kept running.

Bona couldn't believe this shit. Running his ass off because some crazed fucking waitress was chasing him with a gun. Probably his fucking gun, too. It didn't get any lower than this. Thank God Melody wasn't home to see it, he'd never hear the end of it. Not that he planned to be around to hear any more of Melody's bitching anyway, but—

Then he remembered, *Shit!*, he'd left the money pouch in the Pontiac, along with his old man's rifle. Well, there was just no goddamn way, no freakin goddamn way he was leaving that money.

He was off the sidewalk now and running alongside the ten-foot high chain link fence that ran around the Love Canal containment area, a huge rectangular hole in the ground mounded over with dirt and grass and warning signs; a permanent reminder of the chemical dumping and the hysterics that had, for a brief period in his youth, put his neighborhood on the map. He got as far as the northeast corner of the two-by-four block containment area, ducking just around the corner, before pulling up next to a pile of brush.

A fucking waitress. How tough could that be, even if she did have a piece?

🍁　　🍁　　🍁

What with her sore joints and woozy head, a steady trot was about the best Suzzy could do, but she was confident she'd catch up to him. She was a runner, after all, and had the stamina and the lung capacity for the long haul; guys like this Bonawitz thought exercise was something that should be limited to climbing in and out of other people's windows.

She saw him make the right turn at the corner, then temporarily lost sight of him through the interference of the double fence and the overgrown foliage that rimmed the containment site. But she wasn't worried.

Not until she rounded the corner herself, that is, and went sprawling as something hard and low made painful contact with her shins and sent her sprawling.

"Hey, bitch."

She rolled onto her back, opened her hazel eyes wide and rolled away farther just as Bona brought a tree limb down on the spot like a man chopping wood. The gun had come out of her hand when she fell and, as she scrambled to her feet, she tried to spot it. Bona was looking for it too at the same time he was readying the branch for another swing at her.

"I'm a federal officer, dimwit. You're under arrest."

He cackled, half lowered the branch. "Yeah, right. Who you supposed to be with, the Food and Drug Administration?"

She knew it would sound ridiculous, a disheveled woman in a filthy pair of sweats claiming to be the law, but it was pro forma. He'd been warned and he had chosen to ignore the warning. Now she could legally kick his bony ass.

She let him wade in closer with the thick branch, waiting until he was four feet away and beginning to raise it again, then she pivoted and broke the branch with a roundhouse kick, quickly following up with another that knocked Bona back against the fence.

He dropped the branch and began to wheeze. "Fucking cunt—"

Suzzy danced in and crunched his nose with a short right jab, kicked his balls with a flick of her left foot, and danced back briskly to let him fall. Before his moaning form could curl itself completely into a fetal position, she was on his back, pinning his shoulders and rubbing his face into the damp soil.

Of all the indignities Bona had suffered at the hands of this Amazon woman and her boyfriend—the bruised cheek and ribs, the broken nose, the crushed nuts—the only truly terrifying moment came as he felt that wet, oozing Love Canal earth pushing into his mouth and up his bloody nostrils and, at least in his imagination, metastasizing to his brain.

Later, Suzzy would swear his screams could be heard halfway back to the Rainbow Bridge.

🍁　　　　　🍁　　　　　🍁

They were coming slowly up the sidewalk on 97th, Suzzy with barking shins and the .38 in hand, Bona four steps in front of her, sobbing and limping and hunched over like a ham actor doing Richard III, when the champagne silver Lincoln Town Car rolled up the street from the other direction.

"Holy freakin Jesus!"

Bona recognized the car and suddenly his bruised ribs and broken nose and battered nuts didn't hurt so bad. He took off across the lawn at a gallop, angling for the Pontiac and the money and his old man's deer rifle. Suzzy swore and went after him, ready to pummel him again if necessary, but then she, too, saw the gleaming Lincoln as it skidded to a stop at the curb and she realized she had bigger problems.

❈   ❈   ❈

Garth, in the front seat with Coco, spotted them first, pointing and hollering like a kid on the zoomobile. "There he is! See, with the blond do, eh? See 'im?"

While Coco was skidding the Lincoln to a halt, Jimmy Frat, leaning forward between the seats, said, "Aw right, aw ready, we see him." And, "Jesus, lookit the little faggot. Looks like Johnny Ray havin' a bad hair day."

"You want we should grab the broad, too, boss?" Coco Pulli wanted to know.

Jimmy noticed the big honey-blonde for the first time and assumed it was Mrs. Bona, waving the gun to protect her husband. "Shit, I guess we better." In truth, he hadn't thought things out that far, the problems of grabbing a guy in a residential neighborhood in broad daylight, what to do about potential witnesses. So far his anger and his need for revenge had driven him, but now a modicum of caution mixed into his mindset. "Take her along, anyway. Sort out what the hell to do with her later."

"We'll have to kill them both," Prevost said flatly, sitting beside Jimmy in the back seat, enjoying the mafioso's indecision.

"Yeah, prob'ly," Jimmy conceded as he reached into his jacket for his SIG nine.

❈   ❈   ❈

Suzzy saw the Lincoln's four doors swing open and four men emerge almost casually, guns in hand. She recognized the Buffalo capo, Fratelli, and his henchman, but couldn't make the other two and didn't have time to worry about it. She was alongside the Pontiac, backpedaling toward the house without even realizing it. Bona was crouched in front of the car, alternately whimpering and trying to figure his chances of getting into the Grand Am for the money and the rifle without getting shot. Problem was, the doors were locked except for the driver's door, and that was in the direct line of fire from the four coming out of the Town Car.

Suzzy, still backing up, kicked Bona in the butt and told him to move and he did, scrambling crab-like back toward the house. Meanwhile Suzzy tried calling out her identity again—"Special Agent Koykendall of the U.S. Customs Service. This man is my prisoner."—but all she got in return were a few sniggers.

"Lissen, 'Special Agent,'" Jimmy said, as the four moved forward like it was a stroll in the park, "we're here to make a citizen's arrest on your boy there, so you better just move your pretty ass outa the way, *capice*?"

She had Bona by the collar now and was tugging him in the general direction of the front stoop when a burst from Coco Pulli's Glock shattered the glass in the storm door and changed Suzzy's mind for her. She suddenly zagged to the right, back down the driveway toward the side door off the carport, by now half dragging the sobbing Bona.

The initial burst from Coco's automatic was like openers in a Jacks or better poker game. Almost immediately the others began firing, Jimmy pacing himself to conserve the SIG's eight-shot magazine, Prevost pinging away with the prissy little .25 like he was shooting rats at a landfill, Garth taking the time to aim the big Colt Python revolver with its six-inch barrel. Most of the slugs plowed into the vinyl siding or missed the house entirely, but two or three caught the storm door as Suzzy swung it open, punching a pair of holes in the upper plexiglass panel and just missing her head.

They had moved past the Prism by then and were loosely arrayed around the Pontiac, none of them taking seriously the woman with the gun. Coco, at Jimmy's command, walked slowly toward the support column of the carport, taking a semi-circular route and keeping the Glock aimed lazily toward the side door of the house.

"Piece a cake," he called back to Jimmy.

✤   ✤   ✤

"I got your piece a cake," Suzzy muttered. She was crouched just inside the doorway, which opened directly into the Bonawitz's cramped eat-in kitchen, a study in 1970s-era earth tones under a patina of calcified grease. Bona was sprawled facedown across the grim harvest gold-on-avacado green vinyl flooring, still crying over his failures and his fears.

"Shut the fuck up!" She hollered at him. "You got any more ammo for this thing?"

"N-n-no." He lifted his head to look at her, his eyes shot with red and unblinking. "You gotta stop 'em, they're gonna torture me, I'm your prisoner—"

"No shit." Another volley rang out and rattled the house. Suzzy stared at the Smith & Wesson. Fifteen years she'd had her chromed Browning Hi-Power 9-mm auto with its 13-shot magazine, had won a few marksmanship awards with it, but had never fired it in the line of duty. And now, her first fire fight and here she was without it, stuck instead with an old, poorly maintained .38 revolver with only five rounds left in it.

Well, five shots, four bad guys. The math worked.

She saw Fratelli's big bodyguard approaching the car port, his weapon poised.

"Have some cake!" she yelled as she leveled the S&W and put two holes, spaced no more than an inch apart, in the center of his broad chest.

     🍁   🍁   🍁

Jimmy Frat saw Coco's knees buckle, the Glock fall from his hand as he pitched forward onto his face, the whale-like torso heaving but unable to right itself.

That's when that modicum of caution bloomed into a full bouquet. What the fuck was he doing, risking himself like this in broad daylight, just to nab some two-bit punk he could pick up any time? Just to impress some fancy Canuck car thief, prove how fucking tough he was? He must be outa his fucking mind. Temporary fucking insanity.

Coco was still twitching when Jimmy, crouched behind the Pontiac now, decided a strategic retreat was in order and began backing away toward the Lincoln.

Garth was too busy wielding the Colt to notice, but Miles Prevost, hunched behind the Pontiac, had taken that moment to reload his .32. Therefore he came eyeball to eyeball with the Mafia capo as he tried to slink away in his Hickey-Freeman suit and Bruno Maglis. For the split second that they stared at each other, Jimmy read the contempt and revulsion in Prevost's patrician face, and Prevost read the shame and the bald loathing in Jimmy's puffy visage, and each recognized the moment as both an opportunity and a necessity of survival.

Jimmy swung the SIG around, but Prevost was faster, firing three times in rapid succession and sending Jimmy down onto his chalkstriped back. Not even a twitch out of him.

Prevost signaled Garth to keep firing at the house, everything was all right. Then he half stood and leaned over Jimmy's body for a better look. He had just enough time to frown when, instead of oozing blood, he saw beneath the charred holes in the mobster's navy vest what appeared to be some sort of gray synthetic material. That's when Jimmy grinned up at him, said, "You never fucking learn," and shot him twice in the face.

✤   ✤   ✤

Suzzy, hearing all the firing, wondered what the hell the bozos were shooting at. The only one who was even coming close to her position was the hairy bastard with the .357 and he didn't have an angle good enough to do much more than tear up the siding. On the other hand, she didn't have an angle on him, either, not without exposing herself. Still, it was a six-shot revolver, that big Colt of his, and if she was counting correctly, he was about due to reload.

One more heavy slug slammed into the house and she heard a muffled curse. Good enough. She rolled to her right, out the door and onto the gas-and-oil-stained carport, rolling until she was partly shielded behind a colorful plastic kiddy playhouse, then coming up on one knee and sighting with both hands and finding the target thirty feet away, the burly one with the red beard crouched alongside the Pontiac, part of his shoulder and back exposed while he thumbed shells into his gun.

She fired one round and knew she'd missed and fired again, this time seeing him spin and go down, seeing a splash of red as the slug tore off a piece of his shoulder.

Great, she thought. Two down. But two left, and only one round in the Smith & Wesson.

Suddenly the math didn't add up so good.

What Suzzy didn't realize was that she'd already won the battle. At that very moment, one of her assailants lay dead on the crumbled driveway, an elegant corpse; another was blubbering and beginning to go into shock from the wound to his shoulder; and the third was pushing fresh shells into his SIG and trying to decide whether to break directly for the Lincoln and get the hell outa there or to finish the biker off first.

"Fuck it," Jimmy Frat said, and aimed the SIG at the glass-eyed Garth.

Which is when they all heard the screaming sirens.

CHAPTER 36

Habit 4: Think Win/Win

By the time he'd spent two miserable hours in a holding cell at Niagara Falls police headquarters on Hyde Park Boulevard and another hour and a half sitting in the small interview room with only a silent uniformed cop to keep him company, Bona had moved past the shakes and tears stage, had gotten a handle on his abjectness, and was almost looking forward to the inevitable interrogations that would follow.

First off he was planning to try and get the upper hand by lodging a complaint against the Amazon woman for excessive force, kicking him in the nuts and mashing his face in all that contaminated freakin dirt. And the broken freakin nose. The ugly bruise on the side of his face, the one that Monk dude had given him, he'd blame that on her, too. Next he'd raise the cruel and unusual punishment issue, how he'd been kept in custody for like half a day and nobody'd offered him anything to eat or drink except for a bottle of Snapple, which had been good actually, and a packet of peanut butter cheese crackers that were stale and unnaturally orange and probably had enough carcinogens to give a lab rat a deadly tumor. Not to mention the half-assed medical attention, some dipstick with a first aid kit butterflying a couple bandaids over his tender nose and dabbing disinfectant on the abrasions.

After that, he'd start laying out his biggest cards, which figured to be his inside knowledge of Jimmy Frat's hit order on Eddie Touranjoe and the break-in at that Niagara County politico's party house to steal the kiddy porn. And those were his openers. He still had another ace or two he'd keep up his sleeve in case they didn't wanna deal.

He let out a sustained belch that tasted of apples and citrus and peanut butter and grinned at the cop. The cop, a fat guy with a walrus mustache, looked right through him like he was some homeless bum working the tourists on Rainbow Drive.

"Ex-screw me, officer," Bona said, and grinned wider.

When the interview room door finally swung open, seven bodies filed in and surrounded the trestle table and found chairs and stared at him with shining, expectant gazes, like this was the Last Supper and he was Jesus freakin Christ or something. There was the Amazon woman, Suzzy, who it turns out really was a federal agent after all, and her boyfriend the monk—Bona was a little surprised they'd let him in—and a stocky black cop named Hazard that Bona knew mostly by reputation. The other four he didn't know from Adam, but he soon would: Monroe County Sheriff's Investigator Mulvaney, Special Agent-in-Charge J. Ellison Randall of the U.S. Customs Service, a Royal Canadian Mounted Police captain named Morrisey, and Sheldon Fife, a prosecutor from the Niagara County attorney's office. Everybody wearing a suit of some kind except for Decker.

Bona looked at him. "Don't tell me you're a Fed, too."

Decker smiled and shook his head. "A concerned citizen. And witness."

"I'm real sorry about that, man, trying to rip you off that way, but I was desperate. I mean, I had these killers after my ass—"

The county attorney cut in, speaking loud and clear for the recording, "Are you absolutely certain, Mr. Bonawitz, that you do not wish to be represented by counsel at this time?"

"Absolutely. Let's keep it friendly, huh?" The busted nose making his voice sound like a freakin kazoo. "I'm sure, once you hear me out, you'll see I'm as much a victim here as anybody."

Suzzy had cleaned herself up and changed into a gray worsted wool pantsuit, but it hadn't improved her mood much. She leaned forward. "You tried to *kill* us, dipshit. Blow us up in that house, all for a lousy few thousand dollars."

"I wouldn't call forty grand a lousy few thousand, lady."

"Oh, excuse me. That's twenty thousand per life, isn't it. I stand corrected." She rolled her eyes. "Somebody please get God on the phone and tell him to do some repairs on the assembly line. He's putting out too many assholes."

Bona searched the other faces around the room as if to say, Y'See the way she talks to me? But none of the men were interested in challenging Agent Koykendall's choice of descriptors. In fact, they all seemed to be regarding her with heightened respect and with something else, too; a calculating wariness, as if they were remembering the two guys she'd nailed with the Smith & Wesson and that had got them thinking about the women back at their offices and their homes, wondering just how much *they* might be capable of if pushed.

All but Decker, who wore a goofy little grin at the corners of his mouth.

"Okay, first off, people, let's be fair here," Bona said, leaning on his elbows. "Remember it was Jimmy Fratelli, a known Buffalo mob guy, and his crew who showed up at my place and started throwing lead around. This is after this woman here attacked me viciously while I was unarmed and unaware she was a federal agent—" He held his hand up like a traffic cop. "—but we'll let that go for now. The main thing is I know some stuff about Fratelli and his organization that can help you guys put him away and I'm prepared to testify against him in exchange for certain considerations, the key one being I do no hard time on the kidnapping thing and you relocate me somewheres warm through the Witness Protection Program. I'm thinking Arizona."

He didn't like the looks he was getting—too smug by half—so he threw in, "Oh, and that other guy, that was Miles Prevost, right? Is he dead? Cause I got some stuff on him, too, that you Customs people oughta be especially interested in."

He sat back, arms crossed, tiny smirk lurking under the bandaged nose, and waited.

Again, the county attorney spoke. "You expect us to give you a free get-out-of-jail card on kidnapping, extortion and attempted murder charges?"

"Yeah. In exchange for my helping put Jimmy Frat away." Bona had a terrible thought and shot upright. "He's not dead, too? I thought he was wearing body armor—"

"Mr. Fratelli is very much alive. In fact, he's claiming he was only attempting to bring *you* to justice, Mr. Bonawitz, for the murder of his daughter's fiancé, Dale Maratucci."

"Ah, he's fulla shit. It was those bikers of Prevost's threw Dale over the falls. They were after me, too, but I got away from 'em. That's why I was so desperate I had to pull a crazy stunt like I did, going after this gentleman's money." And let anyone prove different, Bona thought, leaning back again.

"Happily, Mr. Bonawitz, there are some other matters," Sheldon Fife said, savoring the moment. "There's the matter, for instance, of the late Gary Graycastle."

The name hit Bona's sternum with more force than one of the Amazon woman's roundhouse kicks, but he did a decent job of not showing it.

"Uh, I don't believe I know the guy."

"Really, Mr. Bonawitz? Well, then, what about Mrs. Graycastle, Marla Ellen Graycastle of Eden, New York. How well do you know her?"

Bona tried a laugh, but it didn't come out right. "I don't know either one of 'em. What's the deal here, anyway?"

Now the little attorney gave a nod to Decker, who put his palms on the table and looked into Bona's eyes and said, "I'm a witness, remember? And what I witnessed was you and Marla Ellen Graycastle together in the Metropolis the day before her husband was abducted."

"No way, man. He's making shit up."

"And then I followed you over to the Rainbow Garage. I'm sure you remember that, the two of you sitting in her white minivan, only she wasn't just sitting there, she was playing Bobbing for Bonawitz. Some sort of down payment, I'm guessing."

Bona sat still as a painting for maybe twenty seconds, while inside he fought to keep the drowning sensation from bubbling up to his eyes and spilling out as tears. You're never truly fucked, he'd always believed, until they put you in the ground and mumble Latin at your dead ass.

He exhaled for so long it felt like his belly button was rubbing against his backbone. Like there was nothing left of him but a pancaked cartoon body in the middle of the road with a freakin tire track across it.

"Oh-kay," he said finally, inching forward again. "Let's just say for a minute I *did* shoot poor Gary."

CHAPTER 37

❊

Based On A True Story

They picked her up that evening for questioning, gave her time to make arrangements for the girls to stay with her in-laws, then, instead of taking her downtown to the Hall of Justice in Rochester, they drove her west to Niagara Falls, an hour and a half of total silence on two-lane state highways and secondary roads.

By the time Marla Ellen Graycastle was plunked down in the same interview room in the same chair that had held Bona a few hours earlier, left there to stew for another forty-five minutes, she had managed to calm her jangling nerves by plunging head first into the rich fantasy life she'd created for herself. When the two sergeants came in, looking tired and irritable and a bit sodden in their cheap sport coats and limp ties, Marla had almost convinced herself that all this was a grievous miscarriage of justice that no recently-widowed mother of young children should have to bear. Now all she needed to do was convince them.

Sgt. Hazard, his face dark and dour as usual, Mirandized her for a second time—"A formality."—and for a second time Marla waived her right to counsel. She could handle these two men and, besides, why begin an attorney-client relationship with some gross and underpaid Niagara County public defender when, *if* the time should come, she would have her pick of high-profile celebrity lawyers?

Marla was sitting at the head of the trestle table. Sgt. Mulvaney of the Monroe County Sheriff's Department took the chair adjacent to her on the right. Sgt. Hazard of the Niagara Falls P.D. sat on her left. Both men stared at her for several seconds, working their wads of gum like masticating bulls. Marla almost laughed.

Until Sgt. Hazard reached inside his coat and extracted a photo and laid it on the table in front of her.

It was a mug shot of Dennis Bonawitz.

She glanced at it, not seeing Bona in it at first, what with the blond buzz cut and goatee and the bandaged black-and-blue nose. But then the eyes popped out at her, and the nascent sneer, and she felt her breath catch in her throat.

The two cops watched, studied, as her face flicked through a gamut of emotions from surprise to puzzlement to anger to resentment to resignation. The expression she settled into, however, proved to be the most interesting, and the most chilling; a vague little Mona Lisa smile.

"Well, I'm relieved, really," she said. "You don't know much I've wanted, finally, to be able to tell someone about the living hell my marriage to Gary Graycastle had become."

Epilogue

Suzzy Koykendall waited for the light to go green, then drove her Pathfinder through the intersection. In the passenger seat, Decker looked out at the empty early-morning streets and up at the sky turning gradually from indigo to robin's egg blue as the sun climbed on the horizon.

"Good day for it," he said.

"Mmm. Trick or treat."

"I meant the weather," he said mildly. "Not it being Halloween."

They rode in silence for a while. Suzzy picked up Rainbow Boulevard South and followed it to the turn-off to Goat Island. As she crossed over the bridge, Decker spoke again.

"So, have they figured out yet what's gonna happen with the punk?"

Suzzy shook her head. "It's in negotiation right now between his defender and the county attorney and the federal prosecutor. It's a turf battle, who gets him first. I'm guessing New York State will end up pleading him out first on the Graycastle hit. Not that it matters a whole hell of a lot; he's gonna get partial immunity in exchange for testimony on the contract killing as well as what he can tell us on the other hit, the one Fratelli ordered." She cleared the bridge and picked up the loop road and chuckled with grudging admiration. "He's even peddling some mob killing he witnessed several years ago, supposedly some snitch that was blown away by Rick the Quick Lemongello, another Buffalo wiseguy. Selling his soul for the best deal he can get."

"I think he sold his soul a long time ago," Decker said. "What about the kidnapping thing, attempting to kill us?"

"He'll do time for that, and the Graycastle hit. The question is how much." She glanced over at him. "My best guess? He'll be out and probably ensconced in the Witness Protection Program he covets within seven years. They'll get him a job clerking at some shoe store in Emporia, Kansas, or somesuch and within six months he'll be out burglarizing isolated farm houses."

"The more things change," Decker said. "Fratelli?"

"Problematic." Suzzy frowned. "The state attorney's gung-ho to put together racketeering charges and the Feds'll probably sign on. I doubt much'll come of the Touranjoe murder, though. Nobody but Bonawitz is talking and Coco Pulli is of course—" Her voice hitched just slightly. "—dead. And Bonawitz doesn't know the name of the other guy, the one he calls the Ghoul. And there's no way a body's gonna turn up—"

He reached over and touched her shoulder. "Here comes a cliche, babe, but it's true. That Pulli guy—you did what you had to do."

"Oh, I know that. It was him or me. It's just, it's still a human life, y'know? It's not something I can just forget about."

"And you shouldn't. Just keep it in perspective."

"Anyway, Fratelli's got his team of shysters claiming he was only acting as an enraged citizen, out to get his daughter's fiance's killer, when he showed up shooting out on 97th Street. They've got him cold on an assortment of weapons charges, but I don't know what else might stick. Maybe attempted murder of a federal agent, but since I didn't have any ID on me, it's iffy."

"He killed that Canadian, Prevost, point blank."

"Yeah, well, he's claiming self-defense on that and he's got three slugs from Prevost's popgun embedded in his Kevlar vest to back him up." She followed the loop road around until the river rapids were on her left, began slowing the Pathfinder as they approached the parking area for the Three Sisters Islands. "Talking about Prevost, turns out that isn't his real name, or at least, the name he was born with. Milos Previc was what he was called when he emigrated from Czechoslovakia thirty years ago. The RCMP have a file on him an inch thick, mostly from his early days as a con man and scammer up in Toronto, but they suspected he'd moved up to bigger and better things. Stolen cars primarily, shipped all over the world for resale. That's another thing Bonawitz offered up. He had a couple first names of customs inspectors, one Canadian and one of ours, that he claims were on Prevost's payroll. We've got a couple suspects we're questioning, which makes Randall happy. Happy about that, at least."

She pulled over in the parking area and switched off. There was only one other car in the lot.

Decker turned in the seat. "He isn't giving you a hard time, is he? You're a hero."

She sniggered. "Yeah, for the moment anyway. I'll get a citation for my wall. But I can see it in his eyes, the resentment—that I not only went off the reservation, got involved with you and broke my cover, but that I walked into a shitstorm and came out smelling like a rose. He won't forget it, believe me. Once things quiet down, I'm gone. He'll transfer my butt someplace a long way from here, probably a station on the Montana-Alberta border doing spot checks on cattle trucks."

Decker reached over again, but this time he pulled her gently to him, mindful of her bandaged arm, and kissed her. "Montana sounds good. Maybe I can open a little bakery, sell donuts to cops and cowboys."

"I'll hold you to that."

"I could build a log cabin, put it on a fieldstone foundation." He got lost in it, thinking back to the gathering of the stones.

Suzzy returned his kiss and for a few moments they held each other awkwardly across the console shifter. Then she let go and sat back. "What if it's not Montana, Decker? I mean, it could be anyplace. Miami, Laredo—"

"Doesn't matter."

"But it does matter. The job, I mean. I didn't realize that until the other day, what it means to me to do my job. I love you and I want us to be together, I just—before you commit to anything I need for you to understand what I do, where I'm coming from—"

He cut her off again. "Back at the abbey, whenever he wanted to drive home a certain concept, the novice master used to use the spoke and wheel analogy on all the novitiates."

"The spoke and wheel?"

His hands drew a circle in the air. "Picture a big wagon wheel. At the hub is God and out on the rim is the secular world. And each of the spokes has a label: student, teacher, lawyer, mechanic, carpenter. Each coming from differ-ent places on the rim, each following his own path, but arriving at exactly the same place. It's a little Zen maybe, but if you change the parameters—"

"Decker, please don't go David Carradine on me."

He laughed. "Sorry, grasshopper. My point is, where you're coming from doesn't matter, where I'm coming from doesn't matter. So long as we both end up in the same place."

She nodded, feeling part of her fear—the long-term fear—lifted. That left the short-term fear; the fear that there may not be any long term. She wished she could keep him right there in the car beside her until the sun made its entire circuit and the day passed into night and it was too late to chase night-mares. But she knew she couldn't do that.

"I suppose we should get going," she said. "Norton's probably going nuts waiting."

"Yeah. That's his Mustang sitting over there."

"Nice old car."

"Yeah, vintage."

Still they hesitated.

"Aren't you scared?"

"Yeah. I'm scared. Scared to go, but more scared not to go. Does that make any sense?"

"Hell," she laughed, "let's not worry about making sense at this late date."

They climbed out and crossed over the empty road and picked up the trail down to the Three Sisters, three small islands that formed a mini-archipelago that extended like a finger out into the rapids some three hundred yards above the Horseshoe Falls. A paved pathway tied the Three Sisters to Goat Island like a string of freshwater pearls, each island linked to the other by a stone and concrete bridge, the green Niagara River rushing and gurgling below.

Decker and Suzzy followed the path from one rocky, wooded island to the next in the dim morning sunlight, until they came to the third island and passed a 'Proceed With Caution' sign. Just beyond, the path turned from macadam to dirt and gravel, then petered off into half a dozen narrow tracks. Without hesitation Decker took a path to his left and led Suzzy down to a small inlet, where the rapids were given a respite on their relentless trek to the rim and where Norton Gage and the Torpedo were waiting.

When he saw them, he jumped up from the rock he'd been sitting on and tossed the stub of his cigar into the water. "All right," he enthused. "All right. Is this a great day for stunting or what?"

"It's a beauty," Decker agreed. "Just like you called it."

The Torpedo lay three-quarters in the water, its nose up on the gravel beach. Norton and Decker and Norton's employee at the newsstand, Lou, had snuck the giant, insulation-padded tube onto Goat Island the previous night using Norton's flatbed with the winch and PTO. After they had lowered it down into the rocky river with a steel cable, Decker had piloted it around to the back side of the farthest island, finding a calm and secluded inlet to stash it until morning, concealing it under layers of broken branches and brush.

"Almost time, man. They'll be turning up the flow in twenty minutes."

"Twenty minutes," Suzzy said. "Great."

They spent the time talking, about the stunt and about the pickup boat that would be down in the gorge with Lou at the wheel. About the above average temperatures for the last day of October and the prospects for snow flurries later in the week. While they talked, Norton lit another cigar and checked his watch every two minutes and Suzzy had her first Virginia Slim of the day and Decker watched the water, his hands in the pockets of his jacket.

"Oh, by the way. You guys realize there's a ten thousand dollar fine for doing this?" Suzzy asked. "I looked it up."

"Nortie and I agreed we'd split it," Decker said.

"Yeah," Norton nodded. "Anyway, it's only Canadian."

Then the time was gone and Decker gave Suzzy a light kiss. She held him close, patted his back and let him go. He pulled off his jacket and shirt and jeans and boots, stripping down to a rubber wet suit. Norton nudged the Torpedo a few inches farther into the water and popped the hatch.

Decker lay on his side on the rocky beach and began to slide his legs down into the stunt vehicle. When he was in up to his shoulders, about to swing the nose shut, he paused and looked over at Suzzy and winked.

"Y'know," he called to her. "Horseshoes are supposed to be lucky."

She found a smile. "And with this one, there's almost always a rainbow at the end."

Afterword

✿

While the characters who populate this novel are entirely fictional, it should be noted that all of the historical figures mentioned—Sam Patch, the Great Blondin, Annie Taylor, and the other stunters referred to in the story—were very real people who performed very real deeds. One such real person's experience on the mighty Niagara was borrowed for this book: The childhood trauma of the character Walter Beidecker was inspired by a true-life incident involving a seven-year-old boy named Roger Woodward, who, in the summer of 1960, was swept over the Horseshoe Falls wearing only a life preserver. He was and remains the only person to go over Niagara Falls unprotected and live to tell the tale. Walter Beidecker is otherwise a fictional creation whose life, as far as I know, bears no resemblance to that of Roger Woodward.

—the author

About the Author

❀

Stephen F. Wilcox was born in Rochester, New York, in 1951. The author of several mystery novels, he has a B.A. from St. John Fisher College in Pittsford, New York, where he majored in Journalism and Political Science. In addition to his experiences as a newspaper reporter and editor and a freelance writer, he has worked as a major appliance installer and a clerk in a liquor store, a personnel specialist for the U.S. Army and a farmhand, an assembly-line worker in an auto parts plant, a tax preparer, and a creative writing instructor, among other jobs. Currently he and his wife and son live in a scenic little village located along the Erie Canal near Rochester.

0-595-22146-7

Printed in the United States
701800002B